SORROW'S LIGHT

Also by Freda Warrington in Pan Books

A TASTE OF BLOOD WINE

FREDA WARRINGTON

SORROW'S LIGHT

PAN BOOKS
LONDON, SYDNEY AND AUCKLAND

First published 1993 by Pan Books

a division of Pan Macmillan Publishers Limited
Cavaye Place London SW10 9PG
and Basingstoke

Associated companies throughout the world

ISBN 0–330–32663–5

1 3 5 7 9 8 6 4 2

A CIP catalogue record for this book is available from
the British Library.

Phototypeset by Intype, London
Printed by Mackays of Chatham PLC, Kent

This book is dedicated with love to MLL,
guardian angel and VIP

CONTENTS

THE BURNING STAR

Try to imagine.

One violet star eyes the night-swathed earth. Its light blooms the great black slabs of the mountains and dusts the path between them with a blood-pink glow.

Down this path the travellers are riding in urgent silence. They feel the star burning them. Under its livid eye they dare not rest.

The leader says, 'There are the domes of Torbyrgi! Can you see the river glittering? Two hours, we'll be there, my lady.'

The Lady Antrid says nothing. Two hours might as well be eternity. She cannot see the domes or the river. She can only see the rock-strewn steepness of the path, the jet shadows and the poisonous light that soaks everything. She does not think of the husband-to-be who waits for her in Torbyrgi. There is no future, no world outside this frantic flight. Only the hot laboured breath of her horse, its muscles straining beneath her; only the clatter of hooves on stone, the capes of the outriders flapping on the wind.

She knows they will never reach Torbyrgi.

They should have spent the night safe in the way-hut, but even way-huts give no real protection; not when the Unseen have gathered outside, and the torches have burned out and there are no more firebrands to keep them away. So the travellers have panicked and fled.

The light of the star, Sudema, has woken the invisible creatures of night. The Unseen won't tolerate travellers through their domain, the part of Thandarkyr that they stole. Antrid can sense them watching. Legions of demons, poised all along the ridges, staring down at the travellers with crimson eyes. She can feel them pursuing. They are invisible but their claws click on the rock and their breathing is like the soft roar of a furnace.

'It's no good!' she cries. 'They're following!'

The leader glances round. 'It's only the wind, my lady.'

'The wind doesn't breathe in and out.'

'Don't look back. Keep going! We'll be safe in no time,' he says, but there is fear in his face and he pounds his heels into his horse's ribs.

The horses stream down the path, a sweating mass of darkness, rimmed by lavender light. Fifty riders, an escort fit to bring a prince's bride safely to him across the Stolen Land. They've come all this way – days and days of vigilance and anxiety – without incident; isn't it unfair, isn't it cruel of the Unseen to pounce at the very last moment, to let them see safety then snatch it from them?

The river glitters. The domes beyond glow like lava. Antrid can see them now. She throws her heart towards them. All they have to do is reach the bridge . . .

Suddenly the leader's horse stumbles and goes down. Antrid's horse is galloping too fast to stop, too close to swerve. It careers straight into the fallen animal and somersaults, flinging her into space. The world cartwheels. The impact as she hits the icy rock drives out her breath.

All around her, horses are swerving, falling, squealing in panic. Shadow-silhouettes begin to flow across her vision.

Antrid tries to move but she cannot. Her back is broken. She is so deep in the well of terror that she has all but drowned there, and she gazes up at the mountains and the stars as if through a rippling weight of water. It is almost over.

Now the legions of Sudema are pouring down the mountain slopes to kill and feast. No longer Unseen but half seen; a gleam here and there like a reflection in a dark shadow. Hints of flanks and limbs, like velvet stretched over stone; bunched paws, each armed with four silver scythes. Gossamer filaments of hair outline gaps where their faces should be, but all she can see are their eyes, glaring like the purple eye of their star.

A man screams. A lingering yell of terror, cutting through the confusion, weirdly isolated from it.

Antrid sees the screaming man, still on horseback, hurtling towards her. The horse is bolting and the man is carried blind. A shadow clings to his back. Claws flash and blood droplets scatter and something like a scrap of flesh tumbles back on the wind and lands beside her on the rock.

That is the last thing she sees. She is staring at it as she dies; an eyeless mask on the rock.

The man's face.

Try to imagine it, Mathrathur. I only wish I could stop.

CHAPTER ONE

THE STOLEN LAND

As I sit here in the half-light, writing this with a white stone on a dark wall of rock, I wonder quite how to explain. I wonder if I should even try; but then my anger rises and I think, by the sun or by the star, I am going to make *someone* understand.

Please try.

I am aware of the differences between us, Mathrathur, between your views and mine. Before you condemn me, understand that I was brought up with these beliefs; only shifting experience or violent revelation can change them, and even then they die hard.

One of the first stories we are ever told in Torlossen, the first we have to learn by heart, is that of the Creation and the Separation which brought evil into the world. My father would make the children sit in a circle round the fire; I can see him now, the flames glowing bronze on the folds of his Perfect-Governor's robe, the dusk blue behind him. Then he would intone the words of the Prophet Hendleiknir, which we only half understood.

'In the beginning there were two great lights, Ama and Sudema. They ruled the heavens together and Sudema was chosen by Ama to be his consort. But she said unto him, "Wherefore should I submit to thee when my light is equal to thine?"

'Ama replied, "If thou wilt not merge thy light with mine, there shall be no offspring of our union. Thy light shall be diminished and thou shalt be separated from me for ever." But Sudema in her pride would not submit. Thereupon Ama created for himself a consort whose name he called Eileah, that is the world, who had no light of her own but who shone in Ama's light and put Sudema to shame. Eileah was fruitful and obedient, and the children of Ama and Eileah are called Men.

'Then Sudema in jealousy and rage fled from Ama, and her light was diminished. And Ama said unto her, "in darkness shalt thou live thy days; but because thou wast once my equal in

3

dignity, over darkness shalt thou rule." And he called her name Sudema the Evening Star; she who brought about the separation of night from day, and man from woman, and good from evil.

'Now Ama rules the day; but the night is Sudema's realm, and there in the bitterness of her exile she avenges herself on the Sons of Eileah and takes congress with them while they sleep. And the offspring of Sudema are called the Unseen Legions of Sudema, against which we must ever be vigilant.

'So may Ama's grace protect us from her. For she can hold dominion only over those who turn from Ama and sin, as she turned away and sinned; those who shun the day and love the night, as she did. The Great Light bless us.'

That is the essence of the story. Obedience, hard work, selflessness, virtue; all these flourish and shine in Ama's Light. But the moment we fall prey to lust or pride, or fail to make our devotions to Ama, we open ourselves up to Sudema. She'll consume us with her evil and drag us to Kvold where it is always night. Even to walk in the night is dangerous without calling on Ama to ward her off. The light of her violet eye will corrupt and burn us. The Stolen Land is full of her Unseen offspring, who hunt and slay any children of Ama who dare to walk there . . . and that, as you know, is true.

So if my dread of Sudema offends you, forgive me; but I am damned if I will let you forget the reasons.

I'll begin with the day my parents took me to Torbyrgi to attend the marriage of Prince Tykavn to Lady Antrid, because that was the day my life began to change.

I come from a village called Vryatan, though it is not truly a village but a mass of caves in a cliff, a day's ride south of Torbyrgi. Don't imagine we're uncivilized, though. The caves are dry and well ventilated; it made sense to our ancestors to make use of them rather than building afresh. We don't call them caves but grace them with the name *heimar*. Around the entrances there are ancient worn carvings, a reminder of the days when Thandarkyr was whole and Vryatan had pretensions to greatness. It's said the carvings were brightly decorated once, but now we have neither the time nor the materials to maintain them.

There are hot springs nearby, streams rich with reeds, and good grazing for the goats and horses. We even have books, made of woven reed-paper, from which we learn to read the teachings of

Hendleiknir. I liked to look at the pictures of things I'd never seen – trees, mountain deer, volcanoes – and dream.

My father, Gaefir, is Vryatan's Governor; he's a cousin of King Vidvikjan, so in theory we are part of the royal family. Yet I have no sense of being noble-born. I've grown up as a villager, living in a heimar, tending the goats, spinning, weaving, sewing; every task necessary to life. So have my mother and father, uncles and aunts. Living in Vryatan there is no quarter for the privileged to live in idleness. Not that we'd want to.

It wasn't the first time I'd seen Torbyrgi. Father had taken me to the city several times in the previous four years since he and Mother had been appointed to the Assembly. Yet in the silver ash-light of that evening the sight of it affected me as it never had before.

Our party were a lovely sight, our thick-set golden horses with their black silky manes and tails and their neat black legs, stepping with arched necks down the rough path. I rode between my mother, Vithrie, and Mehaar, who is pretty and blonde and my best friend, even though she's our bondservant and has no Status. Gaefir rode before us in straight-backed silence. The boy Langyr, who looks after the horses, rode at the back behind Mother's two tall thin brothers, both devout Sublimes who had taken vows of silence.

A trail of villagers followed, bulky figures in layers of dark wool; coats and shawls belted over split riding-skirts, wide-brimmed hats with round crowns. Our clothes are made of coarse goat-hair, in all shades of cream and brown. The finest hair, geitha – especially the rare pure white and black – is sent as a tribute to the city, and reserved for the Palace and the highest Perfect-Ministers. Even my father only wears his fine robes at Court. My idea of Torbyrgi as a casket of wealth enhanced the awe I felt when it came into view.

With the gravel hill a frozen wave behind us, the landscape ahead unfolded into layer upon layer of mountains, fading back into the smoky purple of the sky; and in the valley below us the city rose from an ocean of indigo shadow, its domes dark and soft as thunderclouds.

Don't misunderstand. Torbyrgi isn't a magnificent place with shining roofs and golden statues. The walls are dull ivory, the domes made of blue-grey metal and green glass. It's old and dilapidated and wreathed in the steam of hot springs, and it would be dwarfed by the cave-riddled cliff at Vryatan. Torbyrgi is a remnant of a happier time, before Thandarkyr was split in three by the Unseen. Almost impossible, now, to maintain it in its former glory.

Yet in its greyness and oldness there seemed to be mystery, a magical allure. The city on the very Border.

From Vryatan to Torbyrgi – and throughout Torlossen – roll the black and plum-bronze slopes that were the only landscape I'd ever known. Cold, barren. The soil blows off the slopes and drifts into the valleys, held there by what little vegetation can take root. They say tall strong trees grew here once, but I've never seen any. Grazed by too many goats, the grass dies, the soil shifts, the tenacious plants take hold again . . . just enough for us to scrape a living. Torlossen always seems to be just two tendays away from famine.

The Unseen stole the rich land of Inner Thandarkyr and left us the scraps on the edges. So I was always told.

Four miles beyond the city I could see the flat sheen of a river. The near bank was furred with green fields, glowing vividly in the half-light. The river Torlau is the boundary, the Border between the safe province of Torlossen and the mystical hills of the Stolen Land.

The thought both scared and excited me. I startled my horse, Datha, out of his half-doze, and rode close beside Mehaar. 'Do you know what the river is?' I asked.

'Is it the Torlau?' Mehaar said uncertainly. She knew perfectly well, but she never likes to appear too clever.

'Yes, but you know what it *is*, don't you? It's the Border between our country and *theirs*. The Unseen. Ama's Light, we're looking at the mountains where they live! We can't see them but they are there . . .'

Mehaar shivered. 'Don't, halla Iolithie. It's frightening.'

'Why be frightened?' I exclaimed. 'They never come across the river. We're in no danger. But to know that they are there, just on the far bank, doesn't it make you feel strange?'

'Yes,' said Mehaar. 'And I don't want to think about it.'

'But think of Lady Antrid, Prince Tykavn's bride,' I went on. 'She's travelling all the way from Onafross to marry him. Imagine riding across those mountains we can see, hundreds and hundreds of miles, all the way through the Stolen Land. Can you imagine how thrilling it must be? I almost envy her.'

As I spoke, I became aware of a terrible silence thickening around us. I hadn't kept my voice down. Father was frowning, but I thought, *What does it matter?* and went on brightly. 'I should love to ride down to the river. Just to look. Could we go down there tomorrow, Father?'

No one spoke. Mehaar drew in a breath. Mother made the protective circle of Ama over her heart. I found their fear irritating. I was naïve, you see; everyone whispered of the horrors that lay beyond the Border, but I had a feeling that third-hand stories might be exaggerations. And even if they weren't, how could my family not be fascinated by the unknown?

Finally Father said, 'We are here for a state wedding, Iolithie, not for your pleasure.' His tone was stern. 'There will be no excursions down to the Torlau. It's forbidden. Only those who work the farms are allowed in the river valley; and at night only the Border-guards.'

I never know when to let something rest. 'But has anyone ever been hurt down there?'

'Yes, many times! Hurt and killed.'

'But not on *this* side of the river . . .'

'That is not the point.' Father turned away coldly and I knew I'd gone too far, trespassed on something that wasn't my concern. I hate that feeling. It makes my skin crawl, more with resentment than anything else. 'You know full well the dangers,' he said quietly. 'The Laws are made for our safety, Ama protect us. You are not an idiot and not a child; try to behave with the self-restraint of the adult you will soon be. Don't let me hear you speak of it again. If you make a poor impression on Prince Tykavn it will reflect badly, not only on your family but on the whole village.'

Torbyrgi is a city turned outside in. As you approach it you see only sheer walls rising from the stony ground, hardly a soul about; perhaps a few children playing, a boy leading a pair of horses, some Sublimes coming home from the fields. A ghost city. But inside, it vibrates with life.

When we came to the huge double-doors at the entrance, a committee from the Palace was waiting to welcome us. I counted twelve Perfect-Ministers and Councillors, all friends of my father; one expressed astonishment at how fast I had grown up, but I didn't remember him. They were surrounded by attendant-Sublimes in white, blue and black livery, bearing staves that were crowned by gold suns, the symbol of our Lord Ama. The sun and the Hand of the Prophet were emblazoned on everything.

Our horses were led away to the stables outside the Palace; Langyr went with them. The other Vryataners were taken to lodgings in one of the poorer quarters. While the bustle went on around us, I stood and gazed at the echoing height and length of Torbyrgi.

There's a main thoroughfare, lined with the shops of merchants, with tiers of galleries rising up above them. These galleries give on to schools, workrooms, the apartments of the wealthy, chapels of Ama. The roof is high, domed and inset with ocean-green glass, protecting the city from the storms of winter and the dust of summer. At one end there are vast double-doors, only closed at night or in bad weather, through which the citizens can come and go; at the other, the magnificent pillared entrance to the Palace itself.

Lesser streets fan outwards from the main one, lined with smaller shops and quarters, until they dwindle to the poorest quarters on the periphery; storerooms, workrooms, the homes of the Unstatused, or of Sublimes who have taken vows of poverty. But I was only interested in the grandeur of the centre, with its silvery marble, intricate tiling, glossy blue-black columns rising layer on layer to the light-starred roof. Torbyrgi seemed shrouded in a contradictory haze of enticing dilapidation and wealth.

I began to feel that I'd like to live here.

Because of my father's position and connections, we were honoured guests of Prince Tykavn for the wedding celebrations. When we were led into the Palace, we were greeted by Arch-Perfect-Elect Laasastiuk himself. He is the Head of our Church of Ama; he is a Judge, highest member of the Assembly, Tykavn's adviser. I'd expected him to be a formidable man, but he was grey-haired, soft and kind; such a contrast to the stiff angularity of my father that I liked him instantly.

Mehaar's mouth was hanging open, though I didn't blame her. Although our heimar in Vryatan is clean and comfortable, imagine the grandeur of the Palace by comparison; long bright halls, black columns against silver-grey marble; geometric tiling that made the eyes dance, friezes of coloured stone around the walls, little trees – trees! – growing in tubs, pools and waterfalls with no purpose but to be decorative. My mouth was open too, I'm afraid.

'It is good to see you again, Gaefir,' said Arch-Perfect Laasastiuk, shaking my father's hand and gripping his arms with a great show of affection. Father, never demonstrative, seemed embarrassed. 'We are so glad your family could accompany you. The news, unfortunately, is that the Lady Antrid hasn't arrived yet. She was expected this afternoon.'

The Arch-Perfect's tone was conversational, but there was a tangible stiffening of the air.

'She's only a few hours late,' said Gaefir. 'The simplest thing could have delayed her party; bad weather, a lame horse.'

'Quite,' said Laasastiuk. 'She has fifty men guarding her, armed with fire-brands, and the security of all the way-huts on the Onafross Way was checked before they set off. Every precaution was taken. We expect her at any time and the Border-guards are on permanent alert to welcome her. I fear it has set the Prince a little on edge, but we're doing out best to keep him calm.' There was a murmur of uneasy laughter from the other Perfects, and reassuring comments went round the circle.

I was shocked to realize how desperately worried they were. No one could admit it, though. The notion that Lady Antrid might not arrive safe and sound was unthinkable.

But this fear is all-pervading in a country split into three by Sudema's brood. In the north is Onafross; in my mind, a gleaming, fertile, unobtainable heaven, from which King Vidvikjan rules us all. In the south, chilly old Torlossen, governed by Vidvikjan's son Tykavn. But between the two lies the Stolen Land, where no one ventures without risking their life.

When our previous Governor died, four years ago, the King sent his younger son to govern Torlossen. And now he was sending his son a bride, a specially chosen noblewoman from the Court of Onareyru.

There was a commotion at the far end of the hall, and an impressive young man walked in. He was tall and big-boned, with brown curly hair and a full beard framing a strong face which everyone agreed was handsome; how could a prince be anything else? He wore split-skirts of geitha, patterned with fine black and white stripes, a black shirt and a jacket held in by a belt of gold and quartz, and over that the most stunning cloak I had ever seen. It was bright yellow, like a great splash of sunlight. The Light of Ama, by whose grace he ruled.

Tykavn came straight to me. Oh, he greeted Father and Mother first, but only on his way to me. He exuded energy and masculine power, and his eyes, river-green and shiny, seemed a well of intellect and deep concerns that I would never fathom. Yet there was a trace of vulnerability in them, too.

'Halla Iolithie Gaefir-daughter,' he said warmly. He spoke with the beautiful Onareyru accent which everyone at Court imitated. 'You were only a child the last time we met. Do you remember?'

'Of course, Your Highness. I was twelve.' I'd been awestruck then, too. We'd had a long conversation about horses, and I'd never forgotten how friendly, how natural he had been. Not what I'd expected of a Prince at all.

'Well, don't be nervous of me,' he said. Irresistible, a mighty person being kind. 'We are cousins, after all. Still love horses?'

'Yes, Your Highness.'

'That's something of a miracle, after you've had to sit on a saddle all day. I hope your journey wasn't too tiring.'

'Not at all. It's an honour to be invited to your wedding.'

A shadow came to his eyes. 'If it takes place,' he murmured. He bit his lower lip, blew a soft breath through his teeth. 'It's no light matter, riding through the Stolen Land. Nothing happened to me when I came here from Onareyru, yet I've never been so frightened in all my life. I wish it hadn't been necessary for the Lady Antrid to make this journey.'

His confiding tone took me by surprise. I felt I could ask him or tell him anything. 'You must be very happy that she's joining you at last.'

He shrugged and half smiled. 'I hardly know her, halla. It's a marriage arranged by my father. A suitably accomplished, beautiful noblewoman. Because of my duties I am already several years beyond the usual age of marriage, so it is clearly a matter that cannot wait any longer.' He seemed to grow restless as he spoke; his gaze swivelled from mine and he turned to Laasastiuk. 'Still nothing?'

The Arch-Perfect shook his head. Tykavn sighed. He seemed to have the weight of the world on his shoulders, and I wished desperately that there was something I could do to help.

You may gather I liked him. For the second time, I felt envious of the marvellous Lady Antrid.

Ama forgive me.

Mother, Father and I were each given a guest chamber of our own, and I loved the novelty of having a room all to myself. Mehaar's bed was in the ante-room, but I invited her in so she could share my fascination with the beautiful tiling, the crystal windows and the shutters made of real wood. The bed, too, was made completely of wood. I'd never seen such an extravagance of the stuff, in this land where nothing grows taller than a bush. We make our furniture and tools from woven reeds, stone or metal, and we're masters at preparing food that needs no cooking, so we can conserve scrub for only the most essential fires. The bedframe was ancient, cracked and faded with age, it's true, but it must have been priceless. This seemed the most wonderful luxury. I had no desire to go back to my tedious life in Vryatan.

On a marble cabinet by the bed lay a thick book bound in goat-hide. I opened it and gasped. The pages weren't made of rough flattened reeds, but of real paper, smooth and creamy, turning golden-yellow with age around the edges.

'Look, Mehaar. Have you ever seen anything so beautiful?'

The pictures were exquisite, brightly coloured with real gold leaf burnished into them. We bent over the book together, turning the pages with slow reverence. There was Ama portrayed as a man, dressed in blue with rays of light pouring from his head and hands; Sudema, a black-haired woman wrapped in violet. She was arrogant and beautiful where she was Ama's consort, crone-like and cunning after He banished her into the night. Eileah, her replacement, was round, white and gentle as a cloud.

When we'd seen the pictures, I sat down with the book on my lap. Mehaar sat on the floor, leaning against my legs, and I read to her.

'Now it happened that Sudema was jealous of Eileah, for Eileah was obedient and Ama loved and cherished her. So one night while Ama slept, Sudema stole Eileah away from him and held her prisoner in the darkness of her domain, Kvold.

'Ama could not walk in the night, because night only exists where he is not. So he shone strong upon a tall rock, and to the Shadow that was cast he spoke thus: "I command thee to rise up and live; I charge thee to go into the Night where I cannot walk, and to deliver my wife Eileah from Sudema's cruel hands."

'And the Shadow rose up and answered, "However thou commandest me, I shall obey; for thy Light is the Law, mighty Ama, and I am thy Emissary . . ." Do you want to hear the adventures of Hendleiknir in Kvold?'

'Not now, halla,' said Mehaar. She yawned. 'I'm too tired.'

I turned over pages and pages of the horrors the Emissary had faced until he finally rescued Eileah from Sudema and brought her safely back to Ama. ' "Then in gratitude Ama gave his Emissary a human form and bestowed on him the name Hendleiknir, and sent him to Vivirjosa as his Prophet, there to spread the Word of the Light . . ." '

Mehaar was nearly asleep. I closed the book, sent her to her own room and climbed into the luxurious bed.

11

I couldn't sleep.

More powerful than the excitement of being here was the knowledge that the Border with the Stolen Land was so close. The sight of those mountains haunted me. I was desperate to see them again. I imagined walking by the river, hearing the rush of water, while knowing that the Unseen were only yards away on the far bank . . .

There would be no chance tomorrow. This was the only time I would have to myself. Night.

My candle had burned itself out. One set of shutters wasn't properly closed, and a grainy rose light fell through the congealed crystal of a window, turning the white tiles coral. Our apartments were on the ground floor, and my room was on an outside wall. It took me five minutes to dress, to discover how to open the window and to climb through it.

Outside, the lava-scape swept away under the black sky and the Palace wall of the city rose up beside me. No one wandered outside after dark.

I knew I might be taking a risk, but that only made it more exciting. I said a warding prayer and drew the circle of Ama over my chest as a precaution; but when had the creatures of Sudema ever crossed to this side of the Torlau? I was only going down to the river. Just to look.

As for Antrid, I was too involved in my own adventure to think of her. She was a name, not a real person. How could her journey go wrong when it was merely an image in my mind?

Although it was summer, the wind fluttered cold in my hair and I tightened the string of my hat. People tell me I'm nothing to look at; my hair is bronze, my skin fair, my eyebrows so thick, dark and straight that I look bad-tempered even though I'm not. Well, not very. But sometimes people dislike me just for my eyebrows.

I walked towards the river down long slopes of ash and shale, scrambling down under overhanging brows of rock. The sky was glassy-black with a sprinkling of white stars – one, big and lividly purple, scintillating malignly to the north-west. The Eye of Sudema, goddess of the night and of everything dark and sinful, the antithesis of Ama. I circled myself, and felt a necklace of sweat on my throat.

But when I came to a hill-peak and the mountains unrolled before me, my heart sprang with excitement. At the bottom of the long slope lay the river, not fast-flowing as I'd imagined, but wide, still and dark as volcanic glass. To the left was the Torlau Bridge, the only gateway to the Stolen Land. Specks of smoky yellow light marked the presence of Border-guards down there, armed with fire-brands.

Further down the slope I found a strange rock. It was an oval slab tilting up out of the ground, twin-lobed like a flattened backside, sheened pink in the star's light. I climbed on to it and lay with my face to the sky and arms outstretched, as if on an altar.

Sudema's fiery light suffused me. I was tempting fate. I knew it was wrong to expose myself to it, but I wondered how it would harm me, how it might feel. Would the tainted glow burn me, corrupt me, or call down a mass of the Unseen to carry me away?

I lay there. Nothing happened.

Except that I was becoming aware of a faint drumming in the air, a sound coming from a very great distance, streaming in on the wind. Urgent and imperative it sounded, yet intangible. I visualized a volcano erupting, far away. Or an earthquake fissure racing towards me until it cracked the slab on which I lay and tipped me down into the earth . . . No. It was only the wind blowing through the stones.

The farmlands along the river were bloody-silver in the star's radiance. I could see goats down there, little grey clouds asleep on their shadows.

But the far side, the forbidden country – I'd imagined a nightmare region, a boiling plain of lava where monsters roamed and the air was torn by screams and roars. Yet it was shadowy and still and looked no more sinister than the scoured hills of Torbyrgi. Richer, perhaps; not overgrazed.

Thandarkyr was once whole, they say. How do they know? When did Sudema's Unseen drive the good people of Ama out of Inner Thandarkyr and the magnificent city of Vivirjosa, and why did they stop short of Torlossen and Onafross? Our history is so wrapped in religious euphemism that the truth has been lost. Even though I was young and had swallowed the myths by rote, I knew this.

My heart was thumping as if trying to burst out of this cage of ignorance. I longed to go into the Stolen Land and find out the truth!

I wasn't ready to be an adult. We have some freedom as children, but adulthood, at sixteen, demands conformity. The choice is between marriage and celibacy; there is nothing else.

Marriage brings heightened Status and it isn't for ever; when child-raising duty is done, the parents separate, become celibate Perfects and take their seats on the Assembly. Their reward is a certain amount of authority and power. My father and mother became Perfect four years ago; we still saw Father often, but he lived alone, while I stayed with Mother until my future was decided. I have no siblings; there was a brother who died before I was born, and after me no more children came.

I sometimes wonder if my parents resented having to part. Knowing them, I doubt it. Their devotion to Ama always meant more to them than their own family, and I've never heard them express a word of regret. They took their Vows of Perfection; Father gathered his belongings and left; life went on.

So, I could marry; and any boy in Vryatan would have been willing, despite my looks, to wed Perfect-Governor Gaefir's daughter. Shame there wasn't a single one I thought good enough for me.

Some choose to be celibate from the beginning and devote their lives to the service of our God. They are called Sublimes and they work themselves to death and have no political influence at all; their consolation is that they win society's reverence and the ultimate relationship with Ama.

I don't think I have the strength of belief for that.

There is one more choice, of course. The Vows and Laws that bind us to Ama are sacred. Break them, and we have all Status stripped from us and spend our days as bondservants, forever despised. The menial work they are put to may be tolerable, but the shame is not.

So I lay on the lobed rock in a state of confusion, daring Sudema's fire as if it might burn some kind of sense into me. I was chasing my thoughts round in a trance . . .

The voice dropped on to me like a wave of ice water.

'Here, behind this rock,' it said. 'This will do.' A second later a bulky silhouette loomed up beside the rock, stopped dead and stared down at me.

I almost screamed with shock. I don't know who was more startled, him or me; but his reactions were fast and as I tried to leap up he grabbed my arm.

'Stop there, halla.' It was a Border-guard. He looked brutal, impregnably plated, and the face under the leather helmet was in shadow. 'What in Ama's name are you up to?'

I felt sweat soaking into the collar of my jacket, but as he

14

shook me for a response I saw a smaller figure duck down behind him. I had a quick glimpse of the face and scared eyes as the figure turned and scampered away down the hillside. Finally I squeaked, 'Nothing, mathyr. I came out for a walk.'

He gawped at me in disbelief. 'Have you just fallen out of the sky? Don't you know the Laws of Torlossen?'

'I know them,' I said. 'I wanted to see the Border, that's all.'

'Bloody little fool! The Laws are made for people's safety. I'll have to report you.'

I was trembling. Because of Gaefir's Status I was unlikely to get into any official trouble; but I dreaded my father's wrath, dreaded bringing on him the shame of having a wilful daughter. 'No, there's no need to do that, surely.'

'It's my duty,' he said. He looked furious, and I was scared; but I can think fast when I have to.

I tried to harden my voice. 'You report me and I'll report what I saw.'

His hand tightened. 'You saw nothing!'

'Oh, the lad I saw running off was river mist, was he?'

'Trick of the light,' the guard said thinly.

'A trick of the light . . . named Langyr.'

As I spoke the boy's name he let me go. Mine was not a Status-stripping offence; his most definitely was. His anger frayed into dismay. 'You sharp-eyed little—'

'It was just your misfortune to pick on someone I know!' I was horrified, actually. The Border-guards are all Sublimes. Everyone knows that Vows get broken, but when it happens there is disgust and outrage. And I'd never expected to come so nearly face to face with the breaking.

He let go of my arm, scared now. The star's light shone on him and I saw that he was fair-skinned and much younger than I'd thought. 'You mustn't tell anyone. You won't.'

'You'd no right to entice Langyr up here. He's just a boy. Leave him alone!'

'He was willing. He's not a child. It's almost impossible for men like us – it's loneliness, it's – Ama's Fire, you don't know how it is!' he said. He sounded desperate. 'No one knows.'

'I'm not sure I want to.' I rubbed at my bruised arm. 'All I am saying is, don't tell on me and I won't tell on you.'

'Clever girl, aren't you, halla?' he said bitterly. 'You win. I won't report you.'

'But what harm am I doing? I just wanted to look, that's all.'

'At the scenery.' His tone was sceptical, resigned. 'Have a look, then. Damn all to see.' And he sat down on the rock next to me and we looked out across the fire-tinted sweep of the landscape together. He offered me a drink of beer from his flask, then seemed to relax a little. If he'd been angry that I'd interrupted his tryst with Langyr, perhaps he was glad now that I'd saved him from the sin. He seemed glad of someone to talk to.

'What's your name, mathyr?' I asked.

'Call me Tsevren,' he said. I doubt it was his real name but it didn't matter. 'Up from Vryatan for the wedding?'

'That's right. How long have you been a Border-guard?'

'Two years,' he said. 'God's Light, I hate it. But I couldn't have married, I couldn't have stood it . . . and when you're a Sublime you have to do whatever duty Ama requires – for Ama read Sublime-Elect, miserable old bastard.'

'I'll have to make the choice soon,' I said. 'But all the young men in Vryatan are coarse idiots and no one from Torlossen would have me, so . . .'

'Well, thank Ama they don't send female Sublimes to the Border, halla, unless you like being frozen, scared, bored and treated worse than a goat. There could only be one thing worse and that's being without any Status at all . . .' He trailed off. Perhaps he was still afraid I might report him, but I wouldn't, because I didn't see what right I had to judge him. I sensed that he worried a lot about his weakness being discovered, and I felt sympathy for him. It's hard trying to be perfect when most of us aren't.

I said, 'It's all very well being disgraced for your own sins. But it's an awful thing to be punished for someone else's. Like our Mehaar; she never did wrong in her life. Her parents were Sublimes who broke their Vows. So because Mehaar's illegitimate she can never be anything but a bondservant. It doesn't seem fair. She's such a sweet girl, too.'

He smiled. 'Be careful, halla. Sins of the flesh cut all ways.'

My face went hot. 'She's a sister to me!'

As we talked, the low drumming noise I had noticed before sounded closer, metallic, yet still so distant that I could only hear it in the spaces in our conversation. Yet it filled me with a sense of wild and distant mountains, meadows where flowers grew; a vast mythical land where life was richer and more exciting. The land that Sudema's legions had stolen.

'There must be something else,' I whispered. 'Somewhere else to go.'

'Well, there isn't. We live like this because it works; everyone gets fed and looked after, one way or another. If we all started breaking the rules there'd be chaos; just what Sudema would like, I should think.'

'But people do travel to and from Onafross. If I had the wealth or the power—'

Tsevren cut in, shaking his head. 'Sounds glamorous, the Stolen Land, doesn't it? It's not, believe me. Do you know how many men have died, just trying to keep the Onafross Way open?'

'Have you been over the Border? Have you ever seen anything?'

'I've had to go on the far side of the bridge a few times. Yes, there's danger. You can't see them but you can feel them *watching*. It's said you only see them when they're about to kill you. But you can hear them. You go out weaving circles of fire like a madman to protect yourself and you can hear them snarling and backing off . . .' He shuddered. 'If you want to know how wonderful the Stolen Land is, you can ask Lady Antrid when she arrives.'

He was being sarcastic, but I decided that if I had a chance to speak to her I would do exactly that.

Tsevren took a swig from his flask. In the pause, I heard the strange drumming noise very clearly. It seemed to vibrate up from the earth and right through my bones.

'Do you hear that sound?' I said softly. 'Is it the wind?'

He was silent, listening, and the vibration streamed in on the air, persistent, ringing. He rose to his feet. 'No. That's horses galloping . . .'

I stood up beside him. The sound was distinct now, and it sounded like a headlong stampede. There was panic in it. I shivered with empathic fear. I thought I could hear cries mingled with the hoofbeats. Human screams of terror and pain.

'Ama preserve us,' Tsevren murmured. 'Look.'

I looked where he was pointing and I saw shadow shapes on the far bank. Horses were streaming down into the river valley like a flight of geese, necks outstretched, burnished bronze in the starlight. I counted at least twenty, but only a handful still had riders on their backs. Pure terror and urgency burned from every line of them, man and beast.

17

Tsevren forgot about me and started to run down the hillside towards the bridge. I went straight after him. I knew there were other guards down there but I didn't care.

As I ran I saw the Border-guards forming up on our side of the bridge to slow the stampede, their torches weaving light-lines in the air. But the horses' flight did not slacken. Like sand through an hour-glass they squeezed on to the bridge and came thundering across. The guards, unable to hold their ground, broke and scattered in front of the stampede, shouting.

Tsevren and I were about two hundred yards away by now, with the bridge on our left. As the horses poured on to the near bank they swerved off in different directions, crazed. Two came careering up towards us, scattering foam and sweat as they came, mad-eyed. The flecks they scattered were blood-red.

One horse was riderless, but the other had a man slumped over the front of the saddle, hanging on for dear life. Tsevren stepped out to stop him but the horse pounded on, almost knocking him over. I smelled the hot pungency of sweat, the sickly-sweetness of meat. I caught a glimpse of the rider, hanging over the front of the saddle for dear life, heard a few of the words he was mumbling, 'All that's left... Hordes of them... never saw...'

The words bubbled out thick and guttural from his ruined mouth. He was past us and away, a shadow racing along the scarp; but the moment, the image, scorched like death into my mind.

Dear Ama, I wish I could burn that image out.

Sometimes when I close my eyes I can still see it. The face that was no longer a face; the nostrils two dark slits in a wet morass of blood and frayed muscle fibres. Teeth stretched lipless in a skull-grin. And the eyeballs, with their lids torn away, two white spheres glaring in blind terror.

CHAPTER TWO

SUBSTITUTE

I thought I might be of help to the Border-guards; I thought, in the confusion, no one would take any notice of me. But I'd only been down at the bridge a few moments before I heard someone say, 'What in Kvold is she doing down here?', and two guards came to arrest me.

There was no sign of Tsevren. Anonymous among the other Border-guards, he didn't come to my defence. How could he, without incriminating himself and me? I was led away to the stone guard-house nestled in the side of the hill, while behind me forty Border-guards tried to round up the stray horses, and the torch-fires danced on the black mirror of the Torlau.

The guards didn't know what to do with me at first, and they were too busy to bother. I was left locked in a little storeroom for an hour or more, listening to the people coming and going in the next room, and the murmur of their voices. At least I had company; one of the little wild-cats with tufted ears, who sometimes make us their pets, came and curled up on my lap.

I realized the guards were bringing in the survivors of the Onafross party. I heard a man weeping, another coughing softly as if his lungs were ruptured. I could guess what had happened, but I wanted to be told for certain; not out of morbid curiosity. Out of fear. I strained my ears but I couldn't hear a word they were saying.

An officer-Sublime eventually came to me, and demanded to know who I was. When I told him, he went very quiet and dispatched me back to the Palace on horseback, accompanied by two Border-guards. Shifting the responsibility to someone else.

The guards wouldn't respond to my entreaties for information.

'It's not our position to say anything, halla,' one said gruffly. 'You'll know soon enough.'

'You probably know as much as we do,' said the other.

19

When we reached Torbyrgi, messengers had preceded us and the Palace was in a subdued state of panic.

Feeling like a criminal, I was delivered to the first Perfect the guards could find. There were whispered exchanges, concerned looks in my direction. I seemed to be a minor inconvenience in the midst of a drama. I was given into the charge of a Lady Mynirrie, who took me to an ante-room, brought me a cup of hot wine, and left me there.

I waited, my heart a small hard lump in my throat, for hours. Had they woken my parents? Was Father furious? Yet no one came. I think they'd forgotten me. I was treated neither as an honoured guest nor as a transgressor; I was simply ignored.

To take my mind off the waiting, I studied my prison a little at a time. Columns of black polished stone, veined with blue and speckled with glittering nacre. Intricate tiling of black and white. On the walls, religious scenes had been exquisitely created by inlaying flakes of coloured stone. There was the sun – a golden figure in a halo of flames – quarrelling with Sudema; Sudema the Evening Star running away into the night, turning from a beautiful woman into a grotesque crone as she went; Ama taking Eileah as his consort, Sudema trying to steal and corrupt their children. There was the Prophet Hendleiknir venturing into Kvold to rescue Eileah from Sudema's grasp; and there he was again, bringing Ama's word to the world. I was spellbound.

But superimposed on everything I saw the man with the ruined face, dashing past me again and again and again.

Tiredness and wine extorted their fee. When the door opened at last I woke violently from a nightmarish doze.

Arch-Perfect Laasastiuk himself was standing in front of me. I sprang to my feet, off-guard and nervous. He was dressed in robes of creamy geitha which looked stiff enough to stand up on their own; everything about them, down to the stripes of black and gold woven into the hem, cried wealth and power. On his chest, the golden sun-symbol of Ama glinted at me like an eye, and the chain from which it depended was rich with semi-precious stones.

'Good evening, halla Gaefir-daughter,' he said. 'Morning, I should say. Do sit down, and don't be nervous.'

He spoke kindly, but there was a thread of steel in his manner. I sensed that he'd be fair with me, but not soft. Relaxing a little, I sat beside him on a grey marble bench.

'I'm sorry you've been kept waiting for so long,' he went on. 'Everyone assumed you to be someone else's responsibility, so it was several hours before the news of your presence filtered through to me. As you may be aware, there is a very grave situation.'

'Yes, I – I gathered that, Your Grace.'

'I understand that you may have witnessed a certain event.' He had a habit of running his tongue over his lips often as he spoke, so his wide mouth always looked pink and wet within his grey beard. 'However, it does seem very odd that you were down by the Torlau at night. Can you explain yourself?'

I tried to answer truthfully. 'I just wanted to see the river and the – the mountains. Father had said we couldn't go. It was my only chance—'

'So you disobeyed your father and broke the Law,' he said mildly.

'Yes. I know it was foolish, but—'

'Well, if we were born Perfect, Ama would have nothing to teach us, would he? I would have thought you'd outgrown childish high spirits by now, but let it pass. What did you see?'

I'd decided not to mention Tsevren, and then I grew uneasy, in case Laasastiuk already knew I'd met him. I described the hoofbeats, the horses streaming wild with fear across the bridge, and the man whose face had been torn away . . .

I started to shake as I described it. Delayed shock. The Arch-Perfect put a hand on my shoulder. 'Be calm, halla. Ama is with you.'

'But did they find him? Did he live?'

'They found him. He did not live.'

I put my face in my hands. Laasastiuk's presence was comforting, fatherly.

'I could have hidden or run away,' I said. 'I went down to the bridge to see if I could help.'

'And that was commendable.'

I was afraid to ask, but I had to know. 'Your Grace, they were the Lady Antrid's party, weren't they?'

'Yes.'

'What about – about her?'

He sighed heavily. 'Border-guards have been dispatched to look for her. Nothing will be known for certain until they return.'

My heart was hammering. Antrid was becoming real enough now. It crept on me slowly, the shock and the grief, but this was a tragedy. A tragedy.

'Will you have to tell my parents about me?' I asked dully.

He pressed my shoulder and looked sadly at me. 'I'm afraid so. Perfect-Governor Gaefir is a friend of mine. Disobedience is a serious misdemeanour, as you know. However, in your case it has been overshadowed by graver events. I doubt that your punishment will be severe. I know you are tired, but I have to ask you to stay here a little longer.'

'Why?' I was longing to go to my bed; to cry, to sleep, to find Mehaar; anything, just to unravel this cold pain.

'Prince Tykavn wants to see you.'

I turned colder. Laasastiuk stood up, making the sign of Ama over me. 'Be patient, halla. Ama is with you. Pray for the Lady Antrid, not for yourself.'

I did. With all my soul, I did.

I sensed activity beyond the door, hushed comings and goings. It was still an hour before dawn, but lights burned and no one slept.

I tried to stay awake, but I was dozing again when Tykavn came in. I shook myself and prepared to be alert, deferential, correct, everything one should be with a prince. I was destined to fail miserably, but he was clearly in no state of mind to care how I behaved.

He was alone. His fine clothes were dishevelled as if he'd been in them too long, and his strong face was gaunt with exhaustion and strain. He stared down at me, his large green eyes showing the whites all around. I started to get up to bow, but he was standing too close and his eyes pinned me to the seat.

At last he said, 'You saw it happen, didn't you?' His voice was hoarse, trembling a little.

His manner alarmed me. 'What, Your Highness?' I gasped.

'You saw the Lady Antrid die. Didn't you?'

I felt horribly aware of perspiration trickling down my back, as if I'd filled his exquisite chamber with smells of damp mohair and sweat. 'No, no, I didn't. I only saw what I told Laasastiuk, the rider with the injured face . . .'

'You didn't see her?'

'No, truly.'

'Well, what did you see?' he demanded.

He paced around the room while I described it all again. He seemed to have such difficulty in believing me that I stumbled over the words and began to sound to myself as if I was lying. And when I'd finished he made me go through it again. And

22

again. He asked question after question, most of which I couldn't answer.

'I don't know, Your Highness,' I kept saying. '*I don't know.*'

He wasn't seeing me as a person; he didn't care about my transgression. Why should he? He was distraught. His grief and his endless questions distressed me unbearably.

'You must know! You were there!'

'I swear by Ama's Light, I saw nothing of the lady!' I raised my voice, and I think it shocked him. I was on the verge of tears.

He sank on to the bench next to me, close enough to touch. He let out a heavy, weary breath and said, 'I'm sorry, halla Iolithie. I have had a great shock. I know you could not possibly have seen her. The attack took place miles to the north. I wanted someone to tell me that it was a mistake, she was still alive . . . or at least that she hadn't suffered.'

'I couldn't give you that. It wouldn't have been true.'

'I know. I didn't mean to upset you. Forgive me.'

'Of course, Your Highness.'

'It's been a long night.' He signed again, frowned and rubbed at his forehead. His voice was quiet and grave. 'The Lady Antrid's party were set upon by the Unseen as they crossed the Stolen Land. Out of a party of fifty, only twenty horses escaped, and five or six riders.

'They found my lady on the rock, less than two hours' ride away. Her back was broken. She was covered in claw marks and her eyes were open. Blue eyes, she had. Black hair and blue eyes.'

I choked on a sob. 'Dear Ama above, I'm so sorry, Your Highness.'

'Yes,' he whispered. 'Yes, well. I thought if you could only say one word to the contrary, it might undo the nightmare . . . but nothing can. Nothing can.'

'You must have loved her,' I said.

He shook his head, pinching a fold of flesh between his eyebrows. 'I hardly knew her, but it makes no difference. It's my fault she died, you see. She was on her way here *for me.*'

He made the circle of Ama over his chest, then his hand fell limply to the bench at his side. He no longer seemed a remote figure, but completely human. And I took a gross liberty; I clasped my fingers round his hand, just as I would have done had Mehaar been upset.

Yet he didn't object. He only sat there and wept silently, while I held on to his cold hand.

Sleep descended like a boulder, when I finally went to bed, but the images rolled on through my mind. The drumming of hooves streaming towards me from the far, far distance . . . My imagination tried to put shapes on the Unseen ones, but they remained amorphous shadows, flowing down the hillsides towards the column of riders. In my dream Sudema's creatures made no sound. All I could see clearly was that they had long, curved claws like scythes to tear out the riders' hearts, mutilate them . . .

A man came towards me, pale with terror. I knew they were going to rip his face away. Yet they didn't slash and tear at him; a disembodied claw was cutting very carefully and neatly through the skin under his jaw. The calculated precision of it filled me with horror. Suddenly it was my face they were cutting, and I was watching from outside, unable to help myself . . .

'Halla Iolithie! Wake up, halla!'

I woke, shattered by tension and tiredness. Mehaar was kneeling by my bed. I looked into her sweet face and flung my arms round her neck.

'Horrible dreams,' I said. 'Horrible. Oh, Mehaar, have they told you?'

Her arms were long, slim, comforting around me. 'Told me what?'

'About Antrid. About what I saw.'

'You know they don't tell me anything, but I know something bad's happened.' She pulled back, and her dark eyes were fearful. 'Is it very bad?'

'The worst.'

'It's nearly noon, halla. Lord Gaefir wants to see you.'

A pebble of trepidation fell into my stomach. Laasastiuk and Tykavn had been bad enough; facing Father's questions would be worse. At least he'd let me sleep before the interrogation began.

'You'd better sort out my clothes, then,' I said, starting to climb out of the bed. But as Mehaar turned away I caught her arm and embraced her. 'After I've faced Father I'll tell you what happened dearest. It's not fair for you to be kept in the dark.'

Although Mehaar was our bondservant, I'd never been able to treat her as anything but a friend. She was so perfectly lovable, with her plaited blond hair and her dark eyes; always there, always smiling. She said little, and she never forgot her place, though I often wished she could. But I could pour everything out to Mehaar, who absorbed it all in silence and never betrayed my trust.

There was a communal room for Palace guests; a huge, light chamber, with fountains and seats on different levels and greenery growing wild in the steam of warm pools. But the Palace, which had seemed so strange and luxurious on my arrival, now felt confining. I was used to the open hillside outside our heimar, to coming and going as I pleased. I didn't like the feeling that I couldn't leave even if I wanted to.

I was relieved to find my mother, Vithrie, there on her own. She sat with a huge tapestry spread out on her knees, sewing swiftly and absently, her thoughts elsewhere.

I love my mother. She has long tawny hair and a fair, high-cheekboned face. She's graceful and charming, undaunted by the hard work of living, joyfully devoted to Ama; she's everything I would like to have been.

Sadly, she does not feel the same way about me.

'Where's Father?' I asked, sitting down on a step by her feet.

Vithrie looked sideways at me. 'I think he's still with the Arch-Perfect.' She returned her attention to her needlework.

'I thought he wanted to see me.'

'I expect he does. Just sit and wait for him.'

More waiting. I looked at Mother; Mother looked at her sewing. I said, 'Don't you want to ask me about last night?'

Her tranquil expression didn't change. 'I can wait until your father comes.'

'He's going to be angry with me.'

She glanced at me and smiled. 'I'm sure whatever you have done can't be so bad. Don't frown.'

'I'm not frowning!' Didn't she know by now that I always looked like this? 'I saw something awful last night. I saw Lady Antrid's party come back – what was left of them.'

'That must have been a terrible thing,' Vithrie agreed. 'Wait until your father comes. Do you think this brown is too dark against the beige?'

I gave up. I ventured the opinion that the brown was exactly right.

'No. No, it's too dark,' decided Mother.

Sometimes I think my occasional reckless behaviour was an attempt to get her attention, but it never worked. Her thoughts seemed to be on a different plane; on our God, I assume. She should have been a Sublime; then I would not have existed to plague her.

I gazed around at the marble walls and the rugs scattered on the floor of speckled tiles. Daylight, tinted green by the thick crystal of the windows, shone on the leaves of the trees in their tubs. Real living trees, growing inside, to be looked at like ornaments. Riches.

We'd come here for the wedding. Now there would be no wedding. There was no reason for us to stay. I felt an odd tugging at the thought of returning to our barren home, after tasting the luxury of the city. *I could like this place – if I had the freedom of it*, I thought. *Freedom and wealth.*

I heard footsteps and anxiety flooded through me. I didn't recognize my own father for a moment, so magnificent he looked in his fine Court clothes; geitha robes with needle-stripes of bronze and cream, a dark red cloak. His long hollow-cheeked face was sombre. He seemed a complete stranger to me; which, in a way, he always had been.

Mother remained seated, but I was on my feet. 'Well, Iolithie, I hope you have recovered from your adventures,' he said drily.

'Father, I can explain, I— '

'I wish I knew what to say to you! I've spoken twice this morning to Prince Tykavn and the Arch-Perfect-Elect. The first time, I learned how extremely foolish you had been. I told you there was to be no trip to the river. You disobeyed me and broke the Law in a display of childishness that would hardly befit a ten-year-old, let alone a girl on the verge of adulthood.'

'Yes, Father,' I said. 'I'm sorry. I only wanted to see— '

'If I want a comment from you, I shall ask for it!' His voice rang off the walls and I shivered. 'I hope you have learned your lesson.'

His tone softened a little and he came towards me. 'Why must you always put what you are told to the test? Couldn't you accept your own father's word that the Stolen Land is dangerous? The Laws are to protect us, not restrict us. Perhaps you don't appreciate that what you witnessed last night was part of an appalling tragedy.'

'I do, Father,' I said quietly. 'Out of fifty riders, only six survived.'

He turned away, as if unable to speak for a moment. 'Five,' he corrected me. 'And because of that, your own stupidity will not be punished. Sudema's Legions are real, my daughter. They may be Unseen but they exist. We are at war with them.'

He stopped, and the silence made the room shimmer like heat. Vithrie did not react, only listened to our exchange with a kind of sad acceptance that made me want to weep.

'However,' he said at last. He paused again. 'However, shortly after I had left His Highness the first time, he called me back again and said that he had been thinking. He said that despite the loss of his intended bride the wedding must go ahead. Another wife must be found. He does not want to risk the life of another noblewoman from Onafross, therefore he must choose a high-born young woman of his own province.'

I was racking my brains for noblewomen. There was Lady Mynirrie; but she was too old, had already been married and was now Perfect . . .

Father was looking hard at me. I swallowed and gasped. 'Oh, Ama's Fire.'

Father went on awkwardly, 'Tykavn said that he found you . . . sympathetic. He thinks you will do very well for him.'

I could hardly speak for shock. 'Do I have a choice?'

Gaefir frowned, but he said, 'Of course. He would not want you against your will.'

My first instinct was to say no. I wasn't even sure I wanted to get married. But I did like Tykavn, what little I'd seen of him. Everyone regarded him as a good ruler, hard-working and fair; and a man who could suffer so deeply, over the death of a woman he barely knew, must have a kind and sensitive heart. Hadn't I envied Lady Antrid?

My mind lashed out like a tongue into the future. Wife of the ruler of Torlossen! That would be all the wealth, respect and freedom I could desire. My shock turned to swooping excitement, only to be shot down by guilt. To think I'd envied Antrid – and now to be handed all her good fortune over her grave . . .

I said quietly, 'What do you think I should do, Father?'

He held my shoulders and kissed my forehead. 'You will accept him, of course. We could not be more honoured.'

'I know.' My voice failed. I drank in that rare moment of closeness with my father. We smiled at each other, and there were rims of light round his grey eyes.

'I will go and tell them of your decision,' he said, and left hurriedly. I don't think he wanted us to see him wipe his eyes.

I turned to Mother and hugged her. She hugged me back, but I felt the stiffness of her arms, the way she held her breath until the embrace was over. Physical demonstrations embarrassed her, but I couldn't help it. I wanted her to share it, to laugh, to tell me that everything would be wonderful.

'Mother, I can't believe it!'

She looked at me, and pinned her needle into the edge of her work. 'Why not? You're the daughter of the Perfect-Governor of Vryatan; you're his cousin, however distant. You are probably the only girl with royal blood of the correct age in Torlossen.'

'And he likes me.'

'Why shouldn't he?'

Because you don't seem to! I felt like shouting. 'Aren't you happy for me?'

She smiled, but it looked forced. 'Of course I'm happy for you. But you must realize that liking has nothing to do with this marriage. It's a political arrangement, that's all.'

'Well, I suppose I've no right to happiness, if it was won at the expense of Lady Antrid's life,' I said flatly.

A touch of disapproval came to Vithrie's eyes. At least I'd got a reaction! 'Such bitterness does you no credit. Be glad of what our good Lord Ama has given you. But listen to one piece of advice; don't fall in love with him, because marriage lasts only until you have brought your children to maturity. Give yourself to Ama, not to Tykavn, or in a few years your heart may be broken.'

I couldn't stop myself saying what I said in response.

It's so hard to describe Vithrie; the heart-stealing sweetness she had that she always seemed to be pouring into a void instead of on to me. I seemed to have spent my whole life trying to win her love and approval; even just her attention. I'd stopped expecting it long ago – but I could never stop wanting it.

'Well, thank you for explaining how you've protected your own heart, Mother,' I said furiously. I hated myself, but I couldn't stop. 'By never giving a damn about Father, or me, or even the son you lost.'

The outburst did not make me feel better. It made me feel utterly dreadful, as if I'd stabbed her, even though her face stayed like stone.

I knew I should wait for Tykavn to send for me, but I can't always see the point of doing things the correct way.

I wanted to see him. I wanted to reassure myself that he'd meant what he said, that he was as human and sincere as he'd seemed last night. He would still be in a state of shock, and I wanted him to know that I was there to comfort him if I could. After all, if we were to be married, why shouldn't I go and find him?

I knew where his rooms were. He might not be there or they might not let me in, but I'd talk my way in if I could. Yet when I reached the double-doors emblazoned with a huge golden sun, the attendant-Sublimes let me pass, and there were no Perfect-Councillors in the ante-rooms to stop me. In some ways, life in the Palace was less formal than I'd expected.

The door to a large, dark chamber stood half open, and I could hear someone moving about inside. I could see a bed, and I didn't think I should march into Tykavn's private room. I paused; Tykavn was in there alone, and I wasn't sure whether to call out or slip away unseen.

I saw that he was closing the shutters over the windows, making signs of consecration at each one to seal out Sudema's influence. Then he went to a small shrine in an alcove on the far side of the room and began to light candles.

He was preparing to pray. I knew I shouldn't watch, but he couldn't see me and I was intrigued.

The wall was of dark shiny stone, but the alcove shone sky-blue, with a blazing metal sun set in it. A small altar in front bore the circles of candles, the tiny gong and the symbolic golden hand of the Prophet Hendleiknir. Tykavn's hands were shaking as he lit the candles with a taper. His whole body trembled as he stood before the shrine, his hands, limbs, all his muscles knotted. Then the words began to pour out of him.

'I must protect this land. Lord Ama, give me the strength to protect my people. I implore you, Light of the Sun, don't let the Unseen break over the Border. May their evil be driven back to Kvold and burned and destroyed! Please, Lord, keep us safe from the Legions of Sudema . . .'

I had never heard anyone pray with such ardent desperation. He poured all his strength into it. And I could hear the hoofbeats again, the screams on the wind. Sudema's darkness blew through me and I hugged myself and shivered.

He prayed for fifteen minutes before his own pleas gave way to the calmer words of the set prayer.

Smoke and flame in the darkness of the chamber. The golden chime of the gong, struck by Tykavn to send his thoughts up to heaven. Ritual passes with the Prophet's Hand, flashes of gold.

Now each candle must be blown out in the correct order to seal the prayer. I knew the ritual. We performed it at home every day – though without such rich trappings – to ensure Ama's continuing blessing and protection. It was always comforting.

Here was the ruler of Torlossen, invoking the sun-god's power against the forces of night. He did it with the finesse and power of an Arch-Perfect. So why didn't I feel reassured? Why did I feel only lost and cold, watching him?

Because I felt his pain.

The last wick sent its rope of smoke to heaven, but Tykavn seemed to have found no release. He stood rigid for a moment. Then put his hands over his ears as if, like me, he could still hear the drumming. He fell to his knees, sweat pouring off him, crying, 'No. NO! What did I do wrong?'

I would have run to him, put my arms around him, said, 'Nothing, nothing. It's not your fault!' But I felt a gentle, strong hand on my arm, restraining me.

I jerked round, found Laasastiuk at my shoulder.

'Come away, halla,' he said gently. Sympathetic, not angry. 'You must never interrupt His Highness at his prayers. He is very devout. I know you want to help him, but only Ama can do that. As the Prophet tells us, only Ama can help any of us.'

CHAPTER THREE

THE RITUALS OF THE SUN

The wedding was delayed a tenday, to allow a period of mourning for the Lady Antrid, and to give me time to prepare.

Stroking Mehaar's single sleek plait of white-yellow hair, I told her how I felt. 'I wake every morning hugging myself, unable to believe my luck. Then I feel so guilty . . .'

'It was Ama's will,' said Mehaar.

'How could Ama have wanted that to happen? It's so unfair. Not only that she died, but that you . . .'

Mehaar looked up at me, her dark eyes wide. 'Halla?'

'That you can never have any of this, just because of some misfortune of birth which was no fault of yours. You can't marry, or be anything but a bondservant.'

'That, also, is Ama's will.' She bowed her head.

'I'm going to miss you so much,' I said. 'When you're at home with Mother, don't envy me living in luxury. Just remember that I am going to miss you desperately, all the time.'

'No, you won't, halla,' said Mehaar. 'You won't have time. You'll soon forget me.'

I was sure she was wrong. My new life was rushing at me too fast; I couldn't let go of the old.

A party of messengers was dispatched to Onafross to carry the sad news to Lady Antrid's family and King Vidvikjan. I doubt I was the only one who wondered, secretly, if they would ever arrive. What brave men they were to go at all. What would they see when they passed the place where the attack took place? My imagination painted hideous pictures. Dismembered remains of horses and men smeared across the hillsides for miles, splashes of blood colouring the rock like iron.

Then I'd make the circle of Ama over my breast and drive the images out, thanking the God that there was so much else to occupy my mind.

The moment I became Tykavn's betrothed, it seemed my

thoughts, my body, my time were no longer my own. I'd become part of a larger entity, a circle which sucked me in, revolved around me and possessed me. Married courtiers, Perfect-Councillors and Perfect-Ministers all had advice to offer, endless lessons in etiquette, duty, religious belief. I felt I was being treated as an ornament to be splendidly decorated and revered; while, like an ornament, I was not expected to have any life inside.

While my own parents kept their distance, Laasastiuk and Mynirrie were almost a father and mother to me. The Arch-Perfect gave me religious instruction, polishing my performance of rituals and ensuring I understood the meaning of prayers.

'Prince Tykavn is a very pious man,' he told me several times. 'He is an example to us all. Every action he takes is devoted to our God; he never acts without asking for guidance and blessing. This is in accord with the Prophet's teaching.'

I wondered to what extreme I was meant to carry this. Each time I washed my hands, combed my hair, or selected an under-garment, was I meant to look up and ask Ama, 'Is this all right?'

I wonder Ama didn't strike me down for this blasphemous thought. When the Arch-Perfect-Elect himself instructs you to be devout, you obey. I could only pray that Tykavn would find me suitably holy.

The Lady Mynirrie was the Palace Physician. She ran the royal household and answered only to Tykavn and Laasastiuk – although she would also be subject to me, after the wedding. It was strange to think that I, an awkward sixteen-year-old, would be able to command this mature and accomplished noblewoman. She was tall, with curly coppery hair and a huge nose. I sensed that her intellect would have crushed mine like a boot crushing a river-fly; yet, out of kindness, she held back.

She instructed me in my wifely duties, which came down to one thing: 'Always obey your husband in all respects.'

I must be gracious, holy, compliant; I must sing if he commanded it, read to him, pray, or be silent, whatever his mood dictated. I must never be ill. I would endure the problems of pregnancy and childbirth with uncomplaining fortitude. I would always look presentable, and be a credit to him in public.

I took all this in with great patience until, one day, I couldn't stay silent any longer. 'It sounds awful,' I said. 'I'm sure my mother was never so subservient to my father. Why must women endure this?'

'Hush, before you blaspheme,' said Mynirrie. 'Next you'll be asking why Sudema was punished for not obeying Ama.'

'Well, why was she?'

'It's just the way of things. One has to rule and one obey, or there'd be chaos. But it's not so bad. In years past, women were not allowed on the Assembly, and only men had Status. There have been improvements, even an acknowledgement that men start life almost as Imperfect as us. You don't know how lucky you are, so do the Prince's will and thank Ama for your blessings.' The sensible way Mynirrie advised me made it all seem acceptable. She smiled. 'Don't despair. It's not for ever. You'll be Perfect before you're forty, and then you can begin to live your own life.'

Yet my advisers were talking not about a Prince but about a man who'd let me clasp his hand while he wept in front of me. We'd shared a tragedy and that bound us together. I endured the instruction because I didn't want to displease Tykavn, and at the end of it all there would only be us; two human beings, alone and equal.

I was still nervous with him. Until the wedding we were allowed to meet only formally and that gave us no chance to speak our feelings. I was often uncomfortably aware of his exalted rank, his magnificence, the differences between us.

The day after Lady Antrid's funeral, a party from the Palace went out to ride across the hills round Torlossen. It was a ritual of respect; of reflecting on our sadness and releasing Antrid's spirit to the sky. We rode mostly in silence, and I found Tykavn beside me.

Our horses walked side by side in step, golden necks arched, black manes flowing. The sun-god's light coaxed a warm plum-brown glow from the rocks and brushed the lower slopes with green. Moving away from the others, Tykavn reined in on the crest of a hill and we looked down on the green-blue Torlau, the mountains beyond wreathed in silver cloud. It was exciting to be alone with him.

'You were so curious to see the Stolen Land,' said Tykavn. His voice was gentle, but there was an odd note buried in it. 'So, there it is. Isn't the view better in the light?'

'It's beautiful,' I said. Its loveliness was stunning, and I felt no sense of evil. 'It's hard to believe there's such danger on the other side.'

Tykavn gazed across the river. His hands tightened on the

reins and I saw a glint of rage in his eyes. He murmured, 'Sudema's Legions stole the best of Thandarkyr; they took Vivirjosa, the most glorious city ever built. But they won't steal Torlossen. I shall stand against them.'

'And I'll stand with you, my lord.'

His reaction astonished me. Glaring at me, he snapped, 'I've always stood against them alone. I have no need of your help!'

I exclaimed, 'But I'm to be your wife! If I can't support you, what can I do?'

He seemed to recover himself and spoke more gently. 'I don't expect you to take on my responsibilities. I'll still have to face them alone. You don't understand the evil of them. They're shape-changers, demons. Sudema's ill-begotten progeny.'

'But anything I can do to help you, I will,' I said. 'Please realize that. I want to be a good— '

He cut across me. I don't think he was listening. 'There's only one reason that Ama's protection failed the Lady Antrid, which was that *we* have failed Ama. We didn't pray hard enough for her safe passage. We were Imperfect. For that, we were punished. Imperfection lets Sudema in and feeds her evil strength.' He looked straight at me, blinking, considering. He looked so pre-occupied. I felt helpless in the face of the burdens that weighed him down. 'I fear it will not be easy for you, Iolithie, being my wife. I'm sorry.'

They had explained what would happen on the wedding day, but when it came, my expectations seemed to have no connection with reality.

Bars of green-gold light lay across the communal hall; the air was dusty, light-edged. Everything looked crisp yet imprecise through the glass wall of my anxiety. All the men had been banished and there were only women with me now, fussing over my hands and hair and bridal clothes. When they finished, I would leave my parents and my girlhood behind. One day, I might look back on this morning and smile at my own naïvety; I would have taken my place on the Assembly by then, and might be attending the wedding of a daughter of my own. But that was very far in the future and there was a mapless dark road to tread first.

Half of me was on fire with excitement; the other half wished that I was at home and none of this was happening.

'Try to keep still,' Mother said benignly, tugging at the hand she was trying to wash. 'You're bound to be nervous, but this wedding won't change what you are inside. It doesn't make you special.'

Second-best, I thought, and that sobered me. I'd been trying not to think that it should have been Lady Antrid whom they were grooming and anointing, not me ... And my heart twisted with the pain of leaving Mother and Mehaar. I wasn't ready. I hadn't made Mother love me yet.

But Mehaar whispered, 'You are so fortunate, halla.' Her fair face was alight with excitement. 'I'm so happy for you.'

I held her hands in mine and smiled. 'A mere husband won't come between us, dear. I wish you could stay with me.'

They dressed me in a robe of yellow geitha, fine as silk, patterned with white and gold. They scraped back my hair and plaited it, leaving my face bare and unadorned. Lastly they anointed my hands and feet with oil, lifted me up and led me out of the communal room.

In the main hall of the Palace, Lady Mynirrie organized the procession; Palace officials, Father and Mother on either side of me, the married women of the Palace as my attendants, my silent uncles, Sublimes in the royal livery of white, black and blue. I didn't even know half the people in the train. Ama knows what they thought of me, a girl from nowhere marrying their prince.

We left the Palace and walked the length of Torbyrgi's main street towards the huge doors.

I tried not to look up, but I was aware of the crowds lining the tiers of galleries above. It was a clear, fine day, green-blue light falling through the glass cupolas of the roof. So many people watching. It struck me suddenly that this was terrible, walking through their burning scrutiny to be married to a stranger.

That was what Prince Tykavn still was, after all. When we walked out into daylight it took all my willpower not to run for the hills.

As we walked, Vithrie whispered in my ear, 'Still nervous?'

'Terrified,' I replied.

'So was I. But it's good. The more you sweat, the better. It's the heat of your skin, you see, that makes the purple dye turn white.'

That was, perhaps, the kindest thing my mother was capable of saying.

The walk to the Fane was gruelling. There are small chapels

within the Palace and the city, but the main House of Ama, the Arch-Perfect-Elect's throne, was on the far side of the Assembly. A twisting path winds up a stepped hillside; on either side are huge crazed slabs of lava with cracks that would break your leg if you didn't take care. The slabs stop, suddenly, at a cliff edge. Below, a huge arena fans out, half-circled by another lava wall which tilts up in steps of ideal proportions to make rows of seats for five hundred or so Perfect-Councillors. That is the Thjoth, our Assembly where the meetings are held and the Laws are made. Beyond lies the silver-blue Lake Thjothvatn, on the far side of which, gleaming grey and coppery-green against the distant mountains, stands the House of Ama.

All along the stone tracks and the lakeshore, our route was lined with cheering Torlosseners; children, fishermen, farmers, smiths, Perfects, Sublimes, bondservants. More people than I'd ever seen. I went hot and cold to think that it could be such a cause for celebration, that a wedding could be so important.

I was relieved to reach the Fane. The interior was cool and dark. It took a few moments for my eyes to adjust, but I heard the breathing and rustling of people in the darkness. Glints of gold and bronze, the rays of the gold metal sun winking above the altar. I saw the Arch-Perfect-Elect at the altar, a figure in rich robes of white sewn with gold and ochre, waiting for me. Laasas-tiuk had told me what to expect. Before I could be married, I must be cleansed.

In a trance, I let my parents lead me to him. The rays of the metal sun seemed to radiate from his head. He looked on me as if I were something unclean, and suddenly that was how I felt; godless, a daughter of the Night Star, whose influence always contaminated those who did not offer themselves up to Ama every second of the day.

'Iolithie Gaefir-daughter, you are today given up by your family into the hands of Ama,' he said, and I felt my mother's and father's hands slide from my arms, felt them move back into the darkness. It was as if they had dropped me. I felt rootless suddenly, on the dizzying brink of something I didn't understand.

As Laasastiuk began to speak the words of the ritual, he painted symbols on my forehead, with a gold Hand of the Prophet dipped in little bowls of dye. The yellow circle for Ama, the sun; and within it the purple disk of Sudema, the Goddess-demon of night, confined and constrained by the circle.

Flanked by two female Sublimes, Laasastiuk led me behind the altar and through a filigree door into a small chapel. The altar there was a smaller echo of the main one, the walls black as basalt.

As the door clanged shut, he seized me bodily and threw me down on the altar. I'd been told to expect it but it was still a shock. The cold stone bruised me, and the pain made me indignant; my instinct was to hit back and tell him to leave me alone – but I bit my lip, swallowed the blasphemy until it choked me. The Sublimes glided forward, stretched me out and slid stone loops over my wrists and feet, clamping them down so I was held rigid. Then Laasastiuk purged Sudema out of me.

Heat, Mother had said. The sweat was streaming off me. The Arch-Perfect was sketching signs over me, circle within circle. He struck me with the gold Hand on its rod, symbolizing obedience. He roared out the words that would drive the evil from my body, his voice so loud that I shook as if caught in a thunderstorm. Thank the Light the responses didn't desert my scrambled brain. I screamed them back at him until my throat was sore.

Never in my life have I felt so vulnerable, so humiliated as I did at that moment. I submitted completely, body and soul, but a distant part of my mind was screaming. *I don't want to be here. I'd rather stay a child for ever. Why did I agree to this?*

At last they lifted me up and the Sublimes shook the creases out of my gowns and arranged a veil on my head. Then Laasastiuk led me out and presented me to the congregation. Smiles of satisfaction; the disc on my forehead had turned from the purple of Sudema to the white of Eileah, the consort of Ama. In sheer relief that it was over, I felt drained yet light as air, truly cleansed. White as the disc; calm and receptive as earth. I was purified and ready to receive my husband.

Down the length of the aisle, framed in the doorway, I saw Prince Tykavn coming towards me. He, too, wore the golden-yellow of the God. The purging left me beyond fear; the ceremony of joining was simple, gentle, a prelude to joy. When it was done, Prince Tykavn smiled and kissed my mouth, and I saw real affection in his eyes.

'Do you know what to do?' said Tykavn.

We were alone in the royal bedroom, now our bridal chamber. The celebrations were over; they'd meant nothing. Only this moment mattered. I'd kept Lady Mynirrie with me as long as I could, finding little tasks for her, delaying the moment, but at last she had tactfully suggested that it was time she left us alone.

The bridal chamber was huge and dark. I half-expected a crowd of courtiers to file in and witness the consummation of the marriage. The walls and floor were black marble, figured with spider-lines of white and indigo. There was a giant bed of black wood, with a dark blue coverlet. The golden sun of Ama hung over the bed, and tied by silver cord to the canopy were phials of soil; the sacred soil of Torlossen, on which the Legions of Sudema had never set foot.

I didn't want to make Tykavn impatient, but I was so nervous. All the same I was determined to behave correctly, with dignity. Not to disgrace my family.

'Sit down,' he said, indicating the bed, where a white cloak lay spread out. 'Yes, on the cloak. This is difficult for us both. I am not used to . . . to having someone here with me.'

I bowed my head and obeyed. He seemed so formal. Was it because he was as nervous as me? Celibacy until marriage was the rule; I knew some broke it, despite the risk of losing Status, but I was sure Tykavn had not. This was so awkward.

Tykavn shed his yellow robe. Underneath he wore a thin shirt, waistcoat and split-skirt breeches, all in fine white geitha. Leaning down, he kissed me and said, 'I want you to be happy, Iolithie.'

I smiled. 'I want to please you, my lord.'

I thought the ice was broken, but he managed to seal it again. He straightened up and glanced around the room as if distracted, making me feel shut out, almost as if I shouldn't be there. His gaze lingered on the shrine and his lips moved; I lipread something like, *No, it will be all right.*

He seemed so tense. Was he wishing I was black-haired, blue-eyed Antrid?

'Do you understand what we must do?' he said.

I was brought up with farm animals around me; I'd bred horses and goats since childhood. Sex held no great mystery for me, though I realized – hoped – it must be different between humans. *'The first time can be uncomfortable,'* Mynirrie had told me. *'After that it will be better. You probably know as much as he does – only let him think he's teaching you.'*

So I said, 'I – I understood that it was for you to guide me – my lord.'

'No, not that,' he said impatiently, waving at the bed. 'I mean the warding. The rite we must perform before the marriage can be consummated.'

I was startled. Mynirrie had mentioned such rites, but told me they were considered old-fashioned and unnecessary now. The cleansing and blessing of the Perfect-Minister were enough to sanctify the union. But I recalled Laasastiuk's cryptic words: *'Lord Tykavn will wish to perform certain religious rites before sleeping. You must accord with his wishes in all details. He is very devout.'*

I said quickly. 'That is what I meant, my lord.'

He sat down on the bed beside me and put his arm round my shoulders. He looked anxious. What did he have to fear? He was so strong, yet his moist green eyes seemed focused on some dark place inside himself, not on me.

'Yes . . . yes, I must guide you, of course. We cannot consummate the marriage until Sudema has been warded from between us.'

I had the feeling he was far more interested in devoting this act to Ama than in making love to his new wife.

I ventured, 'The Arch-Perfect-Elect cleansed me—'

'That was for the ceremony. Time has passed since then. This is another matter, a different one. Don't you understand?' He sat forward, hands between his knees, and sighed softly. 'Recall the story of Ama and Sudema.'

He looked expectantly at me. I took a breath and began the shortened version of our story: 'Once there were two great lights in the universe, Ama and Sudema. But Sudema refused to submit her will to Ama and therefore he banished her into the night, never to share the day with him again. Then he created the world, Eileah, to be a more fitting consort for himself. But Sudema is jealous, and because she rules over the night she takes her revenge on the children of Ama and Eileah in the darkness. Any man or woman who sins in thought or deed, or fails to ward her off, she may possess in the night . . .'

'Quite so,' said Tykavn. 'A man and his wife are the Sun and the Earth. But unless the congress is sanctified, Sudema will creep between them, to steal the man's seed and soil the union.'

Writing this now, the notion begins to sound ridiculous. Savage creatures who tear you to pieces on their territory are one thing; evil spirits that can be conjured up by a lustful thought are quite another. But these teachings had been drilled into me. At the time, I accepted his words completely and would not have dreamed of objecting.

'I understand, my lord. I'll do everything you wish.'

'It's not right,' he muttered. He hesitated, looking around the room again, as if not quite sure how to proceed. 'Yes. No. Slowly now, in Lord Ama's name . . .'

He was preparing himself mentally, as if this was a gruelling task, which did little for my fragile self-esteem. Then he reached down to the cloak, drew it up around me and wrapped me in it. It was an exquisite garment, made of the finest cream geitha, trimmed with white fur and stitched with crystals. 'Lie down,' he said.

Trembling with anticipation, I did as he asked. He untied one of the phials from its silver thread and stood over me. Using the phial to sketch the symbols of Ama in the air, he chanted,

'Ama is with us, who wrap ourselves in this pale cloak;
Thou shalt not enter this blessed abode,
Red-clawed demon of the dark;
Here is nothing of thine.
Begone!
Away, away along the winds of the night.
We are wrapped in the holiness of the Light . . . *Say it with me!*'

I repeated the verse with him, struggling not to make a mistake. then he sprinkled some of the holy soil over me – oh, on the beautiful cream geitha! – and placed the phial on the pillow. At last he lay down beside me, parted the cloak, drew the edge up to cover both his head and mine.

I was very conscious of his face close to mine, his breath slightly milky from the food of the celebration feast. It wasn't unpleasant. Only strange. Rather exciting. I waited for him to kiss me; instead he suddenly tore himself away with a groan.

'No,' he said.

'What's wrong?' I said, forgetting to call him 'my lord' in my disappointment.

'I haven't sanctified the room!' He leapt up, seeming angry with himself. He stood still for a moment, then went to the shrine of Ama on the far wall to our left.

'Do you want me to help you, my lord?' I asked hesitantly.

'What?' he said, as if he'd forgotten I was there, and found the interruption irritating. Then, less harshly, 'No, no. Stay there. Don't say anything.' He almost sounded apologetic. 'Be patient, Iolithie. It will not take long.'

A fresh circle of candles stood on the altar. Murmuring a prayer between each, he began to light them one by one.

He certainly is fastidious, I thought, lying back. *We only say one prayer when we light the candles: not a prayer for each. He'd think*

us very slapdash; yet I thought we worshipped in the correct way . . .

He picked up the Hand and began to move around the room, making passes over the windows and the seams of the door. He muttered the warding words to seal all the apertures through which Sudema might enter. My family said such words each night when darkness fell, but only as part of the evening prayer. We didn't repeat them at every window and corner, nor with such intensity. A pang went through me. Had we been putting ourselves in danger, not performing the rite thoroughly? But Father and Mother were Perfect; surely they knew what they were doing.

Tykavn's attention to detail was hypnotic. He was so caught up it was almost a holy fervour. I was moved and fascinated. But when he'd completed his circuit and prayed before the shrine for what seemed an hour, I began to grow tired and impatient.

At last he stood up and came towards me, a strange intentness in his eyes. I didn't see it as an expression of lust or passion. There was a fragility in the way he walked as if he were on a mountain ledge and must concentrate very hard not to fall.

He pulled the cloak around me and we went through the cleansing chant again. Did repetition strengthen the power of the cleansing? I wondered. If so, how did a Perfect-Minister decide when to stop? His intensity affected me. As he uncovered me I dared not say a word. I held my breath as he slid under the cloak and held me tight against him.

'I think it is all right now,' he told himself. 'Yes. It is all right.' He kissed me, and began to remove my clothing, and his own.

The consummation was clumsy, but nicer than I'd anticipated; after the fuss that had gone before, I forgot to be nervous about it. I had a strong, sweet feeling that made my face contort and my breath burst out in gasps. I saw the same happen to him and I wanted to kiss him and hug him with joy; but he rolled away from me and lay staring at the ceiling, eyes shining in the gloom.

Then I didn't feel happy, but hollow. Was he disappointed with me, wishing I was someone else or not there at all? I just didn't know. I longed to ask what he was thinking but I daredn't speak.

Was it such a burden to rule the province? It must be, of course. Being responsible for the lives of all these people, the safety of the land . . . I never saw my father brood about Vryatan, but then we didn't live right on the Border.

I was longing to say, 'But you're no longer alone. I am your

41

wife; you can talk to me, you can trust me completely!' Yet fear of rejection kept me dumb.

The hollowness became a little blunt knife of anxiety in my throat. I'd hoped for affection and laughter; if he was still too upset, I thought he'd let me comfort him at least.

I remembered how self-assured, magnificent and kind he'd seemed, when we'd first arrived. Before the bad news came.

This person beside me in the darkness seemed like a different man.

CHAPTER FOUR

INVISIBLE DEMONS

In the morning, a minor horror awaited.

Three courtiers, led by Lady Mynirrie, came to establish that the marriage had been consummated. Thank Ama they were all female, that's all I can say. I felt like one of Mother's goats.

Then a thin, dark Perfect-Minister, whom I disliked on sight, came to bless me and put the Sun-and-Eileah symbol on my left palm. He did this by pricking gold dye into my skin with a needle. A privilege accorded only to royal brides; if I'd known how it would bleed and hurt, I would have stayed in Vryatan with a blanket over my head.

When it was over, Mynirrie bathed me, dressed me, chided me, and sent me all bright and clean to meet my husband.

We broke our fast together in a small, light dining room that was part of the royal suite. We were waited on by a thin, anxious-to-please nephew of Laasastiuk, called Ofaldiuk, and his blonde wife, Thysar. Thysar reminded me of Mehaar – heartrendingly so because, unlike Mehaar, she was plump and charmless.

Tykavn made no mention of the previous night. After 'Good morning, Iolithie,' he said nothing at all for a long time. There were no jokes, no enquiries after my welfare, no words of affection; nothing at all to lighten the atmosphere. I didn't know what to say to him. I can be garrulous when the mood takes me, but I sensed he wouldn't appreciate my chatter. My own husband and I didn't know what to say!

Although he was quiet, he kept staring at me in a way that made me uncomfortable. Whether he was feeling affection or lust, or simply wondering what on earth I was doing sitting there, I didn't know. My overwhelming impression was that I'd displeased him, though I couldn't for the life of me work out how. I felt myself turning hot, and hoped the redness had not crept to my face.

After a time he said quite sharply. 'Is something wrong?'

'No, my lord. Why?'

'You have a sulky expression.'

As I've said, my eyebrows don't flatter me. But I thought it was unfair to be accused of sulking when all I wanted was to make him smile. 'No, it's only that my hand's a bit painful, I—'

'I don't want you to be unhappy,' he said.

'What reason have I to be unhappy?'

A faint shadow pleated his forehead. Then he reached across the table and took my hands – one bandaged – between his own. 'Iolithie, I cannot change because I am married. I am still the ruler of this Province and I must do my duty as I always have done.'

He seemed to be telling me that he had no time, nothing to give me. This wasn't what I'd hoped for at all. I could have wept. 'Is getting married just another duty?'

There was a knock at the door. He pressed my hands together and put them away from him, as if telling me to comfort myself. 'Come in!' he called in a quite different, cheerful tone.

Laasastiuk glided in, bowed and smiled at me. 'A good morning to you, my lady. Are you ready, my lord?'

'What's happening?' I said.

'I have to go and attend to my duties, of course,' said Tykavn.

'But I thought – I understood we would spend the first few days of our marriage together.' I sounded as wretched as I felt.

Laasastiuk , would you give me a moment?' The Arch-Perfect withdrew, and Tykavn, standing up, spared me literally a moment. 'I'm sorry, Iolithie. You must understand. I have a great many responsibilities and none of them will wait. Of course I would spend time with you if I could but it isn't possible. Torlossen comes before everything else.' He gave me the strangest look, half-warning and half-pleading. 'Lady Mynirrie will look after you.'

And be bowed to me and left.

This was the pattern of my life.

Each morning, Mynirrie would wake us and we would say a brief morning prayer at the altar. Then she would lead me through to the bathing and dressing rooms, where Thysar would attend me, while her ingratiating husband Ofaldiuk acted valet to Tykavn.

Once I went back to the bedchamber to ask Tykavn something,

and found him not dressing but on his knees before the altar. Mynirrie came hurriedly after me and pulled me away.

'But we've already said the morning prayer,' I said innocently.

Mynirrie shook her head sternly, as if she was too shocked actually to reply. I learned fast that to question Tykavn's religious devotions verged on blasphemy.

Then Tykavn and I would breakfast together. He was almost always edgy and uncommunicative. Occasionally he would be in good humour, and talk lightly of everyday matters, as if I was a casual friend. My hopes would rise, only to be dashed again with his next change of mood.

Then a Perfect, if not Laasastiuk himself, would come to escort him to the offices of administration, and I wouldn't see my husband again until the evening. Although I didn't know precisely what Tykavn did, I appreciated the huge amount of work involved in ruling Torlossen. I didn't quite see why Tykavn couldn't delegate the tedious aspects to others; but I had great respect – as did everyone – for the way he took on responsibilities beyond the call of duty.

I only wished it didn't seem that he worked all hours to avoid being with me.

As for me, my days were empty.

I'd expected a rich, exciting life, but as soon as the novelty of living in the Palace wore off I was bored and lonely. In Vryatan, I'd never been idle; there were always animals to feed, mohair to be spun, clothes made and reeds woven. I hadn't done the dirty, menial jobs of the bondservants, but I was used to working as hard as Mehaar. As Princess of Torlossen I was not expected to do anything. The other married women of the Court had various duties or were occupied with their children. When I expressed a wish to help, Mynirrie reacted with disapproval. Hadn't she explained my position? For Tykavn's wife to do any kind of work was unseemly. I was special, set apart.

The married women gathered in a communal room – like the one in the guest apartments, only more lavish – to socialize, but whenever I joined them the atmosphere was strained. They had a curious dual attitude to me. They would have fawned on Lady Antrid, I imagine, but I was unsophisticated and, despite my blood, had the looks and habits of a villager. At the same time I had been set above them, and they were not meant to speak to me unless I addressed them first. I could think of nothing to say to these aloof, knowing women, and the result was silence. I'd retreat to my own rooms and feel sorry for myself. If only Mehaar were here . . .

I was allowed out of the Palace if I insisted, but it caused such a palaver I only tried it twice. A retinue must be organized, people informed, the correct finery worn. I longed just to slip away, no one knowing who I was; just to take my horse, Datha, and ride over the hills, alone, the wind blowing through my shirt. Ah, dreams. Why do we always want what we haven't got?

There was little for me to do, except embroider, or play a musical instrument – which I abhorred – or study the teachings of the Prophet Hendleiknir. I dare say in time I would have rallied, and found some interest to galvanize me. If Tykavn had loved me, if we'd been happy together, any activity, however dull, would have been limned with joy. Instead I spent all day, every day, fretting about him; with that cloud over me, nothing mattered.

Each evening, there was a Court dinner, which took up several hours. At these, Tykavn presented a magnificent front. He was hearty and confident, every inch the Prince. He spoke to me in the same friendly tone that he used with everyone, the way he'd spoken to me before the wedding. Kind, humorous, easy-going. He made me feel involved, as I never felt when he wasn't there. For the first few evenings I relished these times, believing it meant he was growing fonder of me, learning to trust me. Later, they made me feel like crying.

When the meal was over and we went to bed, his bright mood died. He would become quiet and preoccupied; if I spoke to him he would answer politely enough, but if I persisted he grew irritated. His silence made me unbearably tense and fearful, though I didn't know what I feared.

Sometimes he'd look at me, kiss me, ask if I was all right. 'I don't want you to be unhappy,' he would say, pressing my hands together. Then he'd close himself away again in the closet of his thoughts.

I had to say my prayers first, and say them fast. Then he would make me get into bed and lie in utter silence while he made his own devotions. These followed the same pattern as our first night; he'd consecrate every corner and aperture of the room, light the candles, utter prayer after prayer, send them to heaven with a chime of the gong. This ritual, performed with frightening intensity, lasted at least an hour.

I thought the business with the white cloak and the chant before we made love was for the first night only. But no, he insisted on repeating the warding every time. And our couplings, rather than growing longer and more tender, remained brief, guilt-ridden and hollow. As if he wanted me, but hated himself for it.

That hurt me more than I can say. He should have been a Sublime, I thought. It would have suited him better to have no responsibility, no wife, nothing to come between him and his God.

For quite some time – the first two tendays at least – I accepted his behaviour passively. I'd been conditioned to do so. If doubts crept in, that was a fault in me, not in him.

It's a wonder Ama hasn't struck me down for my faults. Another of my sins was that, while Tykavn worshipped. I grew bored with waiting for him to come to bed. But I wasn't allowed to speak or move or even sleep. So I tried to relieve my boredom by timing him.

The first few times I counted almost to four thousand. That was over an hour. Gradually, on each successive night, the count began to creep higher. The ritual stretched to two hours, two and a half; he performed it with an absorption that was truly frightening. The muscles in his neck and arms stood out like wired ropes; sweat tangled his hair and beard. Worshipping our God of the Sun was meant to be joyful and cleansing, but Tykavn pushed himself through it like a torture.

Several times he would stop in mid-ritual, curse, and start again from the beginning. I had no idea why he did this. If it happened – especially when I thought he had nearly finished – my heart sank. Now we'd be unable to sleep for another hour at least.

Needless to say, we didn't make love very often. He had decided that the room had to be consecrated both before and afterwards; I think the extra rituals were so much trouble that he avoided them completely. So, usually, after he had made frantic devotions to Ama for two hours or more, he would collapse beside me and sleep as if dead.

It didn't take me long to work out that as soon as I was safely out of the way in my dressing rooms in the morning he would go through it all again.

Against the beliefs I'd had drilled into me, questions wormed into my mind.

Since when did Ama demand that we pray to the point of

47

exhaustion? The rites were meant to comfort and give strength. Their effect on Tykavn seemed to be the opposite. Was this desirable?

Night after night I lay there, longing to ask him 'Why are you doing this?' But I simply dared not open my mouth.

The awful thing was that I cared about him desperately. Against my mother's advice, I loved him. Perhaps I transferred my need for affection from her to him; but I craved kind words, attention, some sign that he loved me too. And the longer his indifference went on, the more the craving became an actual, continual pain.

No. *Indifference* is too weak a word. He was aware of me; as one might be aware of a splinter under a fingernail, or a wounded stray kitten that demands the kindness of one who hates cats.

Perhaps I misinterpreted his feelings. But that was the signal he sent. Indifference would have been far less cruel.

The sky was pale, clear turquoise, fish-scaled with tiny clouds, above the tilted half-bowl of lava in which the Assembly met. Cliffs of plum-brown lava, splashed with lichen, rose in front of the flat grassy arena; behind stood the House of Ama, reflected in the still silver-blue water of Lake Thjothvatn.

It was my first public appearance since the wedding, three tendays ago. I was determined to look worthy of Tykavn so I walked proudly beside him as we made our way to the royal Seat in the centre of the Thjoth. In our geitha robes of wine-red and butter-yellow, black and white, we shone against the soft colours of the landscape.

Perfect-Councillors lined the tiers, men on one side and women on the other. Each had one vote. Once a woman was Perfect, she was no longer accountable to her husband. This was her reward for child-bearing; equality.

The arena swarmed with non-Councillors. On the lakeshore, booths had been set up to sell food and drink. Children ran and shouted in the distance. The Assembly meeting was always an occasion; the adults would be respectfully sombre while it was in progress, wildly festive afterwards.

Everyone bowed low as we passed. When we took our seats a huge cheer arose, a wave of goodwill for their Prince and his wife. My throat ached. How perfect we must look; thank Ama they didn't know how things really were.

I wasn't expected to contribute anything to the business of the Assembly. All that was required of me was to look charming on Tykavn's arm. I could manage that. But I couldn't shake off the feeling that I was an imposter. *This should have been Lady Antrid, not me. Would she have felt this . . . this emptiness?*

The speeches and the debates, proposals and votes were deathly boring. Tykavn presided over the business, rarely exercising his power to veto anything he did not approve. It was very democratic. He considered every point of view with intelligence and fairness; his charm and easy strength warmed the Councillors like a golden light.

Who would believe that the driven creature I knew in private was the same man?

Sitting in the rows of Councillors, I saw my father and mother. I hadn't seen them since the wedding; they'd gone home with Mehaar, and had returned for the meeting. My chest hurt; homesickness, I suppose. I wanted to run down to Vithrie but I couldn't. I shouldn't even want to – I was meant to be an adult now – but I couldn't help it.

When the meeting was over we all went down to the lakeshore, deigning to mix with the lesser orders for a few minutes. Married couples and children, Sublimes and bondservants all mingled together with no regard to Status. It was a Holy Day.

People formed an avenue for Tykavn and myself to pass between them. It was easy to smile graciously, to play the role. It was fun. Until I suddenly found myself staring into a face that had haunted me.

Mehaar. I stopped and gawped at her. She looked astonished. She hesitated, as if not knowing how to react, then curtseyed so low that her head was almost on a level with my knees.

'Stand up, Mehaar, please,' I said, embarrassed. She obeyed and we looked at each other, not knowing what to say. I couldn't do what I wanted, which was to hug her. I said, 'How are you? I miss you.'

I felt Tykavn's hand on my arm. Our retinue swept us away and Mehaar was lost in a sea of faces. I never saw my parents in the crowd at all.

Later, when we returned to the Palace, Tykavn gripped my arm and took me straight to the royal suite, pushed me into the bedchamber and closed the door behind us.

There was a terrible glint in his eyes, which I hadn't seen since the night Antrid had died and he'd tried to make me say

49

I'd seen her. I was frightened. Why was he so angry?

'How dare you speak to her!' he began. 'To that bondservant.'

'It was Mehaar, she was my mother's—'

'I know who she was! That has nothing to do with it! Don't you even know enough to know that a princess does not address the Unstatused without good cause? Ama's Light.'

'I thought I had good cause, I—'

'You addressed her as an equal! Like a *friend*!' He spoke the word with the utmost contempt, as though it were something dirty. His fury flayed me and I was too upset not to fight back.

'Why not? She was my friend!'

Tykavn, lips drawn back, grabbed me by the upper arms and lifted me up. I was gasping, scared. One thing was clear; this argument was not about Mehaar at all.

His face changed. He released me, then hugged me, breathing hard into my neck. 'Oh, Iolithie.' It was a groan of need. *He needed me*. He pushed me backwards until the edge of the bed caught my legs and I fell back on to it.

He fell with me, removed just enough of my clothing and just enough of his to make the act possible. I didn't resist; just the opposite, I helped him, and I was groaning too. I wanted to draw him right inside me, body and soul, as if I could somehow melt the essence of him into someone different; someone who'd love me, trust me with every secret of his being . . .

When it was over he fell away, sweating, his fingers pressed to his forehead. I lay stroking his arm with my fingertips; and after a time I fell asleep.

When I awoke it was dark, I was alone on the bed, and a manic figure was roaming the room, muttering.

'Tykavn?' I said, too sleepy to remember I must be silent.

He went rigid, swung round and came towards me.

'This is your fault,' he said quietly.

'What is, my lord?'

He didn't sound angry, but in the altar-light his eyes were all white points of fire. 'We didn't sanctify it.'

'It doesn't matter,' I said. 'You consecrate this room every day. How could there be anything bad—'

'It matters!' he cried. His vehemence was alarming. 'How am I ever gong to make up for it, how do I drive the evil out? This is your fault!'

'No, it isn't,' I said, indignant now, but it was impossible to make him listen.

'Shut up!' he roared. 'Didn't I tell you never to interrupt? I have to start again now!'

He turned away and I lay shaking as he pushed himself through ritual after ritual. I had never seen anything like it. I thought he'd kill himself, he was in such anguish; almost a state of hysteria, beyond reason. For hours I lay there, not daring to move, feeling wretched with helplessness; until, as dawn glimmered in thin lines through the shutters, I started to weep.

'Please stop,' I said, beyond fearing his wrath. 'Please stop it.'

To my surprise, he didn't shout at me. He came to the bed and sank down on it. Dear Ama, he looked exhausted. His eyes were red with weariness and tears. 'I'm sorry, Iolithie,' he said, hugging me. I was a cloth doll in his arms, limp with confusion. 'I'm sorry, I didn't mean to upset you. I know it wasn't your fault.'

I was so astonished that he'd apologized, I would have forgiven him anything. 'But what's wrong?'

'Nothing. We have to keep out the demons. You must understand that. I'm doing this for both of us.'

'I know. I didn't mean to make you angry, I—'

'Do you think I'm such a monster?' He sighed. 'You're lonely, aren't you? Finding this hard to cope with.'

Tears were streaming down my cheeks. Pathetic, what a few kind words can do to me. 'I want to understand.'

'There's nothing to understand,' he said. Perhaps that meant he couldn't explain his own behaviour; and I was too glad of this precarious communication that I daredn't risk it by pushing him. 'I can't bear to see you miserable, I know how to change that.'

Yes, yes, I thought. *Talk to me. Trust me. Love me.*

But he said, 'Your little friend, Mehaar. Bondservants aren't normally allowed to work in the Palace, but I can make a special dispensation. Would you like her as your maid?'

In a shaft of green-gold light, which dusted the morning with hope, I clasped Mehaar's hands. Tykavn had gone to his state duties; we were alone in my dressing room. 'It's so good to see you. Are you glad to be here?'

Mehaar nodded. Her smile was like Ama's light; her golden hair blazed white where the sun caught it. 'It's kind of you to send for me, halla.'

'Do I look any different? More like a princess than a goatherd?'

Mehaar put her head on one side. 'You look a little tired, halla.'

She was perceptive, our Mehaar, and truthful. 'Do I?' I said, with a sigh. 'Never mind. Sit with me and tell me how things are in Vryatan. I am so glad you're here.'

'I'm glad too.' Mehaar looked around at the room, awed by its richness. 'How wonderful to live here ...'

'You live here too, now,' I said, laughing.

'No, I mean as a mistress, not as a servant. You have all this now ... yet you don't look happy. Aren't you?'

'Of course I'm happy, but ...' Although it was wonderful to have Mehaar there, I'd already begun to realize that there was nothing she could do to help me. Royalty could not confide in bondservants. I couldn't say to her, 'Tykavn behaves strangely, what shall I do?'

He'd seen I was upset, so, out of kindness – or guilt – he'd given me the gift of Mehaar. But even as he offered it I'd known that it did not signal a change of heart. It was an appeasement. At breakfast the distance between us had reopened its cold throat, and he'd gone with Laasastiuk with only his usual dry nod in my direction. And I'd felt crushing disappointment but no great surprise.

Did I have to weep and plead every time I wanted him to show me a little tenderness? I wouldn't do it!

'Halla?' Mehaar prompted.

'It's only ... I think I expected too much. It has been difficult. Tykavn has ... he has many problems. He prays ... all night, sometimes.'

'They say he is very pious.'

Pious wasn't the word. 'He is. But sometimes it makes him tired, and angry with me.'

'Oh, poor halla.' I'd wanted comfort and Mehaar gave it . All her attention was gathered and held by my face. 'I'm sure he doesn't mean to be.'

'I try so hard to please him.' I was starting to say too much. I must stop. 'No one warned me how difficult he – how difficult marriage would be. I know I shouldn't speak of it, but you are the only one I can tell.'

'You can tell me anything,' Mehaar said softly. 'That's why I'm here.'

Although Tykavn had let me have Mehaar he seemed to resent her presence. He was polite to Thysar, but Mehaar he ignored. He would refer to her, with a hint of a sneer, as 'your friend'. 'Why not get your *friend* to do that?' he'd say, if he saw me engaged some minuscule task, like cutting a loose thread off a garment. 'She has nothing else to do. Which of you is meant to be the maid?'

He'd imply that she was a bone-idle parasite, that I cared more for her than for him, that he'd done me a huge favour for which I was utterly ungrateful. All of this was totally unjustified. It made me angry, unhappy and guilt-ridden. Although I knew, logically, that I had done nothing wrong, logic seemed to play no part in Tykavn's attitude to me.

His obsessive worship I forced myself to accept, but this injustice was too much to swallow. Prince or no, I began to argue back. This got me nowhere; it only made him furious with me. Losing my nerve, I retreated and tried to keep the peace, but he seemed determined to think he'd married an argumentative harridan.

I believed he was beginning to hate me. It was so unfair, and it broke my heart.

He had lost weight since the wedding. I noticed it suddenly, one evening, as I finished my prayer at the altar and turned to see him sitting on the edge of the bed. His fine garments hung on him; even his skin hung on him, roped to his bones by wasting muscles. In the contours of his eye-sockets, the skin was dark and tissue-thin. Had no one else noticed? Was it only to me he looked so gaunt and haunted?

I'd come to dread the night. As the evening passed he would grow more and more withdrawn and tense; his temper could be terrible, though he usually suppressed it unless something irritated him. I think he tried to put off the ritual, because once he began it could take three or four hours. He'd stop and start over and over again, dissatisfied with his own performance for no reason that I could see. He'd go through it in such frantic anguish that it filled me with horror to watch him. On one occasion I'd begun to weep again, but instead of showing sympathy he had turned and screamed at me to be quiet.

We hadn't made love since that one time he'd lost control and spent all night paying penance. I didn't care what Laasastiuk or anyone called 'devout'; there was something obviously, desperately wrong with Tykavn. Why was he fighting these exhausting battles with invisible demons every night?

The demons were winning and I couldn't bear it any longer.

It took all my courage to challenge him, but as he stood up and walked towards the altar I said 'Tykavn, would you let me ask you something?'

'What is it?' he said impatiently, half turning.

'Couldn't you just say the prayer once tonight, and come straight to bed?'

He frowned. 'I can't believe you ask such a stupid question.'

I gathered myself, determined to persist. 'I don't think I'm being stupid, when I see you causing yourself such distress! What harm would it do? We're both exhausted.'

'Oh, *you* are exhausted? Have you worked all day, or given Ama more than the bare minimum of devotion? You make it worse by asking questions. Be silent.'

'I won't be silent!' I exclaimed. 'The Perfect-Ministers, the Prophet himself never said we had to make the warding or blessing rites more than once. What good does it do to keep repeating them?'

My words stung him into a convulsion of rage. 'What you were taught has nothing to do with this!? Don't criticize what you don't understand! The ritual has to be done a precise way or Sudema will enter you, me, the whole of Torlossen. The rituals are all that keep her out!'

I stared at him. I had no way of disproving what he said, but suddenly I seemed to be seeing this passionate belief from outside, and realizing that there was something not merely illogical but ludicrous about it. 'Who sets this standard of perfection? If one ritual isn't enough for Ama, why should he be satisfied with thirty, or a million? I can't see why it should make any difference to him!'

He clenched his fists and I thought he was going to hit me. 'I know it makes no difference!' he exclaimed. '*I know!*'

To my astonishment, he subsided on to the edge of the bed and broke down in tears. How thin he looked, his hands dangling between his emaciated thighs; worn away by nervous energy. His face was distorted, tears of pure mental agony oozing down his cheeks, his whole frame shaking. Almost weeping in sympathy, I tried to put my arms around him but he pushed me away.

His rejection was a knife-thrust in my heart. 'Please let me help you!'

'No one can help me.' He wiped away his tears with the back of his hand. His cheeks were red and white, yet his expression was cold, locked away. 'I know you must think I am mad,' he said flatly. 'But I am not. I know that what I am doing makes no sense, and changes nothing. But I can't stop it. *I can't stop.'*

A moment of absolute shock, revelation; his first admission that his behaviour was abnormal, *and that he knew it.* 'Why?' I said softly. 'Please tell me why.'

'The Perfect-Ministers tell us that we must make devotions to Ama daily. We must do so to keep our houses, our bodies and minds clean. I must do so, also, to keep the Unseen out of Torlossen. Of course, it's easy for those who don't *think* to worship in some slapdash manner and never consider they may have displeased Ama . . .'

'My lord, do you think that you displease Ama?'

He chewed at his lower lip. 'As a child,' he said at last, 'did you never sit in the Fane and think a blasphemous thought? That you were bored, perhaps, and didn't want to be there?'

'I – I expect so.'

'You expect so,' he said sarcastically. 'But you never imagined Ama would punish you for it unless you did penance, did you? I did. All the time. I always felt that I was displeasing Ama in a thousand ways. I had doubts. When I said my prayers, how could I be sure I'd said them correctly? I must repeat them, to be certain. And even then I still couldn't be sure. Some tiny slip, somewhere, might have made the prayer invalid. However correctly I thought I'd prayed, I could never be sure. Do you see, this is how it feels to me? Always, *always* to be in doubt.'

'But I know how it feels. I am uncertain—'

'Don't humour me!' he said savagely. 'You could never know!' He breathed in and out heavily. 'When the King sent me here from Onafross, I prayed and prayed for a safe journey, and Ama protected us. Sudema did not attack us. Thus it must follow that my prayers had been heard.' He spoke with the faintest touch of irony. 'After that, it seemed clear that I must continue to be devout. Bad must be countered with good; every unclean or dark thought must be annulled with a prayer, a ritual. I must be perfect. Nothing else will appease my God!'

'But it's destroying you. Surely Ama doesn't demand that.'

'No,' he said. '*I* demand it. I make the rules and I enforce them; incessantly, brutally, without remorse.'

There was a silence like brass quivering. I was frozen, inside and out. Tykavn's state of mind seemed to lie on the whole room like a nightmare. He said, 'I have done this for years, don't you see? It was under control. But then they sent Lady Antrid . . . and the rituals did not save her.'

'That wasn't your fault,' I whispered.

'I know,' he said. 'My mind knows it, but my heart won't believe it. Still the doubt, you see. What if I *didn't* pray hard enough? If I couldn't save her, how can I protect Torlossen? I must worship harder and harder, just in case.'

A glimpse of his mental torture, a black whip across my mind. 'But what – what would happen if you simply . . . didn't do it? If you just came to bed now and slept.'

'Do you think I don't want to?' he cried in anguish. 'I'd do anything to do that! To be *normal*, like you, floating through life without a care! Dear Ama, you don't know how lucky you are! But trying to resist the compulsion causes me the most unbearable pain and fear. You can't imagine such fear. What if I stopped, and Sudema entered? I just can't take the risk.'

'But if you'd try! The Unseen have never come over the border; Torlossen has always been free of them. Who kept them out before you came?' An awful rush of doubts was going through me. I watched in horror as all my own beliefs collapsed like a cage of twigs on a fire. *If we all stopped praying tomorrow it would make no difference. They're only words. The power they have is only in our imagination!* Ama's Light, if I said such things he'd kill me!

But Tykavn said wearily, 'It doesn't work like that. Knowing it's illogical makes no difference. Reassurance makes no difference. I *have* to do certain things, in a certain order, to find any peace at all . . . and next day they're all there to be done again.' His voice fell almost to a whisper. 'I dread darkness falling, when I can't put it off any longer. Every night I tell myself, "Tonight the ritual will be perfect the first time, and I shall sleep soundly in the arms of Ama. Without dreams, without anxiety." But the harder I try, the more likely I am to make some small slip. A shake of the hand while lighting the candles. An inappropriate thought.'

He looked at me, and his eyes were glittering, too focused on his own pain to see mine. 'Only, Iolithie, having you here makes it all much worse.'

'How?' I said, shocked.

'Because you don't suffer as I do. You lie there, not understanding, watching me, thinking I'm mad. Your presence inhibits me. While I'm conscious of being watched I can't concentrate; while I'm thinking of you waiting for me so you can go to sleep, I feel guilty, and that creates bad thoughts against you and Ama. When the ritual is polluted by a bad thought it has to be scrapped and started afresh.' The anger in his voice was chilling. I hugged myself as he went on. 'I can't bear you to see this weakness in me! Do you know how much effort it costs me, to appear strong and in control to others? But you force this choice on me; either I look weak and mad in your eyes, or the rituals go undone!'

Oh, suddenly, horribly, this explained everything. All the resentment and hatred he had been directing at me. Oh, dear Ama.

I was distressed for him; but at the same time I was offended, upset, and filled with guilt. There aren't words to express the pain he was inflicting on me; how rejected and worthless I felt.

'Why on Eileah did you marry me?' I managed to say.

'I've asked myself the same thing,' he said flatly. 'If I hadn't acquiesced to Father's demands, Lady Antrid would not have died; and you wouldn't have been lying beside me, holding me back from my duty to Ama.'

'We could sleep separately,' I said.

'Don't be ridiculous. How would it look? I suppose it would please you to lessen me in the eyes of others.'

'Of course it wouldn't! Why are you saying these things? I love you and I want to help you!'

My words seemed to make no impression. I don't think he was hearing anything I said; or only hearing what he wanted to. Why did he want to believe I hated him? Because he hated himself?

'You can't help,' he said. 'Every time you try, you make it worse.'

Defeated at every turn, I said hopelessly, 'Tell me what to do, then. Whatever you say, I'll do it.

'You are under some kind of false premise that there's any-thing you can do. Your very presence is an interference in some-thing that's none of your concern.'

'I'll go away—'

'Ama above, don't be pathetic,' he snapped. 'Just shut up. Let me alone; don't speak to me.'

And he turned away and moved to the altar. God's Light, it was so terrible to see him; this driven, tormented man, consuming himself from the inside. I could sense the pressure increasing under the unbearable weight of his responsibilities. Like lava, the longer it was contained, the greater would be the force of the explosion when it burst free; the torrent of his rage, terror, and pain.

Yet the ritual was short that night, and when he came to bed he hugged me in his sleep. Moments like this gave me painful little strands of hope.

I stared into the darkness all night, thinking that at least he'd explained. That was a beginning. Now we'd talked, things must get better.

Every day we worshipped in the Palace chapel. And twice every tenday the inhabitants of the Palace went to a special service in the Fane at Lake Thjothvatn. Suddenly I found I couldn't worship any more.

Every ritual was a cold thin echo of Tykavn's frantic devotions. Every artifact – candles, water, fire, the gold Hand, the gong – was a reminder; every gesture, every word the Perfect-Ministers uttered filled me with revulsion.

Tykavn's obsession had left my own faith in shreds.

He worshipped quite normally in the Fane; Laasastiuk, Mynir-rie and all the others around us seemed sublimely ignorant of his true state of mind. I hated them for it. I almost hated him for hiding it from everyone except me. I was having to bear it all alone; I was in anguish and I couldn't ask Ama for help.

A single prayer to Ama; I used to believe that it had power, that Ama listened and considered my words. But a prayer repeated again and again until it twisted the supplicant's mind into exhausted madness . . . How, if Ama existed, could he let that happen? If such desperation had no effect, how could a single prayer have any power? How could any of it make the slightest difference?

It was all a hollow mockery. Tykavn had made a travesty of faith.

I knew Ama was there; I saw him every day, blazing in the heavens. But I was no longer able to believe that he listened or was even aware of mankind. It seemed to me that the powers of heaven were blind, deaf and dumb as rock. Rituals were self-delusion; false comfort. The whole Church of Ama was deluding itself and everyone else.

Everything to do with religion disgusted me.

That feeling, that anti-revelation, was one of the most terrible things I've ever experienced. And I secretly blamed Tykavn. I knew he couldn't help it – but then, neither could I.

Can you imagine how painful it is to watch someone you love falling apart before your eyes? Not from a clear cause like an illness, but needlessly punishing, torturing, eating himself from the inside?

I had believed that talking would help my husband, that once the problem was in the open we would begin to solve it. As we prepared for bed the next night I felt a faint sense of hope. We'd talk again. He would let me help him, step by step.

I soon saw, from the glitter of grim preoccupation in his eyes, that nothing had changed. 'Say your prayers and go to bed,' he said. 'Hurry.'

A familiar depression and fear hung heavy on me. Far from seeming better, he looked worse. 'My lord, do you have to—'

'Be quiet!' he snapped. 'Just obey me and don't say a word!'

I obeyed. He began his ritual, more frenzied than ever. I endured it for fifteen minutes or so, teeth clenched, silent tears wetting my face.

If reason had had no effect, the only thing left to me was anger. Unable to bear it a moment longer, I erupted from the bed and shouted at him.

'For Ama's sake, stop this! Just *stop*!'

He broke off and turned on me, shaking from head to foot. 'I warned you—'

'I don't care!' I jumped out of bed and strode to the middle of the room. 'I can't stand to see what you're doing to yourself. When we talked, I thought you realized how futile—'

'Shut up!' He turned his back on me and shook his fists. The whole Palace must have heard us screaming at one another. 'Don't defy me! Ama dismissed Sudema for her insolence!'

'If Ama had listened to Sudema, instead of banishing her, there would *be* no demons!' I yelled back.

He fell ominously silent. I heard sounds in the outer rooms, light footsteps, worried voices. When he turned towards me his eyes were burning with rage; more than rage, madness. Then he roared, 'Blasphemy!'

God's Light, he scared me. I shrank back, raising my hands to ward him off. 'You're out of your mind! What use are these rituals? They didn't save Lady Antrid, did they?'

Oh, fatal words. Cruel, too. He came towards me, one hand raised, like some skeletal thing from Kvold. 'You evil bitch,' he said.

Although I saw the blow coming I was too slow to evade it.

I didn't feel any pain as his hand hammered into the side of my head. There was an inky explosion behind my eyes, a sensation as if my skull was folding in on itself, and then a heavy, ringing nothingness.

CHAPTER FIVE

FACE TO THE WIND

The light was a halo of pain round my eyes. The left side of my face was one throbbing, tender bruise; my skull rang with pain, inside and out.

At first I didn't realize I was on a couch in my dressing room. I thought I was at home, that I'd fallen off my pony on to the rock; it wouldn't be the first time. *How stupid to do it again*, I thought ... Then I saw Mehaar and Mynirrie bending over me, and lamplight shining on the silver-grey polished walls. Dawn glimmered in the window.

I remembered.

I raised my head but saw that the door to the bedchamber was closed. I looked up into Mehaar's large, frightened eyes.

'Where – where's Tykavn?'

'Lie down, halla, please,' said Mehaar. 'He's asleep. Please rest.'

Mynirrie was moving about in the background; I couldn't see her clearly through the haze of blood and pain. She put something in Mehaar's hand and I heard her say in an oddly flat tone, 'Put this ointment on Her Highness's face. Don't encourage her to talk about it; and don't you talk about it either, girl. It never happened, you understand?'

Mehaar nodded dumbly. I, too, understood.

I lay back and cold claws of despair tore down the length of my body.

Mehaar sat with me until breakfast time. Then Mynirrie came in again and both women looked expectantly at me. The weight of their gaze hung on me like lead, and I realized that however ill I felt, however battered I looked, I was expected to behave as if nothing had happened. To keep up appearances. The Prince's marriage must not be seen as anything less than perfect.

I got the impression that neither of them even believed he had hit me. I could imagine them thinking that either it was an accident or I had done something so heinous that I'd deserved it. They simply dared not think anything else.

If I'd made a fuss, what good would it have done?

I gave myself up to them, let them bathe me, dress me and smear a flesh-coloured paste over my face to hide the bruise. Ama's Fire, that stung! Every movement caused a new burst of pain that made my head swim.

Yet at the appointed time I gathered my dignity and sat down at the table opposite Tykavn.

I tried not to look at him as I half-heartedly picked at pieces of cheese and salt-fish. He said not a word but I sensed his gaze on me. His eyes weren't regretful, or sympathetic. They were wary and hunted; glass prisons of pain from which he couldn't break free.

It occurred to me then that he simply didn't understand the enormity of what he'd done. He couldn't. The rational, kind part of him had been subsumed by the black fire in his mind.

I wanted to weep; not for myself, but for him.

I couldn't eat. My mouth hurt and my stomach was a solid knot. Tykavn ate only a little sour-milk; then he suddenly pushed his chair back and rushed out of the room. Very faint through the doors I heard him vomit, twice.

I stayed at the table, fossilized. When he reappeared, some minutes later, he was groomed and dressed, trying – like me – to appear his normal self. He had just enough energy left to present a front to others; his sense of duty to Torlossen kept him from breaking down completely. But he had nothing left for me.

His crisp clothes and his hearty smile seemed to fool Laasastiuk completely, when the Arch-Perfect arrived to escort him to his office.

'Good morning, Laas,' he said brightly. 'First thing today is to go through the papers on the fair collection of tax from the villages.'

'Yes, Your Highness,' said Laasastiuk. Tykavn was very convincing, but didn't the Arch-Perfect notice the shadows round his eyes? 'There is a petition to consider from the Sublime-Elect, concerning the goat-breeding regulations. And I hate to raise the matter of the repairs to the Fane roof, but . . .'

Tykavn sighed. 'Well, this shortage of metal . . . but the House of Ama comes before everything else, of course. I'll send out to see if there is a roof in the lower quarter that can be stripped . . .'

And so on, just as if everything was normal.

As Tykavn left the room he nodded to me without smiling; the barest skeleton of civility. I saw how loose the flesh was strung over his skull, how the bones of his hands shone through the skin. How much longer could he keep up the act? I felt like leaping up and screaming at Laasastiuk, the attendants, everyone, 'Can't you see how he really is? Help him, please!'

I didn't, of course. But I knew that if I didn't act there would soon be nothing of him left to help.

Alone, I shed a few tears of self-pity, then stopped because it was so painful. I knew without asking that Mynirrie wouldn't help me; she was too tightly bound to the strictures of tradition. She was the one who'd said 'It never happened.' And Mehaar, of course, had no Status or power to do anything.

I had to think.

Rule one of living in Torlossen is never be ill. There are a few physicians and surgeons in the province, who attend animals as well as people, but beyond bandaging wounds or splinting broken limbs there is little they can do. We have hardly any medicines. There are hints that in the golden age, when we were ruled from glorious Vivirjosa before Sudema sent her Unseen to divide Thandarkyr, there were marvellous medicines for fevers and everything. But because of the invasion, we lost that knowledge and never regained it.

Fortunately, we are a hardy race. We have to be.

I couldn't go to those doctors; if physical ailments were beyond them, how could they begin to grasp some nebulous mental disorder? Madness was regarded as possession by Sudema. It was too terrible to be spoken of. A sufferer would be subject to purgings that were more a punishment than a cure; in olden times, I'd heard, such people had been driven out into the Stolen Land or even drowned. No hint of such horrors could be allowed to touch Prince Tykavn – and besides, he was not mad.

As Palace Physician, then, Lady Mynirrie was more adept at concealing ailments than curing them.

This was more a spiritual complaint than a bodily one. Only Arch-Perfect Laasastiuk had any influence over Tykavn, and he'd always been fatherly and kind to me.

How to talk to him, though? If I went to his office, he might not be there, or Tykavn might be with him. Feeling shocked at my own effrontery, I sent a message asking the great man to come and see me.

I needn't have been nervous. He came to me within two hours and we sat in one of the bright, comfortable ante-rooms, under the dappled shadow of an ornamental tree.

I tried not to shudder when he blessed me with the circle of Ama.

'What is it, my dear?' he said, more gentle and paternal than my own father had ever been. 'You look unwell. If there is anything amiss, it is your husband you should tell.'

My throat hurt as I began to speak. 'I can't. It's not me, it's Tykavn. I fear – I fear he is making himself ill.'

'I am not a physician. He should consult Lady Mynirrie, if—'

'Please!' I said. 'Please listen. I don't know who else to turn to, Father. The – the evening rite and prayers. He says them for half the night, all night sometimes, until he exhausts himself. When I tried to make him stop, he—' I touched the swollen side of my face, where the smudged paste hid nothing. 'I don't think he knew what he was doing. He was half out of his mind. I tried to calm him but he won't listen to me and I don't know what to do . . .'

I felt like a sack of water bursting, so great was the relief of telling this strong, kind man. Yet when I looked at him it came to me that I'd explained extremely badly, if at all.

'You are telling me,' he said gently, 'that Tykavn prays too much?'

'Yes, but—'

'And that it is unreasonable for a devout man to be angry when his wife tries to keep him from his devotion?'

'No, no, I didn't mean that.'

'Well, what did you mean?'

The curve of his moist lips seemed frozen, the kindness in his eyes turning to flint. He made me feel I was committing some unspeakable indiscretion. My words died and sickness squeezed my heart. He went on, 'I did explain to you that Tykavn is unusually devout. You are talking about the son of Vidvikjan. He is Chosen. No one of the blood royal has any imperfection.'

'I wasn't suggesting that he has, but—'

'Piety is not a fault. Rituals are a protection against fear, an affirmation of belief. They bring safety, purification and order. We all need them.'

His complacency infuriated me and scared me, because I couldn't fight his authority. I felt I was stirring the surface of a very dark and frightening lake. 'But Tykavn needs them too much. They're destroying him. If only you could see him! There's nothing holy in it; it's as if he's possessed.'

Laasastiuk gazed at me, unmoved but stern. 'To suggest the hand of Sudema in this is blasphemy.'

'I wasn't suggesting that, Father. I'm trying to tell you that he is ill. Can't you see how thin he is? He's in the most terrible distress and he needs help. He seems to think he's sinning, displeasing Ama, all the time. That's not piety, it's – it's obsession!'

The Arch-Perfect looked contemplative. He cleared his throat and ran his tongue over his lips, as if he felt sad that I was under a delusion that made me say these terrible things. 'Obsession,' he said, 'can be used by our Lord Ama as a trial to bring about higher sanctity. I know this is hard for you to grasp, but Tykavn behaves as he does because he is Chosen by Ama.'

I was speechless. All I found hard to grasp was Laasastiuk's attitude. At last I exclaimed, 'You knew about this, didn't you? You know exactly what's been happening to him! How can you see him in such distress and do nothing to help?'

'He carries out his State duties without difficulty; how can he be ill? I am helping him; I give him spiritual guidance all the time. When he asks for blessing and purification, I give it; if he needs more than I can provide, I can only advise him to pray to Lord Ama.'

Oh, what a fine physician Laasastiuk would have made. He'd cure a man who had swallowed poison by making him swallow some more! But the Arch-Perfect-Elect could not be wrong. In the face of his granite conviction I felt such a child, so sinful and afraid. His kindly authority smothered me like wet sand.

He went on in a soft, confidential voice, 'Ama has some special purpose for Tykavn and it is not for us to question it. To do so is blasphemy. I remember that I warned you, very explicitly, that the duties of the Prince's wife included absolute obedience and discretion. Take this as a kindly warning. I know you are village-born; but, all the same, only so much allowance can be made for you. Do you presume to know better than the Prince and his Perfects? You have no power here. Every word you utter against your husband is treachery. I advise you to learn to keep your silence; of all sins, disloyalty is the most shameful.'

With that, the meeting was over. Laasastiuk rose, but I sat

stunned. I couldn't believe it. Not only that he refused to hear me, but threatened me with some unnamed punishment for even daring to speak.

I'd trusted him. He'd left me feeling stupid, patronized, wicked – and, worst of all, completely without hope. Where could I turn now? Oh, serve me right for falling for grey hair and a fatherly smile!

I spent the day resting, steeling myself against the evening, when I would have to face Tykavn again. Perhaps he would be matter of fact, and expect me to behave as if nothing had happened. I could do that, if it was the only way to keep him calm. Bitterness was eating at me, though; that he could behave so cruelly, ill or not; that he could spurn my help, as if my feelings simply didn't matter.

Did being Chosen excuse anything?

He returned at the usual time, greeted me civilly with neither warmth nor hostility. Despite the pallor of his face, he still carried an intimidating authority. Unusually, instead of going to his rooms with Ofaldiuk to dress for the Court dinner, he dismissed all the servants and took me into our private dining room.

'Sit down,' he said. I obeyed, and he sat facing me across the table. The pink unguent hid my bruises, but he stared at the swollen side of my face as if I had deliberately disfigured myself to displease him. I was trembling; I knew that nothing good was going to happen.

He said, 'You spoke to someone about me.' His voice was low, but it thrummed with accusation. 'You have no right to discuss my private business with anyone.'

I'd guessed Tykavn wouldn't be pleased – but this angry? In his eyes, all the sickness of his soul was concentrated. The tension of his face pulled his lids into an expression of deranged fury; the whites were bloodshot, one pupil slightly larger than the other. Everything within him was out of balance in a way that terrified me.

'But it was Laasastiuk,' I said defensively.

'I know. It was he who told me.'

Damn him, I thought. How could the Arch-Perfect betray my confidence? He must have known Tykavn would be angry – yet he had told him anyway. I felt sick, webbed down with ice.

'You're my wife,' he went on. 'You know you should not

discuss me behind my back. Laasastiuk was shocked at your disloyalty – and so am I.'

Well, I could have grovelled, but to fight back surely couldn't make things much worse. 'I only wanted his help,' I said indignantly. 'What kind of friend is he to you? He knows perfectly well how you're suffering and he ignores it! He says it's Ama's will. Even you don't believe—'

'I do not need help! Your motive in speaking to him was utter selfishness.'

'That's not true!'

'You don't care about me; you only care about your own happiness.' The corners of his lower lip pulled down sourly, baring his teeth. He never once raised his voice, but his vitriolic calmness was horrible. 'I would not be like this if it wasn't for you.'

'That's not fair! You told me you've had these obsessions for years. You can't blame me—'

'But you've made it worse! You *made* me tell you about it.'

I couldn't believe what I was hearing. 'I thought talking about it would help.'

'Well, it doesn't!' he said savagely. 'Talking about it makes me *think* about it, and the more I think the worse it gets! All you think about is yourself. You only spoke to Laasastiuk because *your* quiet life is being disrupted. You are the most selfish woman I have ever met. You're pathetic and useless.'

I was seething. 'I asked to do something useful in the Palace and I was told the Prince's wife isn't allowed to work!'

'But you're not doing the job you're meant to! You're not pregnant yet, are you?'

'No.'

'Then you are utterly useless!'

'I've hardly been given the chance to get with child, have I?' I shouted back, my faced heating with rage.

'Too busy fawning on your grinning friend to spend the time with me,' he said sarcastically.

The wounds inflicted by his words, his hostility, were bitter. I was realizing that it actually didn't matter what I said to him; anything and everything would be thrown back. I couldn't reach him. That was the agony of it. *Nothing I said reached him.*

Injustice, rejection, self-doubt; every painful negative emotion swamped me. In a way, he was right. I *was* selfish. I was thinking as much of my own happiness as his. But was that wrong?

'I've done nothing to deserve this,' I said, my voice fractured. 'If you could hear yourself. Tykavn, you work too hard! That's what's brought this on, too much work. Have a rest; there must be so much you could delegate—'

He glared at me as if I was the unhinged one. 'You don't understand anything, do you? Work is all that keeps me sane. I have to oversee everything to make sure it is done properly. Thinking about my duties keeps my mind away from the other thoughts, do you see? Until you, you little fool, remind me of them again. Every time I look at you it reminds me of the night rituals! By Ama's Fire, I could kill you for it!'

His fists were clenched. He moved suddenly, and I leapt up and fled. I wasn't taking a chance on whether he meant to carry out the threat or not. More than that, I was trying to make him see how frightened I was. To make him stop and *think*.

I rushed through the bedchamber into my dressing room, slammed and locked the door. His fists came down on the other side with a bang. 'Iolithie! Come out!'

'No! I won't be spoken to like that.'

'You're behaving like a child!'

Sometimes it seemed the accusations he flung at me applied equally to himself.

'I can't bear this!' I cried. 'I don't know what to say to you or what to do!'

There was a silence. Then he said more calmly, 'Don't be stupid. Come out.'

'No.' I knew I sounded petulant. Perhaps I should have relented, but I felt too hurt. Acceptance, tears, anger, reason; I'd tried them all. 'It will only start again,' I said wearily. 'I've had enough.'

'All right, if you won't come out, you can damned well stay in there!' He struck the door hard in exasperation. I put my hands over my ears and wept. When I raised my head, there was a long lull; then I heard a faint, insistent chant. Although it was not dark, he had begun to ritualize.

It would go on for hours yet, and I dared not emerge. The dressing room had another door which led out to an ante-room, but when I ran to it I found it locked.

In frustration I banged on it, and after a minute I heard Mehaar's anxious voice on the other side. 'Halla?'

'Mehaar, will you open this door, please?'

A hesitation. 'I – I can't. Lady Mynirrie said His Highness

said you weren't to be let out. I'm not even meant to speak to you. I'm so sorry.'

'Mehaar! Don't be silly! Come on, open it!'

'I'm sorry,' came the frightened voice on the other side, fading as if she were backing away. 'Sorry.'

'Who's your loyalty to, him or me?'

No answer. The door remained locked. Mehaar had deserted me. That was another piece chipped off my heart; that she, of all people, could let me down.

I went to the window and stared out at the blue-brushed twilight. The external walls of the city had a lifeless glow, and the hills were coldly indifferent to my plight.

'Help me,' I said to the air. Pain pulled my mouth taut. 'Dear Ama, if you're so clever, tell me what to do.'

I opened the window, but the royal apartments were on the first floor of the Palace and the wall fell sheer to the rock below. One leap to freedom, yes – but I wasn't ready to die!

One or two people walked by as dusk fell; Sublimes coming back from the fields. I leaned on the sill for a long time, staring longingly at the outside world. At least while no one came to let me out I had some time to think. *I could knot my clothes together to make a rope* . . . I dismissed the thought as ludicrous, and in the same moment saw a thin stable-lad with reddish-fair hair, sauntering past right below the window. I thought it was our Langyr, so desperate was I to see a face from home. In a moment he would be gone, the chance lost. I leaned out of the window and spoke in a hissing whisper, praying that no one but him would hear. 'Boy!'

The lad stopped and looked around him before looking up. His pale eyes were startled, his bristling sandy hair adding to the impression of shock. It wasn't Langyr. I'd known it couldn't be, but I had to to on now I'd dived into this.

'Don't say a word. Go and get a rope, long enough to reach this window. Bring a horse, too. I can't explain, but will you do it?'

He shook his head wildly. 'No, halla. I can't. You're—'

'Exactly!' I hissed. 'I can make a lot of trouble for you if you don't.'

The poor boy turned white. 'Halla, you wouldn't.'

'I will if you don't do as I say. Saddle a horse for me, and bring some riding skirts and a shawl and hat. And don't forget the rope. Go on! Be back here as soon as it's dark, and don't let anyone see you!'

All at once my idle plan had taken on alarming reality. It was unfair, what I'd asked him to do, but I was desperate.

The twilight deepened to blue-black in the pane. Every now and then I heard Tykavn moving about the bedchamber, and I prayed he wouldn't come to the door again. It was the first time I'd wanted the ritual to last as long as possible. My heart was pounding as I put on the plainest clothes I could find. If this failed, what would become of me – and him?

I heard the clip of hooves beneath the window, saw the shadows of boy and horse far below. Three attempts it took him to throw me the rope; then I caught it, knotted it tight to the couch, and climbed out over the window sill.

God's Light, it was horrible going down that wall. I went dizzy. I poured sweat like a hot spring. But I did it.

Watched by the wide-eyed boy, I pulled on the rough mohair split-skirts, the dark shawl and the wide-brimmed hat. The horse tried to bite me, rolling its eyes when the lad slapped its nose away and spoke chidingly to it.

'Thank you for coming,' I whispered. 'But did I have to threaten you before you'd help me? Don't say a word about this to anyone, agreed?'

'But you're – you're the—'

'Swear!'

'I swear, halla – er, Your Highness.'

'It's just me,' I said, hoisting myself into the saddle. Above me, the windows of the Palace gleamed yellow, silver-blue, rose and green. No hint of the pain contained within its walls, nor the imminent uproar. 'I'm still the same. Not a lady at all.'

The horse was a stubborn beast that fought me all the way, jibbing every time I tried to urge him into a canter. I reached Vryatan exhausted. As I rode up the sloping floor of the valley, with the cliff a great blind wall before me, the rain came streaming down in grey curtains. My clothes grew heavy with it. Rivulets ran from the brim of my hat, and the stench of wet goat-hair rose like steam.

It was morning. I'd ridden all night. I dismounted from the recalcitrant horse and tied him in a store-cave out of the rain. Then I climbed the scree slope to the mouth of my mother's heimar, pulled back the waxed flap and stood on the threshold, dripping.

Mother came forward curiously and stared at me as if I were a ghost.

'It's me, Mother,' I said weakly.

Vithrie circled her breast. 'Ama save us. I dreamed you married the Prince of Torlossen. Have I just woken up?'

'I wish it were a dream,' I said wretchedly.

For a brief moment, her gaze brushed my swollen face. 'Did you fall off your horse?'

'I – yes,' I said. 'I'm all right.'

'Well,' she said mildly. 'Well. You'd better come in and get out of those wet things.'

I think if a volcano had gone up under my mother her reaction would have been the same. 'Well. Well.'

She began to pull my wet clothes off me, and I submitted, like a little girl. She wrapped a blanket around me and lit a scrub fire. There was no one else in the cave; I was glad. The heat made me shiver. Vithrie brought me food and drink, never once asking why I'd come home. Although I wasn't surprised, it was disconcerting; I know she'd never been greatly interested in me, but surely this was different? In a way, though, I was glad just to huddle there, not speaking.

'Where's Father?' I said after a few minutes. 'I must speak to him.'

'I'll send – Oh, I keep forgetting Mehaar's not here to take messages.'

'I'm sorry,' I said.

'It's all right, dear,' said Mother, tying on a hat. 'A little rain won't hurt me.'

I sat alone for a few minutes in the familiar gloom of the heimar; smoke curling up into the roof-vents, little pools of lamp-light overlapping the rosy glow of the fire. How simple life had been here. I wished I'd never gone to Torbyrgi . . .

The outside flap opened and my parents came in together, haloed by light and rain. I was glad to see Gaefir, but he looked grave. My coming back alone shocked him.

He hesitated, as if unsure how to address me. Thank Ama he didn't decide on 'Your Highness'. 'Iolithie,' he said, 'What are you doing here? Has something happened?'

'Yes. It's awful,' I said, shaking with emotion and exhaustion. 'I didn't know who else to turn to.'

They sat sombrely on either side of me and I began to tell the wretched story. I told them more than I'd told Laasastiuk; I tried to emphasize Tykavn's distress, not my own. It should have been a relief. Yet with every word I seemed to shed part of my strength,

71

and the telling of it left me feeling naked, vulnerable, humiliated.

When I'd finished, Father put his hand on my shoulder. I waited for a reaction; he and Vithrie looked at each other for a long moment, then at me. But no distress, no sympathy came; only a grave silence, a sense of deep but very distant concern. As with Laasastiuk, I felt I should not have spoken.

Finally my father said, 'I'm so sorry, Iolithie. I appreciate how hard things have been for you, but you do know, don't you, that you shouldn't have come here?'

I gave a short laugh, more a gasp. 'I – I know what you're going to say, but do you think I would have come if I hadn't been desperate?'

'No, no—'

'Don't you believe me?'

'Of course we believe you,' said Father. 'But there is nothing we can do. I'm sorry.'

'Nothing?' I cried. I stared from him to Vithrie; they looked back, grim but unmoved. 'Why? What am I supposed to do?'

'Try to understand,' said Gaefir, his hand on my shoulder suppressing me rather than comforting. 'When we gave you to your husband, we were your parents no longer. We are man and wife no longer. Our loyalty now is to Ama and our community.'

'But Tykavn's health, does that have no effect on the community?' I exclaimed.

'You say you have already spoken to Laasastiuk about this? What did he say?'

'That Tykavn was specially "Chosen for higher sanctity". He refuses to believe he's ill.' I related our meeting, but Gaefir's expression did not change.

He sighed. 'My dear, you have already spoken to the highest Church authority in the province, second only to the Arch-Perfect of Onafross himself. I can't override that. My advice to you is to obey his counsel. If you are still worried, go to him again.'

'But Laasastiuk's wrong! Tykavn could die before he does anything!'

'No one ever died from excessive devotion,' said Mother. 'You seemed to expect marriage, life itself, to be perfect. Well, it isn't.'

I could have wept, but I didn't. My heart became a lump of rock, dead, aching. 'You won't help?'

'We regret it, but you know we can't,' said Gaefir.

I started to stand up. I wasn't going to stay here. But Vithrie said, 'Did anyone see you arriving?'

'I've no idea,' I said brusquely. 'Anyone might have done, if they were looking out. Does it matter?'

'Of course it matters!' she said. 'It will be all over Vryatan that you came back on your own, virtually in tatters. People won't know the truth, because naturally we won't tell them anything; but they'll gossip. It's not that I don't understand your reasons, but others may think you've brought shame on the whole of Vryatan.'

'Damn what they think!' I cried. I pointed to the livid bruise on the side of my face. 'Tykavn did this! Do you think he would have done it if he'd been in his right mind?'

I marched to the entrance, but Gaefir came after me and caught my arm. I stood rigid. 'Hush,' he said firmly. 'No more. You think we are being harsh, my daughter, but you know the way of things. Go back to your husband. Be a good wife and do his will. You vowed to give your life to him, for good or bad; and who knows what Ama's plan is? You cannot run away from it.'

'I wasn't running away,' I said. 'Would Ama want us to submit to suffering, or fight it?'

'You must answer that question for yourself, my daughter,' he replied, kindly dumping all the responsibility on to me. 'Have you thought that Ama may have set this trial not only for Tykavn but for you too?'

'Thank you, Father.' I don't think he heard my bitterness.

'I shall find someone to take you back to the city. Vithrie's brothers will go with you.' He squeezed my shoulder and left the cave.

The truth was, Gaefir didn't know what to do either. Faced with an insoluble problem, all he could do was say 'Ama's will' and turn away. Just like Laasastiuk.

And if my own parents couldn't help, who else was there to ask?

In clean dry clothes, with a day's food in a saddlebag, I turned my face into the north wind and began the ride back to Torbyrgi. I was on Datha, my favourite horse; Gaefir had given me that, at least. Datha's coat was creamy-gold, dappled with bronze as if the sun had burned circles all over his back and quarters. His black mane blew over my hands.

I was flanked by two dark figures, mounted on blue dun mares: my uncles, silent Sublimes, hard-working men with no guile and no humour. I once heard one break his vow of silence with a curse when he dropped a rock on his foot; he had done a tenday of penance for it, after. This had seemed reasonable at the time; now, in the light of Tykavn's condition, I wondered at the use of doing penance for vows that were pointless in the first place.

The thoughts circled through my mind as I rode. I had to find a way to think clearly about this; if I didn't, it would destroy me too. Whatever doom Tykavn was driving himself to, he would not drag me with him.

Laasastiuk had to believe that Tykavn was specially Chosen by Ama. To believe anything else was to admit that something was disastrously wrong with the whole premise of his faith; and that was something a Perfect simply could never do.

And it was the same with my parents. The Prince of Torlossen, mad? Unthinkable. What proof did I have, anyway? It was only the word of a young girl against that of a Prince who appeared splendid and confident in public, and carried out his duties with meticulous perfection. If such a thing were admitted, the waves might overturn our lives.

A physical illness would have carried no shame. But a mental one; that was a stigma too terrible to be borne. It was as if I'd suggested that Sudema's evil had possessed the holiest man in the land. To them, that was exactly what I *had* suggested. That made me the wicked one.

But the truth, the very root of it all, was their fear. They dared not let themselves think I might be right. That would put them in an impossible dilemma, because they simply didn't know what to do for Tykavn. They didn't understand what was wrong with him. They couldn't cure him. In the face of his illness they were powerless. Therefore, deny, deny, deny.

No one is going to help him, I thought, in time with Datha's hoofbeats. *No one except me.*

There must be someone. Surely King Vidvikjan would be furious that his son is ill and no one is doing anything ... My thoughts raced feverishly. Torlossen was a backward province, Onafross the centre of wealth and learning. Their doctors were more skilled than ours. There was a renowned physician at Vidvikjan's court in Onareyru; what was his name? Couldn't remember. But he would help. The King and his Physician would help! But how to get word to them?

74

The hope began to die as soon as it was born. The Stolen Land lay between here and Onafross. Very few people had crossed it in either direction since the Lady Antrid's death; very few dared. And even if someone went, how could I get them to carry such a message? It would be breaking Tykavn's confidence. The King might not believe it. And even if he did, it might be tendays on tendays before any help came.

The more I considered it the more impossible it seemed. But what awaited me in Torbyrgi? More misery; perhaps more violence, or worse. At best, watching my husband slowly killing himself, while I was helpless to do anything.

Ama above, will Laasastiuk listen to me when Tykavn's dead?

There was only one answer. I kept pushing it away, but it kept coming back.

I'd always known I couldn't go back to the Palace, anyway. Not after all that trouble to escape. To walk back into it I'd have to be insane.

I think I'd already decided, but now I made the promise real. I would not go back until I had the power to help him!

The only answer was to travel to Onareyru myself. To petition the King in person. Yes, it was audacious – but wasn't he my father-in-law, if that meant anything?

But the Stolen Land . . . The memory, again, of those horses thundering two-by-two over the bridge, stained violet by Sudema's Light and red by blood. The man who had galloped by with the flesh dripping crimson from his skull. What manner of beast had torn his face away?

But I had nowhere else to go. Terrible, that knowledge. Nowhere else . . . But perhaps it isn't as bad as they make out. It won't happen to me. It can't be that far or that dangerous . . .

Now.

'Can we stop a moment, please?' I said. I nodded at a nearby stump of rock. 'I have to relieve myself.'

My uncles nodded and reined in. I turned Datha and jogged over to the rock, guided him behind it and down a little drop. Beyond was a slope of brown gravel, soft and not too steep, curving down towards the distant pleat of a valley. Out of my escorts' sight, I kept going. I kicked Datha's sides and he plunged down the slope at a gallop, his hooves making little sound in the softness.

Behind me, on the ridge, the Sublimes would wait five minutes or more before coming to see what had happened to me. I leaned forward over my horse's thick neck, urging him on, exhilaration thrilling through me. I would be out of sight by then. The irony was, they couldn't tell anyone what had happened to me because of their vow of silence!

Datha's mane whipped over my hands and I was laughing as I rode. Myself again.

CHAPTER SIX

THE STAR THAT BITES

As darkness gathered, I was laughing no longer. I'd ridden all day and even Datha, a tough mountain horse, was tired. I hadn't eaten since leaving Vryatan. Now all I had with me was one day's worth of food. One horse to feed. I had embarked on this insane journey without a thought as to how I would survive.

I circuited the city, gazing at the domes a couple of miles distant. It wasn't too late to go back . . . to food and a bed, yes, but then what?

Tykavn must have sent out guard-Sublimes to hunt for me. Or had he? Perhaps he was glad to be rid of me! There didn't seem to be any sign of a search; the landscape was deserted.

Long ridges rose on my right, mushroom-dark. Before me was the river Torlau, sliding flat and slow beyond the farmland. I daredn't stop to fish in case someone found me.

And how was I to cross the river? After Inner Thandarkyr was stolen, only one bridge to the Onafross Way had been kept intact, and that was always guarded. Datha and I would have to swim across. Were the currents dangerous? I didn't know. It frightened me, how little I knew.

I dismounted, led Datha down to the farmlands and paused to let him graze. The reed beds along the edges of the river were full of faint sounds; water lapping, birds settling for the night. How good the grass felt beneath my feet; how sweet the air smelled. The night arched above us, infinite and silent.

The air was turning chill, though. Autumn was on us. Soon winter would whiten the land, and if we hadn't reached Onafross by then . . .

I leaned against the horse's withers, feeling his coat warm and silken under my hands, thinking, If only time would stand still. If only this was all there was . . . you and me, Datha. No human complications. How can a man create such torment out of his own mind and use it to cut everyone around him to pieces?

'We'd better cross tonight,' I told Datha. 'If we spend the night on this side we might be discovered in the morning. We'll cross, and find somewhere to sleep.'

I took some pickled fish and cheese from my pack. As I ate, I looked up and saw a Border-guard, a black sentinel on the crest of a hill. He held a brand with a blazing, smoking egg of light on its tip. Just from the way he stood, the stocky shape of his body, I was sure it was Tsevren. I'd come this way half deliberately, knowing it was his area . . . Reluctant, I suppose, to leave behind all possibility of human contact.

Leaving Datha where he was, I began to climb towards him.

I wasn't sure whether he knew who I was; I mean, whether he realized the village girl he'd caught was the same one who'd married Tykavn. Doubtless he'd worked it out.

I heard wild-cats mewing. There were two weaving round his legs, and he was trying to push them away with his foot, saying, 'Clear off to the guard-house, they'll feed you there.'

I hadn't been mistaken. I looked about carefully to make sure he was alone. Then I hissed, 'Tsevren!'

He almost jumped out of his skin. 'Who's there?'

I moved into the light of the brand, let him see me. 'It's me.'

I could tell by his face that he knew. 'Ama above! Halla – or I should say Your High—'

'Don't!' I said. 'Don't call me anything. You haven't seen me. Remember what I know about you.'

He extinguished the brand and the after-images hung in my sight. 'You don't have to drag that up,' he said, crouching down beside me. 'I'm pleased to see you. Gets bloody lonely up here; makes a change to have someone to talk to, even if they're not meant to be here. But, Holy Ama, you've got some nerve coming out here!'

'I have good reason, believe me.'

'Can't settle to marriage?' he said with a half-teasing, half-admiring grin. 'I suppose even the highest in the land feel the need to do something forbidden once in a while. Shame—'

'What, that I'm not a boy?' I said acidly. I was glad that once he was over his shock he did not treat me deferentially.

'I wasn't going to say that. Shame you can't come and talk to me every night. Boys are all right, but you can't have much of a conversation with most of 'em.'

'I can't stop and talk tonight, I'm afraid,' I said. 'Haven't the Border-guards been given instructions to look for me?'

'None that I know of,' he said. Disconcerting, but it was obvious really; the fact that the Prince's wife had vanished was too shameful to be made public. Either the search was very discreet – or, as I'd suspected, Tykavn didn't even care. My mouth went sour for a moment, and I had to swallow hard. Tsevren was looking gravely at me. 'Dear Ama, you haven't run away, have you?'

'Not exactly. It's complicated. Tsevren, would you say you are my friend?'

'Well – well, yes, I suppose so. Yes.'

'Good, because I desperately need your help. I'm going to Onafross.'

He gave an explosive laugh and shook his head. 'Don't be absurd.'

'I'm not. You know about the main route, don't you? How do I travel it safely? I really need a guide. I know it is an awful lot to ask but if you would come with me—' I was beginning to gabble, I was so tired. 'It truly is a matter of life and death; Prince Tykavn's. I wish I could explain but I can't, only please believe me. I need help so desperately. There's no one I can ask but you.'

Tsevren was gawping at me as if I'd gone mad. I didn't blame him. Then he said, 'No.'

'Don't say that.'

'I mean it. The answer's no. There's nothing I can do.'

'You said you were my friend! I told you how important—'

'You want me to help you kill yourself – and drag me along with you? You're crazy. They're not a fairy story, the Unseen; you saw for yourself what they can do. The Onafross Way isn't safe, even with an armed escort. One or two people wouldn't last a day.'

I was so angry I was trembling. 'I have no choice! All right, I can't expect you to come, but at least give me some advice. Is it safe to swim across the river?'

'No, he said flatly. 'Currents underneath. You'd drown. Go home, for Ama's sake.'

'Could you get the guards away from the bridge for a few minutes?'

'No!'

'Damn it, I could have reported you and Langyr to the Assembly, but I didn't. Does that mean nothing? I still could, and I will, if you don't tell me something helpful!'

His small eyes were hard with rage now. He might hit me, as Tykavn had done; he might kill me, even at risk of losing his Status. The way I felt, I would kill him first!

Fortunately, my instinct that Tsevren was not a violent man proved right. 'All right,' he said bluntly. 'If you force me to it. Go upriver; it gets much shallower and there are places where you can cross. Then you must double back along the other bank to the main route; only don't double back all the way, or the bridge guards will see you. Cut across the hills there. Only you *must* go to the Onafross Way; there are way-huts where you can spend the nights. But way-huts didn't save Lady Antrid. It's not safe. It's madness. You'll die.'

'I'll die trying,' I said.

I rode twenty miles, more or less, before the still deep flow of the Torlau narrowed to a rushing cascade. Farmland gave way to scrub. No goats grazed here, and the only sentinels against the sky were columns of rock.

I'd been leading Datha for the last five miles. We were both exhausted. If we crossed now it would mean sleeping on the far bank. In the Stolen Land. At last I stopped, and the horse rubbed his head against me, almost pushing me over.

'Oh, Datha,' I said, catching my balance and scratching his broad flat cheek. His eyes were big, dark and unquestioning. Such a contrast to Tykavn's blood-netted, unbalanced glare. 'We'll rest on this side, I won't tie you up. Go and graze where you like. If you're not here in the morning, I'll understand; I can't ask you to go with me into . . . I don't know what we're going into.'

I removed his saddle and bridle, checked his back and legs for sore places. Then I drank from the river, relieved myself, and curled up in a dusty hollow to sleep.

If Sudema's eerie light burned me to cinders or turned me into a river-fly, I didn't care; if I'd awoken surrounded by guard-Sublimes, with Tykavn himself holding a sword at my throat, I would almost have been glad. All I craved was sleep.

When I did wake up, it was to a delicious tranquillity. The rush of the Torlau filled my ears; a bird piped high and clear above the sound. Datha grazed close by, dappled and pale as the dawn itself, his black mane rippling over his deep-crested neck. He was framed by a mass of river-weeds, their pink spires now turning to white fluff. There wasn't a soul for miles, only the sweep of the landscape, Torbyrgi far behind us, the river winding towards mountain ridges in the east.

There wasn't an inch of me that didn't ache. My head throbbed. My face, healing now, must be black and blue, if not yellow; I was glad I couldn't see my own reflection in the foaming river water. Its coldness set my teeth on edge, shocking me out of the trance of tiredness.

Breakfast was a piece of cheese, some berries and pickled vegetables. I could make one day's rations last for two, but I have a healthy appetite and I already felt weak from lack of food. The journey stretched hopeless and impossible ahead of me. Yet I numbly saddled Datha and rode on.

The river rose steeply, then flattened out and ran shallow over a gravel bed. No excuse for not crossing now. It was a scant few yards to the other side, and the country there looked no different from this; thinly grassed, beautiful, innocuous. I turned Datha and he strode out through the water.

As Ama's diamond fingers stabbed over the horizon, the river drank in the colour of the sky and blazed it back in the richest blue I've ever seen. Skeins of azure silk broke and swirled around Datha's hooves. Silver gravel, and, beyond, a cloud-brown slope studded with domes of grass, with lichen and amethyst flowers.

In the distance I saw a group of silvery mountain-deer grazing. I'd seen pictures of such creatures but I'd never seen them in the flesh before. They no longer roamed in Torlossen because they knew we'd hunt them for food, but they still lived in the Stolen Land where humans rarely set foot. If they were calm, there couldn't be any immediate danger . . .

There's nothing to fear, I told myself, gulping deep breaths. *Lady Antrid was unlucky. Why should the Unseen mind me crossing their land?* Then, aloud, 'Their land? *Our* land! They stole it from us.'

The moment he stepped on to the far bank, Datha stopped dead, skin quivering. I jumped. I was more nervous than I'd admit.

'Now, now,' I chided him. 'There's nothing to be afraid of. Walk on.'

Datha obeyed, but he went with his neck arched and ears flickering, far from his usual placid self. Was he picking up my tension or did he sense something I couldn't see? I tried to calm him. We might inflame each other's anxiety until we were both leaping out of our skins.

As Tsevren had suggested, I rode back along the river for a

while. I heard the roar of the cascades, saw the place where I'd slept. Later, the city came in sight again, like a trail of dark cloud on the horizon. If Tykavn had sent anyone to find me, would they dare to cross the river?

If. It's a horrible thing, to have no idea of your value to others. No idea of your place in the world.

Tears threatened; but they were tears of self-pity, so I set my mouth against them. I thought of Laasastiuk, of my parents, even of Mehaar, and I felt pure anger.

'They can all go to Kvold!' I said. 'I'll catch fish. There must be birds and animals, too. Wild goats for milk. I'll build fires from scrub, like we did at home. We'll survive, Datha.'

The familiar terrain of the Torlau seemed to magnetize me. I was in sight of safety here, if not actually safe; I had the idea that if the Unseen came we could plunge into the water and escape. But if I rode much further I risked us being seen by Border-guards. I ought to strike inland and take a short-cut to the main route . . . even though that meant facing the unknown.

I made the decision and turned Datha away from the river. Again he jibbed and hesitated, picking up my reluctance. I squeezed his sides and he walked on.

Dust danced about his hooves and settled again, silver on brown. I aimed for a hill beyond which no one would see us from the direction of the Torlau, and prayed that it was no more than twenty miles to the main route. I had it in mind that we must be there before nightfall. Under Sudema's light, the danger from her creatures was greatest.

Beyond the hill, we rode into a vast, flat valley. The floor was thick with greenery – a lushness rarely found in Torlossen – but at either side rose black ridges, laced with snow. The cloud-mass on their peaks continually thinned to nothing, reformed and rolled wetly over them again; but above, Ama's Light shone clear and citrine-yellow.

I felt exhilarated. There was nothing sinister in the air, only this shining beauty of nature; and I was free.

The valley came to an end, the mountain ridges curving and dropping suddenly into the earth. As I rode out between them, the landscape changed instantly and dramatically.

A chain of hills stretched as far as I could see, like vast inverted shields of sandstone. Their slopes were dusted with a hundred shades of gold, beige and clover-pink, rust-red and umber. Meandering runnels, crusted with white, yellow and amber, incised their sides. Clouds of steam hung above the ground, some blue-grey, some white, fraying into the air.

Hot streams run under Torbyrgi, giving us the perpetual luxury of hot water; there are others near Vryatan. Fire sleeps very near the surface of Thandarkyr. It turns rock to liquid in places; it drives water boiling up through cracks in the earth, heats the mud and pushes up strange minerals that colour the soil and perfume the air. There are small sulphur pans near Vryatan, but we were always warned away from them as children; their heat is dangerous, and the adults used to tell us that the bubbling holes led down to Kvold, that the steam was the breath of sleeping demons.

Yet I'd never seen a landscape such as this, such an alien sculpted terrain, such gorgeous colours produced by nature. At least I assume this was nature's work. An old fear surfaced that the childhood tales were true; how could I be sure that this wasn't the lair of the Unseen, slumbering under the crust like magma?

No, no. Go on or give up for good.

In all the splendour of these barren hills I couldn't see a single grass blade. I took Datha back to the mouth of the valley and let him graze while I rested. When he'd had plenty to eat, I pulled his reluctant head from the grass and struck out along a narrow valley.

The air was steeped with the round hot smell of sulphur. The crease between the hills led in the direction I wanted, north-west. We would come to the main route eventually, if my sense of direction didn't desert me; oh, but to have no map, no compass, not even the simplest tools of survival – I drove out the doubts. From minute to minute, we would live.

The valley widened out into a pan of mineral crusts, a riot of yellows, ash-white and red. Craters pocked the ground, filled with blue-grey mud that roiled and bubbled like ominous cauldrons. The noises they made were infinitely varied; some sinister, others almost comic. Steam drifted from the surface of unnaturally blue pools, screamed at pressure from strange cones of silica. Everywhere heat, strange colours, weird sounds.

The ground felt fragile under Datha's hooves. I dismounted and led him, keeping away from the edges of the mud pools, where the bright-coloured hot crust might give way and plunge us into boiling mud.

Picking the coldest, safest path between the craters, I didn't look up at the surrounding hills for a long time. When I did, I saw something moving.

I pulled Datha to a standstill. What on Eileah was it? It was moving along the crest of a hill, perhaps half a mile away. It looked like an insect, a river-fly moving on long, swaying legs. Yet at such a distance it must be huge, the size and shape of one of Torbyrgi's domes. Stricken with panic, I hurriedly backed Datha behind a finger of orange rock, terrified that it could see us too.

It was amber-coloured like the hills themselves, walking on four spindly legs at least twenty feet long. Was it alive? I stared and stared. I could make no sense of what I was seeing. Some beast that dwelled among the hot springs, some dreadful creature of Sudema . . . Dizzy with fear, I watched until it went out of sight behind a closer hill-peak.

Beads of sweat broke and ran down my back. Either I was beginning to imagine things or . . . Oh, dear Ama, why had I started this? I waited ten or fifteen minutes but the thing didn't reappear. Datha grew restless and we couldn't stay here for ever, so – giving myself up to the mercy of gods or demons – I emerged from my hiding place and went on.

I saw nothing else of the 'insect' all that day; but as the sun dropped lower in the sky I began to wonder how I'd recognize the Onafross Way. It ran through valleys, and there were way-huts; that was all I knew. I might already have crossed it without knowing. Or I might be travelling at too shallow an angle to have reached it. By twilight, both Datha and I needed rest, and there was no sign of any huts, nor of any end to these sterile, sulphurous hills.

I felt utterly alone. There was only a little of my own food left, nothing for Datha to eat. I gave him my last handful of berries and ate a piece of fish that left me unbearably thirsty. We tried to sip from a tiny spring, but the water was hot and bitter, and golden-yellow sulphur strands grew on the bed like weeds.

'These hills have got to stop soon,' I whispered to Datha, scratching his ears. 'Tomorrow we'll find a river. As long as we're heading north we're going the right way.'

But first we must survive the night.

The sky was clear and Sudema shone small and cold in the blackness. I found a dip in the ground at the base of a hill, half sheltered by a mass of rock that resembled a human fist punching out of the ground. The air was chill, but the ground was warm.

Before I lay down to sleep I hesitated. I'd been so tired last night that I'd forgotten to say my prayers. Had it mattered? Would Ama desert me, for that? He wouldn't be pleased. I desperately wanted to pray now, to beg his mercy and protection. I clasped my hands and bowed my head, but the words wouldn't come. All I could see was an image of Tykavn, lighting his candles with a shaking hand and an intent expression; eyes narrowing in anguish when one failed to light at the appointed moment; the burst of frustrated rage and then his terrible calmness as he forced the anger back and started again. And had any of it made one iota of difference to Ama?

I fell to my knees, tore my hands apart and clawed the grit. Tykavn had left me with an aversion to ritual that bordered on horror. Futile, all of it; the Priest-Perfects before their altars no less obsessive and self-deluded than Tykavn. I couldn't pray. He had taken that comfort away from me.

Yes, there is a fire in the sky that we call the sun; but why should it have consciousness, or care about us? Even a child could not sustain such a belief.

I curled myself tight around my sense of loss and fell asleep.

I was standing by a round pool with steam rising from its surface. The water was luminous violet-blue, Sudema's colour. It was as if the star had burst and spilled its colour in the water. And hanging in the blue glass was a reflection. Not my own; it was on the opposite side. Yet there was no figure to cast it.

The reflection was of a woman, clad in black. In all that shadow, only her face gleamed white as a skull, tinted blue by the water. The woman had one hand raised to her face and she seemed to be tearing at her own flesh, picking it off scrap by scrap. Crimson began to colour the whiteness. Her eyes were wide with horror, but she seemed unable to stop herself.

I knew I had to stop the woman from destroying herself, but there was no way to reach her unless I entered the water. So I jumped into the pool.

The water was scalding. I tried to scream. I knew that I was becoming the reflection now . . .

I went on sinking, sinking through the water as if it filled a bottomless crack in the earth. Suddenly I found myself underground, in a flickering darkness that could have been air or water.

I knew I was at the very centre of Eileah. I was in a little dark chamber like the chapel in the House of Ama. Yet at the same time I was still standing by the same pool, and the shadow-woman was facing me across it, casting no reflection.

'Why have you come into this, where Ama's Light never falls?' said the woman. Her face was whole again, her eyes as blue as the water, but she was clawing at her cheek in a way that turned my stomach. Her words filled me with unspeakable dread. 'The soul of Sudema is the centre of a flower. It is the star that bites. Offer your face to her and she will drink up your soul to feed her children. Feed them with the fire for you are damned like me.'

'Who are you?' I cried.

'This is my face!' The woman tore violently at her cheek and the flesh came away, and I was staring at the moist, pulsing mass of vein and muscle that I had seen before, the face of the man who had fled in terror out of the Stolen Land and died.

The woman said, 'I was the Lady Antrid.'

Fighting for breath, my mouth wide, I struggled to escape from sleep. But the earth, heavy and solid, seemed determined to hold me inside itself. Antrid was trying to warn me. I had damned myself by walking into the Stolen Land. Sudema would destroy my body and steal my soul . . .

I felt a pain in my hip, a physical blow, heard a high inhuman squeal. I broke out of the dream, smothered in heat, choking on sulphur. All was dark. My terror did not lessen on waking; it persisted, shaping and growing. Hoofbeats. I was confused; for a moment it seemed a horse was galloping inexorably towards me, and on its back would be that terrible torn face, which would not be that of some unknown outrider but of the Lady Antrid herself . . .

Then my head cleared and I realized that what I could hear was Datha galloping away. I'd been half aware of it happening even while I was still deep in the nightmare. Something had frightened him so much that he had squealed and jumped right across me, catching my hip with his hoof as he went. And the heavy menace of the dream still hung thick in the air, terrible and real.

'Datha!' I called, scrambling to my feet. I went hot and cold by turns. *There was something watching me.* I turned slowly and saw a disc of violet light, floating as if detached in the shadow of the rock. Just where I had been lying.

I stood petrified, fear soaring like a scream into my throat. As I watched, the disk blurred and divided into two. Two nacreous circles, like animal eyes fixed on me. Another pair rose just above the rock, a cold blood-tinged blue. And another. The shadows were full of eyes.

I opened my mouth but I couldn't make a sound, couldn't move. The crystalline discs were drifting towards me, two by two, cat-smooth. There was a glimmer of light that seemed to hint at a sinuous limb. I thought I'd imagined it until I saw it again. Traces of light on legs, long curved backs, and – *oh, beloved Ama* – claws.

Yet I couldn't see the flesh that threw these faint images. Beneath the highlights there was only clear air, transparent shadow. Nothing there – but that nothing was catching Sudema's sick light in the form of a long-limbed beast.

A flash of teeth; one of the beings was opening its mouth. I expected a growl, a roar. Instead a low, cold voice spoke.

'Child of Ama, we do not walk on your territory. Neither may you walk on ours, lest we bring to you what you brought to us.'

And the creature raised a paw, claws glittering. Claws? I had an impression of a closed hand with four knives protruding between the fingers, four tiny scythes shining deathly white.

I turned and ran, panic flinging my body forwards out of control. I was hurtling downhill towards another pan of mud pools.

'Datha!' I tried to call, but it came out a rasp. I glanced round once, and saw nothing behind me. Only the soot-black sweep of the hill. But I knew they were still following. I could *feel* them . . .

Or were they ahead, waiting for me to run into them? Strange noises rolled towards me. The earth itself was bubbling, groaning, growling.

I tried to slow down and couldn't. Each footfall jarred my knees and by breath burned my throat. The air itself burned. It was so sour with sulphur that I could barely draw it into my lungs. A cloud of moist heat wrapped round me, choking; steam mushroomed from the ground everywhere, tinted purplish-grey by the starlight.

The ground was peppered with holes, with cauldrons of mud and simmering water. From these the steam poured and the sounds rumbled, ceaseless, ominous.

I stumbled to a halt on the very edge of a crater and stared down at the blue mud boiling within. One step more and I would have been a morsel of cooked flesh for the Unseen to pick at.

They had driven me into this place. They meant to drive me to my death. The star's light was too ephemeral, the ground too treacherous, to risk running.

No escape. They had only to circle me, swift and invisible, and I was theirs. Bitter tears of terror and rage stung my eyes, and my breath chattered in my throat. The words of a prayer ran through my teeth like beads, meaningless, but I knew they couldn't help. That I'd been so complacent, thinking, *It can't be so dangerous. It can't happen to me.* That it should happen so *soon.*

I felt I would die of fear before ever they touched me.

A gleam of blue in the corner of my eye. I spun sideways and found a pool in front of me, just as in my dream, its surface contained within a thick rim of silica. But it was milk-blue, too turbulent to hold a reflection, and steam drifted from its surface. Through the steam, on the other side, I saw two amethyst suns glowing.

With the crater behind me I couldn't back away. I could only edge sideways, and that would bring me within the creature's reach. As I stood there, suspended, the surface of the water began to bubble and leap. Pressure was building. Suddenly the pool erupted; a trunk of scalding water thrusting fierce into the heavens. I leapt back, but a breath of wind caught the geyser and tipped it away from me. Clouds of boiling spray and steam descended towards the Unseen on the other side.

All in the space of four seconds it happened. I couldn't believe anything could harm the demon, yet I heard it snarl in anger or pain. It was true they feared heat!

I turned and ran.

I danced and dodged round the edges of craters, between the steam-flags that marked their presence. The hot air was choking me, my heart hammering. There was darkness ahead, a place where no heat rose; a hill rising steep and black. I ran straight towards it, impelled by some mad hope of safety.

My right foot came down on hot ground and went straight through the crust into boiling mud. I stumbled, crying out. My boot protected me from the worst of it, but the heat bit through the goat-skin. Gasping with the shock, my leg stinging, I righted myself and ran on.

I allowed myself a single glance behind. Ten jewelled eyes drifted on the darkness; five shadow-shapes flowed impassively as the Torlau after me. I thought of the scythes, the cold voice. *You don't see them until they're about to kill you,* Tsevren had said. I saw Lady Antrid's face, no longer a face, and it was as if a black energy filled me. It would burst my heart if I went on, but for just these few minutes I sailed up the hillside like a bird.

Then I saw a strange shape nestled in a fold. It was rounded, too symmetrical to be part of the mountain. Purple light glittered off small tiles, caught the edges of a round door and a window.

A way-hut. If I'd been able to stop and think, I would have remembered it was little protection against Sudema's Legions; that it only afforded protection at all when manned by guards armed with fire-brands to keep the night creatures away. But I was beyond thought as I flung myself towards it.

My energy was failing. I thought my skull would burst with the pounding of my blood. I felt the sickly pull of unconsciousness, felt Sudema's ice-breath through my clothes.

I clutched at the wall of the hut. I tore at the circular door and it came open, boulder-heavy in my shaking grasp. I threw myself inside, felt the whole structure shake as one of my pursuers flung itself against the door even as it slammed shut.

I curled up on the floor, out of my mind. I had landed on something soft; I was hugging something that felt like a cushion in my arms, with no idea of how I'd got hold of it, only clutching it like a pathetic shield against the Unseen.

I wasn't safe, of course. It was a few seconds' respite, at most. They would open the door and I was trapped. Perhaps they would simply walk through the walls . . .

I wouldn't have minded dying if only it could have been done with dignity, without this terror, this humiliating scramble to survive.

The door creaked. A crescent of indigo showed. Then I felt the floor heave under me.

The whole hut began to rock and sway. In fresh panic I grabbed at the wall, but nothing was stable. Outside, there was a scrabbling sound, then the door thumped shut again and there was silence. It was as if the hut had shrugged off the demon, like a dog shaking itself; and now it seemed to be rising through the air; soaring, dipping, swaying, turning the star-points to lines of light across my wretched eyes.

CHAPTER SEVEN

PAINTING WITH THOUGHTS

As I drowned in weightless nausea, I heard their voices spinning away on the wind. Thin, eldritch cries, neither human nor animal, trying to draw me back through the darkness. The voices seemed full of words that I couldn't quite hear, but which filled me with terror.

You cannot escape us. Wherever you go, we will be there before you . . .

I crawled to a window and gripped the frame to haul myself to my knees. As I looked out, violent dizziness swooped through me. Hard to make sense of anything I could see through the thick glass. In the dark it seemed I was yards above the ground, lurching through thin air at alarming speed. The mountains against the sky dipped and swayed in the window. Was the hut flying? It would fall at any moment. Vertigo possessed me so completely that I could barely breathe, let alone think.

Suddenly light splashed into the room. Hanging grimly on to the edge of the window, I looked round to see a figure standing against a glowing archway.

It looked exactly like a representation of Ama in a book; a sleek figure outlined with blue, haloed from head to foot with gold. For one crazed moment it seemed Ama himself had come, either to save or slay me.

'Make it stop!' I cried. 'Please, beloved God, make it stop!'

The figure laughed. 'Make it stop, when it has delivered you out of the jaws of the Unseen?' It was a male voice, light and haughty. 'I don't think you know what you ask. If we stop, they'll get in and tear us to bits. Would you prefer that to this?'

The hut lurched, righted itself. I was almost out of my mind. 'We're going to fall!'

'We are not going to fall, daughter of Ama,' the voice said thinly. 'My creation obeys my will.'

'Are we flying?'

90

'Would that surprise you, who addressed me as your "Beloved God" just now? Is not your Ama capable of anything?'

I heard terrible sarcasm in his tone. I was beyond knowing what to do or say. 'Please make it stop,' I said feebly.

'Such ingratitude to the mechanism that saved your life.'

'I'm going to be sick!'

That had an effect. 'Only if you want me to open the door and throw you back where you came from!' the shadow said furiously. 'Don't you dare! All right – wait—' He gave an exasperated sigh and turned back into the doorway. 'If I want sense out of you – *if* there's any in you—'

His voice faded, the light vanished, but a few seconds later the terrible motion ceased and the hut – vehicle – whatever it was – came to a standstill.

I slumped in relief, drawing in lungfuls of air as if I had nearly drowned. Then the glow reappeared in the archway and the man came into the room, carrying a lamp. The light sifted about him, burnishing a straw-gold floor half hidden beneath a drift of bright cushions. I was dazzled. The room was about twenty feet wide, the walls and ceiling a single smooth curve from side to side, and ten feet deep. The dividing walls, one before and one behind me, each had a curtained archway. I could see no more detail than that.

'If you still feel ill, put your head out of the door,' he said brusquely. He did not sound like a god.

'No – no, I'm all right now it's stopped,' I gasped. My head was still spinning, but my stomach was calmer. 'What is this thing? It's not a way-hut.'

'No,' he agreed. 'This is not a way-hut.'

'I don't understand what happened. Did you – did you save me?'

'No, halla, I do not make it my business to save idiot children of Ama. It was my misfortune that you mistook my dwelling for a way-hut. You led them to me; you damned near had me slain alongside you.'

My eyes adjusted. I stared at him. He was like no man I had ever seen in Torlossen. He had a mop of blonde hair, brushed straight back from his face and hanging to his shoulders; his face was thin-boned, lined, with a hooked blade of a nose. His eyes were deep-set, narrow, and glacier-grey. He was wearing the strangest clothes, breeches and a shirt of silky geitha, which moulded themselves to his body. As he moved, their colour shifted from blue to purple – the colour of Sudema. Thick gold bracelets snaked around his wrists and ankles, more gold hung round his neck; and in the centre of his chest hung a round, amethyst eye.

The malign disc focused my gaze like the star itself. What kind of man worshipped Sudema? I'd never met a soul who didn't fear her.

'Yes, stare,' he said. His lips twitched, as if he was pleased. 'You will see nothing else like me, from Onafross to the wildest mountains.'

I made the circle of Ama over my breast. He laughed. I don't blame him.

'What are you, mathyr?' I said.

'Your reluctant saviour. Oh, God's Light, don't look at me with that horrible expression. Look out of the window.'

I looked. There was a silver line of light on the horizon, distorted through the syrupy glass. In the first gleam of dawn I could see that we were motionless on a shallow hillside, twenty feet above the ground. The dome-shaped hut was standing on what appeared to be long articulated filaments like the legs of a river-fly . . .

'This was the thing I saw this morning! Walking across the hills like an insect. It was you, wasn't it? Or are there more of these?' Remembering, I also remembered Datha.

'No, Laufi is quite unique,' said the man. 'So now you realize we weren't flying; unfortunately my powers do not extend to defying the imperative pull of Eileah. We are on solid ground, and we are safe. The Unseen will not reach us here. I'm prepared to consider not throwing you to them if you are at least civil and well-behaved, and stop gawping at me.'

I went on staring at him, feeling cold to my very spine.

'I – I've heard of creatures of Sudema, but never of *men* who worship her,' I said faintly.

He blinked at me. He gave a short laugh, shook his head. 'You poor thing,' he said. 'You look at me and see a demon, even though you don't know what one might look like. If there's any name for what I am, it's Eldur-magian; though that won't mean anything to you, either.' He walked away into another shadowed arch. When he returned, he handed me a glass of water and sat down on a cushion opposite me.

The cold shock of the water was delicious. I drained the glass.

'I had a horse,' I said miserably. 'I knew I shouldn't have brought him . . .'

'Well, we aren't going back to look for him. You Amaians, you think that—' He stopped. 'They will have wanted you, not your horse. They don't attack horses, unless they are *very* hungry.'

I hung my head. This was the worst thing of all, that Datha might have died for my ill-considered actions. I said bitterly, 'We Amaians think – what?'

'You think you are indestructible. You think you know everything. You think that only your own rules, your own ideas, are real.'

'And you Sudema-worshippers,' I said fiercely. 'What do you think?'

The demon – whatever he said, that's what I thought he was – drew away from me, looking at me down the knife-ridge of his nose. He looked at me with condescension, as if I knew nothing at all and wasn't capable of understanding, even if he explained. I hated him for it! I hated everything about him, down to the garish cushions on his floor.

'I think,' he said, 'that you look exhausted, frightened and wretched. So would I be in your place, I suppose. Private – uhm – arrangements are through the arch at the back. You can stay here and go to sleep – if you promise not to be sick on my cushions. I have not protected them from the dust of a dozen volcanoes to be despoiled by the likes of you.'

I lay down, but it took me an age to sleep. I kept drifting off then waking in shock, seeing the unfamiliar curved walls, aware of the stranger's presence behind one of the curtained alcoves. Everything that had happened bounced blindly around the inside of my skull. I couldn't stop worrying about Datha.

But sleep came at last, and it was heavy and luxurious. When I woke, daylight and blue shadow slopped about the room and the floor was in motion again.

It was less of a shock this time. Because it was light and I could see to the horizon, I was able to keep my bearings. The motion of the hut felt like that of a horse walking; a four-beat gait on four improbable legs.

What was this object, which moved like a living thing yet was made of slate and precious wood? A work of demonry. Yet it moved under the light of the sun! I began to make Ama's circle over my breast, then let my hand fall. Habit. A shadow of Tykavn's illness.

My only cause for relief was that we'd left the hot suphurous hills behind. We were crossing a volcanic landscape, choked with age-old lava, thinly jewelled with lichens and mosses.

A plum-coloured curtain, patterned with webs of gold, hung across the archway at the front of the hut. A hand drew it aside, and the magian's face appeared in the gap. His expression as he scrutinized me was half irritated, half friendly. I felt myself closing up like a bud under his attention. What was he seeing and thinking?

'So you've woken to this glorious day at last,' he said heartily. 'You're hungry, I suppose?'

I nodded mutely. He disappeared, and a few minutes later came through the curtain balancing two bowls on each arm. He set two in front of me; in one there were strips of meat and fish, squares of white cheese speckled with herbs, and in the other sweetened sour-milk to drink. He sat cross-legged on a cushion opposite me and ate his own breakfast with relish, never taking his eyes off me. He seemed all energy; patterns of purple light flashing from his strange clothes and his saffron hair sliding over his shoulders as he moved, his grey eyes quick as birds.

I didn't know how to react to him. I was ravenous – but was it safe to eat the food of demons?

He paused, a bowl of milk halfway to his lips. 'Why would I rescue you, only to poison you?' he said.

'I don't know,' I said. 'I don't know what you are.'

'A fool to myself,' he said. 'If you don't eat it, I will.'

My hunger won. The meal seemed the most delicious I had ever tasted, but consuming it felt like a small defeat.

My saviour – or captor – terrified me, but I couldn't refuse what he gave. Food, rest, a refuge. I felt tainted by accepting anything from a man who wore Sudema's colours; I hated my own weakness in being unable to refuse his help.

After a time he asked, 'What's your name, halla?'

'Iolithie Gaefir-daughter,' I said, not thinking to lie.

'I am pleased to meet you, halla Iolithie. I am Sigurthur Athaan-son.'

I was surprised that he had a human name. 'Where – where do you come from?'

'Nowhere. Everywhere. Onafross, once upon a time, though I

prefer not to mention that.' He grinned, but it only made his eyes keener and colder.

'Onafross? I – I thought—'

'What? That I came from Kvold? Fell out of the star herself, perhaps?' He leaned towards me. 'What do you think I am?'

'A child of Sudema,' I whispered.

'Ever seen a child of Sudema?' He almost shouted, making me start.

'I've never seen anything like you anywhere.'

'Thank Ama for that!' he said, and laughed. 'I should hope you haven't. But then, there is no reason I should tell you anything. I would like you to remain suitably awestruck.'

I drained the last drop of milk and put the bowl aside. I folded my arms across myself and looked out at a long blue-green ridge drifting past the window. I was trying to compose my thoughts.

'Nothing to say?' he said.

I said, guardedly, 'I'm grateful to you for feeding me. For saving me. But I think perhaps you should let me go now.'

'Really?' he said flatly. He leaned back on the cushions, his right fist resting on his hip. 'You surely don't think I am keeping you prisoner here for my own enjoyment? I didn't want you in the first place.'

'I didn't mean that!' I said angrily. His flippant arrogance was infuriating. 'You've been very kind, but I have a journey to make. I don't want to intrude on you, either, so if you could let me down to the ground now—'

'And then what?'

'I will try to find my horse. If I can't, I'll have to go on foot.'

'How far do you think you are going?'

'That is really not your concern. You don't want to explain anything; neither do I. Let us part as we met, without questions.'

'Yes, yes, a very fair suggestion,' Sigurthur said impatiently. 'But what I meant was, what do you think will happen if I let you down on the ground? Exactly what happened last night. When it grows dark – or possibly while it's light, because they are never predictable – the Unseen will come after you again. Do you know how to fight them? The only thing they fear is fire, and I can see nothing combustible about your person. And suppose they don't come and you survive another night, where is your next meal coming from? Do you even know where the nearest river is?'

'No. I haven't a map,' I said thinly.

'No map! Your faith in Ama's guidance must be absolute! Do you even know how you are going to cross the next river?'

'There is a bridge on the main route.'

He threw his head back with hard laughter. I felt like sticking a knife through his bony chest. Straight through the violet Eye. 'Have you any idea how far from the Onafross Way we are? We are deep in the Stolen Land. This is Sudema's country, halla.'

'I know!' I said. 'And I have to cross it, and your clever remarks are not helping one bit!'

'Ama preserve us,' he said under his breath. He spoke the God's name as if in mockery. Blasphemy, just in his intonation. In one light, smooth movement he stood up and went through the alcove to the front of the hut.

I remained where I was for a few seconds, seething. Then I jumped up and pushed through the heavy curtain after him.

I found myself in a curved sliver of a room, the front wall of which was set with a huge many-paned window. It faced in the direction of travel, and the ground, ridged and crusted with vegetation, rushed vertiginously towards and away beneath us. Sigurthur was sitting on the floor with his back to me, staring ahead, with his arms crossed loosely over his knees.

'I don't want to be a nuisance,' I said. 'You've done enough for me.'

'If you need my help, why don't you ask for it?' said Sigurthur.

I sat next to him, forcing myself to watch the dizzy motion until I started to get used to it. The legs strode out, fly-delicate yet steady as a horse. 'How does this hut move?' I asked eventually.

He gave a sideways smile, a flash of pride. 'By my will. This was a way-hut once; I adapted it. Stole it, if you like. But please, don't refer to it as a hut; or as an *it*, for that matter. I call her the Laufjallfertha; traveller of rivers and mountains. If you insist on attributing unnatural powers to me, I cannot deny it.'

'But how? It's against Ama's Laws.'

'Against the Laws of Onafross and Torlossen,' he said dismissively. 'Ama never said he minded. Not to my face, at least.'

'But do you live alone in the Stolen Land? Travelling like this?'

'Always travelling, yes,' he said, half to himself. 'One day, I hope to arrive.'

'Where?'

'You must learn not to take everything I say so literally,' he said. 'I was being ironic. Yet ... well, I meant it, too.'

I was growing more and more curious, despite myself, to know what lay behind his obscure remarks. 'But are there others like you?'

'Like me – in what way?'

His tone was sharp, and I was sure that whatever description I gave was bound to offend him. 'Other – magians who live in the Stolen Land.'

'I am quite unique in most respects, I assure you. Yet I'm not the only human who manages to survive here ... but I'm breaking the rules, aren't I? I'm speaking to a child of Ama, who cannot possibly have any understanding of what I am.'

I was caught between desperate curiosity and instinctive revulsion for what he appeared to be. One who drew dark powers from the star of night. The antithesis of everything holy. 'I can't ask for your help,' I said softly.

'Why not? Because you think I worship Sudema?'

'I – yes. What else can I think?'

'If you look at me from the lofty position of an Amaian, there's no way to justify what I am. I could not expect you to understand; so think me a demon, if you will. But I'm quite a harmless one, I assure you.'

I was silent. I was at his mercy. I knew he was right, that if he put me down as I asked, within a couple of days I would be dead. Having met the Unseen, I no longer doubted it. The thought of them turned me sick with dread, but the alternative was almost as bad; to beg the uncertain help of this bizarre stranger.

'I wish I dared trust you,' I said. 'All the people I thought I could trust have let me down.'

'So put your faith in someone you *don't* trust! If I'm to help you, you had better tell me why a girl barely old enough to become Sublime is wandering all alone in this wilderness. What are you about, halla Iolithie? Running away from something?'

Loathing myself, I took the risk. 'I'm going to Onareyru. My – my husband is sick. He needs the help of a good physician, but there is no one in Torlossen who can help him.'

Sigurthur was aghast. 'So he sent you, all alone? He must be crazed.'

'No,' I said sharply. 'It wasn't like that. He doesn't even know where I've gone, or why.'

'Then your husband must be a man of extraordinary virtues, for you to risk your life for him! Who is he?'

'His name would mean nothing to you.'

'Ah well, it is of no interest to me if he's the bloody Prince of Torlossen himself. What I ask myself is, why should I do anything that would benefit people who'd condemn me to be stripped of Status, or worse, if they ever laid hands on me? Not that I give a damn for Status, but that's not the—'

'Yes, why should you?' I cried. 'That's why I won't ask! Let me out!'

'Very well!'

The hut lurched to a halt. My stomach dipped and I shivered. He had simply thought *stop* and the impossible Laufjallfertha had obeyed. What else was he capable of?

Neither of us moved. Finally Sigurthur said, 'I don't want you here and you don't want to be here. It's hopeless. Laufi is designed for one and I am not used to company. I can't feed two, and the sanitary arrangements are less than...' He released a breath through his thin nostrils. 'But we both know what will happen if I cast you out. Do you want me to have that on my conscience? I can take you to Onafross, if you would only ask.'

I felt he was forcing me to humiliate myself, to submit to his superior will. And because he was my only hope, I had to. 'I'm not a complete idiot,' I said. 'I know it's probably the only way I will get there.'

'No "probably" about it. They say swallowing pride is worse than swallowing frozen lava.' Sigurthur's mouth twitched cynically.

'More than pride,' I whispered. Everything I'd ever believed in, in fact. 'I don't know what I can give you in return...' Even as I spoke, a new tremor of dread awoke. It hadn't crossed my mind until now, but the prospect of submitting sexually to him appalled me. I would rather the Unseen tore me to pieces.

How many sacrifices was I prepared to make, to help Tykavn?

Not for the first time, he seemed to read my thoughts, and twist them completely around to shame me. 'Nothing physical, I can assure you,' he said with distaste. 'I am not troubled by such desires, nor have I been for many years. I hope that you will not be, either, at least for the duration of this journey, because you will find me most unwilling to oblige.'

I looked away, my face hot with embarrassment. 'I've nothing. No goods or wealth.'

'Don't insult me. It's true, you have nothing to offer . . . other than your soul.' He spoke lightly, but it was a cruel joke, when he knew I had no idea of the extent of his powers, nor of his true nature. At best, another insult to my supposed religion. 'Failing that, I only ask that you listen to me. It is a long time since I had an audience.'

I glanced at him in surprise. *An audience?* 'What – what sort of things might you want to say?'

He barked with laughter. 'Dear Iolithie, your eyes are the size of mudpots! It has always been my ambition to make just one child of Ama see that things are not always as they seem. If you fear I may corrupt you, it might be no bad thing. Listen to my prattle and bear my abysmal company; that's all I ask. Can you bear it?'

Against my will, I felt a smile pulling at my lips. 'I will try.'

'Are you sure?' Sigurthur raised his head, and without warning the Laufjallfertha came to life and pranced forward like an eager horse.

In the same instant something like a strange-coloured shadow moved in the corner of my eye. Startled, I looked round. All over the curved ceiling and the dividing wall behind us, which had been creamy-blank, were glowing images; meadows and mountains, tall plants that must be trees, lakes and weird creatures out of legend. Unlike the static friezes in the Palace, these pictures glowed as if alive. In red and lavender, azure, green and amber-gold, they scrolled over every surface, clustered round the huge window and the archway, covered the floor.

I saw the city of Torbyrgi, idealized in gold. I saw a girl, riding away from it alone, watched by a dark figure that stood on the path behind her.

The girl was me. And I don't know how I knew, but the watcher was not Tykavn. I don't know who or what it was, but my palms turned clammy and my heart began to race with dread.

The images seemed more dangerous than fire, born of the evanescent power that curled all around me like smoke. Lethal, yet impossible to touch.

'God's Light, what are they?' I cried.

'My thoughts.' Sigurthur smiled thinly. 'I surely hope you don't take exception to them. It's a hellish long way to Onafross.'

CHAPTER EIGHT

TRAVELLER OF RIVERS
AND MOUNTAINS

Sometimes I understood why Tykavn drove himself half-mad trying to ward off unknown terrors.

Here I was, trapped in this impossible vehicle, with a lunatic who – I believed – could read my thoughts and project them on to the walls in garish images as if to mock me.

I left him and went into the central room, panicking a little. My mouth was dry. There, too, every surface glowed with images, swelling from pastel and silver to stunning brightness. The colours were extraordinary, delicate and transparent as coloured glass. Mountains, trees, huge stylized flowers. And although they were motionless they changed continuously; I had only to turn away for a second to turn back and see something new. A subtle change, or a whole new scene out of nowhere.

I rushed back into the cabin, crying out, 'How are you doing this?'

'I told you, with my imagination,' Sigurthur replied calmly. The way the light flared through his hair and caught his face at that moment made him look demonic. Clothed in shades of violet, edged with stripes of crimson and magenta, he looked as if he had stepped out of his own creation. 'I can't abide a blank wall, can you? They call out to my artistic urges.'

'Can you see into the future?'

Sigurthur laughed.

'Into the past?' I said.

'Why, have you dark secrets to hide? You're young ... but then, no one's too young to feel ashamed of something in their past.'

'You're frightening me!' I was incensed. 'If I were you, I'd be ashamed of *that*!'

His smile vanished. 'Why are you frightened, Iolithie?'

'I can see myself in these – these—' I pointed helplessly around the walls. 'I can see things that have happened to me.'

'Dear girl,' he said softly, 'you have told me enough of what happened to you for my imagination to fill in the rest. I don't need to read your mind to illustrate it.'

I looked up and saw, on the arc of the ceiling above the window, my own face, jewelled like a mosaic, staring in dismay at a man lying prostrate on a bed.

I didn't believe him.

'Please stop it,' I said.

'I am only teasing you,' he said. The landscapes and cities remained, but I was no longer in them. A line of deer walked along the base of a mountain, outlined by the dim fires of twilight. An innocuous image, but my apprehension didn't subside.

'Well, I don't find it funny,' I said. 'You should be careful; I might learn something about *you* that you don't want me to know.'

'I have already shown you many such things. You have not noticed or understood a single one of them, halla.'

All our conversations seemed to be like this. Perhaps it was no bad thing; I would have been much more frightened of him if he hadn't been so smug and so irritating.

Oh, but the luxury of being annoyed by someone's company, when you're no longer struggling minute by minute just to survive!

The Laufjallfertha was divided into four rooms; the central room, scattered with cushions, where I'd first found myself; Sigurthur's own sleeping chamber, hardly more than a cupboard, where he kept his scant possessions; a washing cubicle which consisted of no more than a hole in the floor and a pitcher of water; and the cabin at the front, which doubled as a food store and kitchen.

Later, I asked where he obtained food. We were sitting in the cabin, looking out through the crystal panes at black mountains and an eggshell-blue sky. The valley through which we moved was the lushest green meadow I had ever seen.

'This is a fertile land,' he said, 'There are fish, there are wild goats and deer, vegetables in the ground and fruit on the trees.'

'Trees?' I said, startled.

His mouth thinned, as if he had said more than he intended. 'Bushes. I meant to say bushes.'

'They tell us that Sudema's offspring took the richest land from us and left us the scraps,' I said.

'Perhaps,' he said. 'However, when a land is inaccessible, it's easy to make grandiose myths about what lies there. After all, who can prove otherwise?'

'But I've seen pictures of trees and tall flowers like jewels in books. You make them yourself on these walls!'

'I am only creating pictures out of my imagination, halla.' His tone hinted that he knew far more than he was prepared to tell me. Cruelly teasing. I thought, *The more I ask, the more chance it gives him to make me look a fool!* He went on, 'There were trees, forests everywhere once. Men destroyed them, did you know that? They cut them down to build houses, the soil blew away and the forests couldn't grow back.'

This sort of thing was rarely mentioned in Torlossen. We're bad at admitting our mistakes, as I was finding out. Bad at admitting anything.

He went on, 'Our ancestors built great ships to sail on the ocean – I doubt that you've even seen the ocean, have you?'

'Never,' I said sulkily.

'It is bigger and wilder than the greatest lake you can imagine.' As he spoke, green waves flowed over the ceiling, and a strangely shaped dark edifice rocked ponderously on them. I doubted that Sigurthur had ever seen a ship, either. 'But the ships are all gone now,' he said. 'All rotted away, and no more wood to replace them. Sad, isn't it? One thing I can tell you; the city of Vivirjosa exists, and it is as beautiful as its legend. Or would be, if it hadn't gone to ruin.'

Now I saw softly coloured walls and domes nestling on a mountain side. 'Have you seen it?' I asked, astonished.

In reply, he smiled.

I said, 'So the Unseen not only stole it from us but ruined it!'

'But have you ever asked why Sudema's people should have left their enemies anything at all? You should be grateful.'

'For what?'

'For letting you live. They never cross the borders into Torlossen or Onafross, do they? They only kill if Amaians stray on to their territory. Haven't you ever wondered why?'

'Yes. The Perfect-Ministers say it's the power of prayer and eternal vigilance, but . . .'

'Ah, no. Believe me, if the Unseen wanted Torlossen they could take it. They *let* you live there.'

Suddenly indignant, I glared at him. 'Out of the goodness of their hearts?'

'Hardly. The point I'm trying to make is that you don't know why, do you? You – don't – know – why.'

'I wish you wouldn't sound so gleeful about my ignorance,' I said in a low voice. 'Just because you know so much that I don't!'

I wasn't looking at him; he touched my arm and I jumped. 'But I want to show you!' His expression and his voice were different; apparently sincere for once. Laufi came to a standstill, rocking a little like a fidgeting horse.

'What are you doing?' I said suspiciously.

He gave my elbow a slight shake. 'Come with me!'

The sky rushed up in the windows as the hut sank, like a spider sinking belly-down between its legs. Sigurthur led me to the door in the centre room, pushed it open, and jumped out on to the ground.

I looked out, curious but wary. The air was crystalline with coldness. Clouds shone snow-brilliant against a sky of deep, rich blue which dissolved into a lake of delicate turquoise on the horizon. In the perfect clarity of the light, mountains seemed sharp and close enough to touch, yet breathtakingly distant across the plains. It was wonderfully lush and green, this land, though it was scattered with volcanic rock. A herd of mountain deer grazed far up the valley, smudges of silver-beige on the green. Silent volcanoes rimmed the horizon, violet and brown; but far to the north I saw mountains that were black as iron and dappled with ice.

God's Light, what an awful place to be lost and alone.

I hesitated in the doorway. My encounter with the Unseen was fresh in my mind. Leaving the safety of the hut felt like setting foot in a depthless cold lake; the ripples would spread out and alert Sudema's creatures to my presence. I'd never see them coming . . .

But Sigurthur was striding away, almost out of earshot. He turned and shouted impatiently, 'What are you waiting for? Come on!'

Holding my breath, I leapt on to the grass and ran after him.

How sweet the air smelt. But how cold, how desolate.

The magian was crouching down when I reached him, probing at the vegetation. The ground was a mass of tiny plants, dozens of different mosses and sedges, all matted together. There were clumps of amethyst flowers, cream and pale yellow cups, tiny white stars. Most of them I knew. But he foraged between them and plucked a handful of silvery foliage with feathery red spires.

'Look,' he said, spreading the filaments across his palm. 'Do you know the name of this?'

'No. I've never seen it before.'

'The Unseen call it Eldur, the Fire in the Blood. You have never seen it because it doesn't grow in Torlossen, nor in Onafross. The Unseen live wherever this herb, and other rarer ones, grow. That's why they don't want your country; it cannot yield the plants they need. No other reason.'

No one had ever told me this before. I felt the world itself shifting around me, the weight of all the things I didn't know like a freezing gale at my back. A small revelation, a dark excitement.

'But why do they need these herbs?'

'Aha,' he said, shaking the foliage at me. 'They know how to draw the power from them.'

I thought I must be the first Amaian to learn this secret. I said rashly, 'Does that mean that if we could only destroy the plants the Unseen would also be destroyed? Or at least they'd lose their power . . .'

As I spoke, Sigurthur's expression changed. A dreadful hardness came to his face and his eyes were slivers of basalt. I trailed off, suddenly afraid of him. 'Destruction!' he said angrily. 'Is that the first thing you think of, the only thing? Burn the hills black, destroy your enemies by destroying everything else too?' With an exclamation of disgust, he straightened up and walked away.

I was shocked by his reaction. I felt I must pacify him. 'I didn't mean to offend you,' I said, following. 'But why—'

'And you needn't think you're so clever, halla.' He bent down, turning his back on me, to examine another plant. 'They tried it, of course. No easy matter, to make living plants burn; a few acres, perhaps, but not thousands of square miles of land. And they grow back, of course; nature is more tenacious than that. Yet the Amaians tried it. One more vicious act against which the Unseen were bound to respond in kind.'

His rhetorical tone and his back were barriers against my questions, yet I persisted. 'But how do the Unseen use these plants? Sigurthur, I didn't mean to make you angry, I only—'

'And why should I tell you?' he said, mimicking my voice.

He tore out handfuls of vegetation and stood up. 'What's the point in me feeding your ignorance? I need not even take you with me. I could just leave you. Here and now.'

He walked away again. Real fear propelled me after him. 'What have I said?'

'For Ama's sake, if you don't know—'

'But the Unseen are no friends of yours! You have to protect yourself from them; they attacked you! Even if you don't worship Ama, you are still human!'

'Stop following me, will you?' he said savagely. 'Leave me alone.'

Upset, I did as he asked, waiting near the Laufjallfertha until he had finished his herb-gathering. When he returned, I looked anxiously at him to see if his temper had improved. He dashed my hopes with a sour glance, but didn't object when I followed him back inside.

His mood struck fear through me, not merely because I was so vulnerable. The echoes of Tykavn's rages were so vibrantly raw that a single cross word could set me shaking.

'No, I won't tell you,' he said, carrying a bunch of red-flowered Eldur into the cabin. 'But we'll play a game. Perhaps you can guess.'

Laufi rose and strolled on at a leisurely pace, but Sigurthur remained ill-tempered. His unpleasantness waned to mere incivility, but the hardness in his eyes chilled me.

I watched the deer herd scattering around Laufi's alien feet. They were such pretty creatures, small yet tougher than goats. There was a mass of females, led by a hart with antlers like frost-crusted silver; young ones, pale white-blotched gold, following on the fringes, with a group of adult males trailing behind.

'They're so beautiful,' I said. 'We never see them in Torlossen.'

'They've got more sense,' he sneered. 'I don't envy their leader, forever wondering which disgruntled male will challenge him next. How long will he be strong enough to hold on to his power? Will the next young upstart be the one that leaves him gored and dying in the snow? Like humans, like animals. No. It's better to travel through life alone. *Completely* alone,' he said, glaring at me.

I gave up trying to speak to him, and simply watched as he picked over the plants, stripped the flowers and leaves from their stalks. He ground them on a little stone slab, then mixed the red dust of the petals into a dish of sour-milk, and put the powdered leaves into a censer.

Twilight fell. Laufi stood motionless, an eerie sentinel in the lee of a hill. Within the central den, on the bare floor in the centre of a circle of cushions, the censer glowed orange. Sigurthur had apparently lit it with a touch of his finger. The room was infernal with its radiance, and its smoke curled up to a ceiling mind-painted with brown and black and amber. The colours of scorched earth.

Seated on cushions, he faced me across the circle. He smiled, but that was worse than his hostility. He seemed to be laughing at me.

He raised the bowl of sour-milk and Eldur to his lips and drank deeply. The burning herbs gave out a bitter-sweet pungency that made me dizzy. I tried to hold my breath, but it was impossible not to breathe in the smoke. Sigurthur lowered the bowl and offered it to me.

The look of the red-flecked milk turned my stomach. I shook my head, looking suspiciously at him. He grinned. 'You won't understand unless you try it. Bloodfire, the Lightning in the Spirit.'

In Torlossen we rarely used herbs. We did not put them in food; we did not burn them or put them in medicine. In worship, we used fire, water and metal, the good clean elements; but never plants.

I had never wondered why. I had never realized why, until this moment.

The bowl appeared to me as a gateway to a realm of sin, debauchery, evil. The rim of a pit, Sudema's snare. One sip and I would fall into Kvold and be sundered from Ama's grace for ever. 'No,' I said. I edged away, afraid he would try to force me, but he only smiled sadly and set the bowl aside.

I couldn't tell what effect the drink was having on him. Would he become mad, intoxicated? He closed his eyes for a time, not moving. The pictures on the walls and ceiling shifted, the burnt colours gleaming now with jewelled blues, greens and reds. I saw rows and rows of figures with human forms and the antlered heads of deer; incredibly, seductively beautiful, they seemed, and utterly evil. I averted my eyes.

Suddenly his eyes opened and he looked straight at me. The hard lines of anger in his face had vanished, but there was a frightening glow about him. It was as if the invisible power with which he animated Laufi and projected images was visibly sweating from him, a heat that could not be contained.

'Why do you look so tragic, halla?' he said suddenly. 'Sudema curse it, I can't stand tears! Tell me what you are thinking!'

I wasn't weeping, but I was close to it. I had to make a great effort to control my throat before I could speak. 'I am thinking that I have no defence against this. I can't invoke Ama against you. I have no faith left.'

He looked at me searching. 'No faith? How have you lost it?'

I didn't want to tell him. When I'd tried to explain before – to my parents and Laasastiuk – I had realized that no words could encompass the blackness that Tykavn's illness had struck in my soul. I said, 'If Ama won't listen to sixty prayers, why should he answer one? The only purpose of rituals is to make us feel better. They are mind-tricks. They have no power.'

'Isn't making yourself feel better in itself a power?' said Sigurthur.

'No. It's false comfort. All religion is a delusion.'

The curiosity with which he stared at me made me uncomfortable and resentful. The light, the smoke-scent, and the sense of his unnatural strength; although they were strange and threatening, there was no hint of intoxication in his voice. 'Your lack of belief in Ama,' he said, 'does it extend to Sudema?'

I met his eyes, startled. 'What do you mean?'

'Is Sudema any more real than Ama? If not, why fear her?'

I couldn't answer for a moment. Then I said fiercely, 'You mock me with your logic. I don't know whether she exists or not. But the Unseen exist. It's them I fear – and you.'

'Me?'

'I fear humans! I fear the sickness in them, the thoughts they don't express. If "Sudema" is just a word for the darkness inside them, then I do fear her!'

Sigurthur looked at me with astonishment. Shifting shadows underlined the changes of his expression. 'I can't recall the last time I heard such words of sense from one so young. The last time I did, I think I spoke them myself.'

'I wish you would let me go,' I said miserably.

'I wish I could. But you don't understand, do you? And I am so clumsy in my efforts to explain.' He closed his eyes briefly. 'Please forgive me for my loss of temper earlier. It was never my

107

intention to frighten you . . . well, perhaps it was, but that was a singularly childish way to make a point. Have you never considered that the Unseen may not be as unredeemedly purple as you colour them?'

'No.' Now he was calmer, my own confidence was returning. 'Why should I? I've only known them to kill or try to kill. They're evil.'

'I didn't say they were perfect. Yes, they're hunters and killers, but you don't know why.'

'Oh, is there an excuse for it?'

'No. The Amaians' excuse is their religion, isn't it? You do realize that they're as ignorant in Onafross as you are in Torlossen? Never mind.'

There was so much in his words, in the thought-sketches, that I couldn't fathom. But what I sensed in him was pain, some unrequited need.

'What are the Unseen to you?' I said. 'You agree with me that they're savages. They're not human. They're your enemies as well as mine, yet you seem to be defending them! Why?'

With grim patience he waited for my outburst to end. 'When I lived in Onafross, that was what I believed too. My parents were merchants in Onareyru, perfect Perfects, and I was set to be a Sublime. But I was a little like you. I refused to fit in; I would accept nothing I was taught. I had to find out the truth of things for myself. Having made myself extremely unpopular and on the verge of losing all Status, I came out into the Stolen Land and sought out the Unseen for myself. I found them and I survived . . .'

'How?'

'By approaching them in the right way. Generally it is called grovelling. Lying down and saying, "Here I am, kill me!" I think it gave them such a shock that they changed their minds. They let me live with them . . . for a time.'

'What were they like?' I gasped. I couldn't believe this.

'Not what you would expect,' he said sardonically. An odd landscape of glittering leaves and dark, twisted rock appeared for a moment, then the ceiling and walls went blank. He went on, 'They are fierce, but they are not beasts, and not what you'd call evil. Did you know their name for themselves, their true name, is Stjarna? The folk of the star. They know the secrets of the earth, which humans have lost. They shared some of that knowledge with me.' He waved a hand at the censer, making the smoke dip and swirl. 'They know the secret properties of herbs, and they know how to draw the powers of Eileah through certain plants. Their power lies not in the plants themselves, but in their understanding of how to use them; and I remain less than them, because I have only borrowed their knowledge.'

As he spoke, I could taste the smoke in my throat. My mind felt too light, too open to what he was telling me. I wanted to believe him, but part of me held back, afraid I was being deluded, corrupted.

'But you aren't with them now. When they were chasing me, you said they would have attacked you too; and you live in Laufi to protect yourself from them, don't you?'

He looked away from me, his profile sharp against the shadows. 'I have great difficulty in being anything but myself. I took too much knowledge from them; stole it, they would say. In their way, they are as bad as the Amaians in demanding obedience to their rules ... I wouldn't obey, I overreached myself, and I had to leave. I created Laufi to protect myself; another misuse of the power, in their eyes. They'd kill me for it, if they could. But I can create things they have never dreamed of, and I won't let anyone constrain me; not the Unseen, not the Amaians, none of these blinkered beings who believe they have right on their side. I regret the separation ... but freedom doesn't come free.'

I could sense hidden memories moving in his mind. Perhaps they were too precious to put into words or images. He was telling me very little and yet his voice, curling soft as Eldur-smoke across the glowing circle, conjured a desirable, fugitive reality.

'You call this freedom? Being completely alone, continually hunted? If everyone behaved like this, there would be anarchy!'

'But they don't,' he said. 'I don't think you realize that I could march into Torbyrgi and knock the Prince off his little rock throne, if I chose. But I don't. This is all I want. *To be left alone*, to think and invent ...' He held up his hands, glowing red in the censer-light. 'You've seen a fraction of what I can do. This is what Eldur and other herbs can give you. Don't you desire this sort of power?'

I did, but the desire was wrong. Corruption licked around me like flame.

He went on, 'Isn't it worth the risk of throwing yourself on the mercy of the Unseen? I can still let you out to them, Iolithie. If you don't believe Ama is good, you can't believe Sudema is bad ...'

I said quickly, 'I – I'm not sure what I think or believe any more, but I've been a good Amaian until now. I couldn't go to the – the Stjarna for help. It's bad enough having to ask you, but at least there's some good still in you . . .'

'Oh, thank you.' He laughed. 'Thank you so much. I am not completely beyond redemption, then.'

'I don't know what redemption is. I don't know anything,' I said. 'But I must go to Onafross. Please.'

He dropped his hands in his lap. When he looked at me, his face was sad, his voice gentle. 'I don't mean to torment you. When I try to make you see that certain things are good, I only make myself wonder if they are wrong after all. The only way I can prove to you that I am not evil is to take you safely to Onafross, and that is exactly what I am going to do.'

In the morning I felt the first trace of optimism I'd experienced since fleeing from Torlossen. I dared to trust Sigurthur, not because I had no choice, but because my instinct said he could be trusted. He was eccentric, but not insane; misguided, but not evil.

He would deliver me to the border of Onafross, he said, but no further. He wanted no guards pursuing him as a heretic; he would rather they did not even know he existed.

Towards the afternoon the green hills gave way to a barren area scoured clean of soil by an ancient glacier, and then to a ghost landscape of grey rock. When I peered down I saw that the rock was a mosaic of flat-topped boulders, polished smooth and gleaming silvery as opal. Laufi picked her way across ridges and canyons, occasionally jolting as she missed her footing on the uneven ground. Sigurthur's mental steering was less than perfect, and the hut had a personality of her own; jaunty, dreamy, imperturbable.

Sigurthur said that the great river Jonlau lay across our path. There was a bridge on the main route, of course, but we were miles from there. I heard the roar of the falls long before we reached them. Just when it seemed the stonescape went on for ever, and we would never reach the river, we saw a huge and perfect double rainbow poised on the lip of the rock.

As Laufi went closer, we saw clouds of spray massing behind the arc of light. On the far side of the river was the wall of a silver canyon, a continuation of the stonescape we had traversed. I couldn't see how we were going to cross.

110

When Sigurthur brought the Laufjallfertha to a halt on the edge of the rock, my heart sank. There was another ledge below us. Soaked by a continual rain of spray it was vividly green with grass, and the rainbow had shifted to gleam like coloured glass against it. And beyond that, running from our right, roared the Jonlau. A hundred yards wide, its fierce white waters hurtled past us and over the rim of a chasm to thunder into a basin two hundred feet below.

I hung on to the window frame. The height, the hut's instability and the lethal speed of the water made me feel dizzily insecure. But when I looked at Sigurthur, he was grinning.

'Are you ready?' he said.

'For what?' I said breathlessly. 'We can't cross here. We'll have to go upriver and find a safer place.'

'Safe?' he said. 'What's that?'

Laufi swayed and lurched. I caught a terrified breath. 'What are you doing?'

He laughed. There was a mad glitter in his eyes. 'Crossing the river! Hold on!'

Laufi started forward. She slithered down on black mud and water-slippery rocks, gathering speed as she descended towards the lower ledge. She hit the spray-garlanded grass at a canter and kept going towards the torrent above the waterfall.

The edge rushed towards us. I tried to scream, but my stomach plummeted. The Laufjallfertha leapt outwards and was airborne for a long moment before she curved down and smacked hard on to the surface of the river.

Suddenly we were caught up in a roar of white chaos. Cataracts thundered across the windows and Laufi span out of control. I knew we were being carried towards the waterfall. I tried to cry out to Sigurthur to do something, but I had no breath. Hanging speechlessly on to his arm, I felt gravity slice away beneath us, a moment of suspension in empty air, the horrific acceleration as we dropped, with thousands of tons of water falling alongside us.

The cascade seemed frozen in the windows, as if time itself had stopped. Then came the impact, white thunder engulfing us, currents spinning us round and round beyond control. Laufi sank, then bobbed back to the surface, an indomitable bubble.

I was on the floor, hands round my head, deafened and bruised. Water dripped coldly on my back. Surely Laufi would break up under the weight of the water. Surely we'd drown. Yet Sigurthur showed no consternation. Under his guidance, the hut rose and went on rising on long, spindly legs, finding her feet on the river bed. Then she began to stride forward through the water, behind the waterfall itself.

I was incredulous. Sigurthur had done everything deliberately. Plunged over the waterfall – on purpose! In an uprush of fury and relief, I was about to yell at him, *How could you do this?* – only to see that he was laughing.

Head back, hair flying, the Eldur-magian was laughing wildly. On our right was a wall of wet black rock; on our left, a curtain of crashing white foam. And Laufi was forging through it, unbowed, water breaking in glittering streams across her windows.

'Ah, wonderful!' he cried. 'It never loses its glamour!'

'Don't tell me you've done this before!' I shouted.

'It wasn't the first time, and it won't be the last!'

His hilarity was infectious. With the elation of having survived, the exhilaration of the water swirling around us, the sheer craziness of our situation, I began to laugh too. We met each other's gaze, eyes brilliant with the shared thrill of it. By the time Laufi gained the far bank and began to climb, slipping and sliding, on to the rock, we were shouting, cheering and hugging each other like children.

'You're an idiot, Sigurthur,' I said mildly. 'Everything in here is wet. The floor's awash, the cushions are soaked. What are we going to sleep on?'

'Oh, it will soon dry,' he said dismissively. 'Open the door, let the air blow in.'

'If you promise not to plunge from any more waterfalls.'

'Trust me,' he said. 'If I feel like turning back and riding the edge a second time, I will be sure to advise you to close the door.'

'Never do that to me again!' I snapped. 'I almost died of terror, never mind of drowning. If you ever do anything like that again, I shall kill you!'

Sigurthur only put his head back and laughed.

The blue light of the sky seemed to fold down on to the earth, clothing everything in an ultramarine veil. As evening fell, I realized that I'd never before experienced such a feeling of peace. It might be illusory; simple relief at being alive, freedom from having to make any kind of decision; but at that moment it was very real.

Looking out of the open door in Laufi's side, I thought I saw shapes on the ground keeping pace with us. Deer? No. I thought it must be my imagination, the fall of twilight and shadow; but the feeling of peace fell away and cold pincers gripped my neck.

Sigurthur came through the curtain from the cabin.

'We'd better close the door,' he said. He spoke calmly, but his face was grave. 'I think we have unwanted company.'

We looked out of the door together. In the twilight, rising, falling, drifting, were several pairs of cold violet stars. They wove round Laufi's legs, watching the hut with an unwavering intensity. They seemed unnatural and completely inimical. There and not there.

My heart began to pound. 'Do they often follow you?'

'No,' said Sigurthur. 'I think they are still looking for you.'

His words were like a cold fist in my stomach. 'Why?'

'I told you, they will not tolerate Amaians on their territory. They don't give up easily.' As he spoke, I felt Laufi increase her speed. I saw the luminous eyes left behind for a second; then, as if blown on a gust of breeze, they caught up. Sigurthur pulled the door shut with a thump.

'I didn't mean to put you in this danger,' I whispered.

'So, are you going to volunteer to throw yourself to them, while I make a clean escape? Don't talk rubbish, girl,' he said briskly. 'I chose to save you from them in the first place.'

'But you said—'

'Never mind what I said. I am not going to abandon you to them. We can outrun them.'

I followed him into the cabin, losing my balance as the hut accelerated violently. 'Is there anything I can do to help?' I said, pressed against the wall.

Sigurthur opened a cupboard and took out a small bowl containing a red powder. Dust of Eldur flowers. 'Swallow this,' he said. 'Mix it with a bit of sour-milk to help it down.'

I took it from him reluctantly. 'Why?'

'Because it will make you less visible to them! Ama's Light, you did ask! Just shut up and do it!'

Numb, I obeyed. The crushed Eldur made the milk taste sweet, spicy, pungent; a trickle of red fire down my throat. But my mind rebelled; it felt like letting a little of Sudema into my body. The beginning of my surrender to the dark side. *Will I be less visible to them because I am no longer so different from them?*

113

I didn't know how Sigurthur controlled the Laufjallfertha. It seemed he simply willed her to move and she obeyed; and his power came somehow from the herbs he ate. Now it struck me for the first time that it cost him energy, too, and that his powers were limited. The faster Laufi ran, the paler and more drawn he looked.

A sudden vibration shook the hut. Laufi lurched, one leg buckling. She righted herself, but she went on unevenly, lumbering.

'What is it?' I said.

'Something on one of the legs,' he said. 'Can't shake it off.'

I sat down beside him. 'Can I help?'

'Close your eyes,' he said. 'Take my hand. The Eldur will help you.'

The moment my lids shut, impressions clouded in. It was vague, seen and felt through woollen swathes of fog, but it seemed for a few seconds that I *was* Laufi; my body a hollow shell, my legs delicately endless, my awareness everywhere. And there were prowling creatures all around me. I couldn't outrun them. They were leaping, clinging to my legs, gnawing at them.

I couldn't support the extra weight. There was no pain where they bit me, only a sense of weakness, of being borne downwards. No emotion, only a dim registration of what was happening.

With a snap, one of my legs broke. I ran on three, but the Unseen Ones were clawing their way up my remaining limbs. Another fracture and I was falling . . .

'No!'

The cry of agony came from Sigurthur. I opened my eyes, felt Laufi stagger and fall, hitting the ground like a horse dying mid-stride.

The only sound was the insistent scrabbling of claws on the outside of the hut, growing louder and louder. Sigurthur and I stared at each other, and his expression of horror increased my fear.

'Run, Iolithie,' he said.

From the centre of the hut came the sound of the door banging open.

Sigurthur stood up and reached for the window.

'No!' I cried. 'Don't open it, they're all around us!'

'I know!' he said, turning on me ferociously, helplessly. 'Ama save us, Iolithie, I'm sorry . . .'

There was a crystalline explosion. The whole of the front window shattered and crashed towards us in showers of diamonds and ice. A violet darkness flowed all around us. Gleaming eyes, searing as fire, massed in the gap and came pouring through, relentless, irresistible. Powerless, I stood and watched as they overwhelmed Sigurthur. I saw him pulled down by gleams of light, I saw the red gashes appear in his chest and the red blood flowering, pooling on the floor.

My mind untethered by fear, I turned and tried to run. An ice-hard jolt stopped me. Claws in my back, so sharp I felt no pain, only a freezing shock.

My face was pressed into the floor. My own blood was gushing over my shoulderblades, forming a liquid necklace. But I understood that I was dying only when I found I couldn't breathe past the knifeblades in my chest.

CHAPTER NINE

IN ANOTHER LIFE

I was spreadeagled on darkness, the pain through my back pinning me to the floor like a blazing ice-shard. Everything was overdrawn and feverishly vivid. The black gape of the window swirled with broken glass and the cold glow of eyes, as if they were blowing in on a wind straight from Kvold. The air shifted with half-seen shapes and shivered with feral howls.

Claws prickled and scratched me. Eyes circled round and round, blank and fascinated as kittens tormenting a dying mouse. My skin itched, more than hurt. A hundred cuts in my flesh; a hundred mouth-slits, dribbling my life away. And, Ama Almighty, it *itched*.

With my left cheek pressed into the floor, I saw Sigurthur rise up like some bleached monster from a lake, salt-white and blood-dabbled, seeming twice his true size.

Beyond reaction, I only watched, mouth stretched open as I strained to take the breath that wouldn't come. Reality was blurred on hallucination. The only thought in my mind was a wordless understanding that this was how death came; suddenly, undeserved, with everything unresolved. Unfair. And too soon, always too soon.

A dead weight fell on me. There was a shout, right in my ear, though I made out only half the words, 'Get off her... not her...'

My hands were numb. They felt huge. Crushed by the hot bony weight on my back, I began to lose my sight to a fraying black constellation. Such pressure in my head. Surely my skull would explode...

'Can you hear me?' Sigurthur said into my ear. His voice was thin, pain-raw. 'Keep your eyes open. You must stay awake!'

The Unseen were tearing at him, now, instead of at me, while he lay across me to keep them off. Emotion was vinegar on my tongue. *It's too late, can't he see?*

'I'm holding your hands,' he said. 'Can you feel them?'

'No,' I whispered without breath. 'Can't feel anything.'

'Believe it . . . giving you this power. All I can do. Take it, run away and live . . .' His voice was a croak, trailing off into grunts of agony. The black wind and the red-clawed Stjarna plaited death around us, yet I felt a tingling heat flowing into me.

My sight cleared. I could breathe again, with difficulty. From semi-consciousness I flashed into instant alertness. Fresh horror.

Sigurthur was dying on top of me, instilling me with the last of his power. And I didn't want it, but I couldn't move, couldn't stop him.

'Why . . . do this for me? Don't want it . . . ' I tried to say, but the words were lost in a spasm of breath. I was burning. I felt a terrible pulling sensation, worse than pain. Cramps convulsed me. Wars were raging in my joints, while my muscles heaved in frenzied tugs-of-war against my bones.

'S'only way you'll cross mountains,' he hissed, his breath moist in my ear. 'Don't fight me!'

Unbearable, this feeling. *Make it stop . . .* I tried to scream, and as the rasp of breath left my mouth the whole front of my skull seemed to thrust forward with it. The bones of my head were crunching, grinding, popping. My neck lengthened. My ribcage rose with a quickly seized breath and went on swelling and lengthening. I felt the floor sliding under me, as if I was moving both forwards and backwards at the same time, although I wasn't moving at all. And the motion had a strange grainy feel, as if I was covered with hair . . .

My legs and arms were numb but how heavy they felt. Why couldn't I feel my hands and feet? They were bound up and encased in tiny boxes . . .

And my head was heaviest of all. It didn't seem to belong to me.

I was no longer myself.

'Go,' whispered Sigurthur. 'Ah—' It could have been a gasp or the beginning of a word, but he died mid-syllable. I felt the life leave him. The agonizing fire went out, dropping me like hot iron into cold water. And death filled me, like a powerful scent, with a fear that was purely primeval.

Escape. Now.

I lurched and scrabbled up, fighting for a foothold on the slippery floor. I felt Sigurthur's body fall from my back, heard the soft thud as he landed. How strange my vision was; I could see a good way to the side as well as in front.

And I could see the Stjarna. Not clearly; only enough to carry away an impression.

They went on all fours, but were like no animal I knew. Long-limbed, they had the precise look of sculptures. Elegant, sandy-gold and silver-grey with solemn faces under great manes of hair. Perhaps it was a trick of the light, but I thought their manes were braided and woven with beads . . .

As I rose up and thrust forward they did not spring to stop me. They fell back, staring with lavender-crystal eyes like blurred stars. And in a flash I was through them, leaping over the frame of the shattered window, leaping out into the blackness beyond . . .

Leaping like a horse, forelegs tucked up then unfolding to take my weight as the ground tipped up to receive me.

Then galloping. All four limbs the same length, my hands no longer flexible but rigid and horny. A hairy outgrowth of bone flapped at my quarters. My heart felt huge in my chest, and my lungs, though labouring hard, seemed to have endless capacity.

Yet all these were impressions, not clear thoughts. I was a thread of screaming terror in a core of pure, flowing instinct.

I left the ruined hulk of Laufi behind; left the corpse of Sigur-thur, who had died to save me, left the predators to their feast, and flew towards the hills.

Within moments I knew they were not following me. I sensed their eyes behind me, dwindling on the rushing darkness. But I daredn't stop. Driven by the cold fire of denial, I ran and ran and ran.

Iolithie, I thought. It was the only word I could form in my mind. I still knew my own name, at least.

All the rest was shapes and images.

I ran myself to a standstill on the flank of an old volcano, and stood there with my sides heaving, sweat drying on my neck. I was shivering from head to foot. The wind blew cruel on my overheated skin. I stretched out my head and shook it, as if trying to shake myself back into my proper shape.

Only I didn't know what that shape was.

Another word. *North*. I turned and looked up, the landscape swivelling strangely in my extended vision. Mountains loured against a gleaming night sky, unfriendly. But I must climb them. I was on my way to . . .

I couldn't find the name of my destination! But I still knew where I must go. That country beyond the mountains, to look for . . .

I would have wept, but I had no mechanism for weeping. Try to remember, try to think.

North. To Onafross. To find help for . . . for Tykavn. My husband . . . The words came dark and heavy, and it was so hard to keep them in the centre of my mind. A shivering, wretched terror possessed me.

I turned my face into the chill wind, and began to trot downhill. My limbs ached and trembled with exhaustion, and my hooves slipped on the volcanic shale. I had run miles further than I could have done in human form, and now I desperately needed to rest. Yet I dared not stop. I ran as a substitute for thinking, but my burdens came with me.

Iolithie still existed and my memories were intact; distant, but still clear and urgent. Yet I was now another being as well. I was two aspects, two personalities in one; human and animal.

Sigurthur had said it was the only way I would survive . . . and he was right. This was truly the only way I would travel to Onafross. In the form of an animal, I could travel swiftly, endure the weather, live on grass and water with no need to hunt; and the Unseen would leave me alone.

They eat animals only if they are very hungry, he'd said. But would they, with their preternatural powers, know that I was an impostor? Did it matter, did anything matter?

I slowed to a walk as I climbed another slope, and stopped at the top, shaking with tiredness. I was at the boundary of my endurance. Clouds were rolling down between the mountains. On the ridge opposite, the clouds were almost level with my nose, and the valley between them was an opaque sea. A tangy coldness filled my newly enlarged, sensitive nostrils. Blackness and fog rolled to the ends of Eileah. The north rose like an iron wall, impassable.

Sigurthur had sacrificed his own chance of survival to help me, transforming me with the last of his Eldur-fire. But how would I change back? If I was to remain in this form for ever, there would be no point in going to Onafross. No way to make anyone understand the help I needed. No point in going on, nor in going back to Tykavn.

I stood very still on the ridge, the wind stirring my fur and tail. Strange, to feel the hair fluttering; new, and yet so natural I might always have been in this shape. I need never go back. This was freedom . . . but if I had lost the power to help Tykavn, it was no freedom at all.

Freedom doesn't come free.

Sigurthur. We'd been friends for such a brief time.

I was beginning to doze on my feet. I let my knees buckle, gathered my legs beneath me, and sank to the ground. The only discomfort was the ache in my bones; the rock itself felt no worse than a firm bed, and my fur trapped a layer of warmth. In the shadow of the volcano, stretched out on my side, I slept.

I awoke to a thin blue sky, a sun that gave no warmth. Ama was winter-silver. I jumped violently and lay panting in a spasm of pure horror. I'd half-expected to wake in my own body, to remember the night before as a disordered dream. But I was still in the shape of a four-legged beast.

Ama's cursed me. When I came into Sudema's land, accepted her help, ate her plants, Ama withdrew his blessing. But the thought was more in symbols than words, and it faded even as I climbed to my feet.

I shook myself and blew a breath through my nostrils. The horror passed. As I breathed in, a whole new sense opened up, stronger then sight and hearing. A hundred different levels of scent; the sharpness of water, the coldness of rock. Soil, dark and dusty. The sweet-sourness of greenery, awakening my appetite.

Below the ridge was a valley, a stream running silver between embroidered cushions of moss. I sprang into a run from a standstill and galloped down towards it.

I was parched. How sweet the water tasted. Moving, drinking and swallowing came naturally, without me once having to pause and wonder how this strange body worked. With my lips kissing the surface, I sucked the water in and felt it travel the length of my throat in a bright line.

As I lifted my muzzle from the water I saw my own forelegs, in daylight for the first time. Dark brown cloven hooves; delicate, hard legs, furred with ginger-gold that blended to cream above my knees. I stared and stared at the shape of my own legs.

Then I looked round at my flanks, saw that I was a pale creamy-gold, almost white, all over. The fur shone different shades as I moved, like shot geitha. My whisk of a tail was plumed with light gold hair.

I looked at my rippling reflection in the water. A small pretty creature stood there, surely no heavier than I'd been as a human; but because my legs were so slender, my bones so delicate, I looked taller. My head was dainty, with huge dark eyes and two horny buds below my ears.

I was a mountain deer. Just like the deer I'd seen in the Stolen Land.

I wanted to laugh or to cry, but I could do neither. I started back on to my hindquarters then leapt the stream from a standstill, wanting to flee from the shock of it. On the far side I stretched out and flew, the wind streaming over my flattened ears, the rocks racing past in a blur.

This was madness. Perhaps I was mad. And yet there was a wild exhilaration in this incredible speed. That I could run this fast, without tiring! Intoxicated, I went faster and faster.

Almost too late I saw the drop in front of me, a deep fissure full of boulders where an earthquake had rent the ground. I sat back on my haunches and slid to a halt on the very edge. One more step and I might have broken a leg in the bottomless cracks between the boulders. That sobered me. I wasn't invulnerable.

I looked around, my ears sensitive to every shift of the breeze. I was standing in a long, wide valley; the black mountains of the north, which I knew I must cross, still looked very distant. How long would the journey take? I felt the urge to gallop again, but another instinct stayed me.

I was hungry, and the valley was rich.

Nosing over the wiry grass, I found dusty red spires of Eldur, the herb of fire. Its scent was peppery. Should I eat it? Would it give me the power to remain in this shape, or the power to change back? Sigurthur had spoken of other herbs, too, which might have strange effects, and I didn't even know how to recognize them. I nibbled gingerly at the grass, trying to avoid the Eldur and any plants I didn't recognize. The grass tasted bitter, yet wonderfully succulent.

Thus the day passed. A steady trot northwards, broken by frequent pauses for food and water.

When evening came I found I needed very little rest. I dozed for a while, standing up, then went on through the darkness. This, too, Sigurthur had given me; great stamina. But what would be the use of it, if I reached my destination unable to become human again?

I tried not to think too deeply. It was no effort. For frighteningly long periods I would blank out my human awareness and become almost completely animal. Through light and through dark I trotted on.

The stars were thick as snow across the sky, but only Sudema gave any real illumination. Her eerie light turned my coat grey and reclaimed the world as her own realm ... *By day, Eileah is Ama's pure and fruitful consort ... but by night, Sudema wraps her in her cloak of violet and silver and takes her down to Kvold ...*

Whose words? Didn't matter. Human words. I was a moving shadow, cat-grey, floating sinuous and unseen through the under-world. Like Hendleiknir, I went in disguise, fooling Sudema, to rescue my love from Sudema's imprisonment.

That was what I'd become. A shadow-figure in a legend. A creature that sees all, says nothing, and moves on.

I travelled through tall sooty canyons and along river gorges where sweet grass grew, walking on precarious tracks which, as a human, I could never have crossed. But in deer form I was sure-footed and agile.

Distances were deceptive in the crystal air. The dark mountain range on the northern horizon, which looked only a few miles away, crept closer inch by inch. I knew that Onafross lay beyond; I also knew that the dark peaks rimmed a huge glacier. Difficult, if not impossible, to go straight across; but to work my way round would make the journey far longer.

At least when I was human I had known these things. Knowledge now was hardly more than a vague urge pulling me in a certain direction.

One morning, as the dawn swam in through a wet fog, I caught a strong and startling scent on the dampness. The drop-pings of another deer lay on my path. A lightning-strike of reality; what might happen if I met other deer – real deer – hadn't occurred to me.

The hair stood up on my flanks and sweat prickled my skin. I stretched out my nose to the dry black-brown pile without any revulsion, only with a poised sense of curiosity and danger. I smelled grass, fermentation, a touch of sulphur, bound together by the deer's intangible personal scent.

Whoever had left this spoor, my instinct was to avoid them. I began to climb sideways up the wall of the gorge, leaping from boulder to boulder until I found a track that led along the wall, halfway up.

The wall became a great cliff curving away to my right. I forced a way round it despite the stomach-turning drop on my left; the height thrilled me more than alarmed me. If the track didn't fade away, if I climbed high enough, I'd be able to see a way into the mountains.

As I came to the head of the bluff, I stopped and stared, my ears twitching with fear. Above the crystal tang of ice and the bitterness of snow, a more compelling odour rolled in. The steep dark slopes were only five or six miles away, crowned with the stark whiteness of a snow-cap and garlanded with clouds; but between here and there lay a vast flat valley, cut out by a glacier in a past age. And in the valley grazed hundreds of deer.

I watched them, my thin limbs trembling and poised for flight. Had Sigurthur intended that I travel invisibly in a herd? There might be safety in numbers. But they were not humans in enchanted form, they were real animals. Wouldn't they sense something wrong?

For a vivid moment I felt completely human again. An impostor, an outsider. I felt exposed up here on the cliff and my instinct was to run and hide.

There was a musky smell in my nostrils, too strong to be coming from the herd. It came from above. My coat prickled with sweat, hot-cold. I looked up, and saw a hart on the cliff-edge above me.

He seemed twice my size, an earth-god of bronze. His antlers were a crown of branching swords. Staring straight down at me, he stretched out his thick neck and bellowed.

The noise terrified me. *Run. Go, get out of sight!* I began to walk on along the track, fast, my legs swinging and my head down. But the hart moved too, keeping pace with me along the top of the cliff. I spun on my hindfeet and turned back, but he changed direction with me.

His intent was clear. To him, I was no enchanted creature but an ordinary doe, to be captured and made part of his herd. And while I burned to escape, I also felt pulled towards him; not because he was stronger than me, but because I belonged with him . . .

I fought the pull, but whichever way I went, on or back, he could move to cut me off. So I went on, the hart keeping pace above me, until I saw with alarm that the cliff dipped down and he was picking his way on to a path that led down to my track.

My instincts were brighter and faster than I thought. I could turn and run back the way I had come; but he would not expect me to go straight down.

The cliff fell vertically below me, but I noticed a place where a bulge on the cliff-wall formed a tiny ledge. Without hesitating I leapt, felt my hooves land firm and sure on the rock, leapt again, felt the rush of cold air over my coat. The base of the cliff flared out to meet me. I was hurtling down at such speed that I stumbled and rolled as I landed, but regained my feet in a second and raced away.

Rather than running out across the valley I turned right and went along the base of the cliff. Now the hart would not be able to see me from the top.

Yet I could hear his hoofbeats above, echoing mine. He couldn't see me, but he could see the herd in the valley watching me. From the synchronized turning of their heads, he knew exactly where I was.

The cliff-wall dipped lower still and angled outwards. I glanced up and saw the hart bounding over the edge, leaping lightly down the steep side towards me. How beautiful . . .

I wouldn't let him catch me. I would vanish.

I put on a burst of speed, thrusting myself across the ground as if I would take flight. Round the corner of a huge stone block I bounded, and found myself in a flat area, pocked by craters. The ground was treacherously ridged, silver-green with moss and lichen, choked with bushes. Ragged circles of stone thrust up out of the ground.

I saw the cone of a steam crater; a dome of rock, nodular as if a giant-child had made it from blobs of clay. There was a dark narrow entrance in its side. I pushed my way through the slit and found myself in a hollow chamber, floored with earth. Light fell dimly through the vent in the top; I could see the sky, a ragged white oval.

I waited, trembling, in the gloom, ears flicking backwards and forwards. I heard the light thunder of the hart's feet; I heard him fly straight past, hoofbeats fading into the distance. I shivered with relief and elation.

But I'd forgotten, of course, that although he could not see me he could smell me. After a few seconds the fading hoofbeats grew louder again. His scent, sweat-sour and musk-sweet, came probing into the crater. He was coming back, and if I stayed here I'd be trapped.

I burst out of the cone and ran frantically as if the Unseen were pursuing me. The hart saw me, roared and came racing after me, so close I could feel his heat. My heart swelled as if it would explode.

I was very fast, but he was faster and stronger. I was trying to head away from the herd, but he was bearing down on me from the right, gradually forcing me into a curve out across the valley.

He was driving me now. I couldn't outrun him. Eyes bulging, I spun away from him, straight back towards the centre of the herd.

Does scattered around me as I ploughed into them. The hart followed. I tried to dodge but he came at me with his head down, and his antlers caught my flank as I turned on a tight circle. I skidded and fell, winding myself.

I leapt back to my feet, but whichever way I turned, the hart was there. I couldn't escape. With red and gold lights rippling on his coat, he circled me, fiercely triumphant. My sides heaving, sweat soaking my fur, I stood in defeat.

He came closer. His heat and strength were both oppressive and enticing. He was snuffing at me, as he would at any doe . . . to see if she was in season.

I don't know where I found the strength, but I was suddenly twisting away, rearing up and striking at him with my forefeet. I caught him a blow on the shoulder, and blood blackened his fur. He jumped back and stared at me as if he could not believe I had attacked him. Whether he saw something unnatural in my eyes, or saw only a doe not ready to mate, I don't know. He circled me a couple of times then moved off, keeping an eye on me from a distance.

The other does surrounded me, ears flicking. Their grainy scents crowded in; warm skin, cold fur, no two alike. Their regard felt like a physical pressure. They resented a new arrival. I was paler than many of them, more the colour of a fawn, though I was clearly an adult; that also set me apart. When I tried to move away, they followed, chasing me, trying to bite.

I began to run again. The hart was after me at once, chasing off his own does as he went. For several minutes there was chaos. But his will was dominant; he wouldn't let me escape, and the other does must tolerate me.

Instinct told me now to submit, to draw no attention to myself. As long as I didn't try to escape, the hart – whom I'll call Bronze, though I gave him no name at the time – left me alone. I tried to hide in the herd, but wherever I went my paleness set me apart. A small brown doe, the lead female, took a dislike to me and persecuted me without mercy, driving me out to the fringes of the herd. Then Bronze would intervene and there would be running skirmishes between the three of us that left me trembling and tired out.

To survive, I must be cunning, invisible, offering no angles for the wind to blow against. But as in my human life, it was difficult. It isn't in my nature just to accept.

As the days passed, the weather grew colder. Ice winds rolled down off the mountains; rainstorms drove us into the shelter of the cliffs. But there were also days of invigorating sunshine, and the herd's mating season was in full swing. The air was filled with the bellows of harts; a group of bachelors drifting on the flank of the main herd offered challenges to Bronze every day. He was ragged with fighting.

Both through animal and human eyes, I admired his magnificence. He was a pure element. He acted not out of malice but instinct, because the strongest hart was best equipped to protect the herd and produce strong offspring. But I lived in perpetual wariness of him. How real a deer was I? What if I did come into season, and I couldn't fight him off?

I was still too human not to be horrified by the prospect. The unnaturalness of it, the possible consequences. What if I conceived? What would I give birth to? If I became human again, and gave birth to an animal . . . that would be truly demonic, Sudema's work, her laughing revenge . . .

I can say this in words now; but at the time these ideas were only darts of fear that pricked me when the hart came too close.

As the nights grew long and chill, the herd began to graze their way down the valley as it curved to the south. This was not the way I wanted to go. Several times I tried to escape, to leave at night and go north, but every time Bronze came after me and drove me back.

I was covered in cuts and bruises. The other does continued to shun me. Yet I felt no real pain, only a kind of dull misery.

Why had I wanted to go north, anyway? Didn't I belong here? The urge remained, yet the reasons were fading.

Once I found the corpse of a deer lying at the edge of a stream, half decayed, its skin stretched over a rack of bones. Teeth bared, eye sockets empty. The stench was ice-dulled but unbearable.

I backed away. I saw myself there. I saw a ruined face dripping crimson; other human faces flashed across my mind, but I barely knew what they meant. All the image left in its wake was a dull sense of dread ... that I would die here, as all these creatures must die one day, and my journey would never be completed.

Once the stars had covered the sky like snow, but now the clouds thickened like curds over the mountain peaks, roofing in the grazing grounds with iron. Then the true snow fell, and the streams turned hard as volcanic glass, and the bushes glittered with ice.

Bronze led his herd further south in search of grass, nosing over the frozen ground where the droppings of other deer lay in abundance.

I moved with the does and fawns, a little apart, trying not to incur their hostility. Their tension was infectious. Ahead was another herd, dark dots against the white sweep of ground and hills.

Each day the two herds grazed closer together. The air was alive with excitement. The young males of both herds made forays against each other, trying to steal females; and finally the other herd's leader came, proud and furious, to confront Bronze.

I will call him Ember, because that's how he looked to me; his reddish coat was tipped with black, so that he seemed to glow.

He was not beautiful. His body was gaunt, his legs too thick, his neck seemingly too long and thin to support his massive antlers. But he carried about with him an aura that was not so much power as a freezing black coldness. He smelled like iron. If Bronze was energy and fire, Ember was the darkness and bitterness of deepest winter.

Seeing him, a weight like a memory pressed on my mind. I know now what the memory was: a picture Sigurthur had mind-painted, of me riding away from Torbyrgi, and a dark figure watching me.

It seemed to me that Ember, though an animal, was also that human figure. That was the unshaped terror I felt when I saw him, black against the ice-grey twilight. I felt he'd come for *me*.

The two harts confronted each other. Against the frosted ground their colour and movement were vivid; red-bronze and near-black on a sheet of crumpled whiteness.

Heads down, they challenged each other. I could smell their fury, their excitement. They charged and clashed heads with a tremendous *boom* that surely must have shattered their antlers to pieces.

I didn't think of escaping. I was transfixed.

The harts circled each other, their hooves churning the snow-crust, sweat darkening their sides. The eternal battle of light and dark; antlers branching against the sky, night-darkness and sun-bronze in conflict, filling the air with heat and energy and blood. They clashed again and again with bone-shaking force.

What would happen if Ember won? I hadn't realized it until now, but I'd grown used to Bronze. I couldn't bear to see his beauty destroyed. Living under his protection had bonded me to him in a deep animal way I couldn't define. If he lost, I would be lost also. I don't know how I knew this, but the conviction poured through me like the torrent of the Jonlau. I wanted to run, but I couldn't move.

With a deafening bellow the harts charged again and the darker one went down. With antlers and hooves Bronze punished him. Then he drew back and gave a deafening call of victory, while Ember scrambled up and fled, limping and scattering blood and spume.

The tension inside me snapped. The herd were milling around me but I pushed straight through them and ran for my life.

If only I could have been completely invisible against the snow. Cream-coloured against grass and rock, against whiteness I was golden. Bronze sprang after me, curving round to intercept me. The air flowed icy-fresh as spring-water over me as I raced flat out, and for an exhilarating moment I thought I would outrun him.

But he was still on fire from the fight, and I didn't stand a chance. He drew alongside, ran flank to flank, nose to nose; then he overtook, propped right in front of me so I skidded into him and nearly fell.

He pranced around me, head high, a savage determination about his eyes and mouth. What was left of my human mind was alarmed; but my dark warm animal core knew that this could not be prevented, did not *want* to stop him. Such magnificent beauty.

I'd run because I'd felt the receptive rhythms within me and I'd known what would happen if I stayed . . .

He came too close and I lashed out. He dodged my hooves and went for me, mouth open, teeth bared. I tried to spin away but he reacted too fast and his flank bruised mine as he rose up over me.

His teeth sank into the back of my neck as he mounted me, holding me rigid. The pain flowered into an intense pleasure that swept right through me in muscular waves. The pain and pleasure together were a fire, a cataract of invigorating delight simply in being alive.

The joy crested and fell away. We broke apart and danced round and round each other, fighting, teasing, playing. Two whorls of fire, bronze and cream-gold.

This moment was everything. There was nothing else.

I experienced no human response to what had happened. No regret. No sense of closeness or possessiveness; nothing that could be called *love*. There was no need for love. The only need was to live in the rhythms of nature. And that simple truth was a massive release from pain, from all my burdens.

When Bronze cavorted away, the little tough leader of the females came to me, snuffing at me. Accepting me.

And I forgot.

I had no name and no secrets, no future, no past. I lived purely in the present. The herd was the only life, the only home I had ever known.

CHAPTER TEN

DANCING ON THE ROOF
OF THE WORLD

Winter descended on the land, freezing and cracking the ground, sending steel-cold blizzards tearing through the peaks and down the valleys. Flurries of snow blew on the wind. Snow lay thick on the ground and drifted along the bases of the cliffs. The contours of the hills glowed luminous white under the heavy, clotted darkness of the clouds. North or south, there was little grass to be found.

There were other herds competing for the more sheltered places. I sometimes saw Ember, at a distance. The sight of him always made me break out in a panicky sweat, although I didn't know why. Bronze was stronger . . . but Ember was still there, a dark speck, a threat.

Life became a continual search for food. All day the herd would dig and dig for grass, shake the glittering snow from bushes so we could nibble what leaves were left. We stamped through ice-crusts to reach the tooth-stinging water below, and a few hours later the holes would freeze over and the grass be covered again.

Sometimes I found red spires of Eldur poking through in sheltered places where the snow hadn't fallen so thickly. I would eat them, not remembering I'd once been afraid to do so, aware only of the comfortable heat it left in my belly.

I no longer had conscious thoughts. Yet I had never felt more alive. I was all sensation, all sensitivity. The herd had accepted me and I accepted their hierarchy; first doe, second doe, all the way down to the youngest fawn; and Bronze, our guardian, who would have given his life to protect us.

I knew all their different scents, their characters. I knew so much, without even realizing I knew it. I could sense changes in the weather hours before they began; I knew where to seek food. I could hear and see for miles, as if the land had opened up like a box of secrets.

The days were endless. The nights were eternal. The world itself had no boundaries.

This was life. This was reality distilled to its raw silver essence. There was fear, pain and joy – but never those killing human feelings of self-doubt, humiliation, worthlessness. Such bliss to be free of them – if only I could have known, at the time, that I *was* free.

If animals have found the secret of life, their tragedy is that they can never know it. Human sorrow is the opposite. Only now, looking back, can I see what I have lost; I never knew how rich I was at the time. You can see it or you can possess it; you can't do both.

Life moved in my womb.

I didn't wonder what kind of creature was growing within me. I didn't dream of a distant spring when a fawn would run beside me in the fresh green meadows; nor did I dread giving birth to some half-human monster. I no longer thought into the future. I felt only acceptance. Not even that. I questioned nothing.

Yet if I was fully animal, why did I have such long and distressing dreams?

Night after night they disturbed my sleep; strange creatures with oval pale faces, walking on their hind legs. They all looked the same. I didn't know what they were but they frightened me, rushing towards me, waving their arms, shouting, *demanding* . . . But what did they want? They made noises I couldn't understand.

And I dreamed of a pool, blue as ice, with steam rising from its surface. Another of the threatening figures was reflected in the water, but this one's face was all crimson and my nostrils were flooded with the too-sweet stench of blood.

I ran in my sleep all night, trying to escape.

But in the morning, the instant I awoke, I forgot the dreams. It's only now that I remember them; at the time, nothing remained but a vague sadness.

I don't know quite when the uneasiness began. It was connected to the dreams, perhaps, some thread of them running through into my waking hours; but at some stage in this eternal white existence I took to wandering the edges of the herd, staring out into the wilderness. I didn't know what I was looking for. I simply had a vague but persistent compulsion to keep watch.

Slowly it became as imperative as the need for food, and I couldn't remember a time when I'd been without the feeling.

The winter went on, mercilessly bitter. Some of the older ones died and were swiftly buried under feet of snow. Bronze no longer took any special notice of me; I was part of the herd, safely in fawn and with no reason to make trouble.

There came a night when a three-day blizzard had blown itself out, and the herd huddled together for warmth under an overhanging ledge, trampling the snow with our hooves, melting it with our warmth. Our coats were bearded with ice and we were torpid from the effort of surviving.

I couldn't sleep, though. I stood near the edge of the herd, so tense that my fur prickled. Our breath wreathed the air; the thousand different scents that rose from us were muted by the cold. There was a continual undercurrent of sounds; stamping, breathing, grunts. I was acutely aware of all this, but it was only a background to a powerful feeling that there was something outside, watching us. Something calling from the frozen hills.

Was I the only one who was aware of it? Even Bronze, whose senses were as keen as a bird's, dozed as if nothing was amiss.

I drifted asleep for a while, but the dreams came. The voices made a strange mumbling, maa-ing noise like goats. *Remember, remember, remember . . .*

Terror jolted me out of sleep. I awoke to find myself in mid-air, leaping out into the open before I was fully conscious.

The wind had dropped but the snow still fell steadily, in great silent flakes. Through this soft infinite curtain, I saw a speck of blackness; something watching me. Waiting for me. I was shivering with fear but I had to know what it was.

The falling snow seemed to glow with a light of its own. I walked through it, my gaze fixed on the watcher. Once I glanced back; the herd were already invisible behind veils of shadowy whiteness, and no one was following me. I almost wished Bronze would chase me and bring me back; but he did not. There was silence and stillness all around.

The dark shape looked like Ember. I believed it was him, so why did I feel compelled to go to him? I still don't know. Quivering and poised for flight, I stepped straight towards the danger.

The shadow resolved into a clear shape, and I stopped. Not Ember! A strange-looking deer, somehow deformed. My nostrils twitched. This creature was thick-set, rounded and muscular, with a long thick neck and a long bony head. He had no antlers. Instead he had black hair growing along the crest of his neck, a long black fountain of a tail. Like me, he was creamy, but there were darker dapples over his back.

I can see him so plainly even now, but at the time I had no idea what he was. As a deer I'd never seen a horse. Yet recognition stirred, as if this unknown being had once been as familiar as a brother . . .

His scent was strong, unsubtle, yet warm and kindly. He smelt of home. From a distant point deep inside me a word began to form. I didn't even know it was a word; it was an odd sound-shape lodged in my mind like a lump of gravel.

Datha.

The sound rang in my head. It unlocked a flood of terrors. There was something I should remember, something I should know . . .

Datha half-reared, his thick neck curved, his coat colourless in the snow and his mane and tail part of the darkness. This meant something. Statue of a horse in the flurried whiteness. An unspoken call, pulling me away into the night, into a subtly different reality.

Between Datha and me there was mutual understanding, deeper than wisdom, impossible to express in words.

I went towards him, my moist black nose extended to touch his soft muzzle. But before I'd come within twenty feet of him he turned and began to move away, climbing a deeply drifted slope. The curtains of snow fell between us and I lost sight of him. I still sensed danger but I followed his hoofprints, not understanding my own sense of urgency.

I didn't give the herd another thought. No one came after me, and the falling snow soon filled and obliterated our tracks.

In endless curtains the snow fell all night and all day, and I plodded knee-deep through it, scratching for grass and bushes as I went. Sometimes I saw Datha, very far ahead, almost silver in his thick winter coat, almost invisible in the drifting whiteness. At others I couldn't see him at all, and I could only follow the blurred indentations in the snow and his scent.

I don't know why I left safety and my best chance of survival behind. I was like a sleep-walker. An odd compulsion – like Tykavn's compulsion, perhaps – to follow a certain course which, beneath the surface, had no rational reason at all.

We crossed the wide valley between the mountains, Datha leading me straight for the wall of rock in the north. Snow had turned the sides white; only here and there, avalanches had laid bare the rock in coal-dark knives of shadow.

Visible above the wall was the rim of the glacier; a roof of frozen glass-whiteness that never melted, only shifted perpetually under its own vast weight. No food, no life. Datha's tracks turned and led westwards along the base. Why didn't he wait for me? I was lighter and swifter, so why couldn't I catch up with him?

The rhythm of my own hooves hypnotized me. The softly falling flakes enveloped me in my own small world, deadened all sound and wrapped me in an illusion of safety. I thought we were the only beings alive in this white world.

I began to see Datha in different places. Usually he was directly ahead of me; but sometimes he seemed to be further out in the valley, still ahead of me but slightly below. These brief glimpses left me confused and nervous. Something not right . . .

There he was again, a black speck to my left . . . and yet his tracks were right in front of me. For a few minutes the wind whirled the snow away and I saw, briefly but distinctly, two figures. Datha was ahead of me, cobweb pale . . . And the other, the dark one in the valley, was a hart.

My first impression was that it was Bronze. I was torn in half; I was completely animal, and I'd taken the structure of the herd as the natural way of things. But the thread that pulled me after Datha was stronger, and I could accept Bronze's patriarchy no longer . . .

But it was not Bronze. My instinct perceived him more clearly than my eyes. A thin wire of scent reached me; shudders went through me, more of gut-deep horror than fear. It was Ember. And I felt this horror because I knew, had always known, that Ember – like me – was not a natural deer.

Knowledge came, vague but compelling as in a dream; Ember was pursuing Datha. That was why I'd had to follow him. I had to warn Datha, rescue and protect him . . .

Datha clearly knew he was being hunted. I saw him pause and glance back, tossing his ice-heavy mane. Then he turned right and began to climb up the side of the mountain towards the glacier. Did he think Ember wouldn't follow him? I went after him, struggling to catch up, failing. And the ugly, fire-edged hart turned with us.

Step by step I toiled up the steep mountainside, sometimes slipping as a crust of snow broke away and threatened to carry me down with it; always regaining my feet with the surefootedness of a mountain deer. I felt the arctic coldness swirling all around me, but I didn't feel cold; my own fur was a layer of warmth against it.

Ember was ahead of me and he was gaining on Datha. I was falling behind, losing sight of them. In panic I strained to climb faster.

At the peak of the ridge I stepped on to the glacier and was blinded. Wrapped in clouds, shrouded in ever-falling snow, I entered a frigid, utterly hostile new world.

I was exhausted. The weight of my womb made my back ache; I could feel every folded limb of the foetus inside me, every joint sticking into me, the weight of its bones. Head drooping, almost asleep on my feet, I followed the two sets of tracks.

Ember's tracks overlay Datha's now. They were growing less distinct; the more I fell behind, the more the snow covered them. I mustn't lose them . . .

A brief doze, a horrible dream image. I came to the end of the tracks and there was a huge churned circle of snow, stained with blood . . .

A brassy bellow shocked me awake.

My head jerked up. I shook myself and broke into a trot, kicking up a froth of crystals round my feet. The glacier was rough, full of leg-snapping fissures, but I leapt around and over them, driven by fear.

As I ran, the snow-curtain parted and I saw the hart just ahead of me, so close I skidded to a halt and fell down on to my side, rolling frantically to regain my feet.

Ember saw me but he ignored me. He and Datha were facing each other in the ashen gloom; Datha with his neck arched, eyes rolling, hooves pawing the snow. Fearless, beautiful.

But Ember . . . It was the first time I'd seen him so close. He was a creature in a deer's shape, but he was no natural being. He was an ugly mockery of a hart, throwing his head against the sky, his antlers sharp and clear like leading in a window; a thing of twisted and rough-finished metal, red as rust, scorched black so that he seemed to glow. And his iron-cold stench was like blood.

One of the Unseen, or some shape-changing creature from Kvold – whatever he was, he filled me with black, chilling terror. He was a demon from the underworld, unleashed on to the earth to persecute those I loved until I surrendered . . .

These thoughts were wordless, yet they were the abstract images of a human mind, not an animal one.

I watched Datha rear up, challenging Ember. His scream of fury shrilled above the moan of the wind. I realized then that he was giving me the chance to escape; that he'd come, perhaps, to lead Ember away from me. But I wouldn't let him. He looked so small, like a toy under the crushing darkness of the demon. Ember shook his beweaponed head and lunged, screaming metallically.

Datha dodged. I could smell his sweat, hear his quick breathing – but from the iron-demon came no heat or urgency at all.

I couldn't let Datha die. I'd abandoned him once; never again. Instead of fleeing I plunged hock-deep through the snow to confront the beast. I felt stick-thin, frail, weighed down by my pregnancy. It was like trying to dam a waterfall with a twig. But I was incensed and I didn't care.

Ember reared and I mirrored the action. But he twisted aside and it was Datha he struck with his sharp, cloven feet – Datha who was plunging and slithering away, blood pouring down his shoulder. Ember went after him. He would knock Datha down and gore him. How could I distract the demon while he was moving away and ignoring me?

I leapt off my hocks, a high, wide leap, and landed right on the hart's back. His substance felt hard as basalt, cold as a Fane. It seemed to take from me all my heat and all my will to live. I felt boneless . . .

And I knew what evil was. In that moment, in a sickening whirl of blackness, I knew that evil was not strong or mysterious but an insidious despair that feeds on hope and will . . .

Why bother? it seemed to whisper. I was being spun round and round through flurries of snow as the beast tried to fling me off. *Everyone dies eventually, anyway. You, Datha, Tykavn. Why take all this trouble for someone who thinks nothing of you?*

Human words and ideas, yet I understood them. Despairing, I felt my strength giving way. But I wouldn't listen to the whispers. They were true, and their truth terrified me. But the fear gave me a terrible anger and desire to destroy their source.

I bit into Ember's neck with my small, grass-eating teeth. The flesh was like leather, soft rusted metal. His bellow was like the grinding of metal on rock. And I knew I must draw power from somewhere. I gathered my desperate anger and let it go.

I felt myself turn into a column of bronze fire.

All at once I was outside my body and watching from a

distance; I saw a dark shape like a hole in the snow; I saw it enveloped by a whirlwind that glowed from within with coloured radiance. Sudema's purple, and the scarlet fire of Eldur.

Datha was shying away, circling frantically. There was a sizzling crack, like thunder.

I was in my body again. Ember collapsed underneath me. He didn't just fall to the snow; the substance of his whole body was collapsing, leaking rust-brown fluid that was not like natural blood.

The details are vague. The summoning of power had done something terrible to me. I was only half conscious; I think I dragged myself to my feet, but I could not stand properly and I was shivering and burning.

But as I drew back I saw Ember rise up. I shrank away, but it seemed he was being lifted by the wind, as if he had no substance or weight left. Like a piece of crumpled goat-skin, he howled away down a ridge and was gone.

What truly happened, I don't know. But that's what I saw.

I tried to run in the opposite direction. I stumbled into a snow drift and dragged myself out, to find Datha looking down at me.

He whickered. His nose touched mine. We pressed against each other, nose to tail, and slept.

I can only guess at what happened, but I believe the power that Sigurthur instilled in me when he changed me into a deer was the power I used to destroy Ember. That, and the Eldur I had eaten. I have never been able to do anything like it since.

Now here were Datha and I, stranded on the glacier without food, certain to starve or freeze before we found our way down. We turned north, and we walked and walked.

In a dizzying fog of snow and ice we plodded on, eating the flakes when we felt thirsty. When we grew tired we slept standing up, pressed together more for company than warmth. Our coats became clotted and ruched with snow. We were moving drifts, white shadows on whiteness.

A deep lethargy settled on me and I began to feel that we would walk through the wilderness until we sank into sleep and never woke again. Perhaps we were already dead; perhaps we were ghosts, and this was Kvold where Ama's Light never shone . . .

I don't know where these ideas came from. In all other ways I was still purely a doe. But something was changing. Winter could not last for ever.

There came a night when the clouds cleared, and our apathy vanished with them. The sky was a crisp black of unbearable purity; infinite space, glossy as jet. The stars glittered white and hard and separate. But brightest of all, a single intense spot of colour, shone the violet star Sudema.

Her light charmed the glacier to a sparkling field of violet and white. The clarity of the air had frosted the snow to a skin of ice, and on this field, fired with the joy of life, Datha and I played and leapt and galloped. Our breath plumed on to the air, freezing instantly.

Too weak to live much longer, we expended the last of our strength in this mad tribute to life. Datha went skidding over on to his side several times, but I kept my footing. I danced on the hard-packed ice – danced on the roof of the world – intoxicated by the profound icy beauty of the night. The star's light crystallized me.

I didn't remember the names of the sun or the star. I couldn't have comprehended how one could be considered good and the other bad. They only *were*, like the earth itself. And their existence was to be celebrated. Life was so sharply sweet and brief . . .

Datha skidded to a halt, raised his nose to the stars and let out a huge, shivering neigh. The sound seemed to bowl through the silence, out towards the limits of the glacier.

I heard the ice creak. I saw him go tense and try to leap, but the footing seemed to give way beneath him. There was a crash and he vanished, still scrabbling, down into the ice. A flag of steam fountained up where he had fallen.

I dashed forward, tried to stop and skidded on to the edge of a hole. The ice was rotten. The edge crumbled beneath me and I fell after Datha, turning head over heels in cascades of slush, scrabbling to save myself until I slid to a halt at the base of a snow-pile.

I scrambled out of the wetness, shaking myself. I could see nothing, except a trail of violet radiance falling through the crevasse and slanting down the heap of ice. There was space around me, which echoed with running water. It was *warm*. But of Datha there was no sign, no sound or scent.

I dug in the fallen ice for a time, but instinct told me he was not buried there. He had disappeared. I wandered round and round in confusion, but deep in my heart I knew I wouldn't find him.

Perhaps, in bringing me here, his task was over. Or . . .

When dawn came I saw that I was in a cave of ice. The walls shone blue, layers on layers creating different shades from ice-blue to deep cobalt. A stream ran down the centre of the cave, sulphur tainted and so hot I could barely drink from it. And on the floor of the cave was grass!

A hot spring had carved this cave out of the glacier. The warmth and the light through the ice allowed vegetation to grow. We can't have been far from the glacier's edge anyway, nor far from the end of winter. But I knew I would be able to shelter here, warm and well-fed, while the worst of the weather played itself out above me. Datha's accident had saved my life.

Over and over I've asked myself, was Datha ever really there?

He had seemed real and warm. My friend, through everything. Was it a ghost who had walked at my side? Or a figment conjured by my own mind to remind me of my purpose?

I think I realize now that I will never see the real Datha again. Perhaps he perished when the Unseen hunted us, lost amid the sulphur hills; perhaps he found a rich meadow and lives contentedly there now, aware of nothing beyond the present. At peace, as only an animal can be.

I don't think I'll ever know.

After a time I stopped wondering where he was every time I looked round. I was still a doe, and as such I didn't grieve as a human would. I had other concerns. I had to eat and eat to regain my strength, to feed the life which hung so heavy inside me.

Physically, I was emaciated. I remained so no matter how much I ate; while the foetus seemed to be growing big enough to fill my whole skin.

Each day I grazed my way a little further down the stream, in the blue safety of the ice-tunnel. They were tranquil days, with some physical discomfort, none mental. But one morning I awoke with waves of pain pushing through me.

I lay down, stood up, lay down again, not knowing what to do with myself. I sweated and panted. The pain felt as if it was going to split me apart.

I remember the sound of the stream trickling past; that sound had been my soothing companion for many days. I lay half in the water, because it was all that eased the pain; and the sound carried me out of myself.

My body was trying to turn itself inside out.

I began to see visions which made no sense. They frightened me. White oval faces; pairs of violet eyes drifting through the dark; indistinct figures causing little lights to burn in a circle, a simple act which filled me with terror; a painting of a city with a real man watching me from a window, a creature who seemed to be Ember, even though he was human . . . oh, and more. Crazed visions which seemed vitally important, yet at the end of all were only illusions.

This was not the simple, natural act it was meant to be.

It seemed to me that I gave birth to myself.

The deer-shape that had contained me split apart in a climax of pain. The fawn slid out. I felt as if it had grown to fill not just my womb but my whole body, swelling until the skin must burst to release it out into the world. And the fawn was human. It was me.

I was the mother and the child. I was the one who dies to give life. The outer skin was dead. It was time for it to split and release the new form from within, as a river-fly shrugs off its nymph-case. Sloughing off the deer-hide, I emerged and lay, smooth and raw and naked, in the edge of the stream.

I was helpless as a baby, and I knew nothing.

The warmth of the water kept me alive. The water-flow pulled me in and bore me along like a beached twig, out of the snow-cave, down into a spring-green mountain meadow, until at last I rolled to rest on a shallow bed of gravel.

I was only half aware, like a sleeper floating on the edge of waking; but I had the strangest feeling that this had happened to me before.

CHAPTER ELEVEN

JOLITHA'S HANDS

The world was rippling as if I lay on a lake bed. Streamers wafted around me like water-weed, milky-blue. My limbs looked like pearl; slender, pale, fluid. Not a deer's limbs. Not mine. Yet when I stretched, the limbs responded, my fingers curling and uncurling like tendrils.

Fingers. Hands, slim white arms . . . the weed fluttering around my face was human hair. I was in my own form again.

How strange it felt, as if I'd lost all my strength and been wrapped in velvet. I felt boneless. And everything looked weird through my transformed eyes, flat and fluid and veiled.

I didn't know who I was or where I was, yet there were no questions in my mind. Only a kind of puzzled resignation.

I've no idea how long I lay there, but it can't have been long. Away from its source the stream cooled and I was very cold now, yet this didn't matter. I didn't shiver. I simply lay with the water washing over me, the gravel abrading my raw skin, until at length I became aware that there was someone standing over me.

A tall slender girl, with a pale oval face and silver-blonde hair. She stood with her hands clasped in front of her, looking down at me with her head on one side.

My first reaction was almost purely animal. Unknown beings were a threat. The leap of my heart carried through to my legs, but my body lacked the strength to respond. I convulsed and fell back, my stomach rising and falling with the effort.

How strange the girl seemed. She didn't react at once, only stood watching my struggles. Then she crouched down, hands still joined, and said wonderingly, 'This was how they found me, too.'

Each word was like a strand of flame in my mind; spurting, blazing, branching through my head in quicksilver lines. The first human voice I'd heard in months. My brain was dormant, but those words – the passive act of hearing and *understanding* them

– fell into my memory like a spark into kindling.

'There, don't be afraid.' Her voice was quiet, her accent unfamiliar. 'I can heal you. Lie quiet and let me touch you.'

The girl lifted her hands, fingertips linked, and pressed the backs of her fingers and knuckles on to my neck. At the touch a tingling warmth went through me, and the shock of it seemed to jolt me back towards normal human awareness.

'You can come home with me,' said the girl. 'I'll look after you.'

I looked up at her. Her slim form was clothed with pale blue and grey and her eyes, too, were blue-grey. She looked ethereal, as if she had stepped out of an underworld that was a pale thin reflection of this one.

I tried to speak – to make a sound, at least – but my tongue was stuck to the roof of my mouth. The memories started to come swift and heavy, completely at random, hitting me like a rain of rocks. My mother calling my name; a Perfect-Minister striking a tiny golden gong; Sigurthur roaring with laughter under the torrent of a waterfall; Tykavn's glittering, deranged eyes spitting hatred at me. Ama's Light. I tried to put my arms over my head. Dear God, dear God.

'Can you stand?' said the girl. 'Rest a moment. Lean on me.'

I pushed myself into a sitting position, my head reeling. The action and her warmth sent me into violent shivers. But the impressions still reached me; how threadbare the girl's blue robe and grey overdress were, faded with ingrained dirt and repeated washings. Her silver hair was untidy, and there were little lines in the fair skin around her eyes. Too pallid and round-eyed to be pretty, she was emphatically human.

I forced my first words through chattering teeth. 'Who are you?'

'Jolitha Vixl-daughter,' she said, offering her arm to help me stand up. She took her overdress off with the most extraordinary awkwardness, like a little girl trying to undress herself one-handed, and wrapped it around me. Where she touched me, I felt warm. 'Do you have a name?'

'Iolithie,' I said. How weird it felt to say it.

She blinked. Her blue-grey eyes were glass-cold, alien. 'You have almost the same name as me,' she said, as if surprised. 'But when they found me, I had no name at all. I could not remember where I came from. Can you?'

I didn't know what she meant. Too much to take in. 'I don't know,' I said. 'I don't know.'

'They found me like this, naked, in the glacier stream. Perhaps you are my sister.'

I thought she was a little mad. Yet when we held each other's gaze, there seemed to be a tenuous bond between us. Then Jolitha looked at her hands, fingertips pressed together so they formed a cage. 'I want to help you. Sometimes I can make people better by touching them.'

'How?'

She blinked, and a fugitive look came to her expression. 'I don't know how. I don't ask these things. If you ask, they go away.'

I subsided, too tired to enmesh myself any deeper, and let her lead me away from the stream and across a meadow. I was in my own shape again; I was, apparently, safe. It was enough. I was too shaken to take in anything new. 'Where are you taking me?'

'To the farm,' said Jolitha. 'You can stay with us. No one will mind.'

'Are you sure?'

'I always take injured creatures home,' she said without irony. 'Vixl is used to it. I charm the goats and the hens better, too, so he can't mind. Perhaps he will make you Vixl-daughter too.'

Jolitha led me through a flat valley, between gentle hills. The glacier looked a long way behind us. Mountains rimmed the horizon, under a fleece of clouds, but spring had come to this valley. Thick wads of snow lay melting into the fresh green grass.

There seemed nothing strange in the landscape itself, only in the way I perceived it; everything seemed too pale, too large, ghosted with wispy colours that vanished if looked at directly. There was a touch of unreality about the world.

My knees gave way and I half fainted. Jolitha failed to catch me, but she immediately bent down and stretched out both arms to help me up. Her fingers remained pressed together as if in supplication.

'Sorry,' I said, leaning on her arm and standing up shakily. 'I feel so weak.'

'We will make you better,' said my pale saviour.

We came to a fence made of wood. Precious wood, used for fences! Jolitha opened a gate. Just inside it stood the biggest tree I'd ever seen outside books. It was gnarled and bent to one side – streaming out on a wind that wasn't blowing – but to me it seemed majestic. I stared at it open-mouthed.

'Here is our farm,' said Jolitha. She spoke soothingly, as she must have done to her sick animals. 'It's just a little way to the house. Not far now.'

I couldn't see the building until we were almost upon it. First I saw a stretch of grass that seemed to be pleated in waves, fanning horizontally out of the hillside below us. Then, as we came down and round to the front, I saw a row of pointed wooden cottages, set into the hill. The 'pleats' were their turf roofs. Four goats were grazing on them, a sight that almost made me laugh out loud.

Jolitha pushed open a door with both hands. The interior was pitch-black for a few seconds, until my eyes began to adjust.

'Go in,' said Jolitha.

As I stepped over the threshold, three pairs of eyes swivelled to stare at me. Sitting in the shadows, there was a big bulky man with grey hair, a younger man, small and wiry, who was almost bald, and a thin lad with blonde hair straggling from beneath a blue cap. The wiry man went on eating his broth, but the other two paused, spoons in mid-air. No one smiled, no one showed any sign of surprise or welcome. I felt horribly uncomfortable.

All my human feelings were returning, with a vengeance.

Finally the large man spoke. 'What's it now, 'Litha?' he said gruffly.

'This is Iolithie,' said the pale girl. 'I found her, Vixl. She's hurt.'

The man made a *harrumph* sound. ' 'Nother wounded animal,' he said dismissively, turning away. The blonde boy just went on staring until I wondered if he was simple. Then the man muttered, 'Well, sit her down, then,' and continued his meal.

While Jolitha dragged a small chair from a corner, I looked around the room. It was about twelve feet square, with lightless corridors leading off on two sides. The ceiling was of bare turves, and the wooden beams that supported it were garlanded with braces of dead birds, ropes, junk that might have been parts of disused farm tools, herbs drying in bunches. A fire crackled sullenly in the back wall. In one corner, a ladder led up to a roughly built gallery.

The men seemed part of the cottage, carved from the same wood, dusted by the same grainy textures and colours. The firelight, which glowed on the earth floor and multiplied the clutter with layers of shadow, painted their breeches with the same dull-red glow and made their bare chests shine like oiled wood.

Yet Jolitha stood out pale among them as if she was not quite of their world.

The stench was overwhelming; a mixture of animals, sweat, salted fish, smoke, damp, bird droppings, cooking, a myriad other stenches all stewed together. I had a cold sick feeling at the back of my throat, and I passed out.

Voices in my head. A few seconds passed like a thousand years. I came round with someone dripping lukewarm water on to my forehead. Slowly I realized I was lying on the gallery, a rickety construction of planks with two or three straw mattresses strewn on it.

'Vixl carried you up,' said Jolitha, pressing a cloth to my head. 'Most things I can do better than – than ordinary folk, but some things I can't manage.'

I wasn't sure what she meant, so I said only, 'You're very kind.' My head was spinning with memories. A great long silence in my mind, when I had walked on the snow under the burning star, with no thoughts beyond the need to survive . . . and now, now, all the human pain and urgency flooding back in again. I had lived another life, then been torn out of it.

A wave of sorrow started to roll through me. I was beginning, only beginning, to realize what I had lost.

'The place I found you, in the stream,' she said, 'that was where they found me – though I don't remember. I was only a tiny child. They say my parents abandoned me, but I don't think I ever had any parents. I think the glacier gave birth to me, as it did to you.'

'No, I remember my life before, I know how I got there . . .' I gave up. The way she looked at me; I don't think she wanted to hear, and I didn't want to tell her. It really didn't seem to matter. There was a deeper link between us which scared me a little.

I tried to sit up. 'But where is this place? Am I in Onafross?'

Jolitha frowned. After a moment she said something that sounded like, 'Onyafrosa, yes.'

'We're not in the Stolen Land?'

'Stolen . . . ?'

It hadn't occurred to me that they would have different names for things here. The people I'd met from Onafross – including Tykavn – had used the same names as us. The only difference had been their refined accents and superior airs, but these farmers were nothing like that. 'Er – the wilderness, Inner Thandarkyr?'

Light dawned. 'Ah, no. I found you on the very borders.'

'So this is Onafross – Onyafrosa.' She nodded, and a great wave of relief went through me. I'd done it, I'd crossed the Stolen Land. But so much had happened . . . I wasn't the same person. The way I looked at everything had changed. To recall the reason for my journey and drag it into the centre of my mind took a huge effort.

Tykavn. A whole season had passed since I left. I pressed my cheek against the mattress, blotting out the thoughts and the pain.

Footsteps sounded on the ladder, shaking the whole gallery. A man's head and hefty shoulders appeared over the edge. His face was fleshy, weather-lined and dour, with a bulbous nose. 'Nearly time for milking, 'Lith,' he said.

'I know, Father. I'm coming.'

'How is she?'

'Very tired,' said the girl. Her voice was soft, slightly sing-song. 'But we'll make her well.'

'Mm,' Vixl grunted. 'She'll make an extra hand, at least.' The head sank out of sight into the lower room.

I was trying to sit up again, panicking mildly. 'What does he mean? I can't stay here. I'm grateful, I'll find some way to repay you, but I can't stay.'

Jolitha did not react, except to say, 'Shh.'

I thought she was finding my accent hard to understand, so I tried to speak more clearly. 'But don't you want to know who I am, or where I'm travelling to? You don't know anything about me!'

'It doesn't matter. You're safe here. Vixl looks sour but he is good at heart; he has always looked after me well. His son, Ysa, doesn't like me; but he doesn't really like anyone, so I don't mind. The other man is Vixl's brother, Jon. Vixl's wife died a long time ago; I miss her. It was she who took me in and made Vixl let me call them Mother and Father. They're good people. They don't mind that I'm not . . .' She trailed off for a moment. 'You see, I can work as well as anyone at most things. Then they don't mind helping me with the things I can't do. Mother made all my clothes, before she died, so that I could put them on myself. They don't mind . . . that I have this deformity.'

I gazed at her, moth-pale in the gloom, and could see nothing whatever wrong with her. 'I can't see any deformity,' I said, tactlessly, I suppose. 'What do you mean?'

The corners of Jolitha's mouth twitched up in sadness. She

raised her hands, the fingers forming a steeple, the cloth still caged between them. I met her eyes, not understanding. Jolitha simply waited until my gaze dropped again to her joined hands.

Jolitha parted her palms a little and the cloth fell.

Then I saw that she wasn't keeping her hands together deliberately; she couldn't separate them. The fingertips of her left hand were joined to those of her right – not artificially but by an aberration of nature. Each fingertip and thumbtip grew straight into its counterpart, with a joint at each cusp but no fingernails, only continuous flesh.

She could never separate her hands, nor open her arms.

'How did this happen to you?' I said at last.

'They say I was born like this.' Jolitha dropped her hands into her lap and stared down at them.

'It must make your life difficult . . .'

'I've never known anything else. Sometimes I cannot pick up things as easily as other people. But I never drop anything,' she said fiercely. 'I never drop anything.'

Within a few days I began to feel better. Jolitha had a healing touch, a magic about her.

As soon as I was able to get up, I went outside and stood in the farmyard, breathing in lungfuls of the air – which, after the closeness of the hut, was unbelievably sweet. I felt purposeful again, and calm; more like the girl who had first set off from Torlossen, but much stronger. Which way did Onareyru lie? I looked out at the hills, all misted with spring green. I knew I wasn't strong enough to go yet, but the moment I was . . .

Until then, there was the simple joy of being human.

Sorrow, too. The stamina and speed I'd possessed for a short enchanted season; I mourned their loss. The simple ability, which could never be recaptured, to live in the wild without a single item of civilization. Simply to exist, without having to think, or plan, or grieve, or feel guilty. Simply to *be*. And now it was all lost, and reality stared me bleak and uncompromising in the face. Tykavn, hundreds of miles away, was still sick; at least, I must assume he was, since I had no way of knowing otherwise.

Anything could have happened to him by now. He could be better, he could be – No, don't think of that! I was still going to seek help for him. Then, Ama knew how, I would have to make the journey back. But King Vidvikjan would help me. Perhaps he'd travel back with me for the sake of his son.

I'll do it, I told myself, my jaw tight. *After going through all this, I won't give up now!*

For a few minutes, though, I keened in silent agony for the terrible and wonderful existence I had lost. For Datha, my truest friend ... And then, my memory flowing backwards, for Sigurthur.

What a desperate injustice I'd done him, assuming he was evil; that in accepting his help I'd sold my soul to Sudema. Well, if I had, he had given it back tenfold. Saved me – and, in so doing, perhaps redeemed himself.

And I missed him, as I'd never missed my own family, Tykavn or even Mehaar. I ran to the yard gate, tears streaming down my face, so no one would see me weeping.

Through the veil I saw Jolitha crossing the yard from the dairy, a pail of milk cradled in her joined hands. It was full to the brim, but Jolitha never spilled a drop.

Jolitha, I soon noticed, worked like a bondservant would in Tor-lossen. She tended the goats, she milked them, she made the butter and cheese, she nursed the animals when they were sick. And all this she did with the handicap of her fused hands. She never uttered a word of complaint. She had developed the most extraordinary dexterity in overcoming her problem. More out of guilt than anything – although I was still too weak to do much – I took to helping her, and Jolitha's skill at her tasks left me standing.

As the days went by, I learned more about the farm. Vixl was the farmer, and although Jolitha called him 'Father', it seemed he treated her no better than a farmhand. Still, he treated his brother and his son the same, so I suppose he was fair, at least. I found all of them dour and monosyllabic. They didn't exactly make me feel welcome, but neither did they seem to mind my presence. They had a tradition that no traveller could pass by without being offered their hospitality, such as it was. To do otherwise was bad luck. And I was one of Jolitha's wounded, after all; in their eyes, as strange and fey as Jolitha herself.

I sensed no bad in these people. They were like the farmers of my own village, who lived such a hard life that they saw no point in smiling, laughing or even saying anything that was not essential to survival. The oddest thing was that they seemed to have no Status; Vixl had not been made Perfect, Jon was not a Sublime, there was no mention of Ysa and Jolitha being of marriageable age. I assumed they had lapsed because they lived so far from Onareyru – and that in itself was a depressing thought.

It worried me a little that they did not care *who* I was; that they assumed I would be staying and working at the farm, and that I had no identity, no plans of my own. If they knew I planned to leave, would they try to stop me?

Once or twice I tried to find out the way to Onareyru.

'Have you ever been to the city?' I asked Vixl. 'Is it far?'

'Don't know of no city,' he said abruptly. 'Don't suppose I'd want to go there if I did.'

Then to Ysa, 'Hasn't anyone ever told you about Onareyru? Which way would it be?'

But Ysa only looked curiously at me, shrugged and sneered. He was not simple, but so deeply uneducated that he could only mock what he didn't understand. That was why he mocked Jolitha and ignored me altogether, if he could.

If I run away, I thought *I might go in completely the wrong direction for miles and miles. I need a horse, a map, a road. Ama curse it, it's not fair! Someone must be able to tell me!*

I felt trapped, both by their ignorance and by my own physical weakness.

One morning I was standing in the yard, throwing feed to the chickens, when I saw a man passing the gate on horseback. I couldn't stop myself from staring, his looks were so arresting. He was tall and imposing, with grey hair swept back from a wise, serene face.

To my alarm, he saw me looking at him over the wall and turned towards me. Reining in, he dismounted and bowed courteously. He was no villager.

'Good day to you, halla,' he said.

'Good day, mathyr.'

'Can I be of any help to you?' He spoke beautifully. His voice made the accents of the Court of Torbyrgi sound coarse.

I was so startled that he'd noticed me that I didn't know how to respond. 'Well – no, mathyr, I hardly know – I didn't mean to—'

I knew I sounded a fool, but I didn't know how to begin my desperate questions. Yet he seemed to understand. 'Dear child,' he said, 'don't be nervous of me. I stopped because I noticed you looking at me, and I thought you seemed rather pale, a little upset. Have you been unwell?'

'I – yes, I have, mathyr, though I'm much better now. But—'

'Perhaps I had better take a look, all the same. I am a doctor, you see.'

My eyes widened. My heart was racing with hope. 'You don't come from Onareyru, do you?' I spoke in the slightly affected way I'd adopted in Tykavn's Court. He looked taken aback to hear such a refined accent from someone he had taken for a country girl.

'Yes, I do . . . I am from Lor Palace, in fact.'

I almost shouted for joy. 'Oh, I am so glad to see you! I need to go there to see the King's Physician – you are not him, are you?'

His eyebrows lifted over cool, brown eyes. 'No, I am not. But actually I am the King's *Surgeon*. There is a subtle difference. I am Lord Ovinor. May I know who you are?'

'Iolithie Gaefir-daughter, of Vry – Torbyrgi. Are you on your way to Onareyru?'

'Yes, I am.'

'Oh, would you take me with you? It's desperately important that I see the King and his doctor. It's such a long story it would take me all day to tell you. Please believe me—'

Ovinor laughed. He wasn't young – he looked fifty, at least – but in a way he was beautiful. 'Halla, I'm sure it is not my place to question your motives. There is no need to explain anything. Of course I will take you to Onareyru.'

I was so ecstatic I could have leapt over the wall and hugged him. I mastered myself and remembered my manners.

'Won't you come in for some refreshment, mathyr?' I said. 'It won't take me long to get ready, but you must be tired. Have you travelled far?'

'Far enough,' he said. 'But I am in no great hurry. It would be pleasant to break my journey. I can wait until you are sure you feel able to travel.'

Bursting with excitement, I led Lord Ovinor into the living room of the farmhouse. I apologized for the gloom, the smell and the clutter as we went, but the stranger did not seem to mind in the slightest. I introduced him to Vixl, Ysa and Jon, who greeted him with the same enthusiasm as they had shown me. Jolitha turned from stoking the fire, the poker gripped between her palms.

'And this is Jolitha Vixl-daughter,' I said. 'I have something to tell you, 'Litha. I'm very grateful to you for nursing me, for all you've done for me, but I have to leave very soon. Lord Ovinor is going to take me to Onareyru. That's where I was trying to go when I was . . . taken ill.'

Ysa said sullenly, 'No such place as Onareyru! We didn't ask you to come here with your stupid accent and peculiar ways. If you want to go to a place that don't exist – good riddance! That what you say, Father?'

'Be quiet,' said Ovinor, and his voice sliced the thick air like a cleaver. He was gazing at Jolitha as if she had gathered all his attention and held it within her like milk in a pale vase. Then he moved towards her, took her fused hands in his and lifted them up.

'Step into the light,' he said. She obeyed, letting him take her to the open door. 'You were born like this? Of course you were, what am I saying? This must have been a great trial to you.'

'Never bothered her,' said Vixl.

Ovinor glanced at him with contempt. 'With respect, mathyr, have you ever tried going about your daily work with your hands tied together? Perhaps you should try it, to appreciate what this poor girl has suffered. Just putting your clothes on in the morning would be impossible.'

Jolitha said faintly, 'Mother made all mine with the sleeves slit and laces down the side. I can do them with my hands and teeth . . .'

The Surgeon was examining her fingers intently. The shared fingertips, the long digits curved like a ribcage. 'Have your hands given you any pain?'

'No, never, sir. Only if I tried to lift something too heavy.'

'That'd hurt anyone,' said Vixl.

'I hope you don't overwork her,' Ovinor said sharply. He was silent, examining, thinking. No one spoke; the fire popped and spat, a goat on the roof said *maa-a-a*; everyone stared at the Surgeon as he studied Jolitha.

Eventually he said, 'Well, it is very fortunate that I was passing your house today. And you have Iolithie to thank for inviting me in. I can cure your daughter's deformity, mathyr.'

'How?' said Vixl, incredulous.

The Surgeon answered delicately. 'There would have to be . . . what we call an operation. I can separate the fingers quite successfully. There would be some discomfort, and a period of healing, of course, but the result would be full use of your hands . . .'

Jolitha's gaze was fixed on her hands in his as he turned them this way and that in the firelight. Glassy white lights shone in her astonished eyes.

Ysa said, 'You mean you'd have to cut her?'

'That is putting it too crudely. But what is a few moments of pain against a lifetime of freedom for your daughter?'

There was a long pause. I felt the air tightening, pressing down. Eventually Vixl said, irrelevantly, 'She's not my daughter.'

He didn't know how to face the problem so he sidestepped it. I saw the hurt look in Jolitha's eyes. I could've hit Vixl!

'Not yours?' The Surgeon sounded as if he was not really interested in the answer.

'We found her as a child, abandoned in the top valley. Not our fault her hands are like that!'

'Father,' Jolitha said quietly, 'I never said it was. I never—'

'All I'm saying is, it's her decision.' Vixl pushed a hand over his sweating face, bringing blood to his cheeks. 'Don't ask me. Don't look at me!'

The Surgeon gave him a condescending smile and turned to Jolitha. 'Of course it is your decision, my dear.'

I saw her hands start to shake. Everyone was waiting for her reply. 'I don't know. I can do almost everything. Would it – would it hurt?'

'I can't promise it won't. But I am an experienced surgeon. There's no need to be afraid.'

Jolitha hung there as if tethered to the floor only by his grip. She looked at her father, her brother, me, as if pleading for advice, but no one spoke. I couldn't. A heavy vortex spiralled around Ovinor, drawing us all in. He would have his way.

'Imagine,' said Ovinor, 'being able to do this.' And he separated his hands wide and brought them together with a loud clap that made us all jump. He smiled.

'Well,' Jolitha said faintly. 'Well, if you say it's best . . .'

'It will be.' The Surgeon nodded emphatically. 'We'll begin now, if you don't mind. Let me look at your rooms to find the most suitable.'

He put his hand on Jolitha's back and she went with him, malleable as a sleepwalker.

Behind the living rooms at the front of the cottage a warren of corridors and lightless chilly storerooms ran back into the hill. Ovinor chose one such storeroom for his work, because it was cold and uncluttered and had a good-sized table on which he could work. But because it was deep inside the hill, with no windows, he asked us to bring every candle and lamp we had.

The walls were of mud-and-straw bricks and seemed to suck in all the light, giving the brightest flame back as a muddy glow. It was always damp and chill in here. For all the lamps they brought, the room remained in ghostly gloom, with one core of brilliance on the table.

The Surgeon sent me to boil some water. When I returned, he was taking metal instruments from his bag and setting them out on a white cloth on the table, where they glittered and flashed. There was an atmosphere of ritual. All attention was centred on the surgeon, and no one spoke except him. Vixl, Ysa and I obeyed his instructions; and through it all Jolitha sat at the table, her hands resting on the cloth. Her face was whiter than the linen. She sat like someone who has lost all will to live and waits only for the claws of the Unseen to end it.

Ovinor dipped his instruments one by one in the hot water and dried them. Knives of different sizes with strange handles, implements like tongs and pincers, a pair of scissors with long thin handles. Made of some shiny metal I'd never seen before, they looked sinister.

'Now,' said Ovinor, 'before we begin, we must pray. Bow your heads. You too, Jolitha. Pray for Ama's blessing on this operation. This is done in the name of the Prophet Hendleiknir, to whom our hands, our healing hands, are sacred.'

We stood before him as he mumbled a brief prayer, just as we'd stand before a Perfect-Minister. I tried to block out the words. Then he lifted a chain that hung round his neck, half hidden in the folds of his coat. On it hung the sign of Ama; a bronze disc, with a blazing corona of gold. He held it up and said, 'Before we begin, you must all kiss the sign of Ama. Kneel and ask for his blessing.'

Vixl and Ysa obeyed without question. Then it was my turn, but I hesitated.

'What's wrong?' said Ovinor. His voice was sharp and accusing. I tried to move forward, but I felt pegged to the floor. The thought of worshipping Ama, asking him anything, kissing his symbol – all sent my mind and body into revolt. It seemed hypocrisy of the deepest kind.

They were all looking at me. 'Come along,' said the Surgeon. 'You are keeping Jolitha waiting.'

And his stare was like an anchor, dragging me in. Numb, I kneeled and kissed the disc. I tasted the foul tang of metal. My lips curled and my mouth turned sour with revulsion, and my scalp shivered at the Surgeon's touch.

Then he turned and held the symbol to Jolitha and she kissed it where she sat, raising huge scared eyes to stare at him.

He pulled her hands further on to the table, and clamped shackles over her forearms. As he tightened the bolts that held the shackles to the table, Jolitha uttered a very faint sound and tried to pull back. The iron bands held her hard.

'Try to relax,' said the Surgeon. 'Try not to struggle.'

'Couldn't you at least give her a little wine?' I burst out.

The look Ovinor gave me could have cut out my heart. 'Do you think I do not know what I am doing? The more you interrupt, the longer you make this last for Jolitha.' He beckoned to the two men. 'You will sit on the bench on either side of her and hold her still. You must hold her *absolutely* still.'

Vixl and Ysa obeyed, uneasy but held in thrall by the Surgeon's presence.

'Stand behind her, Iolithie. Hold her head. And make sure she keeps this between her teeth.' From the opposite side of the table, he leaned across and put a small pad between Jolitha's lips.

Then he picked up a knife and made a deft, delicate cut around her conjoined forefingers.

Jolitha's body convulsed so hard that the table almost jumped off the floor. She screamed harshly through the gag.

I shut my own eyes tight, held on to Jolitha's head. I moved my hand to keep the gag in place. It slipped; Jolitha's teeth opened, and closed on my fingers instead. She bit me to the bone.

Her blood pooled wet and rich-red on the white cloth. Jolitha fought and we strained to hold her, all of us grunting with the effort, beginning to sweat despite the cold. We were all terrified of the surgeon's wrath if we dared to let her move. But the Surgeon took not the faintest notice of us. He continued his delicate work as if nothing existed above his patient's wrists.

Blood ran down Jolitha's chin, mixed with saliva. That came from my fingers, but I didn't make a sound.

'Notice the way I don't cut straight round,' Ovinor said matter of factly. 'I need to make flaps to fold over the fingertips, you see.'

Jolitha stiffened and writhed. She was utterly silent now, but sweat ran like pearls down her blanched face.

The Surgeon was cutting an S-shape around her forefingers and peeling back the skin. Then, holding her fingers in tongs, he selected a tiny saw and began to rasp through the little rod of raw bone.

Jolitha screamed again, at the very end of her breath. Mercifully, long before all four fingers and the thumbs were severed, she was unconscious.

By ingenious cutting, the Surgeon had left a little flap of flesh hanging loose on each finger. Now he folded each one back to cover the exposed bone-tip, and sewed it neatly in place. There was incredible craftsmanship in this grotesquery, I could see that. He knew exactly what he was doing.

Ysa bore it as long as he could, but halfway through the sewing he leapt up and ran out of the room, retching. Vixl did not move or react. And, for Jolitha's sake, I simply bore it, my own fingers torn and bleeding in sympathy.

The Surgeon cut the last stitch and sat back, dipping his hands in the bowl of water, long turned stone-cold. He glared at me. 'Well, bring some more hot, girl! I'll bandage her and then you can put her to bed.'

He leaned forward again and inspected his gory handiwork, nodding with satisfaction. 'A job well done, I think. She'll thank us all for this.'

But Jolitha hung so cold and heavy in our hands that I feared she had died of shock and pain.

CHAPTER TWELVE

THE FIRE AND THE BLOOD

When Lord Ovinor left, I refused to go with him. I told him I wanted to stay with Jolitha to make sure she recovered.

But he said, smiling, 'I shall come back in a few days to check the girl's progress. You can come with me then.'

I hoped he would never come back, but I daredn't say so. Wise, beautiful, authoritative – however fine his qualities, I loathed him.

Jolitha was recovering, physically at least, but she drifted through the days in a semi-trance, seeming indifferent to everything. When I re-dressed her hands, as Ovinor had instructed me, the fingertips were already healing well.

'That's good, isn't it?' I said, sitting beside her on her straw bed on the gallery. 'The pain will soon go and you'll be just like everyone else.'

'But I was never like everyone else,' Jolitha whispered. 'I don't want to be. It's not the pain. You don't understand.'

'What don't I understand?'

But Jolitha shook her head. 'You can't. No one can. Because I don't understand either . . .' And she stared down at her hands, which lay separate on her thighs, the fingers like thick white sausages. She sometimes stared at them for hours.

And I loathed Ovinor, because I knew, with a chilling soul-deep certainty, that the Surgeon had not cured her. He had destroyed her.

The days went by, and Jolitha got up and began to take part in the life of the farm again. But there was no light in her eyes any more. She moved like an old woman and when anyone spoke to her she took minutes to answer. Sometimes she did not respond at all. Vixl, Ysa and Jon began to skirt around her, uneasy and fearful. But no one dared to say that the operation had been a mistake.

As Jolitha's hands healed, she seemed to fade.

Once I found her in the dairy, trying to lift a bucket as she had used to do, hands linked underneath it. But the bucket slid straight between her hands and clattered on to the floor, spilling a blue-white foam of milk. Jolitha stood staring at me, her eyes filled with horror.

'I can do nothing now,' she said. 'I can lift nothing. Everything falls through my hands.'

'You shouldn't be doing that,' I said helplessly. 'It's too soon.'

'No.' Jolitha stood with her hands curled like dead things she couldn't control. 'There's no pain. But everything I had is lost.'

'You'll get used to it. Don't be sad. You have the healing touch.'

'No more,' Jolitha said flatly, turning away. 'I go to the sick animals and stroke them, but nothing happens. I feel no warmth, no light. I touch them but they don't get better. They never will again.'

I wanted to put my arms around her, warm her as she'd once warmed me, until she felt better; until she could smile again and say, 'Well, perhaps it will be all right.' But I couldn't. I knew she'd push me away, as Tykavn had; I couldn't bear the rejection. I knew I couldn't comfort her. Her pain was too deep, too personal to be reached – and I was the one who had invited the Surgeon into the house.

When someone you love is dying and there is nothing you can do to help them, how, how do you let them go?

Before two tendays were up, Lord Ovinor came back. He was on foot but dressed all in black and gold geitha, like an Arch-Perfect.

He was all smiles, delighted with Jolitha's recovery. He seemed utterly oblivious to her depression or her family's unease. When I tried to tell him how she dropped things now, he was stern. She must do no heavy work until the healing was absolutely complete; Vixl had had no business allowing her to lift buckets.

I couldn't get through to him how things really were. He smiled and said again and again how wonderfully successful the operation had been.

And no one dared to say he was wrong.

'Come, halla Iolithie,' said the Surgeon. 'Make ready to leave, and I will take you to the city.'

I wanted to protest violently. *'She's not better! You've destroyed her! I'm not going anywhere with you. I'm staying here to look after her!'* But I couldn't say it out loud. The point is, he *knew* what he'd done; he knew it, yet he smiled and smiled and said it was good. How do you fight that depth of evil?

The Surgeon, with his beautiful strong face and his steel-and-silver hair, dominated me completely. The feeling was intangible but ghastly. It was as if he was a shadow across the sun, sucking out all my will to resist.

So when he said, 'Time to go,' I obeyed. I didn't want to, but it was as if an invisible hand controlled me, body and mind. Numbly, I packed the few extra clothes the family had given me, took some cheese, meat and sausages. Then I stepped out into the yard, saw Ovinor waiting at the gate, and Jolitha a few yards from him, staring at him.

The morning was gloomy, steel-grey as a storm. Jolitha was a milk-pale window of light on the darkness; Ovinor a door into blackness. Their hair lifted on a cold breeze that came straight down off the glacier.

I approached the girl, feeling terrible, not knowing what to say. I would have done anything to stay with her. Why couldn't I? Was she less important than Tykavn? 'I have to leave now,' I said.

Jolitha turned to me. The blank, haunted look had not left her eyes since the operation.

'Don't go with him,' she said, low and urgent.

'I don't want to. I wish I could stay with you.'

'Don't go.'

My throat ached. Leaving Jolitha was as bad as losing Datha and Sigurthur. She'd saved me, healed me; and in return I had invited this man into the house, this knife-wielder who had severed Jolitha from her soul.

Ovinor said, 'Time to leave.'

This was my fault. I despised myself, but I couldn't resist the Surgeon's dark magnetism.

I said, 'I'm sorry, Jolitha. Thank you . . . for everything you did. I'm so sorry . . .'

But the words sounded hollow, and Jolitha's white face didn't change. As I went through the gate and followed Ovinor, the sky darkened and Jolitha seemed to blow away like paper on the wind.

The track to Onareyru was narrow and stony, winding between the roots of scrubby hills. No herbs grew here, only thin grass and grey lichens. Ovinor strode out and I struggled to match his pace. My legs ached and my chest was sore, but I seemed to be pulled along behind him like a ploughshare behind a horse.

No Unseen dwelled in Onafross; there were none of the herbs here that they needed. But I began to think that no humans lived here either. There were no signs of habitation, no goats on the hills. The darkness deepened. I'd never seen clouds so black, so gravid. Only the Surgeon seemed outlined by an eerie light, the silver streaks gleaming bright in his grey hair.

I walked in a state of suspended terror. Eventually I could bear the silence no longer.

'It's not even noon,' I said, 'so why is it so dark?'

Ovinor spun round and glared at me. His chiselled face no longer looked beautiful; it looked cruel and forbidding. 'You asked me to bring you, child! You chose to follow me.'

'How far is it to Onareyru?'

He did not answer, but he smiled. The smile was purely evil, terrifying. He marched on and I struggled to keep up.

When I dared to ask him to slow down he responded with harsh anger, all pretence of concern and humanity gone. I feared that if I spoke again he would kill me. Not swiftly, but slowly, with surgical precision. *For my own good.*

We walked down, down. Two gnarled white trees stood by the track, one on each side, their branches wound together as if in endless antagonism. They reminded me of Jolitha's hands. As we walked under the arch of their branches, I felt terror building up inside me beyond endurance.

'This isn't the way to Onareyru, is it?' I said.

'It is the road into light,' said the Surgeon, although darkness rolled over us. 'Look,' he said.

Away to our left, in a distant valley, I saw a phantom illumination, like sunlight slanting through a gap in a thunderstorm. There were flames flickering over the meadows, black ash whirling in blue smoke. The air rippled stiff as a gel with heat. Dust-red, Eldur blazed orange with fire.

I saw people fighting in the smoke. I heard their cries. I saw banners of gold and of purple, but these were not armies, only random groups of people. Those under the gold banners were mounted and robed like Perfects; those of the purple were on foot, being chased and driven into the fire. A wall of flame leapt up to consume them. I could no longer see them but I heard their wails of pain, the terrible screams that went on and on like Jolitha's pain . . .

Ovinor was laughing.

'Dear Ama, what's happening?' I cried.

'That which follows the Separation,' he said, a razor-smile in his voice.

The fire dwindled. The mounted party rode home victorious. They did not see the ghost creatures pursuing them from out of the ashes. Too late they turned to face a nothingness that was full of teeth and rending claws and knives. The flesh of their enemies had bubbled and crisped in the fire; now their own blood fell to douse the last embers . . .

The Surgeon's hands fell on my shoulders like axes, and I jumped violently. 'What do you see?' he hissed.

'People dying,' I said, sobbing.

'I call it life. The eternal conflict between the fire and the blood. Without it, what life is there?'

'But it's horrible.'

'But it's real,' he said, mocking my tone. 'Won't you come with me into life, Iolithie? Won't you open your hands and take what you want?'

Finally the terror blossomed like fire inside me. There was no logic to it, but when I looked at him I saw Ember.

I saw someone else, too, someone I didn't recognize. A faceless figure that watched me riding away from Torbyrgi . . .

I twisted and pulled out of his grasp. 'You've been following me, haven't you? You followed me across the glacier! Why? What are you?'

'You know my name. You've heard my name a thousand times.'

'No, I haven't.'

'I come from Vivirjosa.'

'That's impossible.'

'Do you know what the name Hendleiknir means, in the old tongue, when they used to call Onafross "Onyafrosa"?'

'It's the name of the Prophet.'

'But it means "healing hands",' he said, taking a step towards me. 'It means "surgeon".'

'You're no Prophet. I don't know what you are,' I said, backing away. 'No. Let me go.'

There was a big standing stone beside me. I backed round it, but he came after me. As he did so he opened his bag and felt around inside it – for a weapon, one of the surgical instruments he had used on Jolitha?

I reacted with a flash of deer-like instinct. He would expect me to run away. If I did, he'd catch me. So instead I rushed towards him.

I succeeded in taking him by surprise for one moment. As his hands came up to grab me, I seized the chain that hung round his neck and pulled it with all my might. It dug so deep into his flesh he grunted with pain. His eyes glittered white-hot with rage but I dared not let go now. Even as his hands closed on my arms I went on twisting it tighter and tighter.

He moved one hand, and I felt something sharp pressing into my back.

'Let go,' he rasped, 'or I'll cut you.'

A line of blood sprang out on his neck. Suddenly the chain broke. He gave a grunt of agonized rage. I was pressed against him but straining backwards, and in my right hand I held the symbol of Ama with the chain dangling from it.

His face was distorted, lips raised in a sneer of contempt. I felt the knife pricking my back through my clothes and I reacted, lightning-swift, in the only way I could. I drove the disc, with its corona of sharp metal spikes, straight into Ovinor's throat.

I caught him hard under the larynx, bruising and crushing his windpipe. His mouth opened but the merest rasp of pain emerged. Then he staggered back, blood spurting from his throat, and collapsed at my feet.

The blood sprayed me and I jumped back, wide-eyed. He hit his head as he fell and lay still, eyelids showing two slivers of white. I stood and stared at his dark form, spreadeagled at my feet like a sacrifice. Ama's golden sun stuck out of his throat.

I'd killed him. I couldn't believe it. The wave of shock and relief that poured through me was so powerful that it seemed to shake everything around me. But I was horrified, too; this was worse than destroying Ember, because this was stark and real.

A shadow in my mind; some dark unknown *thing* was pursuing me, and every time I destroyed it, it would come back again in a different form . . .

The world was shifting, as if a great weight had been lifted from it. Layers of darkness began to peel away, like veils going up into the air. One by one they lifted, and light glimmered beneath them. Colours scintillated. Ovinor-Ember-Hendleiknir –

161

whatever he was – lay stretched out at my feet, a dark flat shape . . .

The increasing brightness dazzled me. Pure daylight, so suddenly! I squinted skywards, saw the inferno of the sun blazing down. When I looked down again, I saw the standing stone protruding from the ground, and a sharp black shadow that the sun threw from the rock to my feet. Ama's shadow. The words of the Prophet's story reverberated. *Ama threw a shadow upon the ground and from the shadow he made a man who would walk in the night where Ama could not go* . . .

There was no corpse. Where Ovinor had fallen there was only the shadow in his shape.

I turned and fled. I ran, sobbing for breath, until I could run no more.

The fjord was wide as a lake, shimmering azure blue. The hills that rose on either side were palest green, dappled with ochre and rust-pink as light and shade moved across them. Rooted in the peaks on both sides, a thick roll of cloud spanned the river like a bridge.

I sat on the hillside, my knees drawn up and my elbows resting on them, looking down at the city on the opposite side of the fjord. Onareyru was not at all what I'd expected. With its white houses and bright red roofs, it looked the most friendly and welcoming sight I'd ever seen.

But I stayed on the hillside, where I'd been for two hours or more. My legs were shaking so much I could barely stand. I desperately missed the deer's ability to run and run; my flight from Ovinor had left me drained and aching all over.

At some stage I'd collapsed in the lee of a cliff and slept. My memories of that time are hazy. I'd woken at dawn; found the world still in its normal guise; eaten some of my food and walked wearily on.

I had then found myself not on a stony goat-track but on a proper slabbed road. There had even been a milestone and a sign to Onareyru. With renewed hope, I'd walked all morning until, in the spring afternoon, I saw the city below me.

I'm safe now, I thought. *The sun is shining, I'm nearly there, no one can touch me here.* But I'd thought the farm was safe, too. I had thought Ovinor was a safe person.

I looked down at my hands. There were still pink scars where Jolitha had bitten my fingers in her agony. Nothing to the scars

Jolitha bore. And now these hands had killed someone . . .

Did it count, to kill a demon? If Ovinor had been sent by the Unseen, would they come after me to take revenge? Questions had haunted me all the way here. The only good thing was that I was too tired to feel afraid any more.

But if he was a man, I've committed murder . . . But when the light came back, he wasn't there! Was he real? Of course he was, you fool! Look what he did to Jolitha!

The corpse had seemed to vanish, but there was still blood spattered down my shirt, blood under my fingernails.

I wasn't sorry I'd killed him. There was a little thread of hardness inside me that had never been there before. I thought, *I'd do it again. He would have killed me, or worse. That darkness . . . where was he taking me?* It was like the stories, the Prophet going down the path into Sudema's realm, wearing Ama's sign. But the Prophet was meant to be the most Perfect man who ever lived, not evil. Sudema trying to kill my ailing faith by trickery? My thoughts churned round and round. Nothing made sense.

The one thing that truly hurt was that I couldn't pray. I longed to offer my soul up for guidance. I'd hoped that, away from Tykavn, I would find my way back to Ama eventually – but not now. Ama had betrayed me. There was no god I dared trust.

I flexed my grimy, scarred fingers. I remembered how it felt to trust my own instincts completely; I'd lived a whole season in an animal's shape and mind. That hadn't brought wisdom . . . but freedom from human confusion, at least.

I drew myself to my feet, brushed the grass off my breeches, and set foot on the road that led down the gorge. I wasn't going to give up, not while I still lived.

A land-bridge lay across the water, and there were a few people coming and going across it, some on foot and some on horseback. They looked clean and well-fed; their split-skirts, coats, shawls and hats were of a similar style to those of Torlossen, but made of finer mohair and sleeker goat-hide. I became horribly aware of my own wretched appearance. I was dirty from travelling, and the threadbare rough clothes that Jolitha had given me bore little resemblance to anything these people wore – even those who were obviously farmers. My long hair was a mess, my shirt stained with sweat and droplets of blood. People glanced at me in distaste as I passed, but no one spoke.

As I reached the edge of Onareyru and stood looking at the

white walls gleaming in the sun and the narrow stone-paved streets that ran between them, a man approached me. He was dressed in bright blue, and it took me a moment to realize that he was a Perfect-Minister.

'Are you all right, halla?'

He spoke kindly enough, but I trusted no one now. From his expression his intention was to get this ragged outcast off the streets with all speed. I drew away.

'Yes,' I said.

'But where are you going? Perhaps I can help . . .'

'I'm looking for the Palace.'

He looked dumbfounded, as if he couldn't believe I didn't know where it was. 'At the top of the hill, above the town. But—'

I was away from him, and running. Where I found the stamina, I don't know. But no Perfect was going to stop me!

I found my way on to a broader street that led straight up the hill. A sign informed me that this was King Lor's Way, and above me I could see white walls with foliage massing over them and trailing down their sides. There was a golden roof, with a huge sun-symbol shining above it. Below the symbol, the roof was forested with crests and banners, with stylized trees and animals, all fashioned out of gold. But as I went closer it sank out of sight behind the forbidding white wall.

In the wall, facing the end of King Lor's Way, I saw a monumental pair of gates, decorated in turquoise, blue and gold. Nothing could be seen through them. There was the huge aureate disc again, one half on each gate, a holy sign to ward off unwelcome creatures. Did that include me, grubby and so deeply contaminated by Sudema I'd never be clean again?

I stopped and stared disconsolately at the gates. Well, I had reached the Palace; but how on Eileah was I to get in? If I demanded to see the King, what would they do but laugh and send me on my way?

A darker thought wormed through me. If a miracle happened and they let me into his presence, should I mention that I had murdered the royal surgeon on my way here? I pressed a hand to my head. Damn it to Kvold! It was for their son's sake I was here and in this state.

Simple. I'd bang on the gate. Insist the guards let me speak to a Palace official. I had the proof of who I was in my palm.

I approached the gate, lost my nerve, and went straight past. Ahead of me, a goat-drawn cart crossed my path and vanished round the corner of the white wall, accompanied by three young female Sublimes on foot. Strangely, their dress was almost as drab as mine, and the cart was packed with a mass of swaying foliage.

When I reached the corner, I saw a sign on the wall that said 'By Royal Order, the citizens of Onareyru will enter the Gardens of Lor Palace by the side gates only'.

My heart hammered. Suddenly I was excited, not afraid. Turning the corner, I saw the Sublimes and the goat-cart ahead of me and I hurried to catch them up, trying to look as if I was with them, while not actually attracting their attention. One of the women glanced at me but looked away without reacting. Onareyru didn't seem to suffer the insatiable nosiness of Vryatan. The side street was bounded on my left by the Palace wall, on my right by low red-roofed houses.

Fifty yards along, a gate of golden metal-work stood open, and the Sublimes went through unchallenged. I followed them, and found myself in a vast garden that took my breath away.

I'd never seen such a place before; the only 'gardens' in Torlossen are scrubby vegetable patches. But here were vast expanses of grass, plants growing in profusion with huge flowers nodding on their stems. And the growth wasn't random but composed like a tapestry in velvet-green and jewel-colours. There were trees everywhere, with white and grey branches and tiny glittering leaves.

In the middle, half concealed by trees and shrubs, was Lor Palace, its roof glinting like fire between the leaves. Nothing was as I'd imagined. I'd heard only the vaguest descriptions of Onareyru, and I'd still visualized it as a covered city like Torlossen, only ten times bigger and more magnificent. But the houses were all separate, and the Palace itself was an unexpectedly simple building of grey shale, long and three-storeyed, the top windows protruding from the roof amid the golden menagerie.

And ordinary people were walking about in all this glory, in twos and threes, enjoying this extravagance which had no purpose but to look beautiful. There were guard-Sublimes at the gates, wearing uniforms of intricately patterned leather and armed with staves, but they were doing no more than keeping a relaxed eye on things.

I shouldn't have been surprised, I suppose. We have no internal enemies in Torlossen or Onafross – only the threat from the Unseen. I was half in love with Onareyru already, its mild sunny weather and its air of peace.

I followed the goat-cart along a path which wound behind the Palace through huge flower beds. The mystery of the Sub-limes' dull clothing and cart-load of greenery was solved; they were gardeners. On an impulse, I hung back until I was sure no one was watching me and pulled a small shrub from a bed, roots and all. Carrying it, I felt I looked official.

The Sublimes went through a small gate in an inner wall, a private garden within the main one. There was a guard there. I walked briskly, looking straight ahead, the shrub clutched to me and shedding earth all down my breeches. I held my breath, but all he did was nod as I passed through.

Within, there were banks of shrubs and trees rising in tiers up the hillside, criss-crossed by walkways. I lost sight of the gar-deners and climbed faster, unsure which path they'd taken. When I came in sight of them again, they'd halted on a path by a stretch of freshly dug earth and were unloading the cart. They were watched by two elderly men leaning on spades, and a tall yellow-haired woman.

I stopped dead, but they'd seen me. The woman waved at me to come to her and to be quiet; she was inspecting every shrub as it was unloaded, talking non-stop – 'Is this really the healthiest one Gudryr could send? It's rather straggly. Never mind, we'll nurse it along; put it further back, behind the stronger ones, so that if it doesn't thrive it won't leave too much of a gap,' – so the Sublimes had no chance to point out that I was not meant to be there. Or perhaps they assumed I was.

Ama, I'm glad I had those few minutes to think. I didn't recognize the woman at once because the portraits I'd seen showed a much younger, more waif-like being. In the flesh she was tall, thick featured and well built, with a mass of straw-coloured hair and a natural air of authority. There was nothing haughty about her. People would still have jumped to attention if she'd been a Sublime or even Unstatused.

I was sure she was Queen Raunigia, Tykavn's mother.

This was so easy, yet so terrifying.

Presently she finished sorting out the contents of the cart and turned to me. 'Well, what have you brought me, dear? Some-thing special?'

I stepped forward. She was so intent on the bush in my arms that I didn't like to interrupt her. 'Oh yes,' she said, turning its little leaves over to inspect the undersides. 'This is a very nice Vaxa. Mature, too. It's very like the one I've got down by the side of the Palace. I wonder where to put it because they're so fussy . . .' She frowned suddenly. 'Wait a moment, this *is* my Vaxa. I'd recognize it anywhere. Are you trying to sell me my own plants?'

She glanced round at the Sublimes, who started edging away as if to disown me. They looked mortified. I was going to be in a great deal of trouble unless I explained, fast.

I did the first thing that occurred to me. I opened my left hand, wiped it on my leg, and held my palm out to the Queen. She looked at it and her face changed. 'Ama's Light above!' she gasped. She seized my hand and rubbed her thumb across the Sun-and-Eileah symbol as if to wipe it off. 'How did you get this?'

'The Perfect-Minister gave it to me, Your Majesty,' I said softly, 'the morning after I married your son.'

It was very unfair of me, to give her such a shock. I suppose I did the wrong thing, as usual. But it worked. With immense composure she lifted the shrub from my arms, set it down on the earth and turned to her bemused gardeners with a thin, fixed smile. 'If you would excuse me,' she said. She put an arm round my shoulders and guided me swiftly away down the path. What-ever revelations I was about to unleash on her, she was deter-mined it wouldn't be witnessed by lesser Statuses.

She gave me no chance to speak until we were safely inside the Palace. She propelled me through a side-door into a long narrow hall, where tapestries of the legends of Ama brightened the dark walls. When she turned to me, her face was absolutely grey with shock.

'Who are you, girl?'

'Iolithie Gaefir-daughter. I'm Prince Tykavn's wife.'

'But where are your outriders, your attendants, your horses? Where is Tykavn? Why are you in this state?'

Then I realized why she was so agitated. Her immediate thought must have been that, like Lady Antrid's party, we'd been attacked by the Unseen and I was the only survivor.

'Your Majesty, please forgive me,' I said, bowing my head. 'Tykavn is in Torlossen. I came here alone.'

'Completely alone?' she said in disbelief.

'I've had a very difficult journey and I didn't know how to

reach the King or yourself without being turned away by some petty official.'

'My dear,' she said faintly, 'any citizen of Onafross may speak to us if they have good cause. If you are our daughter-in-law . . . But I don't understand. Why are you here? What's wrong?'

Ama, how I was shaking. Not with fear, but with desperation to make my case, to get the help Tykavn needed.

'Tykavn is ill. No one in Torlossen can help him. He needs the King's Physician, but I couldn't make anyone—'

'Ill?' she said sharply. 'In what way?'

'Since the Lady Antrid died, he's blamed himself. He was making himself ill, with guilt; he was breaking down before my eyes. But—'

'Not physically ill,' said Raunigia. She pressed her lips together, looked at me, both upset and thoughtful at once. I could see Tykavn in her.

'He wasn't eating or sleeping properly when I left. But it's taken me all winter to get here. I couldn't travel any faster—'

'And was he praying a great deal?'

'Praying?' I said. 'I couldn't make him stop. He was possessed, destroying himself . . .'

The Queen looked away from me, closing her eyes briefly. She didn't want to hear this about her son. 'All winter? Tykavn must have chosen the toughest woman in Torlossen as his bride. Well.' Her thoughts made minimal changes to her thick-featured, strong face; she was distressed and bemused, but mastering herself. 'Well, the news you bring is a season old; no one has come more recently from Tykavn to say that anything is amiss. I think, my dear, that you need a long rest before you will be in a frame of mind to explain this to us properly.'

The Queen sent two female Sublimes to attend on me while I bathed, to bring me fresh clothes and a meal. There were delicious foods I'd never seen in Torlossen, and the silken geitha felt gorgeous on my skin. It was pure physical paradise; enough to soothe the discomforts of my mind, for a time.

The room was on the Palace's second floor, overlooking the gardens. The walls were ash-dark, but the floor was of pale golden wood, and light fell in rainbows through a stained-glass window. The combination of darkness and melting light was beautiful. The furniture was sparse; a bed and a few chairs, a loom, a harp, simple but exquisitely made. Outside the crystal window, birds chirped loudly. The sound was sweet and reassuring. I lay down on the bed and drifted half asleep for a long time. It was so peaceful here. I dreamed I was riding back towards Torlossen with a huge party from the Palace, all of us fired by my concern for Tykavn; riding urgently to bring him help, while in their midst I felt the exquisite relief of being justified in everything I had done.

The Sublimes came back later to wake me and comb my newly washed hair, making me presentable to receive the Queen again. When Raunigia came in, she dismissed the two Sublimes and turned to gaze at me.

'So you are the one Tykavn took instead of Antrid,' she said. Her blonde hair, though dressed in elaborate loops, had a dishevelled look, and her strong, plain face had a tendency to pinkness. She looked me over, then turned away. 'Messengers reached us six tendays after the Lady Antrid's party set out for Torlossen,' she went on quietly. 'They said that she had been slain by the Unseen. We were all distraught, not least her father. Antrid was a sweet girl, much loved. However, the messenger also informed us that my son had decided to find a wife in Torlossen itself so that no one else's life would be put at risk.' Raunigia moved to the window-seat and looked out over the gardens and the town beyond the Palace wall. 'Sensible of him. Noble, I suppose.'

I wasn't sure how to interpret the Queen's tone. She sounded pensive, more concerned with her own feelings than with my presence. I said, 'Lady Antrid's death was a great shock to us, too. I could never aspire to replace her. I was greatly honoured when Lord Tykavn asked me to be his wife, and I could only hope to do my utmost to support and comfort him . . .' My voice faded. The words seemed a mockery of themselves. He'd found no comfort in me at all. The memories were sour blows; his rages, his violence, the distress within him that was too terrible to be soothed . . .

'You seem a nice enough girl,' said the Queen. 'But you must realize how irregular your presence here is. Princes' wives simply do not . . .' She shook her head. There were footsteps outside. 'My husband, my eldest son and the Physician Lord Breithir are coming to see you. Lord Breithir is Lady Antrid's father, as you know.'

I hadn't known. Thank Ama she told me, one second before the three men came into the room.

I stood up and bowed. I was in the presence of King Vidvikjan himself; it was much less awe-inspiring than I'd anticipated.

They greeted me politely, with a sort of embarrassed delicacy. Only Tykavn's brother, heir to the throne, smiled. He bore a close resemblance to Tykavn, except that his hair was receding and he was clean-shaven. I assessed him in a moment, and I don't think I was wrong; a cheerful, flippant, very masculine man, with little understanding of other's weaknesses. Sensing he wouldn't be of much help, I concentrated on the King and Lord Breithir.

Vidvikjan had a bald pate, circled by a ring of wild white hair; a sharp-boned face, imprinted with introspection and long years of responsibility. It struck me he was in rather fragile health.

But it was to the Physician that I looked with hope. Solid, serious, with curly grey hair and a woolly beard, he looked understanding. His blue eyes were like the ones that had haunted me in dreams; Antrid's eyes.

'The Queen has told us the circumstances of your arrival,' said Breithir. 'Would you like to see a Perfect-Minister, before you speak to us?'

That was the last thing I needed! 'No, no, I'd rather explain everything to you.'

'Good. You say Prince Tykavn is ill . . .'

This moment was so important. It was what I'd risked my life for, again and again. But I was safe here, I was with people who'd listen.

I began to explain Tykavn's condition, dredging it all from my memory before the strange time with Sigurthur and Bronze had begun. His worsening rituals, his distress, his emaciation. It was a difficult thing to put into words, especially with Breithir's critical intelligence silently dissecting everything I said. But I thought I described it eloquently. I didn't mention that Tykavn had hit me or even shouted at me; I described only his anguish, not mine. All the mistakes I'd made with Lassastiuk, I tried to rectify.

A few minutes in, Vidvikjan sat back in his chair and began to drum his fingers on the arm. I paused, but ploughed on. Occasionally they would all glance at each other, exchanging secret communication without words. Like Judge-Perfects, they seemed, absorbing and weighing information without any kind of involvement or emotion. The longer I spoke, the colder I felt inside.

To my shock, long before I was near the end, the King stood up and left the room.

I was dumbfounded. As I faltered, the Queen and Tykavn's brother also rose and left, as if they felt bound to go after him. Only Breithir remained.

'Please go on,' he said gently.

I could hardly demand to know where the King had gone. Trying to recover the thread, I finished the tale, describing with bitter passion how everyone around me had refused to help. I didn't mention my journey at all.

When I came to the end, though, I didn't feel unburdened. Only drained. I'd expected sympathy, passionate concern, instant action. Instead there was only a strained, almost indifferent silence.

The Physician mused on my story. I felt a cloistered Palace atmosphere creeping into me, a sense that everything was available – except freedom. A sense of truth being shut out with the rest of the world.

'There are one or two questions I need to ask,' he said. 'Why did you make this journey alone?'

'Because no one would help me.'

'Surely the fact that no one would help you indicated that no help was needed? You seem to have acted very rashly.'

I almost laughed. 'Rashly? Only because I was desperate!'

'But how on Eileah did you survive?'

'I – I had a good horse. We were lucky almost until we reached the Border, then the Unseen came after us and I lost him . . .' Only half a lie. The journey was irrelevant. All that mattered was Tykavn.

He pressed his fingers together – like Jolitha – but he wouldn't quite meet my eyes. I said, 'Don't you believe me? Tykavn needs your help!'

Breithir sighed. 'You seem to have come here expecting an instant answer, Iolithie. But this is a very complex matter. I could ask myself, why did you survive the Stolen Land alone, when my daughter, with an armed escort, died? Why are you married to the man who should have been *her* husband? But it is my job, as a physician, to be impersonal about this. If anything was really amiss, an official message should have reached us long before.'

'But they wouldn't have sent a message, because no one else would believe he was ill! That's the whole point.'

He leaned forward. 'The point is, no official word has been sent. That makes this very difficult.'

'You can't not believe me!'

'I didn't say that. All I am trying to say is that I can't give you an immediate judgement. I am going to discuss what you have told me with the King, and come back to you with his decision. Until then, be patient. Relax and don't worry.'

I couldn't relax and I wasn't reassured. As soon as he'd gone I went in search of Queen Raunigia. Security in the Palace was informal, and no one tried to hinder me.

I made a sensible guess, and found Queen Raunigia at one of the flower beds, cutting back the stems of a bush with what appeared to be unnecessary savagery. As I approached her, she glanced in my direction then went on with her work, saying, 'They have to be pruned back or they go wild.'

She wiped her forehead, leaving a streak of soil on her skin. I don't think any amount of dirt or sweat would have made her look less regal. Strangely, I liked her. Or I could have done if it hadn't been for what was happening.

'Your Majesty,' I said quietly, 'the King and yourself didn't listen to my whole story.'

'We didn't need to. It's only what we already knew. Aren't these flowers lovely?' She bent down to a clump of white blooms, sniffing them, stroking their soft petals.

She really didn't want to listen. 'You knew Tykavn was ill?'

'He's not ill.' She went on inspecting and trimming her plants all the time she was speaking. 'What you described . . . He's always been like that.'

I was astonished. 'Always?'

There was a touch of irritation in her tone; not with me, I realized, but with Tykavn. 'He was strange as a little boy. Not content to be ordinary like his brother. There were certain doors he wouldn't go through, certain paths he wouldn't take. If we tried to make him, he'd panic until he thought his own heart was going to stop. It wasn't, of course. He often had to say his prayers twice, just to be sure. Silly things like that, hundreds of them. It was a foolishness I thought he'd grow out of.'

'But he hasn't. It's not foolish. It's deadly serious.'

'It's something he could stop if he wanted to!' she said brusquely. 'He should take more exercise. If he had a child, of course . . .' Her gaze touched me, accusing. 'There's no time for that sort of nonsense when you've children to look after.'

172

'Ma'am, he looks after a whole country. It makes no difference. He wants to stop but he *can't*!'

'Of course he can!' Raunigia turned on me, her hair dishevelled, her pruning blade held like a weapon. Her temper, like Tykavn's, had a truly frightening quality to it. 'There's nothing wrong with him that he couldn't put right if he wanted to. He needs a wife to make him pull himself together, not one who indulges him then runs away. A strong wife.'

Her words sliced deeper than the knife could have done. 'How strong do I have to be?' I cried. 'You're the strongest woman I've ever met; how much notice did he take of you?'

She sawed brutally at a twig, splitting and tearing it. Her face was rigid, but her eyes glittered. 'It's beyond me. Why must you harp on about it when you know there's nothing to be done?' she said. 'It's beyond my control.'

The next morning, as soon as I was up and dressed, Breithir came to see me again.

'His Majesty and I have talked over what you have told us,' he said, courteous but distant. 'After careful consideration, I'm afraid we've both come to the conclusion that you've had a wasted journey.'

'What do you mean?'

'Everyone you've spoken to has assured you that there is nothing actually wrong with Prince Tykavn, haven't they? That what you describe as his extreme piety is merely an aspect of character that he's always possessed?'

'But he—'

'Answer yes or no.'

'Yes,' I said. A sense of helplessness was creeping over me.

'I know you disregarded what you were told – even by Arch-Perfect Laasastiuk himself – with what you thought were your husband's best interests at heart. But I think you must realize now that you should have listened to those who are more experienced than yourself, and better acquainted with the Prince.'

His obduracy floored me completely. 'I don't know what else to say to make you believe me. You haven't seen the distress he's in!'

'A period of agitation and mourning is natural after a death,' he said, lowering his eyes. 'I went through it too. It is natural, also, for one of Tykavn's strong faith to call on Ama to help him

173

through it. If he married too hastily it was your duty to appreciate that and tolerate his more extreme behaviour with patience and forbearance.'

I'm only surprised he didn't add, *As my perfect daughter Antrid would have done.*

'You're wrong.'

He looked sternly at me. He was seeing me as a misguided and naïve female; nothing I said or did would shake his point of view. Tykavn's parents had shifted the entire burden on to him, and this was how he discharged it. 'I don't think so, Iolithie.'

'What are you going to do?'

'Nothing,' he said. 'There is nothing to be done.'

'After I've come all this way?' I cried. I shed tears, I'm ashamed to admit. I could have killed him as I'd killed Ovinor, set the Palace on fire and burned them all for their blindness, their indifference.

'I'm sorry you have had a wasted journey,' he said blandly. 'I'll give you some wine to calm you down.'

As if I were upset for no reason! I scrubbed the tears away. 'Perhaps my father-in-law the King would at least lend me a horse and a guard for the journey home.'

He looked uneasy. 'Ah . . . we have discussed that, and in fact we all feel it would be best if you remained in Onareyru, at least until we have informed Prince Tykavn of your whereabouts. You'll be very comfortable here. We cannot simply let you ride out into the Stolen Land. I would never have let Antrid go, if I'd known . . .'

He stood up, ending the meeting. As he turned to leave, I said. 'Lord Breithir, are you the King's only doctor?'

'Why do you ask?'

'I . . . I once heard that he had a surgeon as well. A man called Lord Ovinor.'

He shook his head. 'Someone misled you, my dear. I attend to all the King's medical needs. There is no one named Ovinor here.'

When I had finished beating my pillow in frustration I sat on the bed and thought.

Someone had followed me all the way to Onafross. Some*thing* that took different shapes . . . Ember, chasing Datha across the glacier. And then Ovinor, who was no royal surgeon. What was it – and *why*?

Now I felt the darkness tightening around me again. Their smiles did not reach their eyes; their eyes were so narrow, so glass-slippery, that smiles would slide off like light off frozen pebbles. There were breathing silences under their honey words.

I was getting quite good at reading between the lines.

When they saw me, they saw – as Laasastiuk had – a girl who had forfeited her nobility by being born in a village, growing up like a farmer's daughter. My father might be the King's cousin, but he had got his hands dirty. I could never compare with the beautiful, the high-born Lady Antrid, who had been Tykavn's true intended. I was a second-rate replacement, a usurper, a nothing. I'd had the ill-judgement to make a journey all alone across the Stolen Land, the bad taste to *survive*, the effrontery to come begging for help. And, worst of all, I had dared to suggest that a son of the Blood Royal might not be right in the head.

So incapable were they of admitting it that they had sent him all the way to Torlossen, to rid themselves of the problem. And I had brought it right back to their door.

Breithir's daughter had died and I had taken her place. He hated me for it, naturally.

Everything I had done was unforgivable.

They weren't going to let me go home. They were going to keep me here for my 'own good'. And they were not going to send any help to Tykavn!

They'd send a message to Laasastiuk, asking for the truth about Tykavn. The reply would be, 'There is nothing wrong with the Prince and never has been. His devotion to Ama sustains him in his duties. I will continue to pray with him, and for him.' I could just imagine the smug pomposity of it.

No one knew where I was. As an unsuitable, undesirable wife, I could simply ... *disappear*. Indeed, hadn't I disappeared more than a season ago?

I sat shivering, knees bent up, arms wrapped round myself.

I saw the mistake I had made. I shouldn't have told the truth.

I should have pretended that there was a big official party and I was the only survivor. They needn't have found out the truth until we reached Torlossen – and once they saw Tykavn, they might have appreciated why I'd lied.

All lost, for want of a simple lie.

I jumped off the bed. One thing I knew; I wasn't staying here to be patronized, cosseted, murdered – whatever they thought they could do to me. I'd go now, while the doors were still unlocked.

I'd rather have spurned their charity, but they'd thrown away my dirty farm-drabs, and the fresh clothes they'd lent me would at least prove to Tykavn – if necessary – that I had been to Onareyru. Over my fine striped split-skirts I put on a coat of warm red geitha, a black shawl trimmed with gold, the matching belt, hat and goat-skin boots.

I don't think they expected me just to get up and leave. But then, they didn't know me very well. They didn't know me at all.

CHAPTER THIRTEEN

THE GATE TO KVOLD

I was going back to the farm. Back to Jolitha.

If I couldn't help Tykavn, I thought, at least I could help her. We'd help each other. Somehow.

From Onareyru I walked back exactly the way I had come, across the fjord, along the slabbed road that led east between the hills. I walked all that day, and the next; I was expecting the road to fizzle out at any time into the stony goat track that led to the farm. But the third morning broke, and the road went on, winding broad and clear ahead of me.

Anxious, I stopped several times to take my bearings. The hills were familiar; I was certain I was going the right way. I simply knew that the last time I had passed this way – with Ovinor – *this road had not been here.*

The stone surface was weather-pocked and worn by cart wheels, with mosses and wildflowers crusting the slabs. It had been here for many, many years.

The landscape felt different in other ways too. When I'd been with Ovinor it had seemed barren, deserted, but grass now rippled on the lower slopes, goats grazed, and there were a couple of farmsteads that I didn't remember seeing before. They weren't like Vixl's farm, roofed with turf; they were white cottages tiled with red, like the houses of Onareyru. The sky was a tranquil veil of aquamarine.

I had felt that the Surgeon was taking me into some dark realm that wasn't quite part of this world. If that was so – and I didn't altogether believe it – how was it that the contours of this landscape and that were identical?

Some time later, on a stretch of grass to my right, I saw the standing stone where I had killed Ovinor. The sight of it turned my guts to ice. I half expected its shadow to spring into three dimensions and come soaring after me. Nothing happened; the stillness seemed to consume me. I can't put into words how strange I felt, how alone. If only I had a companion I could trust. But I'd never really trusted anyone except Datha.

Further on, I saw the two white trees that had arched over the track. They clasped each other's branches no longer; one was black and hollow, the other a stump. Lichen lay thick on the road's surface here, as if for years no one had travelled beyond the last farm I had passed. A few yards on, a milestone protruded from the ground.

I ran to it, eager to see what it could tell me. The distance between Onareyru and the eastern border once had been crudely scored through and a somber message carved below.

'Good disciples of Ama, be Warned. East of this stone Thandarkyr is Stolen. Go no further.'

I ignored the warning and went on. I could see that it wasn't far to the farm, because its immediate surroundings had become as familiar to me as my own home. Recognizing them, I broke into a run. My heart was leaping.

A minute later I skidded to a halt. I think I cried out 'NO!'

That's the essence of dread. Fearing the worst doesn't deaden the hellish moment of revelation; it only sharpens it.

Where the farm had been, there was nothing.

At first glance I could see no trace of it at all. There was only the low green hill and the flat area in front where the yard had been. Dazed, making unconscious faint noises of denial, I drifted towards it. As I did so I began to see evidence that I hadn't been dreaming and wasn't in the wrong place. The yard wall was delineated by a ridge of stone, barely above ground level, crusted with years of lichen and moss. There was a discoloured oblong patch where the dairy had been. All that was left of the cottages were ghost shapes in the side of the hill, as if the structure had slowly collapsed, been assimilated into the ground and overgrown. But my eyes translated the faint undulations into the five roof-ridges I remembered.

A farm *had* stood here once. Countless years ago.

I almost wept, but the emotion, the disbelief, stayed shut inside me.

Only days ago, I was here, I thought. 'Days!' I said aloud.

I stepped over the wall-ridge and scuffed at the grass with my foot. If I dug down, I would probably find the bones of chickens in the soil. Other bones, too?

The people who'd lived here ... 'Jolitha,' I whispered. Dear Ama, whatever had become of her?

A white streak in the corner of my eye. I turned, heart thumping. There was nothing there, but in my mind's eye I saw Jolitha standing by the gate, saying, 'Don't go with him!' Jolitha, white as a candle; a candle that Ovinor had snuffed out.

And I asked him in. I shut my eyes.

Had I just stepped years into the future? Or had Vixl's farm existed centuries in the past?

I dredged my mind for clues. They'd called Onafross 'Onyafrosa'; they'd known of no city called Onareyru, and hadn't known what I meant by the 'Stolen Land'. Perhaps life in Thandarkyr hadn't changed greatly over the ages, but I'd put the subtle differences of speech and dress down to their culture . . . not to time.

I felt sick and dizzy with the impossibility of it. When had I passed through? It must have been some time between leaving the glacier and being found by Jolitha . . . perhaps at the moment I changed back into human form. Or before that. When Datha had disappeared?

And when had I returned to my own time? That was easy. The moment that I'd killed Ovinor; that was the moment when the whole world had seemed to change around me, and the clouds had peeled away, and the road appeared . . .

'I don't want this,' I said bitterly. I started to run, past the green mounds and the lines of stone. I shouted to whatever gods would listen, 'I don't understand it and I don't want it!'

I ran through the meadows until I passed the place where the outer fence of the farm had stood. The gap where Jolitha had led me through the gate was still marked by the stump of the lone tree, the first real tree I'd ever seen. Its absence meant something to me. I kneeled down by it, shaking with a grief I couldn't express.

This was the border between Onafross and the Stolen Land. I didn't know what to do now. There was no Sigurthur to transform me into a deer, no Jolitha to help me. If I couldn't go back to Tykavn with some way to help him, I felt I couldn't go back at all. And if I went back into the Stolen Land, I wouldn't survive anyway.

I couldn't bear to remain here, though. Go back to the nearest farm, ask for work and shelter; that would have been the sensible thing to do. But there seemed no sense in the world, and certainly none within me.

I looked up and saw the glacier rimming the horizon, forbidding and frigid-white. While spring charmed the lower country, it was always winter on the glacier. If I went there now it would kill me; but I had been happy there, for a time. I had danced with Datha under the stars.

So I walked back into the Stolen Land. I went towards the glacier as darkness fell and felt the cold wind streaming down off its sides.

I wasn't unafraid. I was numb with fear. But the compulsion overrode self-preservation. I think I was still looking for someone; I was looking for an answer, even if the only answer I found was death.

'Jolitha,' I said, under my breath. Then the pain welled up and I shouted, 'Jolitha!'

My own voice startled me, but the stillness that folded down afterwards was worse. The darkness breathed in and out. It moved. It began to follow me. And a voice said, '*Iolithie.*'

There are worse things than death, I knew then. There's the terror of an enemy who comes back again and again when you thought you'd destroyed him; the horror of anticipating his revenge. And worst of all, not knowing what he was, or why he pursued me . . .

Did Ama really send shadows into the night to seek out those who'd offended him?

I turned in my tracks. I was going back into Onafross, before I froze, before I went mad with fear.

As I turned, I saw a face on the darkness in front of me. An elongated face half drawn in silver dust, floating. Terror squeezed the blood black across my eyes. Two starbursts of violet light rested coldly on me; the eyes of an Unseen creature, not Unseen now but half seen, just as in those moments when Sigurthur had transformed me and I had seen with a deer's vision.

It knew my name.

Something Sigurthur had told me surfaced from the back of my mind. I knew I couldn't run from this thing. Instead I fell to my knees and bowed my head, offering my exposed neck, offering my life.

'I don't know whether you can understand me,' I said, 'but I don't worship Ama. I don't give a damn about their stupid god or your stupid goddess, or the disgusting things everyone does in their names. If you're going to kill me, do it! Only please do it quickly. That's all I ask.'

The face went on looking at me. Tendrils of hair floated from the crown of its head. There seemed something maddeningly familiar about the features. Then the face tilted a little to one side and the soft male voice said again. 'Iolithie.'

The voice, too, I half recognized. Madness threatened and I almost screamed, 'Why are you doing this? Stop, please stop!'

The face drifted nearer and the voice filled my ears. 'Iolithie, don't be afraid. I know this is hard for you to understand. Imagine how *I* felt! I've been searching for you for a long time.'

'Why? What do you want? I never meant to—' I was confused. I was so sure it must be Ember-Ovinor in another form, but the voice was striking different notes in my mind.

'Don't you know me? I can't blame you. Look at me, don't be afraid.'

I was looking. I simply couldn't believe what I thought I saw. He said, 'I'm not your enemy, and I'm not going to hurt you. Before you look at me with such incredulity, remember that you too have been in another form; only my transformation is rather different, and it is for ever. But let's be clear; whom do I sound like?'

'Sigurthur,' I said. 'But he died.'

The violet eyes seemed to narrow as if with a smile. 'No. I didn't die. The last I saw of you was a clean pair of hindfeet disappearing over the rim of Laufi's window. I know it's a shock to you. There was no way I could approach you without it being a shock; but come along, my friend, this isn't the first fright I've given you. You should be used to it by now. How do you rate this against the waterfall; better, or worse?'

That sounded like Sigurthur. It truly did. 'Worse,' I said. I was halfway between laughing and crying. 'But how can it be you? What happened?'

'Watch,' he said. With every moment I could see him more clearly. 'I am letting you see me by degrees. It takes a little getting used to.'

I saw a sleek, handsome body, more like a sculpture than a living being, with four legs that ended in paws. Vicious-looking spurs sprouted from a tail which was scaled like a fish. His head was crowned with a thick mane in mingled tones of copper and silver. Some of the strands were woven in complex patterns and threaded with beads and charms. From his chin a beard hung in long, smooth plaits. But the face under the mane was human. Changed, certainly; longer and finer, with eyes that seemed both animal and angelic – but still Sigurthur's own eccentric face.

I reached out to touch his hair, but paused with my fingers in mid-air. He'd never liked to be touched, and I was awestruck.

'Now I understand why Tykavn was going mad,' I said. 'It's because the world is mad. I saw you die and you're alive again; I lived here on a farm and now the farm's gone as if it fell down a thousand years ago. How can this be you?'

'I didn't die,' he said, 'although I thought I was going to. I gave all the power I had to let you escape.'

'I know,' I whispered.

'I lost consciousness, but I have a vivid image of you jumping over the broken frame into the night. After you'd escaped, the Unseen didn't finish me off. I came round to find them licking the wounds they had made. As if they were trying to lick me into another shape . . . as I had reshaped you. Then they took me with them. They took me back to answer for my crime of stealing and misusing their wisdom.'

'Is this how they . . . punished you?'

'Punished! No, no . . . there was no retribution. I saw the error of my ways and we reached an understanding. I didn't have to live with them long before I became like them.'

I reacted without thinking. 'That's awful!'

'Is that what you believe?' His pupils enlongated. 'You're wrong. I was halfway there already, you see. They knew it. They saw that I only needed a little guidance . . .' His pearl-sheened eyes looked beyond me, as if the experience was too precious to explain in detail.

'You don't mind what they've done?'

'I'm alive, aren't I? Do I look as if I mind? Besides, they didn't *do* anything. I became this by my own choice.'

'But are you really . . . exactly like them?'

'I am not *like* them. I *am* one of them, a Stjarnin.' He paused, but I couldn't reply. 'They only showed me what I was searching for.'

'Which was what?'

The fountain of hair trembled as he shook his head. 'You don't want to know, now, 'Lithie. You're tired. You only want to know that you can trust me, don't you?'

'I don't trust anyone.' I shivered.

'Even after I gave my life for you? Tried, at least.'

I couldn't speak. At last I dared to touch his mane. It felt strange, cool and silvery, as if zinging with electricity. Finally I said, 'If you know so much, tell me where the farm is.'

'What farm?'

182

'There was a house here . . . A girl who helped me . . . And then a man who tried to kill us both and take me into a place like Kvold where it was always night. Who vanished when I killed *him*, and then never existed in the first place. Answer that, with your wonderful wisdom!'

'I never claimed to be wise,' said Sigurthur. 'I think we have a lot to talk about; it's lucky we'll have plenty of time to talk. But your friends in Onafross; didn't you reach them?'

'Friends!' I twisted away from him and struck the ground with my fists. My hand caught a rock. I picked it up and gouged the soil with it. 'Oh, I found them, for all the good it did me. What's wrong with them? They'd rather believe I'm an idiot, a trouble maker, anything except that Tykavn could possibly be ill. Why won't anyone listen? Goats, all of them. *Unstatused!*'

I hurled the stone away and it arced into the blackness, hitting the ground with a distant thud.

'Feel better?' said Sigurthur.

'Perhaps everything makes perfect sense, and it's me who's crazy. I've missed something.'

'Now you're beginning to sound sorry for yourself.'

'No!' I cried. 'It's not that. I just want to understand and I'm angry because I don't!'

'I'm listening,' he said.

His tranquil tone stalled me. 'So?'

'You said no one would listen to you. Well, I am listening, my erstwhile companion; and I want to know everything. But we can't stay here for ever, so you can tell me as we go.'

'Where are we going?'

'You'd better climb on my back. My purpose in life seems to be to provide you with transport, one way or another; why fight it?'

I did as he asked, wary but without any reason to refuse. Under my legs and hands he felt like metal and stone, air and cold fire. When he stood up, his shoulders were the height of a man's, and the ground seemed a long way below. He said, 'Now I'm taking you home.'

'Where's that?'

'To the place where I live now, and to the people—'

'Not to the Unseen!'

'The Stjarna.' He sighed softly. 'I'm sorry, Iolithie. I owe it to you to be honest; the Stjarna sent me to find you. They don't like Amaians wandering about in their land and they seem to perceive a threat in you. It didn't matter what I told them about you; they have to see for themselves. So I was sent to bring you to them.'

'What if I refuse?'

'You have no choice. I won't . . . hurt you, but I'll take you anyway. Please come willingly.'

I swallowed hard. With a few words, Sigurthur seemed to switch from my friend to my betrayer. Another one. Beyond responding with any violent emotion, I said bitterly, 'So now you're taking me prisoner? And I thought I could trust you.'

'I know,' he said, 'and I'm truly sorry. But they won't harm you, while I am there, I swear.' His words cut through my feeble protests, which died like a breath. 'Well, after the way your trust-worthy civilized humans have used you, why not seek the help of demons? You may well get a kinder response.'

The journey wasn't easy. Sigurthur ran at a speed that frightened me and it took all my concentration to stay on his back. Twice he took off into a run before I was ready, and I tumbled on to the ground and bruised myself. He was exasperated with me and we quarrelled. But for all the discomfort of it, cold rain blowing against us and comfortless blue hills all around, there was magic in the journey.

In every part of my travels there has been magic; all subtly different, all of it filling the deepest crevices of my mind like snow that will never melt. My heart aches for Tykavn that he can never taste the magic inside the pain.

Sigurthur skirted round the northern edge of the glacier, where Datha and I had danced under the stars after we'd defeated Ember. Ama, it was cold, and Sigurthur seemed to give out no heat at all. Yet he must have given me something. The will to live, surely.

In a day or two the glacier was behind us, no more than a black and white wall along the horizon, as I had first seen it. Before us was a great purple-grey mountain, with smoke and steam blowing along its naked sides.

'That is Mount Hrafna,' said Sigurthur. 'You must have heard of it.'

'Yes, of course. Only as a name in a book, though. A place no human has seen and returned from alive for hundreds of years. Am I the first, do you think?'

'You haven't returned alive yet,' he pointed out. 'But no, you aren't the first; though you are one of a privileged few.'

There was such enchantment in the sight of the great cone rising against the moody black and cream sky. The Perfect-Ministers tell children that demons sleep under sulphur pans and that volcanoes are entrances to Kvold itself . . . and in me the fight between reason and superstition went on. I could feel the unquiet ground trembling but I thought I was imagining things, that my own body was vibrating with a surfeit of wonder.

There was a long ridge to the left of Mount Hrafna, and Sigurthur ran up the slope as easily as he did on level ground. As we reached the top and came in sight of the other side of the mountain I saw, nestling at its base between two vast arms of rock, a city.

It looked like Torbyrgi; a domed city turned in on itself. But it was twice the size and its walls were not grey but a soft watered pink, like a sunset. It glittered against the landscape, like a jewel thrown into black sand. I stared with amazement at its towers and domes.

'Is that where we're going? Is that where the Stjarna live?'

'No, no,' said Sigurthur. I think he laughed, just a breath. 'That is Vivirjosa.'

Vivirjosa. I knew its name, just as I knew Mount Hrafna; it was once the capital of the whole country, before the Unseen invaded and took it from us. Now it was only a legend.

I couldn't speak for a long time. I sat easily on Sigurthur's back, forgetting to cling on, as he swung down and around the city. I watched the city until my neck ached from being twisted around. The walls shone. Glass sparkled. Despite the broken panes, the dust and lichen on the roof, it seemed enchanted, ghostly and magnificent. Eventually I said, 'It's deserted, then?'

'Yes. For many years now.'

The knot in my stomach, to my surprise, was becoming anger. That the Unseen had taken this beautiful place from us! I imagined them coming in the night, padding through the covered streets and entering the chambers where people lay sleeping. I saw a battle of fire and blood, like the one Ovinor had showed me. Had the citizens fled? Had the offspring of Sudema left anyone alive?

'Why don't the Unseen live there?' I asked. 'What was the point of taking the city if they didn't want it for themselves?'

'They wanted this land, not the buildings on it,' he said, as if exasperated by my questions. 'You don't know what happened here . . . why they couldn't let the humans stay. You'll find out when it's time. Not before.'

I hated him when he spoke like that. He could be so smug. He was still Sigurthur, no question of it.

I'm not sure when I first felt the ground begin to shake. I was too occupied looking at Vivirjosa; I put the jolts down to Sigurthur's swift progress down the rugged hillside.

Beyond the city, the landscape reminded me of the Thjoth near Torbyrgi, where the Assembly meet. Great tilted slabs of volcanic rock, mottled grey and ochre by weather and lichens, criss-crossed by deep fissures where you'd break a leg as soon as put a foot wrong. But Sigurthur flew on without slackening speed, and I trusted him. It was that, or throw myself off.

Suddenly the ground seemed to lurch sideways and he staggered. I only stayed on his back because we were immediately thrown the other way. He came to a halt with me hanging on his neck and spun round to look back at Mount Hrafna.

The rock beneath us was trembling. Black plumes of smoke were rising, not from the cone but from the ridge over which we had just come. I saw a thin, bright gold line splitting the mountainside. Fingers of fire stood along the skyline, mounting towards the clouds.

Then, in a huge, splintering roar, the whole ridge exploded into fountains of red fire. Sigurthur turned on his haunches and ran, with me clinging helplessly on to him.

Many times during my journeys I've been terrified. But this happened too fast for fear. I remember only some vague thought that the volcano was erupting to punish us, because we'd seen Vivirjosa . . .

Golden rain and black ash fell around us. I felt the scorching heat and I could smell singed hair as red flakes landed on me. A strange sound began to chase us, louder than the receding thunder of the explosion; a kind of liquid tearing noise, like thousands and thousands of rocks tumbling after us in a fluid avalanche . . .

I glanced back and I saw the thin gold line spreading down the ridge in streams of brilliance. The sky was on fire. And the sound was that of lava flowing down after us, faster than Sigurthur could run.

CHAPTER FOURTEEN

THE CITADEL

All my life I'd heard about volcanoes, but I'd never seen one erupt. Nothing could have prepared me for the reality. Easy to believe that a gate to Sudema's deadly night-world was rupturing Eileah's crust.

The lava flowed fast as a river, crackling and roaring as it came. Although Sigurthur raced down the mountainside at full stretch, the molten stream was gaining on us. I couldn't help looking back at it. There was such fierce beauty in the danger.

The sky was full of smoke and fire, choked with livid light. In sheets and rivulets of boiling rock the flux came rushing down after us; red-hot, white-hot, thick as porridge. The crust that formed and cracked on its surface looked black against the yellow brilliance. Fires blazed on the flow and were subsumed as it poured on. The boulders themselves caught fire.

Searing heat radiated from the eruption, but far worse was the stench. Choking sulphur and smoke filled my throat. I knew the fumes would kill me if we didn't reach fresh air soon.

Sigurthur, too, was gasping for breath as he ran. He leaped from boulder to boulder, twisting this way and that as he went. I dared not close my eyes; if I hadn't anticipated each jump, I would have fallen. I could feel his ribs heaving beneath me. His coat was slippery beneath my thighs, and there was no saddle or stirrups to help me keep my balance. I clung on until my legs locked with cramp; I buried my fingers in his hair and hung on so hard I must have caused him agony. I was galvanized to him.

We weren't going to outrun the flow. Of all the ways to die, dear Ama . . .

Suddenly, to my alarm, he swerved sideways and started running parallel to the edge of the flow instead of away from it. The heat blew up like a wall; the air was stiff with it. Ash covered us, red-hot flakes showered down. And I saw that the ragged scarlet lumps flying around us were pieces of solid rock. One landed almost on us, scraping Sigurthur's leg and leaving a stink of singed hair along its path.

'What are you doing?' I tried to shout, but my throat was swollen. I coughed until I retched. Then I could not breathe any more. My lungs were sacs of acridity. All the air had burned away. A sea of lava was running down towards us and Sigurthur was all but running to meet the tide.

Then I saw a chasm in front of us. The rock – old, crusted lava – fell away, and a ravine lay between us and the tilted rock-mass opposite. I couldn't guess at the depth – a hundred feet, two hundred – or the width of the gap between us and the far ledge.

I tried to yell a warning, but Sigurthur had already seen the drop. Instead of swerving, he accelerated, screaming out a great battle roar as he went—

And he leaped clear out over the edge of the cliff. I left my stomach on the other side. Sharp, fresh air hit us and we were hurtling through it, suspended. Behind us, the lava reached the ravine and plunged down into it like a waterfall.

Sigurthur's arc carried us right over the gap. When his paws found the edge of the far cliff he landed so hard I thought he'd drive right through the solid rock. He stumbled but I was clinging on hard, and his head came up to stop me tumbling off forwards. Then he sprang upright again and turned to look back.

We were both choking for breath. Behind us the mountain was webbed with lines of bright gold. It shook, pouring thunderous clouds into the atmosphere. And the lava flowed, plastic and lethal, into the chasm in front of our feet.

In time the ravine would fill up and overflow. All the old lava, which had lain here for centuries, weathering into the landscape, would be buried for ever beneath the fresh flow.

I let my gaze travel further up the mountainside, and I saw what was happening to Vivirjosa. A river of burning magma was flowing straight into it, surging through its streets, shoring up against its walls and setting them alight. I heard the distant shattering of glass and the roar of fire and collapsing walls.

I was witnessing the final death of Vivirjosa, which in truth had died centuries before. Go there now and you'll find nothing but rock and ruins. But I saw it die. I saw its last moments of glory. My eyes stung, not only with sulphur.

There seemed nothing to say. Sigurthur turned and loped onwards.

A long time later, when we halted by a stream with Mount Hrafna an angry grey pyramid on the horizon, I slipped down from his back and fell down on my hands and knees in the stream. How cold, how good the water felt. He bent his face down to it beside me and I said, 'Did we wake the mountain?'

He looked at me in amazement. His face was so much more expressive and subtle than that of a human. 'Why do you ask that?'

'We saw the city. They say no one can see Vivirjosa and live . . .'

He blew out a long breath, which rippled the water. 'I think you have a touch of Tykavn's condition,' he said. 'How long have you lived in this land? Haven't you always lived under the shadow of these mountains, these tender boils whose crusts are always ready to burst into fire at a touch?'

'I've never seen it happen before.'

'It was only a matter of time, believe me,' said Sigurthur. 'Damned stupid place to build a city, anyway. They knew Mount Hrafna was volcanic. Humans all over. "It won't happen to us." '

'Are you sure there was no one living in the city?' I whispered. My throat was sore, my eyes still streaming.

'If anyone was, they certainly aren't now. No, Iolithie, I don't think so. Only ghosts.'

When I climbed on his back again and he walked on he was limping. I sensed his exhaustion and weakness; it transmitted itself from his body to mine with every step. Strange, I'd thought of him as indestructible; now I realized he was not.

Fire, of course. The only thing that the Stjarna seem to fear.

I leaned down and rested my head on his. 'I'm sorry.'

'What for?' he said sharply.

'Not realizing you were as afraid as me.'

He cursed under his breath. 'Do you think you are the only creature in the world who gets frightened, Iolithie? Strange kind of egotism, but that's what it is. I'm not immortal.'

'I did apologize,' I said. 'There's no need to make me feel guiltier. Let me get down and walk.'

'Why?'

'Because you're tired.' The new Sigurthur was just as infuriating as the old. 'Because I need the exercise!'

So I came the rest of the way on foot, walking beside Sigurthur. Physical exertion and the survival of a terrifying experience had purged me. I no longer felt tired. I felt light, calm and peaceful, as if nothing else could hurt me.

Later, Sigurthur led me along the side of a hill and as we came round a curve I saw a lake below us. It gleamed sapphire blue, and on the far side I saw three table mountains; old volcanoes, long silent. The land around the lake looked green and fertile. Midges clouded the air.

'Lake Vivatn,' said Sigurthur.

He led me along the hillside and up a ridge, facing away from the lake. The climb made me breathless, but as we reached the top I saw an incredible valley sweeping away beneath us.

'Welcome to the Citadel of the Star,' said Sigurthur. 'Stjarnator.'

'I can't see a citadel . . .' I began, but then I realized. The valley itself was the citadel.

There was a mass of birch trees – more trees than I've ever seen – making a sea that glittered bright fresh green. The birches flowed around outcrops of rock which thrust out of the ground in fantastical shapes; twisted spires, gnarled fingers, cones and towers, and long jagged walls broken by oddly shaped holes through which the sky shone. There were stumps connected by precarious bridges, humped shapes like monsters turned to stone, tors with yawning cave-mouths.

It was a citadel of lava. Eileah herself had spat this place into existence from an ancient eruption like that of Mount Hrafna. Eileah, or Kvold; appropriate, for the folk who lived here.

I looked down at the paths winding between the trees and saw a group of men and women making their way down a slope. Humans! Their hair was long and wild, and they wore strange thin garments of blue and green; but there was nothing remarkable about them. Ordinary people, walking unarmed and unsuspecting in the heart of Sudema's domain . . .

'Who are they?' I exclaimed. 'What are they doing down there?'

Sigurthur butted my shoulder with his head, as if he thought I was about to rush down screaming warnings at them. 'They live here.'

'But I thought you meant the Stjarna lived here.'

'We do,' he said. 'And humans live among us. Are you so shocked?'

'You never told me there were people here. Do the Stjarna keep them as bondservants?'

'No.' There was a smile in his voice. 'Not all humans are vehement Amaians, after all. There are some who have left Onafross or Torlossen over the years to seek the Stjarna.'

I was astonished. 'But why?'

'You may never understand,' he said infuriatingly, 'or you may understand at once. You will have to work it out for yourself.'

'But I never knew.'

'It's Torlossen's best-kept secret. After all, those who leave don't go back; and those Perfects who suspect the truth are not going to admit it. Easier to believe that the Unseen have killed them.'

'But they do kill humans.'

'Often. But those who make it this far alive are given a chance to explain themselves, at least. You must realize, though, that most of the humans you will see here were born here, and know no more about Amaians than you know about us.'

I've given up imagining I understand anything. Every time I turn round, what I thought was the truth is shaken apart.

By the time we walked down into the valley, the men and women had passed out of sight and we saw no one else. The twisted rocks towered above us, ragged and fantastically deformed. Although there were shades from peach to umber to grey in them, their predominant colour was black. They felt watchful, sentient. The wind rustled the trees; when it blew harder, it fluted and moaned through the rocks themselves.

There is such an atmosphere in this place.

But then, the whole of Thandarkyr has presence; it is vivid with life, not only that of plants and animals but of the overwhelming energies of Eileah herself. The howling cold of winter; the heat and sulphur and fire that can move the mountains themselves.

If I hadn't made this journey I would never have known.

I looked around anxiously for other beings like Sigurthur. Foolish of me to expect them to be visible. But I could sense them. They were in the rocks, in the wind. Electric waves of nervousness ran over my skin like spiders. Sigurthur was different; I wasn't happy that he'd brought me here but I didn't fear him. But the Unseen had never given me anything but cause for terror.

'I'll take you straight to Mathrathur,' he said. His voice was low, rather uncertain. I could tell he was afraid for me, and that was so unlike him.

'Who is he?'

'She,' he said. 'Mathrathur is our Matriarch. She is the one who insisted that you be brought here. If there's a decision to be made, she will make it.'

'You mean . . . decide whether I live or die?'

He didn't answer.

I didn't want to see the Matriarch. I resented being judged. What business was it of hers, who I was or what I felt? I wanted to be left alone, to sulk, to lick my wounds. But Sigurthur was leading me up a sandy hill strewn with boulders, which swept up into a dark tor. Where the light rock met the dark I saw a cave mouth.

As we reached it I saw that the cave was open at both ends, a tunnel through the lava with a low, wide entrance. The darkness inside was intense. Although there was daylight at both ends, the roof vanished into depths of blackness. The ground beneath me seemed to crackle and tingle.

There was a presence in the cave that made me very afraid. I turned to Sigurthur – only to find that he'd vanished. I was alone . . . and yet I wasn't. Something was watching me, breathing softly through a mouth that might bite my flesh and lap my blood.

A face began to shimmer out of the gloom. I thought for a moment it was Sigurthur, reappearing. But this face was different; larger, big-boned. Strong, female. A Stjarnin materialized on the darkness, shimmering with silvery colours. She lay on her belly, paws stretched out before her, head erect on her short neck, hair falling in long braids from her crown as if carved from wood. A huge pair of wings swept up from her shoulders.

I thought her eyes would turn me to stone. They were all colours and no colour at all, like oil on water.

And although I hate obeisance I fell to my knees. She was like a goddess on an altar. Without a qualm, this creature must have torn the guts out of any Amaians who dared to tread on her territory, and I knew she would do the same to me if I displeased her.

She said, 'Well, in what heart do you come to us?'

I wasn't sure what she meant. I am always taking these life-or-death risks of being honest. 'Halla – my lady – I didn't come here of my own free will and I don't mean to trespass on your territory.

Sigurthur brought me here; he said you wanted to know why I was wandering about in your land . . .' I trailed off. I was perspiring, halfway between anger and terror.

'And what is your reason?'

'It's simple. I crossed your land to find help for someone I care for. He's ill and I will go anywhere and ask anyone until I find someone who can help him.'

'And did you find no help in Onafross?'

'No. Sudema herself could not possibly be less helpful to me than the man's own flesh and blood have been,' I said.

A swipe of her paw would have killed me, if she thought me insolent. But she said drily, 'And no less helpful than Ama, either.'

I couldn't take offence at that. It was true. You could almost say it was Ama who had destroyed Tykavn. I said, 'I know your people hate us and kill us if we come over the borders. I don't even know why. But I never meant the Stjarna any harm. I just wanted to be left in peace to seek help. I haven't deserved this! I know you despise Ama but I'm none too impressed with him myself now!'

Her expression was withering. There was this great, calm, alien intellect shining in the darkness; I was trying to rail against it but I felt inarticulate, lost.

'You misunderstand,' said Mathrathur. 'We do not despise Ama. Ama is the name of the sun. How can we despise the sun, or not believe in something that is clearly there? We revere the life-giving sun as we revere Sudema; but we do not worship either of them. Do you think we shun the day and dance in the night, worshipping a demon? You assume a division between dark and light, that one is evil and the other good. But there is no division between dark and light. The people of the star have not rejected Ama; it is the Amaians who have rejected *us*. Your troubles have stemmed from your ignorance. Yes, the Stjarna kill; but only those who attack us – or who run away. Those who stand and face their pursuers are given a fair hearing.'

'How was I meant to know that?' Even though I felt powerless before her, I was indignant. 'My lady, I didn't come here to argue with you. But the Stjarna came from outside and invaded Thandarkyr; they stole most of it and they keep it by violence. At least, that's what I was taught. How can I know any better if that's all I've ever been told?'

She picked up the irony in my tone and realized, perhaps,

that I was aware that what I'd been taught might not be the absolute truth. She seemed to soften a little.

'Sit down,' she said. 'Sit between my paws.'

I obeyed. I felt like a mouse between them.

She said, 'Sigurthur is on trial too. It was he who saved your life, without truly understanding who or what you were. He has been a wild element in our land, taking and using our powers without guidance. Happily, he found his way back to us in the end. Then I had to ask him, who was this wayward child you rescued and protected? And everything he told me distilled to this; a child of Ama, seeking help for another child of Ama. And when I asked why, he could only say that you were young and in despair, and he liked you. So I told him that if he did not really know what he had done, he must go and find you and bring you back to me so that I could decide for myself.'

'What I told Sigurthur was true. But I don't worship Ama any more. I can't.'

'Why not?' Her tone was gentle, but it stroked along me like a fistful of knives. 'Someone with no faith rattling about the land may be dangerous in ways that even she does not understand herself. Your loss of faith and your reason for this journey; are they connected?'

'Yes. I suppose they are.'

'Then you must explain them to me.'

I thought for a moment. I sat there between the paws of the Unseen Matriarch, completely at her mercy, and I knew that this was vitally important. It was like the first contact with another race, between Eileah and Kvold. I *must* make her understand or I'd be lost.

But words always seem to betray me. Laasastiuk, my parents, Tykavn's own family; the burning passions inside me had seemed to translate as the pointless whingeing of a child when it reached their ears.

I said, 'Would you let me write it down, rather than speak it?'

'Why?'

'Because I've tried to explain before, and I could never make anyone listen. I don't know why. Spoken words just dissolve and I won't remember what I've said or how well I said it. I want to write everything that happened so that I can sort it out in my own mind.'

Mathrathur looked unmoved. 'Do you think we have paper and pens here, like a human city?'

I said rather sharply, 'Of course, if you can't read—'

'We can read,' she said with icy forbearance. I had insulted her. Good!

'Then I'll write on anything, with anything. Please grant me this. My lips don't express a tenth of what's inside. I know it's my fault, but it's dreadful, it's so painful, not to be taken seriously when someone's life and sanity are at stake.'

She breathed out and I felt her breath in my hair. 'What makes you think I have the time or the patience for this?' Again I was horribly aware of my own insignificance. But she added, 'Still, do it if you wish. I will always be here. The urgency is yours, not mine.'

So here I sit in the gloom and write, with a white stone on a dark wall, making each step of the journey into a section, and each section into a neat page as if I were writing a journal.

I'm not imprisoned, yet I can't escape. I have nowhere to go and no reason to leave. I could stand up and walk away, but I know the Stjarna would come after me and hunt me down and tear me apart within the day – oh, unless I turned and faced them, perhaps. Then they would bring me back here again.

So I stay here building the only defence I can; words against the world.

And I cannot let you, Mathrathur, think I've forgotten what you are, or what you have done. I didn't see Lady Antrid die; but I have heard enough and seen enough to reconstruct what happened. She has come to me in dreams and shown me.

I could weep for her, a woman I never met in my life. Antrid never came against you with firebrands, crying *demon*! She was simply a traveller.

So, I begin with her. And I continue with the stories I was taught as truth. And I try to explain how that 'truth' has fallen apart all around me ... and in so doing, to comprehend the miracle that I'm still alive, here in the darkness, writing.

I sit at one end of the wall, the little white stone scratching persistently. The Matriarch is at the other end, reading what I have written so far.

When she has read it, she will decide what to do with me. As if she had any right! But I'm at her mercy, anyway.

Some time ago, Sigurthur came and sat with me as I wrote.

He read over my shoulder and said, 'I hope you are portraying me in a good light.'

'I'm being honest,' I said. 'If you're unhappy about it, bad luck.'

Then he lit up the cave walls with his visions of what had happened to me, until I shouted at him to leave me alone. Gloom billowed in like smoke; I was sorry he'd gone.

A short time after that a young man – human – came into the cave with some food. There was fruit and fish – the sweetest I have ever tasted – and cold spring water and wine.

He said his name was Hannis. He was younger than me, slender, with floppy dark hair and an open expression. A plain, ordinary young man, like any inhabitant of Vryatan, but with a sweetness about him I'd never sensed before. I was just glad to see an unthreatening face.

I asked, 'How long have you lived here – among the Stjarna?'

He looked surprised by the question. 'All my life. I've never lived anywhere else.'

'But are you here to – I don't know – to serve them?'

He looked at me as if I was some incomprehensible being, an alien – which, to him, I was. An Amaian. 'No, we're not slaves. We don't have bondservants or Perfects or anything like that. We live in a different way.'

'Sudema's way?'

He shrugged. 'I don't know how to explain it. I was told that everyone in Onafross and Torlossen has to have Status, but I don't really know what it means. When you know more about us, you can tell *me* the difference.'

When I know more about you, I thought. Oh, will I ever?

'But where do you live? The Stjarna don't seem to have houses or dwelling-caves.'

'They don't need them,' Hannis said. 'The trees, rocks and water are their homes. But the rest of us have farms around the lake.'

I laughed under my breath; part relief that they were so ordinary, part shuddering memory of Jolitha's farm. He smiled. He was as wary of me as I was of him, but we both wanted to be friends.

After he'd gone I lay down and slept for a time, awoke and wrote again. Sigurthur paced through the cave, looking sourly at me; he blew on my hair, a kind of sarcastic kiss, and left. Hannis brought more food. Once or twice I got up and went to the cave entrance to breathe the sweet air. The lava tors were black with the sun behind them, and the sea of leaves glittered silver. I couldn't see a soul. I felt so eerily alone I could have cried like a child.

I did not. I went on working.

As the cave mouths turned to deep blue pools of twilight on either side of me, Hannis came back. He had a girl with him, and from their closeness I guessed they were together, if not married. She had a mass of crinkled, sand-red hair, which half obscured a rosy face.

Hannis said, 'Halla Iolithie? We're gathering to eat. Sigurthur sent me to fetch you, if you want to come.'

I put down the stone and stretched. Ama's Fire, I was tired. 'I would love to,' I said. 'Who is your friend?'

'I'm Tattri,' said the girl. 'I'm Hannis's sister.'

I liked them both. Perhaps I was just starving for some gentle company, but I liked them so very much; they were both friendly, merry, undemanding. I had never met anyone quite like that before.

I followed them out of the cave and down the side of the slope. Twilight was gathering over the birches, blue and mysterious. It was hard to believe they could seem so kind, and yet revere Sudema . . . even harder for me to stop thinking in this Amaian way.

They led me down a slope, up another ridge, and through a huge circular hole in a wall of lava. I thought of it as the door of a rough Fane built by the gods themselves; only there was no inside and no outside. The Fane was everywhere. It was the world itself.

On the other side, a hill sloped down to the edge of the Lake Vivatn. The waters were sparkling indigo, the grass intensely green in the half-light. The table mountains stood purple-grey against a watery sky. In the shadow of a small stand of trees I saw people gathered on the grass, mingling with Unseen folk made visible.

Hannis and Tattri led me down to them.

I hadn't lost my fear of the Stjarna. The terror they'd inspired in me was still raw. They were like wild animals, moved by some high, cold intelligence I did not understand.

The sight of them filled me with awe. They sat as Mathrathur had, heads erect, paws in front. Some were winged, others weren't. Some were small, almost solid; others were larger and more difficult to see, as if their substance was more rarified. I couldn't say they were beautiful, exactly; some verged on grotesque. But then, they can hardly be judged by human standards of beauty.

There were such colours in their glassy-silky coats; from a distance they looked silver-grey with touches of gold, but when I came closer I saw that colours of immense subtlety rippled through their skin and hair. The merest hints of blue and copper and plum, hypnotically lovely.

Mathrathur was at the centre. I sat between my new friends at the edge of the group, hoping to avoid her attention, but she looked straight at me. She said, 'Tonight there is a child of Ama from Torlossen with us. She claims that her faith has wavered, so perhaps there is hope for her yet.'

The others, human and Unseen, were all looking at me. Oddly, I didn't mind. There was no hostility in it; and no paradox in that, either. Everything was grey and blue and wrapped in tranquillity like mist. Fire and blood might rage around the borders of our lands, but here, at the centre, there was peace.

Mathrathur said, 'Iolithie, have you heard the legend of Hendleiknir, who rescued Eileah from the night-world Kvold, where no light but Sudema's ever shines?'

She seemed to expect an answer. I nodded.

'We tell the legend too, but our version is different. I tell it to show that there is no great division between our cultures, but that we all shape stories to suit our own beliefs.

'This is the Stjarna's story. Ama and Sudema loved each other once, and they created the world Eileah together out of their love, and the bright rain of their thoughts became mankind. But Sudema was afraid that Ama's fierceness would burn the world, so she took it in her hands to protect us from Ama's fire. Then she made a vow that she would never let Eileah fall, so that it would always be a safe and peaceful home for mankind. In those days, all beings revered Ama by day and Sudema by night, and no one said, "My beliefs are right and yours are wrong."

'But Ama became jealous. As long as Sudema held the world, she prevented him from touching Eileah and wielding his full influence over Man.

'Perhaps Sudema did wrong, in trying to keep the world from Ama. But she was only trying to protect us, as a mother cradles her child.

'Well, Ama tried everything in his power to prise Eileah from Sudema's grasp. He could not enter Night and she could not enter Day. Only in the twilight could they meet. So every dawn and every dusk he reasoned with her, he railed at her, he threatened her – but nothing availed. Finally he peeped through the window to her land in the twilight and saw why. In order that she should never let Eileah fall, Sudema had caused her own fingers and thumbs to grow together. Nothing Ama did could make her separate her hands – even if he broke her will.'

As the Matriarch spoke, I felt my heart starting to pound. It was hitting my throat like a hammer.

'But Ama was cunning. He could not go into the Night, but he cast a shadow from a tall rock, and sent the shadow as his emissary, Hendleiknir, into Sudema's domain. Disguised as a man, Hendleiknir faced many dangers – which have formed other legends – before he reached Sudema.

'In your story, Iolithie, Hendleiknir went to rescue Ama's lost love Eileah from Sudema's imprisonment; but in ours, Eileah was not being imprisoned but protected, and Hendleiknir did not go to rescue her but to steal her.

'When he reached Sudema's dwelling he pretended to be a wounded creature, so that instead of sending him away she took pity on him and let him in. Then he waited until she slept with Eileah in her hands, and he crept up on her and cut her fingers apart.'

I sat rigid, unable to breathe in or out. But Mathrathur's voice went on, relentless, suddenly rising in pitch. 'Sudema woke screaming with the pain, crying, "What have you done? What have you done?" Then Hendleiknir revealed himself in his true form and answered, "It was for your own good, Star of the Night. With your fingers grown together how could you sew, or spin, or plant your garden or tend your creatures? How could you be a true goddess?"

'But Sudema's fingertips burned with fire and blood, and the World fell from her hands. And from that moment the division between the worshippers began.

'Some said, "Ama is wicked to have hurt her and wrested the world from her." Others said, "Sudema should never have taken Eileah from Ama in the first place." Some sided with her and some with him. And the hatred and bitterness grew and grew until the veil between the Day and the Night came down, and neither side could see anything but evil in the other. And men began to tear each other apart, with words and with knives.

'And that is what we refer to as the Fall. The night Sudema's fingers were hacked apart like the ribs of a kid and our world Eileah fell from her kindly hands. It has been falling ever since.'

There was a moment of stillness. I don't know what I did, how I looked, but everyone seemed to be turning and staring at me. Their faces expanded and contracted in my fading vision.

'Iolithie, what is it?' came their voices from a long way off. 'She looks so pale!' 'Why are you weeping?'

But I was pinned against the tree trunk by the weight of an immense, unseen glacier. For a long time I couldn't say a word. Then all I could say was, 'Read the wall. Read the wall!'

CHAPTER FIFTEEN

SORROW

When Mathrathur had read my story she looked at me differently.

It wasn't what she had expected. There was something to *me* that she hadn't seen.

I would like to think it shook her a little, though nothing shakes her for long. We sat together in the darkness. At each end of the cave shone a window of deepest blue; and a gossamer light came from the Matriarch herself, as if her hair was dusted with luminous pearl.

'It's all true,' I said.

And she said, 'I know.' I sat between her paws, and I wasn't afraid, only . . . suspended. She said softly, 'The story I told of Hendleiknir and Sudema was a myth. Unlike the Amaians, we don't believe such myths to be the literal truth. They are symbols; ways of putting names to unknowable mysteries.'

'But it really happened,' I said. 'I lived it. It happened to *me*. I betrayed Jolitha . . .'

'Did you not know that the ancient name of Onafross was Onyafrosa? That "Jolitha" is an older form of your own name?'

'I thought they spoke differently in the north.'

'They spoke differently in the past, too.'

'But how could I have gone back—'

'When Sigurthur transformed you into a deer he was using his power in a dangerous way. There is much that we can do that we do not . . . Strength lies in control, in knowing when to stop, not flinging power about at random. But his actions may have had nothing to do with it at all.'

'Then why did it happen?'

The Matriarch rested her chin on my head. The weight of it sent shivers cascading from my skull all over my body. They seem full of cold, crackling energy like stars, the Stjarna; so full they can't contain it. She said, 'Myths can spring from events that were once real. You went back to the origin, which was not what the story eventually became. But I don't know why, Iolithie. Perhaps to be a witness to the abyss between myth and reality.'

'The worst thing is that I'll never know what happened to Jolitha,' I whispered. 'Did she die? Did she find a way to live and heal again?'

Mathrathur fixed me with her terrible, colourless-rainbow eyes. 'Perhaps you *are* Jolitha. Her reflection, her other-self. The name "Ovinor" is not a real name. It simply meant "enemy".'

I can't begin to describe how I felt as she said this. There were snakes of ice worming through me, a wind from infinity blowing into my mind. 'What was Ovinor, then?'

'I wish I could tell you,' the Matriarch said softly. 'Jolitha wanted to keep the enemy out, but her other-self let him in. She was destroyed but her other-self survived and slew him. And the moment you did so, you came back into your own time . . .'

'I think so. That was when everything changed.'

'Perhaps your presence has always been entwined in the story in a way we didn't see. Sudema is in all of us. She could dwell in a milkmaid and she can dwell in you.'

I was mortified. 'No!'

'Don't react with such horror. We are all aspects of Sudema, every one of us, even those who deny her. She is the power of our will.' The Matriarch paused, then went on. 'You've heard many myths, haven't you? I doubt that you will ever have been taught the true history of Thandarkyr.'

'I don't know,' I said. 'Truth seems to be as elusive as the Stjarna. Does it exist?'

'A man called Hendleiknir really existed, though we do not perceive him as the Amaians do. They call him a saint and Prophet of Ama. We call him Destroyer and Enemy.' I should have expected this, but it still shocked me. 'Before Thandarkyr was divided, there was peace, and Sudema and Ama were equally revered. The herbal arts were part of everyday life; our rituals had real magic.'

'The Stjarna used to live among humans?' I said.

'We did not *live* among them. We *were* human. There was no division. We were the herbalists and healers, dreamers, poisoners, manipulators; we were those who understood that the energies of the earth come to a burning culmination in the flowers and leaves of plants. Different herbs have different properties. Knowing them is our wisdom.

'But then Hendleiknir came to Vivirjosa, claiming he brought rules directly from the God's mouth. Ama must not be merely revered but worshipped. All needs of the body were to be subjugated to the spirit. The pleasures of the flesh were unclean. Celibacy must be the rule, except for the purpose of procreation. Hendleiknir informed us that Perfection came in a particular form to which we must all aspire; anything else left us open to the wiles of evil. The night and Sudema must be shunned.

'That was how he cut Eileah from Sudema's protection and exposed her to Ama's Fire.

'His teachings were powerful, but there were those who would not conform to them. The herbalists knew he was misguided so we ignored him and went on practising the arts from which healing and wisdom came. But will is powerful too. Hendleiknir swiftly gained power and formed evangelical armies to impose his will on us. He saw the herbal arts as magic, and magic was evil. Ama, he said, allowed no supernatural forces within the earth except his own.

'Perhaps naïvely, the herbalists thought their practices would be tolerated by the new religion. How painfully we found we were wrong. We were persecuted for not forswearing Sudema. We were first ostracized, then captured, tortured and slain. But we weren't weak, you see; we had never been weak. And we didn't forget. Many of us escaped or were driven out, but we gathered in the mountains and the wild places and vowed to take revenge. We became the Stjarna, people of the star.'

I said, 'You speak as if you were there.'

A smile ghosted her face. 'I'm not that old. But the history of our ancestors is also our own.

'For many years the Stjarna gathered strength through our knowledge of herbs and our affinity with Sudema. With Ama, too, for he never deserted us. Hendleiknir's followers said we had forsaken him, but they were wrong. The Stjarna hid; we built no cities; we lived completely with Eileah, like animals. And as our power grew, we began to change. Our bodies mutated. We could make ourselves visible or invisible at will.

'By the time we were ready to come back, the children of Ama did not recognize us.

'Then the wars began. We drove the Prophet's followers out of Vivirjosa as we had been driven out; we tormented and killed them as they had done to us. We are not forgiving. But once we had claimed all the land we wanted, we were satisfied. Everywhere our precious herbs grew, we possessed; we let our enemies have the rest. If their land was barren that was their misfortune. If they did not want our herbs – if they rejected the power of plants to heal, to transform, to elevate – then so be it.

'Yes, we have been violent and vengeful; but we gave back only what they gave us. We do not want this war; we never wanted it. They began it. We cannot forgive.'

Her words gave me a sick feeling. I said, 'Perhaps one side should try.'

Her voice was a glacial hiss. 'While they cannot accept us, we will not accept them. They don't even believe that we were once human. They think we are invaders, a demonic hoard showered on the world by Sudema. Can you tell me how anyone should shake that belief?'

She was right, of course. It would be easier to move Mount Hrafna a foot to the left. Hate and fear ingrained for centuries would also take centuries to weather away; perhaps they would last for ever.

'I don't know,' I said helplessly.

'Is that all you can say?' She sounded angry and I was afraid again. 'You, who would risk her life time and time again, rather than accept the word of an Arch-Perfect – of the King himself – that your husband could not be helped? Have you no opinion?'

'I don't see how you can excuse what happened to Lady Antrid,' I said.

'I cannot,' she said coldly. 'But the men who sent her out into our land knew the dangers.'

'Well, I can't forget it. If not for her death, Tykavn wouldn't have become so ill. But I'm on no one's side. I just want my husband well; I don't care about you or your wars!'

In a fluid arc Mathrathur rose and stepped back, so I was no longer within her paws (did I want them to grow together around me?). She had severed the link between us; she was distant as a judge. Or a surgeon.

'You've given me much to consider,' she said. 'You can stay with Hannis and Tattri while I decide what to do. They will come and fetch you.'

She was beginning to fade from my sight. I said, 'Wait!'

'What is it?'

'If you are going to kill me, please do it quickly. That's all I ask.'

Her head tipped a little to one side, but I saw no warmth in her expression. 'I am not sure I can send you back to Torlossen, when you know so much about us. But if you are not in sympathy with us you cannot stay.'

'But—'

'Wait. I shall speak to you again. Until then, be patient.' She vanished as she spoke; her last words came from thin air. Then I was alone.

Should I have been more diplomatic? Professed myself humbly enlightened and in sympathy with the people of the star?

You'd think I could lie for once, if it meant saving my skin.

I lived with Hannis, Tattri and several others at the farm for several days. Time passed with undefined laziness. They had no houses, only a complex of shelters formed by walling in overhangs of rock with branches and oiled mohair. They were places to store tools and food, to work and sleep if it was too cold outside. They lived as close as they could to Eileah, with as little as possible. Their clothes were few, simple and threadbare; everything must be saved and carefully patched, and re-dyed in the soft blues and greens they liked. Even the plants from which the dyes came had some subtle power.

They didn't like to answer questions; perhaps it was because I was an outsider. But Tattri was very curious about me and made any excuse to spend time with me. I was glad. She was always laughing and joking; if I'd expected these people to be sombre and sinister I was wrong. They made my own people seem dourly humourless.

'I read your story,' she said one day. I was sitting with her on the hill above the lake, plaiting her wiry rust-coloured hair. Clouds of black and white smoke rose on the horizon from Mount Hrafna, but the wind was carrying them away from Stjarnator. 'You don't like us very much, do you?'

'I like you a lot,' I said. 'I don't like some of the things the Stjarna do. I don't know how you can live among them.'

'But I am a Stjarnin too. We are all the people of the star.'

'Hannis said you had always lived here, but where are your parents?'

'Our father left some time ago ... but Mother is still here.'

'I should like to meet her,' I said, wondering if she'd fled Torlossen or Onafross to come here.

But Tattri smiled. 'You already have. Our mother is Mathrathur.'

I stopped plaiting. I couldn't believe it. She said, 'Are you surprised? She told you that the Stjarna are people who know a way to become other than human. Hannis and I will change, too, as your friend Sigurthur has.'

'When?'

'When we're ready. I think it will take me a long time . . . I don't feel ready yet. I'm a little afraid, although I know there's no need. We'll be like Mathrathur . . . and, in time, like Father.'

'In what way?'

'Truly Unseen. Part of the wind; part of Eileah.'

'You don't mean . . . that he's dead?'

'I don't think so. You can't really know until it happens. Mother says it means to live so completely within the elements that you don't need anything else. Almost to become animal . . . But anyway, it's a long time in the future.'

I went on plaiting her hair. Thinking. After a while I said, 'And when you become like your mother . . . will you go out and kill my people?'

She went quiet, frowning a little. I could see she was worried, very worried. 'I hope not,' she said. 'I don't want to. I would only do it if someone I loved was in danger. We're not all the same, 'Lithie. Your people have done bad things, too. We have to protect ourselves; but most of us are gentle and only want peace.' She leaned back against me and twisted her head to look at me. Her face was fine-boned, pretty, but prematurely lined by the weather. She had no vanity at all, almost no self-consciousness. She seemed so ordinary, but there was a bubbling happiness inside her that I envied. 'You're afraid of Mother, aren't you? Don't be, 'Lithie. There's no need.'

Over the days, a little at a time, I learned more about the Stjarna. Those who were still in human shape had the ordinary needs of humans while they were waiting for the slow transformation to make them Unseen. The wisdom of their elders, meditation, Sudema's Light and the slow effect of herbs would bring about the transformation. It could take years or it could happen very suddenly, as with Sigurthur.

I was waiting, too, like a criminal, for judgement to be passed on me. And I had done nothing to deserve judgement. I should have felt resentful, or apprehensive, yet I didn't; I passed the days in a kind of dream. The azure lake, the soft green-brown folds of the hills, the wind shivering the birches in the Citadel and the trees by the lake; all these entranced me. Hannis, Tattri and the others were unfailingly kind, as if they could forgive me for coming from Torlossen – or see the human being beyond the lapsed Amaian. In this simple tranquillity, I could live for ever.

Perhaps I was running away.

At dawn one morning Sigurthur and the Matriarch came to me together. I was down by the lake, washing clothes. The two Stjarna seemed to swim up through the grey light, their solemn faces grainy-silver. I could see the light slanting on to their flanks and limbs, yet I could also see straight through them to the hills and the lake. They were reflections; there and not there.

'The Matriarch wants to talk to you,' said Sigurthur.

They both looked grave. I was shivering, but I braced myself for the worst. I really thought Mathrathur would kill me if she saw fit, and I didn't want to die; not yet, not while the morning was so shimmeringly new. I'd prepared a speech about the unfairness of it. I wouldn't die without dignity or without protest.

The Matriarch said, 'Come and walk with me.'

I walked with her along the lake shore. Sigurthur stayed behind; there was only this strange, shining, other-world creature beside me, and the haze of the volcano spreading above the shimmering silence of Eileah.

'You know, of course, that I am not going to condemn you to death,' she said. 'We want to help you.'

Following the surge of relief I felt immense anger. 'No, I didn't know! Has it taken you this long to make your mind up? What right have you to decide whether I live or die, anyway?'

I heard her breathe out; I could see her so clearly she was almost solid. 'Don't hate us, Iolithie, until you truly know us.'

'I don't hate you. It's not me who needs help, it never was; it's my husband. But I can't make anyone understand what's wrong with him.'

'On the contrary, you described his condition very clearly. You say his compulsion to perform rituals has given you an aversion to all religion; but rituals are not always harmful. They are not magic in themselves; at their best they are a way of changing your awareness, so that you may look at the world in a new way. They can cleanse, calm, invigorate; anything you wish. But if that is not understood – and clearly the Amaians do not understand it – rituals can be dangerous.

'Your husband's illness is not unknown to us. Nor is it as rare as you seem to think; many sufferers conceal it all their lives – as he did until it became impossible for him to hide it from you. It isn't madness. Before the Fall and the Separation, the herbalists called it the Disease of Doubt.' She paused. 'There are tears on your cheeks; why?'

It was the relief of someone telling me that Tykavn's sickness was real, that it even had a name. 'I wasn't imagining it. I wasn't making a fuss about nothing!'

'You wrote of his feelings; that however many times he did a thing he could never be absolutely *certain* that it was right. We take it for granted that a duty is done or a prayer said properly, because we simply *know*. But what of someone who has lost the ability to be reassured by their own eyes, their own memories? When you can't be certain of even the simplest thing, doubt becomes tyranny, an abyss.

'You could wash and wash and never be sure that you were clean; pray and pray and still feel that the god was dissatisfied. Or there might be pointless gestures which the sufferer believes must be repeated to ward off catastrophe; and being prevented from carrying them out causes unbearable distress. This condition was well known to the herbalists in the days before Hendleiknir. Sadly, when he began his teaching, the Disease of Doubt also began to take the form of extreme religious scrupulosity.

'We didn't know what caused it, but we understood that it was neither possession from without nor insanity from within. The sufferers were otherwise sane, and they could be treated kindly and helped. But this wisdom was discarded when the Prophet's followers drove the herbalists out; the Amaians lost and destroyed more than they'll ever know. They preferred the safety of ignorance to the cold edge of the light . . .

'It is possible your Tykavn would have suffered this sickness in some form, whatever his culture. But the Church of Ama is to be condemned for making it a thousand times worse, with their strictures, their talk of sin and guilt and pollution by Sudema. Onafross and Torlossen are sick to their souls; Tykavn is only a symptom . . .'

This angered me. 'Torlossen isn't that bad!' I said. 'Life is hard for us but we're happy. I know Status isn't fair on everyone, but no one starves, everyone has work, and most people have the chance to sit on the Assembly and make the rules for themselves. Do you think we're savages?'

'Forgive me,' she replied. 'I am sure it could be much worse.

In the past it *was*. You have perhaps never heard how Hendleiknir hated women; how he had them treated like bondservants, and bondservants used as slaves. In his day, a child like your Mehaar would not have been given a place in your family; she would have been drowned, and her "sinning" parents with her. A lesser man with Tykavn's illness would have been tortured and executed. But I won't go on. Only be aware. Iolithie; it *could* be worse.'

I didn't want to argue with her. I tried to be calm and distant, as she was. 'You must admit, though, that Tykavn had something real to be frightened of. The Unseen. It's just that he wasn't fighting them in a real way.'

'He had nothing to fear, really,' said Mathrathur. 'He knows the Stjarna don't want Torlossen. If he planned to take part of our land, that would be different; but we stay on our own territory; and the Amaians know what will happen if they don't stay on theirs. But you are right; his fight wasn't real, *and he knew it*. He saw the futility of his rituals, yet he couldn't stop them; that is the essence of the Disease of Doubt. He may have lived on the edge of breakdown for years. It only took Antrid's death to tip him into it.'

She stopped on the shore of the lake, where a lone tree leaned out over the water. Mist clouded its reflection, and ours. 'You do understand,' I said. 'No one else did.'

'And can't you see, that's why they refused to help you? Because they dared not admit that they didn't know what to do. But you wouldn't be quiet about it, would you?'

I looked round at her and saw that the Matriarch was smiling. 'For all the good it did,' I said unhappily.

'Although we don't know what causes the sickness, there is a medicine that sometimes helps,' she said. 'If he could have been given it a season ago he might never have become so ill.'

The hope that welled up in my heart actually hurt, like a stone. 'What is it?'

'The sap of a root we call Sorrow. It revives the spirit of those who are depressed, and it can work for doubt as well. Not always, but it's all I have to offer you. Sigurthur will give you a flask of it to take home.'

I was astounded. Of all the help I might have been given, I had never expected a simple medicine. 'But why are you helping me?'

'I've asked myself that,' said the Matriarch. 'Why should I help you give aid to the Prince of Torlossen, who would burn me and my people as soon as look at us? Because I can. Because you have been through enough, and I don't want you to go away thinking we are evil. What you think of me, my dear, seems to mean something, though I don't know why . . .'

She turned and began to walk back along the lakeshore to where we had left Sigurthur. As I hurried to stay with her, I was trembling so much it was all I could do to walk.

That was what made me realize how close I had come to giving up. I'd been calm, drifting, almost. The prospect of going out across the Stolen Land, facing Tykavn again – and what I would find when I did – filled me with incredible terror and excitement.

Mathrathur seemed to feel emotions like heat. 'I've offered you what you wanted. What's wrong?'

'Nothing, I – I never expected this. It's a long time since I saw Tykavn and anything could have happened to him . . . And I keep thinking about the thing that was pursuing me. I have dreams about it. What if it comes after me again? What is it, anyway?'

'I can't name it,' she said, 'but it is something that fears you.'

'Fears *me*?' I was astonished.

'You destroyed the creature you called Ember; you killed Ovinor.'

'In self-defence . . . But whatever it was, I can't destroy it properly. I know it will keep coming back.'

'Are you afraid?'

Her question wasn't as pointless as it seemed; it made me stop and think before I answered. 'I've been afraid for so long that I'm used to it. The fear is just *there*, like a toothache. No – it makes me feel depressed. Takes all my energy away so I can't fight.'

'Then you must take control. *Find out what it is.*'

'How?'

'You say you are so good at reading between the lines. Read between them, Iolithie.'

Sigurthur was waiting for us; human head on the body of a mythical animal, a mass of braided hair giving him a look both of wildness and dignity. I could see him so clearly that he seemed completely solid; his coat was pearl-silver.

On one paw rested a stoppered flask, the size of my hand, on a leather thong. He raised his paw, and I took the flask from him and tied it round my neck.

Mathrathur said, 'Sorrow is very strong. It would kill you if you drank it all at once. You must give your husband three drops each day, two in the morning and one at night, until the flask is finished. I must warn you, though, that it does not work at once. It may take a tenday or more before he even begins to improve. And in some people it does not work at all; if he is no better within three tendays, then there is little chance of a cure.'

'But it's something,' I said, all bitterness gone, clutching at the slenderest hope. 'It's something I can *do*.'

'Go now,' she said. 'Go back to your land. Sigurthur will go with you to guard you on your way; the Stjarna will not touch you.'

'Can I say goodbye to Hannis and Tattri?'

'If you wish. Do they mean so much to you, in such a short time?'

'They've been my friends. I don't have many. Is it true they are your children?'

She inclined her head. 'I know it's hard for you to believe.'

'And they will become like you, one day?'

'I hope so. There must be someone to replace me. I am not the oldest Stjarnin by any means; but I am the oldest who still chooses to be seen. A time will come when I choose to fade completely from sight and become a part of the wind ... Like those who have gone before me, eventually to give my energies back to the earth and to the burning spires of the Eldur, the fire of the spirit ... Is there something you want to say?'

'Only that I wish I knew what to believe in,' I said. There was an ache in my chest. 'I don't believe in Ama, I don't believe in Sudema. What else is there?'

'Then I will tell you something,' said Mathrathur. 'They are only names for things we can see, and things we can't see, and things we feel. Your gods and goddesses can be as real as you want them to be.'

She leaned down and kissed me on the forehead. Her lips opened against my skin and I felt the touch of her tongue like a hot flower. 'Go with our blessing, in the Light of the Sun and the Light of the Star.'

And I didn't want to, I didn't want to go.

*

Sigurthur said that I should write down the rest of the story while I still can. While I still care.

He took me south to Torlossen, but the journey was mercifully uneventful. Riding on his back, eating, resting, riding again. Other Unseen ones came with us, prowling at a distance. Not a danger now but a protection against Stjarna who didn't know me. If we did encounter any others, I wasn't aware of them.

The hills and the gravel plains, the achingly blue rivers and the steaming yellow-golden pans of sulphur floated towards us, around us, and away. We talked of my adventures and of Jolitha, though Sigurthur, like Mathrathur, could give me no answers.

'I don't see why you should have been sent back to see how history turns into myth,' he said. 'Who could have sent you, and what would be the point? But there might have been a warning for you, in what the surgeon did to Jolitha . . .'

'What warning?'

'That the cure can be more terrible than the disease.'

I clutched the precious flask of Sorrow that hung round my neck and said nothing.

I began to recognize the landscape. The sand hills where Sigurthur had rescued me from the Stjarna; the hot springs and the milky-blue pool where I had seen Antrid's reflection. The green skirts of the hills were hemmed by the loops of the river Torlau.

We came down towards the Torlau bridge as night fell.

The other Stjarna started to lope soundlessly forward around us. My sight isn't as keen as theirs; I didn't realize what they were doing until I saw a solid, many-headed mass of carved leather against the night.

A patrol from Torbyrgi. And the Stjarna were going down to attack them.

'Sigurthur, make them stop!' I hissed.

'I can't . . .'

There was a single spurt of light. It swayed, split and multiplied, leaving streaks of purple criss-crossing the darkness; two, four, eight spires of flame. The patrol were lighting firebrands.

The Stjarna went plunging down, all metal claws in the darkness; and the fires came sweeping from side to side, disembodied as the Unseen.

I didn't hesitate; I only knew I had to stop the fight. I leapt off Sigurthur's back and flung myself towards the guards, shouting, waving my arms – anything to make them see I was human. I was yelling, 'Can't you see it's me?' as if I thought they would

212

recognize me. 'I'm Iolithie Gaefir-daughter. I'm your Prince's wife! Don't – don't—'

Someone said, 'It's a trap.'

Then flames came shooting towards us. The guards were catapulting burning missiles towards us. The night danced with blinding brilliance and multiple shadows. I heard my companions keening with inhuman rage – and then I felt the air swirling with sudden emptiness. They were fleeing into the cool safety of the night, leaving me behind.

I didn't blame them for an instant. Only as they went I felt the flames catch on my clothes.

I didn't realize what had happened for a moment. I smelled burning; I saw flames licking blue and yellow on my legs and arms and I stared at them, stunned. Then I began to feel the flesh-melting heat and in a panic I rushed forward, trailing fire like a comet, and leapt out and into the dark waters of the river.

The impact filled my mouth and nose with water. I went under and I sank and went on sinking. When I realized I was not going to rise again I began to panic and thresh about; the weight of my sodden clothes was dragging me down.

Panic, choking blackness. The roaring of water and blood in my ears . . .

But then I was being lifted, dragged, hauled up out of the water and dropped on to the bank like some monstrous fish. When I had finished coughing the water out of my lungs I looked up and I saw the leather-muzzled faces of five guards staring down at me.

And one of them was Tsevren.

'Ama's Light, it *is* her,' he said.

'What're you talking about? How in Kvold would you know?' said one of the others.

Tsevren said tightly, 'I'm telling you, it's Princess Iolithie. We're taking her to the Palace.'

All I could think of, as they carried me up the bank and put me across a horse, was the tincture Mathrathur had given me. If the flask had burst in the heat, or if the river water had got in and washed it away – all of this would have been in vain.

CHAPTER SIXTEEN

WORDS AGAINST THE WORLD

I woke to the sound of a voice, low and monotonous, chanting near my ear. It sounded familiar yet it sent shivers of denial through me, like the echo of a nightmare I thought was long over. A blurred golden disc filled my vision. There was a Perfect-Minister praying over me, one who might also be a surgeon . . .

I went rigid with fear, my eyes wide. For a moment I couldn't breathe or even blink. The chanting stopped; the Perfect stood up and as he moved I saw a man and a woman on the far side of the room near the door. They were embracing as if comforting each other.

'I think she is awake,' said the Perfect. He was the sallow man who'd pricked the marriage tattoo on to my palm; I'd never trusted him. As he turned, the couple quickly broke apart and I saw that they were my mother and father.

'Leave us,' said Father, waving him out of the door. When he'd gone, Gaefir came to my bedside and gazed down at me, His hand felt cold on my arm. 'Iolithie, we've all been praying for you. How are you?'

My eyes focused on his bony face. It was a shock to see him. I'd blocked my parents almost completely from my mind, as if I'd never expected to see them again. After they'd refused to help me I hadn't wanted to.

I didn't want their prayers. I hardly even knew who they were.

'I'm all right,' I said. 'My throat hurts . . .' He helped me sit up and gave me a sip of water. I knew I was in one of the Palace guest apartments from the luxuriance of the tiling, the shining black pillars and the wooden bed. Mother stayed by the door as if she was afraid to come any closer. Watching from a distance.

'Where have you been, Iolithie?' Father said, his voice soft and grave. 'What happened?'

I opened my mouth, then realized I couldn't tell him. Not one word. If I even started, 'I went to get help for Tykavn . . .' I would have to explain everything and I couldn't, I couldn't. Not to him. Not to anyone here.

I said bitterly, perhaps unfairly, 'You didn't care where I went after I came begging for help and you refused me. Why do you care now?'

There was such pain and tension on his face. He looked ten years older. 'We would have helped you if we could. You must understand ... Nothing is that simple. Answer me, Iolithie. The guards fished you out of the Torlau; they said you were being chased by a group of the Unseen, and you were nearly burned as they drove the Unseen away.'

A flash of panic went through me. Where was the flask of Sorrow? 'My clothes,' I said, trying to sit up. 'What have you done with them?'

'Don't upset yourself,' he said, restraining me. 'Finding something for you to wear is the least of our problems.'

'But where are they?'

He indicated a corner. 'Lady Mynirrie threw everything you were wearing on that chair,' he said. 'Was there something important?'

I could see the cord of the flask hanging down beneath the blue-green heap of material. I prayed silently that it hadn't been damaged; although the most important thing was not the flask but Tykavn himself. 'It doesn't matter,' I said. My heart began to beat thickly as I forced myself to ask the question. 'How is Tykavn?'

Father looked down at his hands and slowly shook his head. I said, 'Better, worse? Still alive? Tell me!'

'Oh, he is alive ...' He sighed. 'I'm sorry we didn't listen to you, Iolithie. He has been ... afflicted all winter, and he shows no sign of recovery.'

'Please tell me. There's no point in concealing anything from me.'

He brushed a strand of hair out of my eyes, and rested his hand on my forehead. Mother was leaning against the wall, her arms folded, her tawny hair swept back over her shoulders. Expressionless. 'I know,' he said. 'It's difficult to remember you are a woman now, not a little girl. But much has been concealed from me; I can only tell you what I know. Your uncles came back and broke their vow of silence to tell us you'd run away from them; we assumed you'd gone back to Torbyrgi alone. It was several tendays before a rumour reached us that you had disappeared. The word was that Tykavn had given orders for no one to be told, and no search to be made.'

I bit my lip. So Tykavn had considered me expendable, after all. I hadn't wanted to be pursued, but it still hurt that he hadn't even tried. Gaefir continued, 'When I went to Torbyrgi for the winter Assembly meeting, Tykavn refused to see me. He was seeing hardly anyone. He made only one public appearance, which was at the Assembly, and I could see he was unwell; he'd lost weight and could barely sit still through the meeting. I tried to make enquiries about you, but Arch-Perfect-Elect Laasastiuk sent us home. We spent the winter in Vryatan.

'When spring came and the weather cleared, Laasastiuk sent for Vithrie and me. He confessed that you had run away and were now almost certainly dead, and that Tykavn was barely in a fit state to govern.'

I said, 'You mean he's so ill that even Laasastiuk can't deny it any more?'

Gaefir nodded gravely. 'We've been in the Palace three ten-days, and in that time I've seen the Prince only a few times, when I've taken documents to him for his signature. I can't put a name to what's wrong with him. He's very thin. His face is grey as old snow, and his hands shake. His eyes have a tormented look, as if it's all he can do to concentrate on anything outside himself. The strangest thing is that it takes him hours, sometimes, to sign the papers. He keeps beginning, stopping, muttering to himself, as if he can't trust himself to make the simple decision to sign his name. If you try to coax him he flies into a rage. Truly, it's terrible to see ... and he's getting worse. He continued with his duties most of the winter, even when it was clearly very difficult for him to do so. But for the past tenday he's been confined to his chambers. Mynirrie says he barely eats or sleeps. He is either frantically active or in a deep stupor, staring at nothing. He has to be constantly watched to stop him from injuring himself. If no one can do anything for him it may only be a matter of time before he destroys himself. I don't know why Sudema has brought this affliction on him.' Father bowed his head and I could see he was deeply upset, trying not to weep.

Throughout my journey I'd had a strong feeling that this would happen; not that Tykavn would die or get better, but that he'd gradually deteriorate. 'What has been done for him?' I asked.

'We have prayed.'

I nearly laughed, but stopped myself. 'And even Laasastiuk couldn't pull him out of the darkness?'

'Laasastiuk has prayed over him, purified him and purged Sudema out of him several times. It seems only to have made him worse. No one dares say anything ... but to be honest we are all at our wit's end.'

'What's going to happen?'

'That won't be decided until the spring Assembly meeting, in three tendays' time. A proxy administration will have to be appointed, until word can be sent to King Vidvikjan. The King may send a regent in Tykavn's place or let us choose our own replacement ... Dear Ama, it doesn't bear thinking about. Until then I and various other Perfect-Councillors are administering Tykavn's affairs as best we can.'

'Where's Laasastiuk?'

'On a pastoral tour of the villages. His purpose is partly to prepare them for bad news and gauge what their reaction will be. He's due to return just before the meeting.'

One less authority to argue with, at least. I breathed out, wishing I didn't feel so tired, so battered and sore. I needed my strength now, 'I must see Tykavn.'

'I don't think that's a good idea,' Father said gently.

'I must. I'm still his wife, aren't I? Or does that count for nothing? Please don't try to stop me!'

He shook his head, looking troubled. 'I don't think I have the authority to stop you. The only people who have are Laasastiuk and Tykavn himself.'

'Well, one's away and the other is hardly in a fit state to make the decision. I'm going to see him,' I said firmly.

Father seemed to have no strength or will to argue with me. He stroked my forehead and stood up, sighing. 'I'll send Mynirrie to take you to him,' he said.

As he left, I thought Mother was going to follow him. But she hesitated, as if held back by guilt, then came to my bedside. I'd started to get up but when she came to me I stopped, sitting on the edge of the bed. She was embarrassed. So was I.

'You don't have to pretend you're glad I'm not dead,' I said. 'I'm sorry it's given you such a shock.'

Vithrie just looked at me. The lump in her slender throat rose and fell as she swallowed. 'Of course I'm glad you're back. Try to forgive me; it's not my fault ...'

'What isn't?'

217

'That I was never able to feel anything for you. I tried.'

'*Tried?*' God's Fire. I didn't know what to say.

'I never felt any bond with my children; not you, or your brother who died. I never felt you were mine. You were like a stranger who just happened to be in my charge. I don't know why I felt this. I've tried and tried to change. It doesn't mean I don't care about you . . .'

I nearly broke down at that. I seized my mother's hands, but they remained stiff and unresponsive in mine. 'Haven't you ever loved *anyone*?'

'Oh yes,' she said quietly. 'Yes, I have.'

'Who?'

She didn't answer.'

'Well, I love you anyway,' I said fiercely.

Vithrie pulled her hands free and turned away, her hair swinging across her face. It was only when she reached the door and I caught a glimpse of her profile as she left that I realized she was crying. I don't know why.

Washed, dressed and looking as respectable and composed as I could manage, I walked with Lady Mynirrie along the corridors to Tykavn's apartments. The flask of Sorrow was safe, deep in the pocket of my fine geitha split-skirts.

'This may be very difficult for both of you,' Mynirrie said warningly.

'Tykavn and I will find that out for ourselves,' I replied. It was pleasant to feel that tiny spark of power; that although no one wanted me to see him, no one could actually stop me.

'Your Highness, I am on your side,' she said. 'You have every right. I am just trying to warn you that he may not be as you remember him.'

It had struck me that I couldn't tell anyone what was in the flask. They must've assumed it was a water bottle. If I told the truth not one of them would understand. They'd think I'd gone straight to the source of all evil and sold my soul to Sudema to obtain an unholy elixir. If I was to give Tykavn the Sorrow, it must be done secretly.

Two attendant-Sublimes at the doors bowed to us as we went in. Inside, the ante-rooms were weirdly familiar yet alien to me, ingrained with memories I didn't want awoken. Perhaps it was my imagination, but the air seemed saturated by Tykavn's sickness.

We were at the door to the bedchamber. Being here brought back nightmares. I was trembling.

Mynirrie knocked, and there were light footsteps on the other side. The door opened a little, and there, peering through the gap, was Mehaar.

I hadn't realized she was still here; I thought Tykavn might have banished her when I left. Thank God he'd let her stay. I was overjoyed to see her, but she was staring at me as if I were a ghost.

I pushed into the doorway, seized her and hugged her hard – but the moment I loosened my grip she wormed free, took several steps backwards and made Ama's circle over her breast.

'Don't do that, it's me!' I said. 'Oh, Mehaar, I'm so glad to see you.'

I waited for pleasure to replace the shock. The moment didn't come. She went on gaping at me as if I were a Perfect catching her out in some crime, an Unseen creature with claws unsheathed. Then she came into the ante-room and shut the door behind her.

'I thought you were dead,' she said at last.

'Well I'm not! Aren't you pleased to see me?'

She smiled then, but the curve seemed painted on. 'Oh yes, halla. But what – what—' She faltered. I thought I understood what was wrong.

'Dear, have you been looking after Tykavn all this time?'

'Yes. Lady Mynirrie and I between us.'

'It's been hard, hasn't it? You've had almost no help.'

She nodded. She looked as pretty as ever, and she was wearing geitha clothes almost as fine as mine, a shade of cream that made her hair look intensely golden. But I saw shadows under her eyes, and I felt sorry for her. I even felt a little guilty, for she had borne with Tykavn all this time, while I hadn't been here.

'Don't worry,' I said warmly. 'I'm back now. Things are going to be better.'

I liked to mother Mehaar. It made me feel strong.

Mynirrie said flatly, 'Princess Iolithie would like to see Tykavn.'

A slight emphasis on *Princess*. Ama, I'd never expected to be called that again. She and Mehaar held each other's gaze for a second; a secret communication, perhaps even a touch of antagonism. Then, slowly, Mehaar opened the door and stood back for me to enter.

The chamber, expansive and dimly lit, enveloped me like watered ink. I'd expected Tykavn to be in bed, but he was up and dressed, sitting on the edge of his bed, as I had seen him many times before. He was staring at the door as if we'd been conspiring against him. His appearance shocked me so much I almost broke down in tears. He was losing his hair; he was bone-thin, and his face seemed all eyes; hag-ridden, tormented eyes in great pouches of shadow.

What could I say? Only the obvious. 'I've come back.'

He did not look at all surprised to see me. For a moment I thought he didn't recognize me. 'Tykavn, I'm Iolithie. Your—'

'I know who you are!' he snapped. 'What do you want?'

It was torment to see him. I don't now what reaction I'd expected; surprise, anger maybe, but not this – this *indifference*. It was as if I'd only stepped out of the room a moment ago, and irritated him by coming back too soon. 'I've come to see how you are.'

'Well, now you can see,' he said bitterly.

I sat down beside him and took his hand. It felt cold and limp, as if he were already dead. He neither welcomed my touch nor rejected it.

'Tell me,' I said.

'It's the same. But it's bad now. It's very bad. The thoughts are like wildfire, they never give me a moment's peace.' Suddenly he gripped my hand so hard it hurt, and there was sheer anguish and despair in his voice. 'Where am *I*, Iolithie? This isn't me! Where is my *self* in all this?'

It was unbearable to see the hunted look in his eyes. But trapped in his black cage of possession or compulsion – whatever horror rode him – he was frighteningly sane. 'Still there,' I said. 'We'll find the real Tykavn again.'

But he pushed my hand away as if I'd patronized or insulted him. 'I don't know why you bothered to come back,' he whispered.

Be detached. Don't get upset. Standing up, I said, 'Is there anything I can do?'

'Yes,' he said. His voice, deformed by self-loathing, went into me like a skewer. 'Go away and send Mehaar to me with a glass of water. I'm thirsty.'

I did as he asked. While Mehaar was attending to him, I sat at the dining table, alone with Mynirrie.

'Did he know you?' she said. 'I was afraid he might not.'

'Yes. He knows perfectly well who I am. But I think – I think his illness has possessed him so completely that he can't see beyond it to communicate with me. He knows I'm back but he doesn't care. He *can't.*'

'That's what I was afraid of,' she said softly. Then she began to tell me something of what he was enduring.

Tykavn's rituals had taken him over completely. He could not do the simplest thing without them. His reality had become a fractured window on to a storm; there was lightning and there was utter blackness, and nothing in between.

They'd tried binding him, drugging him with wine, but they could not keep him like that indefinitely – and as soon as they released him, or the draught wore off, he would begin again, worse than ever, as if the pressure building up while he was restrained had to erupt like Mount Hrafna.

Nothing else existed for him now. Ritual had become an end in itself; not related to protecting Torlossen, nor connected to reverencing Ama. If Ama himself had come down from the sky in glory and told Tykavn that he could stop now, Tykavn would not have believed him.

While Mynirrie talked, I cried and cried. She made no humiliating remarks, only pressed her hands over mine. 'I am meant to be a physician and I can do nothing,' she said.

'You can't cover it up with a cream and pretend it never happened,' I retorted savagely.

She knew what I meant. She had the grace to flinch. 'I'm sorry. But—'

'It's all right. I understand. Only it's a little more difficult to pretend nothing is wrong now, isn't it?'

Mehaar was a long time with Tykavn. When she came out I asked Mynirrie to leave me alone with her.

I was calm now. It was time to plan, not to grieve.

I took Mehaar to the window, put my hand on her waist and spoke in a whisper, wanting to be sure no one overheard.

'Who prepares Tykavn's food and drink?'

'Ofaldiuk and Thysar, as they always have done. But it upsets him too much to see anyone other than Lady Mynirrie and me, so I take it to him. He won't accept it from anyone else.'

'Why not?'

She looked helpless. 'I don't know. He doesn't trust people.'

'Not even me?'

'Least of all you, halla.'

Another wound. 'Why?'

She floundered, trying to appease me. 'You've been away. He trusts me; it would upset him to try to change things. Anyway, it's all I can do to make him eat anything. He thinks Sudema might get into the food . . .'

I could see that if I was to get the Sorrow into him I would have to let Mehaar in on the secret. 'Is there anything he will eat or drink without argument? Wine?'

'Not wine. He says the dizziness makes him worse. But he always takes a cup of water or sour-milk, even if he has nothing else.'

I turned her towards me, looking her straight in the eyes. I don't know why I felt so apprehensive of telling her – except that she had refused to let me out, that time Tykavn had had me locked in the dressing room. 'You want him to get better, don't you?'

'Oh yes, halla.' A spark came to her eyes. 'I'd do anything.'

'I have a tincture that may cure him. That's why I went away, to fetch it. He must take two drops in the morning and one at night, but we must give it to him secretly in case he objects.'

Mehaar was looking warily at me as if I possessed some arcane knowledge she hadn't suspected. 'He would think we were trying to poison him.'

'So we'll put it in his cup, night and morning. There's a good chance it will make him better; if it doesn't, it won't cause any harm. No one else must know. Will you do it?'

Mehaar agreed enthusiastically. After that, it was easy.

For the first few days the Sorrow seemed to have no effect. Although Mathrathur had told me this would be the case I couldn't stop myself beginning to despair. What if it never worked? Tykavn was slowly killing himself and I couldn't bear to watch. It was burning my heart up with pity, every day, to see him suffering.

Mostly I left him to Mynirrie and Mehaar. I felt guilty if I wasn't with him; I felt worse if I was. If he was calm he reacted to me with a mixture of indifference and hostility that tore me apart. If he was immersed in ritual I might as well not have been there.

He no longer left his chamber; the devotions needed to make it safe to go out had become too demanding. He worshipped Ama and purified the room for hours, only stopping when he collapsed with exhaustion. Then he slept restlessly, ate if Mehaar could persuade him, dragged himself up and began again.

There was a heavy, whispering atmosphere in the Palace, as if someone had died. Married courtiers, Sublimes and Perfects alike moved and spoke softly when there was no need; everyone was on edge. Tykavn's chambers seemed to be at the heart of this darkness. People looked askance at the doors as they passed, hesitated before they entered as if the black aura of his sickness might be infectious.

I found it difficult to be in the Amaian culture again. The talk of Ama as God and Sudema as Demon was jarring and artificial. I was expected to attend the Palace chapel and the Fane, but the services made me break out in such a sweat that it was all I could do not to run out in a panic.

The Palace was like a decapitated chicken, all flapping wings and no head. No one seemed to know what to do about me. Thankfully, even the Perfect-Ministers left me alone and asked no questions, but I found the holy atmosphere smothering. Religion was the very thing that was killing Tykavn even as it purported to help him.

After a tenday, though, the miracle began. And it truly was like a miracle, at first.

Tykavn began his morning ritual with a kind of half-heartedness, rather than his usual manic urgency. A few minutes into it he stopped, as if he could not quite understand why he was bothering to do this. Then he returned to his bed and slept heavily for hours.

When he awoke, he came to the room where I was sitting – actually came out of his chamber – and asked if I would send for Mehaar to bring him something to eat. He looked like a tousled child, with great shadows under his eyes. And he spoke to me calmly, as if nothing had happened, and as if he wasn't quite sure who I was.

Tykavn's recovery was slow. He was so physically weak and drained that it would take many tendays to build up his strength again. There was still a sense in which he was not quite 'there' mentally; he seemed barely aware of anything beyond his own feelings, and liable to misinterpret the simplest thing that was said to him. We walked on eggshells around him. But he seemed to be shedding a burden; his rituals became more a habit than a necessity, and within a few more days he stopped them altogether. He slept a great deal, began to eat normally, and even spent time looking out of the window as if he had realized the outside world still existed.

His compulsions had vanished, washed away by some strange occult property of the Sorrow.

Mynirrie, Mehaar and I agreed to keep his recovery a secret for the time being, in case it did not last. Mynirrie thought it spontaneous; Mehaar and I knew the truth, and hugged each other in tenuous joy.

'I've been somewhere else,' Tykavn once said in a more lucid moment. 'It wasn't me at all. I knew everything I was doing was irrational, but I just couldn't stop. I don't know why. It was worse than a nightmare; it was Kvold. I want to forget it happened.'

After this he didn't refer to his illness again. For a time, his moods swung to extremes; one day, while he was in good spirits, he sent for his senior Perfect-Councillors. They came, but went away shaking their heads, having found Tykavn over-cheerful and full of grandiose ideas that had little to do with reality.

At other times, although his rituals did not return, he was deeply depressed. We kept giving him the Sorrow, praying that it hadn't yet taken full effect.

I passed the days in an odd state of suspension. Tykavn spoke to me civilly, distantly, as to a stranger; he touched on only the most basic everyday concerns, and never referred to my absence. Sometimes he would berate me savagely for some minor failing, then wonder why I was upset. He would play Mehaar and I off against each other, so we quarrelled – or rather we had long strained silences, for Mehaar would never argue with anyone. His behaviour made me anxious, miserable and uneasy every waking moment, and in my sleep too, but I pushed these feelings into the background. I didn't feel like his wife any more. I slept in another room. I had to detach myself from the slow, stumbling pain of his recovery or I would have been dragged down into the blackness with him.

The Sorrow was a balm, not a miracle.

I didn't expect anything of Tykavn, but I couldn't stop hoping that he'd show me some sign of affection, recognition, anything to show he cared about me. When there was nothing, I tried not to mind. I told myself his recovery would take a long time yet.

A few more days, and Tykavn started to seem more like his

normal self. His renewed interest in Torlossen's affairs took a down-to-earth turn, and he talked of returning to work.

Our hopes rose. It was only twenty-eight days since we had first begun to give him the Sorrow. Even if the healing wasn't complete, at least he seemed able to cope again. The wonderful thing was that *he was no longer in distress*.

That was all I'd wanted. That was the whole point of my journey.

There came a poignantly beautiful spring morning; the birds were singing loudly, the sun casting bars of glittering pale blue and green through the windows. The light seemed to come from the kindly Ama of the Unseen: not from a fierce fire-god who demanded perfection or damnation.

I was sitting in the communal room with Mother. Despite the harsh words we'd had there was an uneasy kind of bond between us. Almost a closeness, though neither of us ever spoke of it. She hadn't asked about Tykavn, and I hadn't told her.

There was commotion in the corridors outside. The marble walls tended to echo, and sound carried a long way. We looked at each other and Vithrie said, 'It must be the welcoming party for Arch-Perfect Laasastiuk. He was due back today. Do you want to go and see?'

An odd feeling in my stomach. He'd be shocked to see me, though no doubt he'd already been told I was back. I couldn't forget the way he'd refused to help Tykavn, but in a way I forgave him; Torlossen's legacy of ignorance wasn't his fault.

'No,' I replied. 'I don't really want to see him at all.'

We stayed where we were, sewing. I didn't think the great man would be that interested in me. So I was startled when a party of Perfect-Councillors and Ministers suddenly came into the Communal Hall itself, with Laasastiuk leading them and my father at his side.

Too conventional – or cowardly – to be downright rude, I stood up and bowed to the Arch-Perfect-Elect. He bowed in return. Then he gripped my hand, smiling warmly.

'Your Highness,' said Laasastiuk, 'when the news reached me that you had come home, I was tempted to cut short my tour and come straight back to welcome you. I hope you will forgive me for not doing so. I knew you would be in safe hands here.'

He was just as I remembered; friendly, fatherly, stern, easy to look up to and trust. 'Of course, Your Grace. Your duties must come first.'

'Your safe return is truly a sign of Ama's grace,' he said emphatically.

I tried not to grimace. Laasastiuk turned to my father and said, 'Has Her Highness received the cleansing of Ama?'

'We blessed her and prayed over her with a Perfect-Minister when she first returned,' said Gaefir.

Laasastiuk pursed his lips. 'But she has not actually received a ritual purification.'

I looked from Gaefir to him. 'Why do I need to be purified?'

'Because you have been outside the borders of this country, in the Stolen Land. You must be cleansed of the contamination.' I knew this would be the answer, but I resented it. I'd been changed by Sigurthur and the Stjarna, certainly – but not contaminated. Laasastiuk went on, 'Ideally, this should have been done as soon as she was brought back. However, as I wasn't here you were right to wait for me. I shall perform the purging myself.'

My father inclined his head stiffly. 'If my daughter were to be cleansed by the highest authority in the Church, we should all be honoured indeed.'

Laasastiuk beamed at me and said kindly, 'We'll go now, Your Highness, if you don't mind. I have an hour or two in hand, plenty of time to go to the Fane.'

As he spoke, two Perfect-Ministers moved smoothly to my side. Escorts – or guards? My heart was kicking, my palms turning clammy with sweat. I was on the verge of panic, as if I had Tykavn's sickness in reverse. I hadn't realized how far I'd travelled from this old feeling of oppression; the heavy will of Perfects impelling us all to behave in certain ways or drown in guilt and Ama's Fire. To find myself a victim of it again was terrible. I wanted to refuse, even to laugh and say, 'Don't be stupid, you don't know what you're talking about!'

As if I could.

Instead I let Laasastiuk take me to the House of Ama on the far side of Lake Thjothvatn. Better not to make a fuss. It would be humiliating, but over swiftly, like the 'cleansing' before my wedding.

The day was so lovely but a shadow lay on me. I was a prisoner – of convention, if nothing else. I had a sense of danger, which was more than the antipathy I'd developed towards the Church. It was as if the influence of the Eldur that I had consumed, wittingly and unwittingly, in the Stolen Land, was permanently inside me, expanding my perception beyond the surface of Eileah.

There was a lot of activity around the lake; I'd forgotten that today was the day of the spring Assembly. Outside the Fane, in a landscape of volcanic rock and mirror-blue water, a great many people were coming and going. The majority were Sublimes, dressed in a style I'd never seen before; split-skirts cut so slim they were almost trousers, with long tabards belted over them. The material was burnt-brown, almost black, with broad gold stripes that gleamed in the sunlight. There were banners everywhere; a bright gold sun on an umber background.

It seemed Laasastiuk had been making changes since I had been away.

They led me through the cool half-light of the Fane – where Tykavn had married a woman he didn't really want – and to the small chapel behind the altar, where, with the help of two Sublimes, Laasastiuk had 'purified' me for my wedding.

This time, however, he dismissed the two Perfects and led me through the filigree doors alone. I remembered vividly the dark basalt walls and the small altar with its spiked golden sun and the little stone loops for securing the hands and wrists.

There was a whispering movement out in the main body of the Fane, the distant boom of a door, then silence. The Perfects had taken everyone who'd been in the Fane outside with them. My senses were extraordinarily sharp; I could almost see the deserted aisle, feel the silence on my skin.

I was alone with the Arch-Perfect-Elect, and I was terrified. It was nothing in his manner. The fear came from outside me.

'My child, is something wrong?' he said, turning to me. 'You've been here before; you know me well enough. There's no reason for you to be trembling like this . . . unless you have something to feel guilty about.'

He took my shawl and coat, and said, 'Lie down on the altar. Relax.'

I obeyed. The stone was hard and cold. I started to sit up again, but he pressed me down, slid the stone clamps over my wrists and ankles, and tightened them in place. Now I couldn't move. 'The whole point of the purification is that Ama lifts your guilt from you. He takes the contamination away; but you must be willing to confess all the sins in your soul. You must be receptive to Ama's grace, and utterly repentant. Are you repentant, or is there still some pride left in you?'

I was finding it hard to breathe. I said, 'It's a sin to lie, isn't it?'

227

'Yes.'

'I can't lie, then. I don't think I've done anything wrong.'

Laasastiuk looked down at me. His moist pink mouth was grim. His robes smelled musty with ingrained body odours, dust and the dampness of the Fane, and there was a taint on his breath. Not strong, but the longer he stood over me the more he seemed to reek, as if I had the sensitive nose of a deer again. I started to feel sick. 'Why did you go into the Stolen Land?'

'I went to find help for Tykavn. No one here would help me!'

'And did you find it?' I didn't answer. His voice was gentle, slightly sardonic. 'Where did you go for this . . . "help"?'

'To Onafross.'

'Onafross! Now how could you possibly reach that land alive . . . unless you made some kind of pact with Sudema?'

I gulped in a breath. My back and ribs hurt. What could I say? I had and I hadn't. 'Sudema' was not what he thought, anyway; but here, Laasastiuk's view of the world reigned supreme. Anything I said in the Stjarna's defence would condemn me utterly.

'Why won't you answer my questions?' Laasastiuk said. 'You must tell me everything, Iolithie. Why you left, where you went, what happened to you, how you came back alive. If you hide anything, Ama will know.'

I was very afraid now, but angry too. I tried to pull my wrists free of the stone bands, but they were too tight. My hands tingled. 'Then let him be my Judge! You didn't tell me I had to answer any questions. I came here voluntarily, so purge me and let me go.'

He shook his head at my outburst. 'I cannot purge you until you confess.'

'It's none of your business! I don't need purging! Let me go!'

He moved away, indifferent to my pleas. When he turned back, he was holding a golden Hand of the Prophet on a black staff. He began to sketch signs on the air over me; then his face changed, and he brought the staff down hard across my stomach.

Even through my clothes it was agony. I convulsed, gagging with the pain.

'Must I beat Sudema out of you?' he said thinly. 'I can do that and worse.'

'Wait until I show Tykavn and my father the bruises!'

He smiled, but there was nothing paternal about him now. 'What do you think they'll do? Tykavn won't care; your father will tell you to keep quiet. Your father, my child, lives in the palm of my hand. The shame will be all on you, that you had to have evil beaten out of you. So tell them; if you can with your tongue cut out, your fingers crushed, and your eyes blinded . . .'

A metal finger circled above my left eye. It actually touched the white and I closed my eyes tight against the blinding pain. Laasastiuk made a soft noise of satisfaction.

'I know more about you than you think,' he said. Then he whipped me sharply across the breasts. As I cried out and squirmed, he shouted, right in my ear, 'Answer me! What happened to you in the Stolen Land? No one will care if you die, but it could take days!'

'Stop it!' I yelled. 'I've done nothing wrong!'

I braced myself for another blow, but the Arch-Perfect fell quiet, holding the staff between his two hands and flexing it as he looked thoughtfully at me.

'People like you are a cancer, Iolithie. You must be cut out before you strangle us all from inside. There are too many like you. The Prophet Hendleiknir knew how things should be; his was a Godly age, when men and women knew their different duties, when transgressors were punished properly, and the Unstatused treated as they should be – like slaves, not pampered house-pets. This soft age has corrupted us all. It is a slow slide down into moral depravity.'

I seemed to be speaking Mathrathur's words. 'Do you want us to follow Hendleiknir's teachings to the letter? No women on the Assembly? Wrongdoers to be punished by torture and drowning instead of losing Status? A full-scale War against the Unseen?'

I don't think he was shocked that I knew so much, only that I'd admitted it. His mouth moved wetly. 'To the letter,' he said. 'The time is coming sooner than you think. It may be harsh, but it is the only way the Children of Ama will be saved. You've seen too much and you are too defiant. Now speak.'

And he raised the staff to strike again, the Hand streaking yellow across my sight.

I could feel something dark and hard building up inside me. I felt as if my fingers and toes were glowing like the red spires of Eldur. The staff seemed to buck and twist in Laasastiuk's hands. His face! He gripped the wood harder, brought it down towards me, but it swerved off in thin air. Then, as if in anger – my anger – it wrenched itself from his hands and flew straight into the wall behind him. It stuck there, quivering, the golden fingers buried up to the middle joints in the stone.

I heard myself say in a harsh voice, 'Whatever you give me, you'll get back tenfold!'

He was staring from his hands to me and back again. His palms were raw and bleeding. Then he said, '*Demon.*'

'Touch me again and I'll kill you,' I whispered. I didn't know whether I could or not. But I meant it.

I pulled at my bonds, and my hands and feet slid out as if soaped. I don't know how I did that, either. But Sigurthur had made a heavy way-hut run across the hills as lightly as a deer, using the power of Eldur and other herbs; what I'd just done was nothing by comparison.

I stood up and confronted Laasastiuk. He was plainly terrified. So was I, but I didn't show it. 'Let me go. Open the doors or I'll burn them down and shatter the windows; and how will you explain that to the Assembly?'

CHAPTER SEVENTEEN

AMA'S SHADOW

I ran for my life along the lakeshore towards the laval bowl of the Thjoth. Where they were setting up the Holy Day fête, I seized a horse from a small boy and galloped the rest of the way, leaving the child crying behind me. Awful, how easy it was to be a bully in an emergency.

Reaching the city, I rode right in through the double doors and along the covered street, breaking one of Torbyrgi's strictest rules; no horses inside the city. People scattered in front of me, shouting indignantly, but I didn't care.

Laasastiuk hadn't sent anyone after me; I don't think he dared. But I didn't know whether he might have means of sending swift messages to the Palace. I had to reach Tykavn before an agent of Laasastiuk tried to stop me.

At the Palace doors I leapt off the horse and ran past the startled guard-Sublimes. I sprinted across the hall, up flights of stairs, along the corridor towards Tykavn's apartments. Then I did my best to look calm and enter nonchalantly, to avoid alerting the attendants at the double doors.

Once inside I tried to go straight into the bedchamber, but found it locked. I banged hard on the door, shouting Tykavn's name; Ama knew what he'd think, but I didn't care.

Half a minute's pause, then Tykavn opened the door. The room behind him was empty; no sign of Mehaar or Mynirrie. He was half dressed in split-skirt breeches and a geitha shirt, and I could see that the bed was rumpled. He blinked at me, frowning a little, and said, 'What's all the noise?'

'I must talk to you. It's urgent.'

He came out into the room, pulling the door to behind him but leaving it slightly ajar.

'What is it?' he said tiredly.

'Are you going to the Assembly this afternoon?'

His frown deepened. 'What concern is that of yours?'

231

'Are you?' I asked sharply. I didn't have time for his defensiveness, I was going to get through to him if it killed me. 'I've got something extremely important to say and you must listen!'

His green eyes were fixed on me, angry but intent. 'You know quite well that I can't go to the meeting. It's heartless of you to suggest it! I don't feel ready; I want to be left alone.'

'Do you know what business is going to take place?'

He shrugged. 'The same as always, I suppose. They'll manage without me.'

'Don't you realize that they intend to appoint a proxy to rule in your place until the King decides what to do about you? Haven't they told you that?'

Tykavn sighed and sat down, his gaze unfocused on a window. 'The Assembly and Laasastiuk have managed to run the country quite satisfactorily without me all winter.'

'You think Laasastiuk's governed well in your place?'

'I've hated being away from my duties!' he exclaimed. 'But Torlossen hasn't collapsed! What does it matter if they govern a tenday or so longer, until I'm well again?'

'If you're so nearly well, go to the Assembly today.'

His fists knotted. 'I can't. It's too soon.'

I had an awful feeling that he might never be ready; that he had lost his nerve. I said, 'If you don't go today you'll never go again.' He stared at me, but his accusing eyes no longer unnerved me. 'You're going to be deposed! The plan about the proxy is a sham. Laasastiuk is going to declare you unfit to rule, and he's going to take over Torlossen himself.'

Tykavn gave a sneer of disbelief. 'He wouldn't do that.'

'Yes he would, and everyone knows it! What do you think Laasastiuk's been doing all the time you've been ill? He's gathered an army round him and no one's done a thing to stop him. No one dares! He thinks you're soft, Tykavn. He wants to bring back the harsh laws of the old days, all the cruelty and slavery. He wants to start a war against the Unseen! You don't want that, do you?'

At last, a flare of concern. 'He can't.'

'Yes he can! He's been waiting for you to get too ill to govern; he's been trying to make you worse. He must have planned this for years!'

'But it would get him nowhere. Even if he tried, King Vidvikjan would put a stop to it.'

'No, he wouldn't. Laasastiuk wouldn't even let a messenger

reach your father. But even if a messenger did get through, I can tell you what King Vidvikjan would do; precisely nothing.'

'How do you know?'

'Because I've met your father! I've been all the way to Onafross for your sake and he wouldn't do a damned thing to help you! He'd let Laasastiuk do whatever in Kvold he wanted, and pretend it wasn't happening!'

Tykavn was staring at me as if I'd confessed to some huge crime. I was sick of this. I was sick of everything.

'For Ama's sake, go to the meeting,' I said quietly. 'Show them you're well and in charge. Surely Torlossen still means something to you, even if I don't.'

He sat there, shoulders slumped, hands dangling between his knees. Eventually he said, 'You're making things impossible, Iolithie. As if I haven't had problems enough, you bring this – Look, just go away.'

I could have argued myself to death and still got nowhere. He was closed off, refusing to hear what I was really saying; seeing some strange image of me that wasn't me at all. 'All right,' I said. 'I've warned you. I don't know what else to say.'

As I turned to leave, the gap in the doorway to the bed-chamber caught my eye. Through it I saw Mehaar, making the bed. I wondered why she was doing her morning duties so late. She must have gone into the bedchamber through the dressing room . . . unless she had been in there all the time.

I caught her eye for a second. She didn't smile, only gave me a wide-eyed blank stare. The look suddenly filled me with the most horrible creeping coldness and suspicion.

I turned away quickly and left the apartments, trying to push the feeling out. It doubled back and stabbed me.

It seemed there were not merely words and motives hidden between the lines, but black, fathomless trenches. I wondered how many more there were to dig up before it ended.

So this was where I found myself. Torlossen was about to fall to Laasastiuk's idealistic rule; and the moment it did so he'd have me killed, in public or private. Those infected by Sudema would no longer be purged or punished but executed. There wouldn't be a soul to speak in my defence.

I'd called on a power I hadn't even known I possessed to protect myself against Laasastiuk, but I couldn't rely on it. He'd find a way to overcome it. I should have fled for my life there and then, but some perverse desire for justice held me in Torbyrgi.

As I walked along the corridor from Tykavn's rooms, I met my father. Gaefir stared at me; I'd forgotten how dishevelled and exhausted I must look. 'Iolithie, what's wrong? I thought you were with the Arch-Perfect . . .'

I was so glad to see him I almost told him everything. 'Do you know what's going to happen at the Assembly this afternoon?'

He hesitated. His eyes darkened. 'Why? For Ama's sake, what's happened to you?'

'Your precious Arch-Perfect's idea of purging me was torture and beating.'

'What?'

I shook my head, dismissing it. 'Father, you know we've got to do something to help Tykavn. Laasastiuk's got to be stopped.'

An awful change clouded my father's face, as if the flesh had turned to paper. Blank. 'Be quiet,' he said softly. 'I beg of you to be quiet. There's nothing to be done. Don't make trouble.'

Something Laasastiuk had said stopped me in mid-breath. *'Your father is in the palm of my hand.'* I didn't know what it meant, but the words wrapped round me like a cold shawl of treachery. No use appealing to Father; *he was on Laasastiuk's side.*

'How long have you known what he plans to do?' I cried. Gaefir didn't answer. 'You've known for ages, haven't you? Yet you've never tried to stop him! Aren't you even going to try?'

'Iolithie, don't,' he said woodenly. 'You don't understand.'

'I think I do. He beat me! Can't you see what sort of man he really is?'

Gaefir said grimly, 'It's because I know exactly what he is like that I can do nothing.' Holding my arm, he lowered his voice. 'If Laasastiuk finds out you oppose him you'll be in terrible danger. Don't draw attention to yourself.'

I smiled without amusement. 'Too late for that. He knows.'

My father was turning paler and paler. He looked so old; but I couldn't feel sorry for him because he'd always been so strong and yet he wasn't using his strength to fight back. He started to say something, when Lady Mynirrie came hurrying down the corridor towards us. She looked harassed.

'Lord Gaefir, His Highness wants to see you urgently. Would you come with me?'

Father and I looked at each other. 'Of course, my lady. Just give me a moment with Iolithie.'

As Mynirrie began to walk away, he whispered urgently, 'Leave Torbyrgi now. Take a horse, go back to Vryatan, go anywhere; but go now. I won't say I've seen you.'

And that was all my own father could do to help me. I backed away, brushing my arm where he'd held it. 'Thank you,' I said coldly. 'Thank you so much, Father.'

As I watched him walk away, I wondered what Tykavn was going to say to him. Did he know Gaefir was in Laasastiuk's power? What concern was it of mine, anyway? If no one would listen, I should do exactly what Father suggested; flee, and leave them all to the mess they were making.

I should have fled, but I didn't.

Some crazy compulsion found me walking in the crowds to the Thjoth, dressed in the plainest clothes the Palace could afford. With my hair tucked up under a hat and the round brim pulled down to shadow half my face I doubted that anyone would recognize me.

This was a contrast to the time I'd sat on the Assembly at Tykavn's side, the focus of everyone's attention in our bright Court clothes. Now I stood in the fringes with Sublimes, married citizens, children and the Unstatused, like the villager I'd once been. No one had taken any notice of me leaving the Palace; there was an undercurrent of mild panic, and the laxness of security verged on anarchy.

Laasastiuk would soon change that.

I don't know what kind of morbid curiosity impelled me to go and watch. I was almost beyond caring what became of me; I just wanted to see what would happen.

The Perfect-Councillors were taking their seats on the rock tiers. Laasastiuk came surrounded by his brown-and-gold clad acolytes, with a forest of banners trailing like smoke and fire. A murmur ran through the crowd, but no one seemed greatly surprised. I imagined Laasastiuk had been easing into this all winter, swelling the ranks of his supporters gradually, slowly transforming them from Sublimes to soldiers.

There was uneasiness, but not fear. He must have been preparing people for a change, planting rumours, talking them round to his point of view. What else had his tour of the villages been for but to win them over and recruit for his army?

The takeover would be gentle, shrouded in holiness. Ama's Word and Ama's Will. The Torlosseners would follow like mountain does, mute. As the seasons turned and the Laws were tightened and their lives became ringed about with restriction and terror, then, too late, they would realize.

It entered my head that I should kill Laasastiuk. Seeing him stern and vibrant with dark authority, though, I felt utterly incapable of action. Still I pushed forward through the crowd, trembling.

As I did so, four gold-striped Sublimes surrounded me. They drew little attention and did not even look at me; but as I tried to worm out from between them they moved with me, trapping me.

I felt no Eldur-power within me. Perhaps I'd expended it all, escaping Laasastiuk. What had I done with it, anyway, except throw a stick through the air? My ribs ached where the Arch-Perfect had beaten me and my legs were like reeds. I felt mortal and strengthless. Once the Assembly was over and Laasastiuk ensconced, I'd be taken away by these men and there'd be nothing I could do to resist.

The acolytes ringed the Assembly, holding their holy staves like weapons. Laasastiuk was moving towards Tykavn's empty seat.

Suddenly there was a stirring among the tiers of Perfect-Councillors, people standing up to gaze out beyond the Thjoth. The crowd turned, though it was a few minutes before most of us could see.

From the direction of Torbyrgi a group of courtiers and attendant-Sublimes were approaching, ranked like Border-guards. They wore the white, blue and black livery of the Palace, and they bore a single blue banner held square in a frame, with the sun emblazoned on it.

Under the banner strode Prince Tykavn.

As he came into the arena, the murmuring and the movement stopped. Everyone seemed frozen, watching him and his supporters progress towards the centre of the Thjoth, where Laasastiuk stood.

Tykavn looked magnificent. It might all be in the padded majesty of his robes, the bright yellow cloak and his confident bearing; but from a distance you couldn't see the gauntness of his face, nor the effort it must be costing him to put on this show.

He strode up to Laasastiuk, forcing the Arch-Perfect to step aside so he could take his rightful seat.

I had tears in my eyes. I should have been there beside him!

The Assembly settled and Tykavn spoke. His voice, weak at first, swiftly regathered its strength and authority.

'As some of you may be aware, I have been confined to the Palace with a slight but inconvenient ailment for the past few tendays. However, you will no doubt be dismayed to learn that I am fully restored to health and ready to take up my duties again.' Laughter, people looking from one to another. Smiles. 'Any rumours you have heard to the contrary are unfounded. The business of the Assembly will be conducted as usual.'

And a great wave of clapping and cheering built up and thundered over the arena.

Laasastiuk stood frozen, stooping slightly, as if someone had just punched him in the stomach and he was trying to hide the pain.

Tykavn continued: 'I would like to extend my thanks to those Assembly members who have administered the province during my indisposition, and particularly to Arch-Perfect-Elect Laasastiuk, who has worked with tireless energy in the service of Torlossen and our Lord Ama. In fact, so hard has he worked that no one is more deserving of a long rest than he. I would therefore like to take this opportunity to announce Arch-Perfect-Elect Laasastiuk's retirement, and the imminent appointment of his successor.'

Tykavn went on to extol Laasastiuk's virtues; I've never heard such an outpouring of elegant sarcasm and ambiguity. It was delicious. As a wave of innocent applause swept through the crowd, affirming their appreciation of Laasastiuk's term of office, Palace officials were moving along the back of the Assembly, speaking to the uniformed supporters. They were giving up their staves, leaving, sitting down, mingling with the crowd; deserting Laasastiuk as fast as they'd joined him. The four that surrounded me melted away.

As the cheering faded, Tykavn said, 'I'm sure the Arch-Perfect-Retired would like to say a few words in response to your appreciation.'

With a face black as volcano-smoke, Laasastiuk turned on his heel and marched away. Only a handful of his acolytes went with him. As they reached the edge of the rock-tiers a group of Palace officials were waiting to escort them quietly away.

Astonishment was flowing over the crowd like a palpable wind. It whirled up into excitement, euphoria. They loved Tykavn and they'd dreaded Laasastiuk – only they hadn't dared admit it until now. The lifting of fear turned the rest of the meeting into a celebration.

I'd never seen or heard of an Assembly so disorganized, so full of laughter. And at the end of it even Tykavn looked genuinely invigorated, his spirits lifted by his people's support.

As the meeting ended and the crowd began to move down to the fair on the lakeshore, I pushed diagonally through the flow to find my father. From the moment he left his seat I kept my eyes on his tall, thin figure until I caught him up.

We stood and looked at each other, oblivious to the folk milling all about us. His eyelids were creased with concern and shame. He said, 'How did you persuade Tykavn to come to the meeting?'

'I didn't think I had,' I said.

'You did, believe me. He called everyone he trusted to him and told us we must rally and stop Laasastiuk's coup before it could begin.'

'Well, that's ironic!' I said. 'Tykavn trusted you when you were going to support Laasastiuk!'

'No, I wasn't—'

'But you weren't going to stop him! Why?'

'There are things you don't know—'

'I know I'm not Perfect, but I'm not a child. Just tell me the truth! Please, Father.'

Gaefir's shoulders slumped. He took in a breath, made to speak, let the breath go. Eventually he said, 'You know when your mother and I separated and took our Vows of Celibacy . . .'

'Yes?'

'We . . . broke our Vows.'

I was aghast. After all that has happened, it takes more and more to shock me; but these were my parents, my strict, Perfect father and my spiritual mother, who lived their whole life by Ama's Law. I simply couldn't believe it. 'How many times?' I said.

'All the time.' His voice was low with shame. 'Our separation was a charade. I know you must be horrified, Iolithie, but try to understand; we love each other. It was agony for us to separate. You can't imagine the suffering of being torn from someone you love; all the arguments in the world about it being "Ama's will" have no power to comfort or constrain you. We simply weren't strong enough. Don't condemn us.'

'Condemn you? Me?' I could have cried. All those years I'd thought my parents were somehow above being human; to learn of their fallibility was devastating. 'Oh, Father. I think the Laws are insane.'

He looked at me grimly, because he still believed in the Laws, even though he had broken them. 'Unfortunately, Laasastiuk found us out. If he'd told the Assembly we would have been stripped of Status and would never have seen each other again. And you would have been made a bondservant like Mehaar.'

'It would have been even worse under the Laws Laasastiuk wanted to bring in,' I whispered. 'We might all have been executed.'

'Well, he kept our secret, but the price was our unquestioning support of everything he did. He held the threat over us for more than two years.'

'So that's why you wouldn't help me when I came to you.'

He seemed webbed in shame. 'There was nothing we could do for Tykavn, anyway. But to have listened, come back to the city, given you any support at all – that would have meant acknowledging Tykavn's sickness, and we simply couldn't risk it. Laasastiuk was laying plans even then to take power.'

'Waiting for Tykavn to get worse,' I said. '*Making* him worse, with his talk of prayer and guilt and Sudema. And you daredn't defy him. Not even for me!'

'My dear, I had to think of what Laasastiuk might do to Vithrie. I can't tell you how sorry I am.'

'Neither can I.' I felt numb. 'What do you think will happen to Laasastiuk now?'

'He's been arrested,' Gaefir said wearily. 'He may have to stand trial, and if he's found guilty of trying to take power illegally he'll be stripped of Status. And so will your mother and I, once Laasastiuk tells Tykavn about us.'

'No, you won't,' I said fiercely. 'I won't let it happen!'

Gaefir put his arms round me. We hugged each other hard, for a very long time.

When I went back to the Palace I sat in the communal room and did some sewing, to convince myself that I was not waiting for Tykavn, that I was completely detached from anything he might have to say to me.

But at last Lady Mynirrie came in and said that Prince Tykavn wanted to see me. To my shame, my heart was beating hard as I walked beside her. Seeing Tykavn perform so magnificently on the Assembly, it was as if I'd fallen in love with him again.

I'd never stopped loving him, actually. For all the things he'd said to me, his hostility, even – on that one occasion – his violence, I'd never really blamed him. I blamed his illness.

I suppose everything I'd done had been to prove I loved him. To make him love *me*.

He received me in the ante-room, still bright and imposing in his Assembly clothes. He looked so much better, like the confident, radiant man he had used to be. We sat in chairs opposite each other, like strangers. I felt ridiculously nervous. In spite of everything I still felt intimidated by him; apprehensive but hoping desperately for something from him. Approval, warmth, recognition. Anything.

He fixed me with his bright green eyes and said, 'Thank you for warning me about Laasastiuk.'

'That's all right,' I said awkwardly. 'I felt it was my duty, that's all.'

'Duty?' he said sharply.

'Yes. Someone had to tell you.'

He lowered his eyelids. 'Yes. Well, thank you.' He was on a knife-edge of some kind, as if being civil to me by only the most extreme effort.

'I thought you were wonderful . . .' Ama, there was so much I wanted to tell him: *I knew you could do it. I'm so thrilled you found the strength . . .* And I couldn't. It would all sound patronizing in the extreme.

'I'm finding this very difficult,' he said. He cleared his throat. I thought he was trying to apologize; then he said, 'Iolithie . . . I am sorry to have to tell you this, but I cannot accept you back as my wife.'

His words startled me. I wasn't sure I had come back to be his wife; I wasn't sure of anything. I'd made no plans beyond forcing the Sorrow down his throat. But this bald statement made me feel utterly sick with dread.

'I haven't asked you to! But – what do you mean?'

'There are certain Laws regarding marriage in this land, one of which is that a husband and wife will stay together for the allotted span. There are certain additional dispensations for Kings and Princes. You broke the Law, which entitles me to select someone else.'

I was shaking now. 'What do you mean, someone else?'

His voice was soft and cruel with recrimination. 'It wouldn't have happened if you'd stayed here. It wouldn't have happened if I hadn't realized . . . what it really means to love someone.'

'Who – who is it?'

'Mehaar,' he said. 'I love Mehaar.'

If he'd swung a pole hard into the pit of my stomach he would have left me more breath. Betrayal gutted me. *'Mehaar? But you were too sick to know what day it was, let alone have time to fall in love!'*

'I needed someone! And she was more comfort to me than you ever were!'

I tried to say, 'Don't you know *why* I wasn't here?' but he went on, 'She's everything you're not. She's unselfish, she's understanding, she was always with me at the worst times and never defied me or caused a fuss.'

'Even when you hit her?' I cried.

'There was no need!' he shouted back.

I thought I was going to weep. Instead I started to shake with mirth.

'What are you laughing at?' he demanded.

'At myself! Ama, what a fool I've been. Of course you'd love Mehaar, with her blonde hair and pretty face, the way she always smiles, and never argues and agrees with everything you say. I'll bet she was always there! I know I'm not pretty and I have a vicious tongue – but didn't you have any sense of duty to me as your wife?'

My words only inflamed Tykavn more. Never, never would he back down.

'What would you know about duty?' he replied viciously. 'I needed you, but you weren't here! I was sick and you deserted me! *You weren't here!'*

I was dumbfounded. For a moment I simply couldn't believe what he'd said. 'But haven't you realized why I wasn't here? I went to find help for you! Maybe I didn't support you very well, but, Ama knows, I tried. All I got in return was abuse. Not that I blamed you for it; I blamed your illness. But no one would help you, least of all Laasastiuk. He wouldn't, would he? And the others just didn't want to know, because they couldn't cope with it either! Don't you remember me telling you where I've been? To Onafross and back!'

If I thought this speech would impress him, I was wrong. He

said acidly, 'Then that is the most incredibly stupid thing you have ever done. If it's true.'

'It's true! Why would I lie? Why do you think you're feeling better now?'

'I don't know,' he said. 'Because Ama heard my prayers at last.'

'No. Your own family in Onareyru couldn't help you either. Do you want to know who did? The Stjarna.'

'What?' he said, frowning.

'The Unseen! Sudema's children. They knew what your illness was – they call it the Disease of Doubt – and they gave me a medicine called Sorrow to cure it. You've been taking it in your cup night and morning for three tendays.'

'You're lying!'

'No I'm not! Ask Mehaar! She knows all about it, because I trusted her, more fool me. She was the one who gave it to you. She would, of course; it was in her interests to have you well again, wasn't it? I could've been killed on my journey – I nearly was, several times – but I did it for you. And in return you dare to tell me you're in love with *Mehaar*?'

I suppose he knew I was in the right; but guilt only made him furious, not placatory. I never knew anyone with such a terror of thinking he might be in the wrong. 'I didn't ask you to go. You had no right, nor to accept the help of the Unseen. And you gave me that stuff secretly! How did you know it wasn't poison? Perhaps you *were* trying to poison me!'

'You know that's not true.' I felt weary suddenly. I couldn't shout any more. 'You might not admit it, but you know it. The Stjarna aren't what you think—'

'The fact that you've been among them is all the more reason for me to discard you.' He sat back and made the circle of Ama as if I were contaminated. And I felt dirty and helplessly angry.

'I hope you warded off Sudema before you took Mehaar into your bed.'

His lips twitched in an unpleasant smile. 'There is no point in sanctifying an act that is not sanctified by marriage in the first place.'

'You can't marry a bondservant, anyway. It's against the Laws. You've broken them too!'

'But I am the Prince of Torlossen. I can do what I like.'

We both fell furiously silent. The rage burrowed down inside me; I couldn't sustain it any more. I was thinking now of what happened to people who broke the Laws. I would lose my Status. I saw myself mining rock from the hills in some barren corner of Torlossen. I felt completely wretched; I wanted to sink through the floor, down into soil and rock and to sleep there. I switched into a state of detachment, purely to save my sanity.

'Where will you send me?' I said, cold and distant.

His answer proved that, despite his words, he was still as constrained by the Law as anyone. He could bend the rules in private, but he dared not break them openly. 'Nowhere. You and Mehaar can change places. No one will ever know; outside, you will function as my wife. But within these walls, Mehaar will be my wife and you our servant.'

It was not losing my husband in this way that tore me apart like the claws of the Stjarna. By now I think I hardly had any feelings left for him at all. It was the betrayal.

And the treachery that hurt most was not Tykavn's but Mehaar's. After we had grown up together. After I had loved her all my life. Had I ever treated her as a bondservant? No, as a sister, surely.

And yet . . . perhaps she had resented our positions all along. Perhaps she thought I'd patronized her. Perhaps I had.

And yes, I had words with her. If we were expected, humiliatingly, to live in the same apartments, we could hardly avoid each other. I wanted to behave towards her with crushing dignity, but when I got her alone at last my feelings came flooding out.

She actually tried to sneak past me, but I cornered her in the dressing room. 'This is what you wanted all along, isn't it? To lie in the bed of a prince at any cost. You'd take advantage of a sick man and betray your best friend!'

Tears came readily to her eyes; tears from being found out, I imagine. 'That's not fair! I was here and you weren't! Tykavn needed comfort.'

'What comfort could you give him that I couldn't?' I screamed. It was the only time I raised my voice. I couldn't help it.

She backed away, her pretty mouth trembling. 'He loved me. He didn't love you. It was me he loved!'

'You knew you were breaking the Laws.'

Sulky defiance glittered from her eyes. 'What does it matter? I had no Status to lose!'

'But I was your friend!'

'No, you were my master,' she said flatly. 'It amused you to pretend we were friends, didn't it? Because you had power over me. But Tykavn preferred me to you! He used to say you were . . .'

'What?'

Her voice was almost a whisper. 'He used to say "Iolithie is a bitch." He said you didn't care about his problems, that whenever he tried to explain them to you, you would only argue.'

'That's not fair! No one could have cared more than me—'

'But you *did* argue. I heard you.'

'Yes, but only because I was worried about him.'

'But it only upset Tykavn more to argue! He said I didn't upset him because I didn't ask stupid questions. I soothed him. He just wanted someone to listen and understand!'

'And you were there,' I said grimly. Oh, yes, I could picture it. *'You can tell me anything'*, Mehaar had assured me. *'That's why I'm here.'* I could hear her saying exactly the same thing to Tykavn, the moment my back was turned; a cat transferring her affection to whoever fed her. 'Traitor,' I said, though my heart wasn't really in the insult. I hardly felt anything. Hollow laughter echoed through me.

'I didn't mean to betray you,' Mehaar said helplessly. 'It was meant to happen. I'm better for him than you are. I'm sorry.' I think she meant it.

'Well, it must be very nice for you to condescend to me for a change,' I said bitterly. I wasn't proud of anything I said to her. 'I can't blame you for taking whatever you could get. You're welcome to him. The Light of the Sun go with you.'

If they thought I was going to agree to this deceitful arrangement and stay around to be humiliated, they were wrong.

Yet, even now, I felt like saying to Mehaar, 'Leave Tykavn and come with me! Where there's no ridiculous hierarchy, no Laws to say, "do this, be that, or Ama's wrath will roast you to charcoal".'

If she left him for me, you see, it would mean I had won. Not the best of motives.

But I was going alone.

If Tykavn ever imagined I'd accept his condition, he was deranged in a deeper way than I had ever guessed. Escaping would be easy; I was angry and upset, but I wasn't afraid. In some ways, Tykavn was too soft for his own good. He might have once locked me up in a fit of pique, but now it didn't occur to him to make me a prisoner. That was partly because he didn't understand the first thing about me.

I decided to go the day after the Assembly meeting. I'd rather have gone the same night, and not suffer the humiliation of sleeping in the dressing room while Mehaar shared Tykavn's bed. But, being coldly practical, I needed a good night's sleep.

In the morning, Lady Mynirrie came in to me and closed the outer door behind her. Her strong face was pale. 'News has just reached us that Arch-Perfect Laasastiuk took his own life last night. I thought you should know.'

'Oh,' was all I said. I must have looked indifferent; what I felt was a gentle and refreshing wave of relief. The storm's blown the other way. Oh, good.

'It's such a waste,' she said sadly. 'He was a great man.'

'He wanted to be too great, didn't he?' I was dressing as we talked. She didn't intimidate me any more, even though she was much grander than me. It's difficult to be awed by anyone after the Stjarna. 'He just had a few faults . . . like beating people who disagreed with him. Do you want to see the bruises?'

She blinked at me, unsure of whether I was asking for help or needling her again. 'I have some ointment, if you want it,' she said.

I shook my head. I didn't feel like being sarcastic after all. 'We shouldn't have to hide our hurts and keep quiet about it. We should protest with all the breath in our bodies.' I raised my voice. 'Try it: "I won't put up with this!" '

Lady Mynirrie inclined her head towards the closed door of the bedchamber, as if to shush me.

I said, 'You know what's going on, don't you?'

'I suspected Mehaar has been rather more than a serving maid to Tykavn for quite some time, but there was nothing I could do. Even if you hadn't come back it was wrong of them. I think it's disgraceful.'

'I can't stand it, Mynirrie,' I said. 'I'm leaving.'

She looked stunned. 'But where can you possibly go?'

'I have friends.' I took the flask of Sorrow from its hiding place and showed it to her. It was still half full. 'Look at this; a medicine that *works*. It's what cured Tykavn of his obsessions. Please could you remind Mehaar to make sure that he finishes the flask?'

She looked from the flask to me, incredulous. I was belting my shawl over my coat, putting on my hat. 'Imagine what a physician you could be if you had such herbs.'

I smiled at her and left.

I walked along the corridors of the Palace for the last time, Ama throwing lozenges of light across the silken marble tiles. I didn't hurry. I felt like whistling.

But as I turned a corner I felt a change in the atmosphere. The corridor was deserted and utterly still; the windows were so small and high it seemed night had fallen, and it was Sudema's violet light that fell through the crystal.

And at the far end of the corridor, barring the door, stood Laasastiuk.

The fact that he was dead seemed irrelevant. He was there, waiting for me, and I had to go past him to escape. I walked towards him, slowly and steadily. He appeared hard and solid, and yet I could see the door through him, as if he was made of smoky glass.

His eyes were black pebbles. Twin replicas of the tiny, hard soul within him. He radiated bitter hatred, and it drew me to him even as it terrified me.

He was too real to have been conjured by my imagination; it was as if I'd stepped into an older, stranger world where the impossible was real. The disc of Ama hung round his neck. It was a huge, heavy thing with vicious spikes of rays. I saw Ovinor's face in Laasastiuk's; I saw myself thrusting those spikes into his throat, heard the crunch of the larynx and saw the wet gush of blood . . . I visualized it, as hard as I could, over and over again, as I went towards him.

He said, 'Your hands will never heal.'

But I remembered the staff tearing itself from his fingers, the Hand of the Prophet burying itself in the chapel wall, Laasastiuk's palms all raw and bloody.

'Neither will yours,' I replied.

And he remembered too. Fear came into his eyes. Although he did not move perceptibly, he seemed to draw back and I knew he wouldn't dare touch me. I edged past him, went through the doorway, and walked away, fast.

All the way along the track from Torbyrgi, every time I glanced back, Laasastiuk was watching me, like a paper silhouette set on the path behind me. Grey, triangular. He couldn't touch me, yet in broad daylight his shadow followed me. Only the light of the sun could cast such a dark shadow.

I ran over the lava hills towards the river, I ran across the Torlau bridge in full view of the Border-guards. No one tried to stop me. And that was the power of my own will, an aura flaring around me like warning colours. *You cannot touch me. I am something Other*!

Out into the Stolen Land I ran. I took nothing with me. As night fell, I sensed the darkness beginning to take shape and prowl around me.

These were not Stjarna I knew. I was just an Amaian to them, one who had strayed into forbidden territory. And yes, I was afraid. But I turned to face them and let them come to me. I lay down on the earth and put myself completely at their mercy.

'Please let me come to the Citadel with you,' I said, as their eerie human faces browsed over me, coloured now with curiosity rather than bloodlust. 'I want to see Mathrathur.'

A silver-dust shape came swelling up through the darkness, pushing between the ranks of the other Stjarna. A face I knew and loved.

'I've been waiting and waiting for you, Iolithie,' Sigurthur said gently. 'I had a feeling you wouldn't be staying in Torlossen. Are you ready to come home?'

Well, I have been in Mathrathur's cave, writing again, and she has been reading. I think this will be all I have to say.

It is so wonderful to be with Hannis and Tattri and all their friends again. To be greeted with real affection, without suspicion or judgement. To feel that I belong.

Sigurthur and I have spent a great deal of time together, although we still get on each other's nerves. I think we thrive on it, in some strange way.

The morning we arrived, before I'd even seen Mathrathur, he took me past the Citadel, past the Lake Vivatn, and over the flank of a table mountain. When I asked where we were going, he only smiled.

And the place he took me to was like one of his fantastical mind-paintings come to life; trees in endless rows, tall as hills, with trunks so thick I couldn't have put my arms around them. Light poured between the trunks and between the tracery leaves against the sky a thousand shades of jewel-green.

'Welcome to the Last Forest,' he said. 'Men cut down all Thandarkyr's trees, not realizing they wouldn't grow again. But one forest escaped, and it will remain as long as the Stjarna are here.'

I couldn't speak. He said, 'No one is brought to this place until they are ready to stay with the Stjarna for ever.'

'How do you know I'm ready?'

Sigurthur smiled. 'I know everything. Haven't you realized that yet?'

We walked side by side through the glory of the forest, and I was so in love with it I knew there was nowhere else I wanted to be.

'I don't understand you,' I said. 'I never thought you'd surrender your precious independence to anyone. The Stjarna aren't perfect. They are aggressive and unforgiving and as dogmatic as the Amaians in their way. You never really explained why you gave up your freedom to join them.'

'Freedom does not always reside in the most obvious place,' Sigurthur said quietly. 'Do you think I'm so different from you? Anyone's entitled to change their mind.'

'That's not an answer.'

He snarled at me then sighed. 'When I was on my own, I was trying to prove something to the Stjarna. I thought they were wasting their power, when they could have been doing such magical, wondrous things.'

'Making way-huts walk,' I said.

'Poor Laufi.'

'Turning unsuspecting women into deer.'

'Poor you. Well, I had to get it out of my system, I suppose . . . before I understood that I was wasting my time transforming the things around me, when I could have been transforming my *self*. That's the real trick. It happened very fast and you can't stop it once it starts . . . no longer to feel separate from Eileah but part of her. When you have that, you don't need anything else.'

'And do you go out slaughtering travellers on the Onafross Way?' I said acidly.

'No. Most of the Stjarna don't, actually. But if you can't reconcile yourself to the conflict, don't let it keep you apart from us. I feel the same as you. It's easier to make changes from within, isn't it? Imagine: the Amaians could have medicine, and we could stop killing them.'

'I love you, Sigurthur,' I said impulsively. I was intoxicated by this place, the shimmering green light and the grandeur of the trees.

To my amazement, he said stiffly, 'I feel immense affection for you, too. However, I conquered all desires, whether for women or men, a long time ago and I don't think I'm going to change now.'

I exclaimed, 'Then you'd better try conquering your conceit in thinking I'd want you to! Never mind the anatomical differences between us, which you seem to have overlooked anyway. I love you *because* you're my friend, nothing more; but I don't know how far you expect my friendship to stretch to encompass your ego!'

'Well, that's put me in my place,' said Sigurthur. 'Shame. By the time *you* become Unseen I was hoping I might have changed my mind.'

I love Sigurthur, yet somehow I couldn't talk to him about Tykavn. It was Mathrathur to whom I told everything.

'I don't think I'll ever understand Tykavn,' I said. 'I thought it was his illness that made him so cruel to me. I thought when it was over he would be different; so why did he still treat me so coldly?'

'Ask yourself,' said Mathrathur, 'where the illness ended and his personality began. For most of his life his compulsions were part of his character. They always will be, to some extent. They only became an illness when they could no longer be controlled, and made his normal life impossible. The Sorrow gave his mind the chance to rest and heal itself, and I hope he will never be ill again. There is a great deal of good in him; his sense of responsibility towards his land, his ability to plan and organize with huge energy. He could be fair and kind. But there are also great flaws. An impulse to hurt those closest to him, and never even realize the harm he is doing; an inability to acknowledge viewpoints that seemed to threaten his own. Immense selfishness. Now which of these were the legacy of the illness, and which were *him*?'

'I don't think there's a clear boundary,' I said. 'I don't suppose there ever will be. The real problem was that he never really wanted me. He didn't love me; that's not his fault. He'll treat Mehaar differently because he loves her.'

I could say it without bursting into tears. Miracle.

'I doubt it, but never mind,' said Mathrathur. 'If he's unaware of his faults, you're only too aware of yours; but you've done well, Iolithie. You did everything humanly possible, and more.'

'Even against Laasastiuk? I know what the darkness that followed me was, in Ember and Ovinor; it was *him*. Yet I don't think he was aware that it had happened . . . I don't know how to explain.'

249

'Hendleiknir started the War,' she said. 'He created the Separation. He wants the War and the Separation to go on. Like Ama, he feeds on fire. Hendleiknir is the spirit of those who try to cure that which is not sick; and the only cure they know is cutting.'

As she spoke, I felt an odd wetness on my fingers, a sudden soreness. I looked down and saw that the ends of my fingertips were oozing blood.

'I was Jolitha,' I whispered. I don't know where the words came from. 'The glacier gave birth to me. I was a healer until the Surgeon cut my hands apart. But then I lost myself somewhere . . . I was severed from her . . . I came back through the glacier again and betrayed my own self, and now I can't find her . . .'

I was shivering, staring in horror at my hands, but the Matriarch breathed on my hair as if to calm me. 'You are Iolithie; you must learn not to give others this power to divide you. Listen to me. You saw the Separation; you understood how terrible it was, but it can't be healed. The severed fingers can't be rejoined; you have to find a new way.

'Evil does not emanate from a distant violet star. We always seem to see it as coming from outside ourselves; reposing in the hearts of our enemies but never in our own. But it lies inside all of us. The Stjarna are as guilty as the Amaians. Neither race is truly wicked, yet the War goes on.

'There aren't many who are deliberately evil. Not even your Laasastiuk; but narrow-mindedness and fanaticism may produce the same effect. You say that some darkness detached itself from him and followed you, and that you're not sure he even knew it was happening. Well, the Enemy may have been an other-self formed of Laasastiuk's unconscious will – or it may have been the Shadow of your own fears, trying to hold you back. So have you defeated him, or yourself? I couldn't say.'

'Neither, I don't think,' I said, staring at the blood.

'But that's why you are a Stjarnin now,' Mathrathur said gently. 'So that you can gather the strength to try. The Shadow thinks he can live without Jolitha, but he cannot; one day he will learn, too. Welcome to the People of the Star.'

She kissed my hands, and the bleeding stopped.

'Your hands will never heal,' said Laasastiuk, but he was wrong. They have healed, and now they will heal others.

What I've started to learn is that true power comes not from Ama or Sudema, but from Eileah; she who is ignored and trampled on, yet still retains the calm strength to nurture us.

I don't know what my beliefs are; they shift and change from day to day, and perhaps will for ever. I no longer believe in one strict God and a devious Enemy embodied in a violet star; yet Ama and Sudema are still real to me in a different way. What was Jolitha, if not an aspect of the star made flesh; and what was Ovinor-Hendleiknir-Laasastiuk, if not the paradox of evil shaped to seem good and holy?

For Laasastiuk, I somehow became the earthly incarnation of Sudema. And he couldn't overcome me. Dead or alive, he'll never forgive me for that.

As long as I live, I shall never stop looking over my shoulder for his shadow. But he won't win. Wherever he is, Jolitha cannot be far away, outside or inside me.

THE BRIDGE

I've been with the Stjarna a year. I thought there was nothing left to say, that everything to do with my life in Torlossen was in the past. I was wrong.

This morning, as I stood in the meadow in the dawn light, I saw a figure come riding up the trail from the lake. The valley was misty-red with Eldur and the first deep blush of the sun. Out of this rust and ruby mist the solitary figure came towards me, a tall man on a solid red-gold horse.

I recognized him at once. I simply couldn't believe it was him. I felt a rush of panic; how had Tykavn found me, and why had he come?

Further down the valley I saw a group of riders; his escort. He had left them behind to ride the last part of the way on his own.

I didn't go to meet him, but I didn't try to hide. I stood there in full view, let him see me, and waited for him. Ama knows what I must have looked like to him, with my hair long and wild, and the faded green of my long tunic and trousers. Like some spirit of the trees, perhaps.

Tattri came out of the shelter behind me and said, 'Who is it?' but I didn't answer.

When Tykavn reached us he halted his russet stallion and sat looking down at me as if he couldn't believe his eyes. I thought how well and strong he looked, just as I remembered him from my youth, before I really knew him. But now the strength seemed to go all the way through him, solid and deep-rooted. His eyes no longer had that accusing-defensive look. They were clear and sad, even wise – but he was still Tykavn. I daredn't trust him.

He jumped down from his horse and stood, one hand resting on the saddle, gazing at me. Then he blinked and frowned a little.

'You are Iolithie, aren't you?'

252

I almost smiled. He wasn't sure! 'Yes, I am Iolithie, Your Highness.'

'Aren't you – aren't you surprised to see me?'

I was aware of Tattri, Hannis, and others, who had seen Tykavn arrive, gathering around to see what was happening. There were Stjarna among us, not showing themselves; I could sense Sigurthur close by. This must be the first time a party from Torlossen had ever come to the Citadel.

I said, 'I can't believe it. I thought I'd never see you again.'

'You don't look very pleased to see me.'

I had to keep myself from laughing. What did he expect? After everything, he could still want me to be pleased to see him, and make me feel guilty that I was not. 'It's a shock,' I said lamely. 'But how did you get here? You knew the danger from the Unseen.'

'I remembered what you told me. Don't attack them and don't run from them. I ordered my men to stand and face them and I asked them to bring me to you.'

Moment by moment, I was seeing him in a different light. To do what he had done must have taken immense bravery and the suppression of all his beliefs. But why had the Stjarna brought him here? The answer came at once; to face the judgement of the Matriarch. I felt slightly cold. She would not deal as kindly with him and his men as she had with me . . .

'I don't understand,' I said. 'Why have you come?'

'I want you back, Iolithie,' he answered simply.

His words dumbfounded me. A flame of defensive anger leapt up inside me. 'This is a long way to come to employ a serving maid. What about Mehaar – your *wife*?'

I expected him to flare up as he used to, but the sadness in his eyes deepened. 'Mehaar is nothing,' he said. 'She is not my wife. You are.'

His words, his expression, devastated me.

I looked at his guards, waiting down in the valley. Had he brought them to compel me? My friends wouldn't let it happen, and there would be a terrible fight, Stjarna against humans. I knew who would win.

The red sun spilled blood on the lake.

And yet, what I felt wasn't dread. It was completely unexpected; an actual pulling at my heart, a frightening tenderness. There was still a quality in Tykavn that moved me, something I could have loved.

I glanced round at the others, as if to say, *Help me*, but no one could. I was on my own.

'But you said you loved Mehaar! You humiliated me, you tried to take away my Status!'

'I know how you feel, but please give me a chance. It's taken me all this time to realize what you did for me. Look at me; I'm not ill any more. I think it's the first time in the whole of my life I've been free of the demons. Now I can look back and see how irrational it was. I could never see it before. And I couldn't see your goodness *because* I wasn't rational. Now I realize what I did to you, and what you went through for my sake. You were a true and loving wife to me. I came to ask for your forgiveness. Please come home with me.'

I stood speechless, the world changing around me, everything spinning and falling. He moved forward with his arms held out, and I couldn't move. He embraced me and held me tight against him. And I let my arms move around his back, over the layers of mohair and leather, and hugged him hard in return.

'I love you,' he said. 'Dear Iolithie, I'm so sorry. Do you love me?'

'What about Mehaar?'

His arms relaxed a little. 'I never loved her. I only thought I did, because you weren't there.'

'I wasn't there because—'

'I know. I know,' he said. 'I've sent her away.'

'Where? She didn't do anything to hurt you, either.'

'No, it's all right; I rescinded her lack of Status and made her Sublime. She is happy. Mehaar only ever loved herself.'

'I know that,' I said. It was true. 'I always knew it, but I tried to convince myself that if I loved her enough she would change. People don't change, not really. They only become more themselves.'

'I've changed, truly,' said Tykavn. 'Ama's Light above, please forgive me.'

Such desperation in his voice and eyes. I couldn't resist him. 'Of course I forgive you.'

He hugged me again. 'Can you love me?'

I still couldn't answer that question. 'How do I know you don't just think you love me?'

'I know, believe me. Come home. I miss you. You're my wife.'

I was on the verge of tears, as if the pressure of his arms was squeezing all the old grief out of me. This was all I had wanted from the beginning. He was different. He was well. He said he loved me and he meant it.

Yet he could ask me if I loved him, without understanding for a moment how cruel the question was. That alone told me that nothing could really change; it was all too late.

I pulled myself gently out of his arms. 'I can't.'

'Yes you can!'

'No. I live here now.'

'You can't, not with these—' He went on protesting, insulting the Stjarna with every syllable, but I let the words wash over me, not growing angry. Only feeling sad to the roots of my soul.

When he'd finished I said, 'Come with me. You can't condemn these people without understanding. I've something to show you.'

I took him to Mathrathur's cave and showed him the story I'd written on the wall. The tiny writing made ghost-grey squares on the rock. As he read, I sensed the presence of the Matriarch in the cave with us, and I suddenly understood something.

She hadn't let her people bring Tykavn here so she could judge him. She'd brought him here so *I* could decide his fate.

When he had read the story he was subdued. 'Was I like that? Did I seem so mad, hurt you that cruelly?'

I hadn't meant to fling it quite so violently into his face. 'I had to explain to Mathrathur. I had to drive out my demons . . . It's over. I hold no grudges. How could I?'

He walked out of the cave – I think he found the darkness oppressive – and I followed. We stood together on the slope with the dark spires of the Citadel and the trees shining silver-green below us, the sweet wind blowing off the lake. He held my arms and said, 'What are you going to do?'

'I wish I could come back with you Tykavn. I forgive you, I love you, but everything has changed too much. I belong here now.'

Tykavn stared at me, his eyes basalt-dark with a touch of his old anguish. The look twisted my heart so savagely that I began to relent. 'I'm imploring you . . .' He clasped my right hand, looking down at it, tugging at it as if to pull me with him. 'Iolithie, please . . .' His eyes widened suddenly. He paused, then said, high and sharp, 'Your hand! What's wrong with it? *I can see through it!*'

I snatched my fingers out of his grasp and stared at them.

The flesh looked translucent, with a silver sheen. Through it, the stones on the ground were like shadows through frosted glass.

I felt a jolt in my stomach, but no real surprise. This was how the change began. I was too much part of the Stjarna ever to leave them.

'This is why I can't come back,' I said quietly. 'I don't expect you to understand now, but I hope you will, one day.'

He was silent; shocked, I think. We walked back to the farm without speaking, but as Tykavn took the reins of his horse from Hannis he turned to me and said helplessly, 'What am I supposed to do?'

I looked beyond him and the Matriarch was there, a few brushstrokes of silver-dust on the landscape. She seemed predatory, dangerous – but I knew that whether I said '*Kill him*' or '*Let him go*' she would carry out my wishes. 'I'm sorry. Go home. The Stjarna won't hurt you.'

Without anger, with only a quiet, deep sadness in his eyes, Tykavn began to turn away. 'This wasn't what I wanted,' he said, so soft I only just heard him. 'But if this is your choice, I accept it. Fare you well, Iolithie. Ama bless you.'

I gave the blessing of the Stjarna in return. 'The Light of the Sun and the Light of the Star go with you.'

He mounted the red-gold stallion and began to turn away, then hesitated, frowning. 'The story on the cave wall – I wish I could call it evil! Everything I thought was true ... You don't know what you've done!'

He pulled the horse round briskly and kicked it into a canter, trailing dust like clouds of confusion.

As he rode away he seemed to drag my heart into long fibres of pain behind him. But the emotion I felt was for him, not myself.

All around me my friends watched without comment. They had given me their strength but they hadn't interfered; I was so glad of that. I saw Tykavn reach his companions and exchange a word or two. Then the party moved off. I went on watching until they dwindled to specks and vanished altogether.

And the pain disappeared with them. I could breathe again. I felt Tattri's hand through my arm and her head on my shoulder, and I turned and hugged her.

'Don't be sad,' she said. 'We love you more than he ever could.'

'I've found my place,' I replied, 'but he hasn't found his. That's why I'm sad.'

Write, said Sigurthur, while you still can, while you still care.

He's right, because I know that the more I become a child of Sudema, the less this human story will matter. Just words on a wall. Nothing to compare with the singing of the wind, the high cold peaks of mountains and the sapphire waters that draw me more powerfully every day.

I thought Tykavn had left in rancour after all; but now I realize his anger was born of the bitter pain of change. He must go through it. A worse journey than mine, perhaps.

Just words?

Prophets are dangerous, and I would not want to be one even if I could. I can only record what I experienced and discovered. And when Mathrathur said, 'Can you tell me how anyone should shake that belief?' I knew it was beyond my powers to transform anything except myself.

But not beyond Tykavn's, perhaps. After his journey I hope he will return, as I did; not as husband, or as prophet, but as the first to make words into thoughts, and thoughts into the first thin bridge between the night and the day.